FORGIVING HEARTS
by Christina Cordaire

P9-ELW-711

FORGIVING HEARTS

CHRISTINA CORDAIRE

DIAMOND BOOKS, NEW YORK

This book is a Diamond original edition,
and has never been previously published.

FORGIVING HEARTS

A Diamond Book / published by arrangement with
the author

PRINTING HISTORY
Diamond edition / October 1994

ISBN: 0-7865-0047-6

Diamond Books are published by The Berkley Publishing Group,
200 Madison Avenue, New York, NY 10016.
DIAMOND and the "D" design
are trademarks belonging to Charter Communications, Inc.

PRINTED IN THE UNITED STATES OF AMERICA

10 9 8 7 6 5 4 3 2 1

CHAPTER
One

CATHERINE FOSTER PLACED THE FLOWERS GENTLY ON THE fresh grave of her husband. Kneeling in the damp grass of the old family burial ground, she pressed a hand gently to the mound of earth that covered her beloved Jonathan. A burst of longing threatened to overwhelm her. If only she could have touched him just one more time. If only she could have felt his arms around her just one more time. If . . .

She bit back a sob and whispered the words she had come to say. "I do solemnly promise that I shall do my very best to raise our son as I think you . . ." Her voice faltered and stopped.

She drew a ragged breath and pressed the handkerchief in her other hand to her eyes. With an effort, she continued, speaking more firmly, her voice husky. " . . . As I think you would want me to."

Pain tore through her as the memory of him filled her mind, and she struggled to her feet, eager now that her promise was made to leave this windy hill overlooking the glittering gray sea. She wanted with all her heart—what was left of it—to be gone from this long, narrow mound.

With a sob, she turned from the grave and the stone that would proclaim for a hundred years to come, *In the Service of His Country, Captain Jonathan Wells Foster, June 20, 1836–June 3, 1864, Beloved Son, Husband, and Father*. She recited the simple message by memory, as her tears prevented her from seeing the words graven in granite. She would flee this place, would flee the grave

1

that marked the end of love; but no matter where she might go, she knew she would never escape the heartache.

Blinded by her tears and stumbling over her heavy black skirts, Catherine reached the little cemetery's wrought iron gate. Clinging to it with black-gloved hands, breathing deeply the tangy air from the sea, she fought to regain control of her emotions before she rejoined her son and father-in-law.

"Are you all right, my dear?" The senator's deep voice was full of concern as he helped her into the carriage where her son waited, his eyes wide with anxiety.

"Thank you. I am . . . all right." She turned toward him and spoke with grave sincerity. "Thank you for giving me this time to . . . say good-bye." She didn't phrase it well, but the silver-haired man understood.

"I said my own good-byes last night, my dear," he reassured her.

Closing the carriage door behind them, he called to the driver, "To the station, Seth."

The vehicle rolled forward, heavy with their trunks, and began a slow descent of the hill. Outside the gates of the Foster estate, it turned away from the sea and continued into the town. Soon it reached the gleaming tracks that would take them westward to begin a new life.

"Get along, Reb." Sergeant Jack Keefer gave his prisoner a shove that sent the painfully thin man staggering. "What the hell Washington thinks they're doing letting the likes of you out of prison camp to go West and fight Indians is beyond me." He scowled at the man who stood before him, unconquered in spite of his chains.

Shifting his wad of tobacco, Keefer spat at the Rebel officer's feet. He might have saved himself the trouble. The Confederate captain never even blinked. Keefer had to content himself with the blaze he'd kindled in the man's blue eyes.

He tried another tack, striving to push his prisoner over the edge. "How're those two sisters of yours? Real beauties they were, though one was a mite young. Made me real upset when you snuck in and carted them off. I'd been looking to get to know 'em better. A whole lot better." He watched the muscle jump in the Reb's jaw with satisfaction. "Where'd you take 'em off to, anyway?"

His prisoner stared through him, his aristocratic features haughty. For an instant, Keefer considered striking him for his insolence, but further down the train platform an old gentleman was looking their way as he assisted a pretty little thing in black onto the train.

Keefer could wait.

Many soot and coal dust–filled days later, the train chugged into Saint Louis and settled with a wheezing sigh beside the station. The passengers were as weary as the crew that served them.

Senator Foster caught the conductor as he trudged toward the stationmaster's shack. "Can you arrange for our trunks to be held here until I make further arrangements?"

"Yes, sir. I'll show you."

The senator's grandson followed, fascinated.

Catherine, left alone on the platform, was sick from the long-endured motion of the train. She moved down to the far edge of the wooden cargo dock, where she hoped to find a breath of fresh air.

The air was still as death, and the sun beat relentlessly down to add to her discomfort. She felt as if she would stifle in the black cocoon of her widow's weeds.

Moving toward the narrow shadow cast by the eaves of the depot, she glanced down the length of the train. A man jumped gracefully down from one of the last cars, blond hair gleaming in the sunlight.

Catherine was startled to see chains on him.

Her stomach clenched as she recognized the uniform he wore. Rebel cavalryman. She could tell by his yellow collar. She remembered learning somewhere that yellow stood for courage.

Sorrow and anger welled up in her like the tears she so often had to hide. General Hancock had written that

Jonathan had been killed when Confederate cavalry overran his company's position.

"Devils on horseback" her beloved Jonathan had called them with grim admiration. And they'd killed him. Maybe this man had been one of them. Perhaps he'd been the very one.

Fighting down the emotions that threatened to undo her, she forced herself to look straight at the Rebel.

Even as she watched the man loaded with fetters, an army sergeant lumbered down behind him and shoved the Rebel viciously.

The man, hampered by his chains, staggered and barely caught his balance. The Union soldier struck him hard between the shoulder blades and hooked a foot around the man's shackled ankle, which sent him sprawling.

Catherine now turned her anger to a more useful purpose. "Here! You! Sergeant!" She pushed herself away from the building.

Even as she called out, the sergeant drew back a booted foot and kicked the fallen man. Everything was forgotten as Catherine's rage at such unfair treatment swept away her caution. "How dare you! Stop this instant!"

Feet pounded the wooden platform behind her. "Catherine! What is it?" The senator's voice bordered on panic.

Catherine whirled to face him. "Only see, Senator! This sergeant is abusing his prisoner. I saw him deliberately knock him down."

The Rebel rose lithely to his feet. His face was expressionless. His eyes watchful.

"What is the meaning of this, Sergeant?" Senator Foster's face was stern.

"Who's asking?" The sergeant tried to keep his tone neutral, but scorn edged it.

"A United States senator is asking, Sergeant." The senator's voice had a cutting edge. "I was unaware we were in the habit of mistreating prisoners of war." He stared the man down.

The sergeant shifted uneasily. "He tried to escape back to his own lines. He almost got away. Then he gave me a helluva fight." The man's shifty eyes flicked to his silent prisoner and back again to the senator. "I had to chain him, sir."

Catherine saw one corner of the prisoner's mouth quirk. He had a nice mouth, finely chiseled, with laugh lines at the corners, as if his smile had once come easily. With a quick intake of breath, she saw a little tear in his lower lip.

Looking more closely, she discovered a fresh bruise along the clean line of his jaw. There was an abrasion, too, on the arch of his brow at his left temple.

When their eyes met, she felt as if she'd been slapped. Clearly the Rebel resented her pity.

Her father-in-law heard her tiny gasp. "Are you all right, Catherine?"

She answered him boldly, defying the man in chains. "This man has been beaten, Senator. See the bruises on his face."

"Is this true, sir?" His tone was harsh as he addressed the man in chains.

The Rebel regarded him steadily, his eyes sardonic. Though his eyebrow rose in silent derision, he disdained to answer.

The man's attitude spoke more clearly than words could have.

The senator turned on the sergeant. He was so angry, bright spots of color stained his cheeks. "If there is a repeat of your abuse, sergeant, I will see you court-martialed. Is that understood?"

The sergeant's eyes glittered dangerously, but his gaze fell. "Yes, sir," His answer was sullen.

The senator glared at him a long moment, his eyes making silent promises. The sergeant colored and looked away.

The prisoner spoke. Bowing slightly to the senator, he said in a soft accent, "Captain Jonathan Foster thanks you, sir."

At the sound of her dead husband's name, Catherine was struck with a sudden numbness. As it washed over her, she felt the world spin crazily, then tilt and slide her off.

Blackness closed around her and she slipped gracefully toward the rough wooden planks of the railway platform with a soft sigh.

CHAPTER

Two

CONFEDERATE CAPTAIN FOSTER MOVED WITH STARTLING speed to catch the fainting woman. He swept her up into his arms—awkwardly because of his bonds—and held her carefully cradled against his chest. His blue eyes sought the senator's. "Is she ill, sir?" he demanded.

"No," the senator shook his head, dealing with his own shock, every reaction delayed. "It must be the heat." He realized he wasn't coping well with this.

"You should get her to the hotel then." Impatiently, Jonathan regarded the man staring at him. "You should get her out of this heat and dust, sir," he urged.

The senator shook his head. Looking with distaste at the sergeant, he decided he didn't want the brute touching his boy's Catherine. His mind was clear now. He ordered, "Remove this man's chains."

"But, Senator, he's dangerous!" the big man protested. His beefy face colored with ill-concealed chagrin.

Concerned only for the pale girl who lay so still against the Rebel's chest, Senator Foster snarled, "Do as I say!"

The prisoner transferred his soft burden to the senator's waiting arms as carefully as if he handled a newborn. Then he held out his wrists to his blue-clad captor, his eyes mocking.

The bully snatched hard at the chains, deliberately digging the manacles into the prisoner's already raw wrists.

The Rebel refused to utter a sound as the man roughly removed his fetters. He ignored the fresh blood that seeped into the festering wounds on his wrists. Only his eyes, bright and dangerous, gave away his feelings toward his jailer.

"I hope you don't regret this, Senator." The sergeant spoke through gritted teeth, then stood back, scowling.

Senator Foster coldly ignored him. Giving Catherine back to the stronger man, he turned to lead the way to the street.

Startled, he heard the man say softly, "Come along, Button. Don't you fret. She'll be all right."

Dear God! Between the shock of hearing his dead son's name and his concern for his daughter-in-law, the senator had momentarily forgotten Jonny! Throwing his arm around the boy's shoulders, he clutched him to his side. "Forgive me, lad. It was . . . so . . . unexpected."

Jonny's shoulders began to shake. His voice was muffled as he hid his face against his grandfather's side. "Grandpa? Can he really be . . . can he really have my papa's name?"

His grandfather just held him tightly and walked after the tall, blond cavalry officer and the unconscious girl he carried in his arms.

They followed the desk clerk to the suite the senator had engaged. Shouldering past the man holding open the door, Jonathan Parke Foster, Captain, Confederate States Army, strode across the spacious room to the stiff Victorian sofa. Kneeling beside it, he tenderly shifted his burden to its velvet surface.

Her face was as still as death, but when he checked, he found her breath was even. He untied the ribbons of her bonnet, ignoring his own involuntary response to the softness of her cheek when his fingers brushed it, and placed it with its long black veil on the floor beside him. She was so lovely, his gallant little defender. Her flawless, pale skin was so delicate it was almost translucent.

As he watched, a little color returned to her cheeks. Her lashes quivered, and he started to move away. Let the first face she saw be one of her family.

Rough hands grasped his shoulder. "You get away from my mama, you dirty Reb!" The boy's eyes, long lashes wet with his recent tears, blazed at him. He faced his enemy bravely, but in spite of his best efforts, his lower lip trembled.

Jonathan rose easily. "I guess I am a bit travel worn, son." He smiled lazily down at the boy, seeking to put him at ease.

The boy's shoulders tightened, resisting Jonathan's offer of comfort. "Rebs killed my pa." It was an accusation. His eyes burned with reproach and incipient tears.

"Where, son?" His voice was deep and quiet, softened by his Southern heritage.

"Cold Harbor. And I'm not your son!"

"No," the Rebel's voice was infinitely sad, "you're not my son. But I didn't kill your daddy, boy. I was up in Camp Douglas when they fought at Cold Harbor." His eyes turned bleak with memory.

Tenseness filled the air between the two as the boy fought to keep his dislike of all Southerners alive in the face of the tall man's sympathy. A tap at the door to the suite broke the moment, and a maid entered with a pitcher of water.

Bustling to the nearest table, she poured a glass. "For the poor little lady." She held it out.

The senator took it from her with a low, "Thank you," and came over to the two beside Catherine.

Putting a hand on his grandson's shoulder, he gently moved him from his defensive position between the Confederate and his mother. "Here, Catherine. Drink this and you'll feel better."

Jonathan looked away from the suffering child. The woman's eyes were open, soft brown and a little dazed. They met his wonderingly. Confusion lurked in their depths.

Something deep within him stirred. She'd remember in a moment, and then the warmth in those lovely eyes would vanish like mist in the sun.

Catherine obediently swallowed from the glass the old gentleman held to her lips, and her gaze sharpened. When it did, she blinked and her nostrils flared with scorn. Obviously she, too, was remembering that a Confederate had killed her husband.

Jonathan took a deep breath and braced himself for whatever was to come.

The senator stepped into the awkward moment. "Thank you for your assistance, Captain"—he hesitated slightly, as if the word were giving him trouble—"Foster."

Jonathan understood. He had heard the boy's anguished remark as they left the train platform. He had the same name as the boy's dead father.

"My pleasure," Jonathan answered with the ease of a gentleman long used to polite exchanges. He bowed his farewell to the young woman. "Miz Foster." He bowed again, "Senator." He crossed the room to the door in long, easy strides.

There he waited a moment to see if they would call him back to demand that he await his jailer. When no such suggestion came, he bowed once more, flipped a casual salute at the ten-year-old boy, and was gone, closing the door softly behind him.

Catherine looked at her father-in-law. Moments passed, then she said softly, "I'm glad you did that."

"What?" Senator Foster directed a tight smile at his daughter-in-law. His eyes clearly told her he understood what she had said.

She answered him anyway. "Just let him go."

The senator was silent a long moment. "Somehow I had no stomach for handing him back to that sergeant."

Jonny spoke earnestly. "The sergeant's probably waiting for him downstairs, anyway." He frowned and said truculently, "He won't let that Reb get away."

Catherine sighed. "You're right, of course." Somehow she wished he weren't.

How she longed for life to be pleasant again. To let men trust one another again. To have done with making widows and orphans. With making enemies of men . . . and of children. Of her son.

The senator finally replied to the boy, "I'm sure you're right, Jonny." But when he said the words, his voice was curiously flat.

As a retired lawmaker, he was bound to assume the sergeant would be waiting for his prisoner. As a humanitarian, he hoped he wasn't.

He made a short, harsh sound in his throat. As a student of human nature, he knew there was no chance that the bulldog of a sergeant would miss reclaiming the prisoner he had so obviously abused.

Captain Jonathan Foster wasted no time once he closed the door behind him. His habitual, languid Southern manner disappeared.

Moving with quick, catlike stealth, he passed from door to door on the opposite side of the hall. He pressed an ear against each, listening intently. When he found one that had only silence on the other side, he eased it open. Empty! The gods were smiling.

With a low, exultant laugh, he slipped into the room and quietly turned the key in the lock. Crossing the red, patterned carpet, he flattened himself against the wall beside the window. Moving the lace curtain only enough to give him a glimpse of what lay outside, he observed the alley for a few minutes, scarcely breathing.

Finally satisfied that the alley was unoccupied, he raised the window and straddled the sill. One more look the length of the short alley, and he was through the aperture and hanging by his hands. Dropping lightly to the ground, he stood pressed against the wall of the hotel, getting his bearings.

Hoping the family of his West Point roommate still lived in the house he remembered, he went on his way through the deepening shadows of the twilit town, questing.

Behind him in suite number three, an irate Jack Keefer tried not to let a United States senator know how many kinds of fool he thought he was. "You let him go?" His voice was incredulous. "You let my prisoner just walk out of here?"

"We were certain you would detain him as he came out the door, Sergeant." Senator Foster kept his voice calm—almost disinterested—in the face of the man's insolence.

"I had to go take a—" Keefer's face turned as red as the

carpet on which he stood. He glared, then growled, "I'll have to go to the fort to file a report, Senator. And when I do, I'll be sure to tell them—" He bit off the rest of his sentence with difficulty.

Foster turned toward his daughter-in-law. One look at Catherine's face, and he could easily see she was exhausted. She didn't need this man's bluster. "Do as you please, Sergeant, just go," he said irritably.

The heavy man slammed the door on his way out.

Catherine tried valiantly to smile, her expression wry.

Senator Foster walked to where she sat, smiling back in the same grimly humorous manner. "It's late, my dear. Tomorrow we begin our stagecoach journey." He placed a hand on her shoulder. "Try to get some sleep."

She covered his hand with her own for an instant, both drawing strength for herself and comforting him. She said simply, "Thank you."

She rose and went to her room, knowing her father-in-law would keep her son's nightmares at bay in the room they shared.

What would she do without him? How fortunate she was to have him to accompany her to her grandfather's ranch in Texas. She could never have made the journey alone. Not in her present state. She didn't know where her resoluteness had gone.

She was so tired from the long train ride and all the upset of the day that she got ready for bed by sheer force of habit. She didn't even try to brush her hair the required one hundred strokes.

In her bed, she remembered the blue-eyed Rebel. She wondered if he were safe and far away. She wondered if she wished him well.

He had helped them, but in doing so he had engineered his own escape. How was she to think of him? As a man who helped an old man, a boy, and a fainting woman, or as one of those who had killed her beloved husband and put an end to life as she knew it?

She had no answer to her disturbing questions by the time sleep overtook her.

CHAPTER

Three

"JONATHAN, COME RIGHT IN HERE AND SIT DOWN AND EAT. This minute! I declare, you look as if you haven't seen a good meal in months." Katy Dunston gestured to a place at her spacious dining room table with all the authority only a mother could command.

Jonathan smiled and obeyed, his hair gleaming a darker blond in the lamplight, still damp from the luxury of his bath. He moved toward the clean linen, bright china, and silverware with as much hunger as toward the steaming dishes full of wonderful smells. He hesitated, one hand on the back of the chair, his eyes feasting on the appointments of gracious life.

It had been so long. Everything, every furnishing, every accoutrement of the gracious life that had been his was gone. Silver, china—even the portraits of his long-dead ancestors, founders of this now torn nation—all of it gone in one long hour of agony. Gone in response to the order to burn the plantations of his beloved South.

Something infinitely more precious had gone, too, but his mind shied, screaming, away from that. That memory was a raw wound for which there would never be healing.

"Sit down, boy. Don't just stand there staring. You need to start getting some meat on those bones." Jason Dunston clapped him on the shoulder and moved to his own place at the head of the big mahogany table.

His plump wife fluffed her skirts as she sat at the foot. "Jonathan, you surely do look nice. More like your old self now you're all cleaned up. How lucky we are that our Tom is so tall and thin. Skinny as you are right now, his things look just right on you."

Katy Dunston beamed at him, clearly happy to see him. "After supper, I'll get some more of his things together for you to take with you on your trip." She waved aside his protests before he could voice them. "Tom'll love the excuse to get new. He wouldn't appreciate your doing him out of the opportunity, either."

Jason grinned at his wife's chatter. "Give up, Jonathan. You can't talk Katy out of mothering everybody she gets ahold of. She's gotten real bossy in her old age."

"Well, I never!" Katy bristled for him, knowing he expected it, her fond smile denying she'd taken offense.

"Bring us up to date, boy." The heartiness went out of Jason's voice and he said softly, "We heard about your wife. We're sorry."

Jonathan's head bowed, "Thank you." An instant later he looked up at his host. "Perhaps it was for the best. Melinda was . . . so gentle."

Katy sought to bring him back from his grief. "At least you have the boy."

Jonathan drew in his breath sharply. The pain was worse than the Yankee bullet that had knocked him from his horse into Union hands. After a moment he managed, "No." The single word was all it was in his power to utter.

Katy turned a stricken face to her husband. There was no comfort there, for he was as shocked as she was. He shook his head at her. Finally, he forced himself to clear his throat and say, "Would you, as our guest, please ask the blessing, Jonathan?"

Long habit came to his rescue, and Jonathan stirred from his nightmare to ask the Lord to bless them and the food for which no one now had any appetite.

Catherine and the senator didn't recognize him at first. Shaved and without the ragged uniform with the blood-stained shoulder, the Rebel looked like a different man. "You came back," she gasped.

"I made a bargain, ma'am."

"But the sergeant is gone."

He smiled, his even teeth white against the bronze of his face. The smile was iron hard. "I didn't promise the sergeant anything."

The senator cleared his throat and stepped forward. "What sort of bargain did you make, Captain?"

"To go west and fight Indians." His voice tensed. "And to stay out of the War for Southern Independence."

The senator decided not to correct the man's misnomer for the Rebellion. He couldn't forgo his question, however. "Unusual in a man such as yourself, isn't it?"

Harsh bitterness sounded in the Rebel's voice. "I can't support my sisters sitting in a Yankee prison, Senator." His level blue eyes held the other man's, the white flecks in the irises giving the impression that they were turning to ice.

Catherine put her hand on her father-in-law's arm and turned him with a pretended comment about her son, who was watching the horses being hitched to a sturdy stagecoach. She couldn't bear to look at the tall Confederate officer just now. She didn't know why she'd done as she had; perhaps it was to give him time to recover himself.

A large golden dog clung to the boy's heels, frantic with joy at his liberation from the cage he'd endured on the train. Leaping as high as the boy's shoulder one moment and slamming into his legs the next, he brought the first smile Jonathan had seen on the child's face.

The stagecoach driver came out of the bleached wooden building that served as the ticket office. The man who was to ride shotgun tagged along with him.

Hearing the boy's glad laughter, the driver looked his way and saw the dog. He reached a hand toward the boy. "Hey! I hope you don't think you gonna bring that dog along."

The boy looked stricken.

"He'd have to run after us," the driver told him. "He wouldn't make it beyond the first change of horses. If he even got that far." He turned away toward the coach, throwing back over his shoulder, "Better find somebody to give him to here in Saint Louis."

The boy's eyes filled with tears, and he dug his hands into the thick fur on the dog's neck. He struggled for the words to answer—for the breath to answer.

The big golden dog caught his mood instantly and dropped to the ground at his feet, whining and confused, half on guard.

"I can't leave him. I can't!" It was an anguished cry.

The senator hastened forward. "I'll buy him a seat."

"That's against policy, mister. Besides, stage's full." The driver pushed past and slung his gear up into his box.

Jonny collapsed to his knees in the dusty street and buried his face in his dog's neck, manfully trying not to sob aloud. The dog whined and pushed his muzzle against the back of the boy's neck.

Catherine Foster ran to her son with an inarticulate cry. She sank down in a cloud of black skirts there in the dust beside him. *Why hadn't I thought of this? How can I bear having something else he loves torn from him?* Helplessly, she patted his back.

The senator moved to them and placed a comforting hand on her shoulder. "There, there. I'll arrange for the dog to be sent back to Massachusetts. Old Dawson will take good care of him."

Jonny raised a tear-stained face, outraged at such blasphemy. "No! Scout is mine! I don't want him to go to Massachusetts! I don't want Dawson to take care of him! He's my friend!"

Jonathan was torn by the boy's anguish. Quietly he stepped up to the driver. "You heard the boy. What about letting the dog ride on top with you."

"What?" Obviously the man had never heard such a suggestion.

"Come on." Jonathan smiled winningly. "There's bound to be space enough on top. The dog'll sleep the whole trip. Why not?"

"I dunno." The man shoved his hat to the back of his head, scratched his forehead, and shifted uncomfortably.

"Where's the harm? Remember your dog when you were his age?" It was a shot in the dark, but it hit home.

The driver looked at the boy and the dog—really looked—for the first time. Something surfaced from his memory, and he relented. "Awright. But who's gonna put him up there? That's a mighty big dog."

Jonathan grinned. "I'll get him up there," he promised. Walking over to the little group by the dog, he cleared his throat. They all looked up at him, unwelcoming. "Will you introduce me to your dog?"

"I don't want him to know some dirty Reb!" The boy lashed out from his own pain.

Catherine looked straight at the tall Rebel. With a woman's instinct, she knew he'd come to help. Somehow, unreasonably, she believed he would make things right. The knowledge caused a little flutter in her chest.

Rising and shaking some of the dust from her skirts, she spoke firmly. "Scout." The big dog rose and moved to her side with a backward glance at the boy. "Scout, this is a friend." She put a strong emphasis on the word *friend* and tugged the big dog forward. Stiff-legged he came, eyeing the stranger warily.

Jonathan reached out with the back of his hand toward the golden dog. Liquid brown eyes became friendly, and Scout touched his nose briefly to Jonathan's hand. Immediately, Jonathan fondled the dog's ears and scratched its ruff, hard.

Scout wagged his tail and let his tongue loll from the side of his mouth.

Jonny fell against his mother's side, hugging her waist, accepting her decision to introduce his dog to the Reb but not liking it, not understanding. He felt betrayed. His eyes burned at the tall Southerner.

The flurry around the stagecoach subsided. All the baggage had been loaded, the last trace and buckle checked, and the two men who would see them to their next stop were on the box. Two more passengers, both men, waited to get in the coach.

Dust whirled around the feet of the impatient horses as the driver called to their group. "Better git aboard. I got a run to make."

Jonny panicked, unaware that his mortal enemy had made arrangements to take his dog. "Mama! Gran'pa!" His cry was full of anguish.

"Take it easy, Button." The Reb swooped Scout up and tossed him up on top of the coach. "Stay!" he ordered, his hand thrust, palm rigid, toward the dog. "Lie down." His eyes commanded the dog's obedience.

Jonny's mouth dropped open. "Oh! Gracious! Oh! Oh, do lie down. Lie down, Scout. Lie down boy." He added his own commands. Joy sang in his words. He felt as if his heart were going to leap from his chest. Seeing his dog settle on the roof, he ducked into the waiting stagecoach, afraid that if he didn't get out of sight, the whole town would see him blubbering with relief.

He could keep Scout! It was worth even having to thank a Reb!

CHAPTER

Four

JONATHAN COULD SEE THAT THE ROCKING OF THE STAGE-coach had gotten the boy green around the gills before they were three miles out. Jonny sat beside his window and stared out at the passing landscape with an awful determination.

Jonathan noted his pinched nostrils and his compressed lips. He didn't have to look hard to see that the boy was inches from losing his breakfast. He felt sorry for the child, but admired the way the boy glared resentfully at him when he saw that sympathy on an enemy's face.

Finally he said, "You'll feel better if you look way up ahead." He kept his voice carefully devoid of expression. "You'll get sick if you stare straight out at everything rushing past."

Having said his piece, he riveted his gaze on the space just above the woman's head. He didn't want to give the boy any further reason to dislike him. The lad had enough against him now. He'd worn a uniform the color of the one that had killed the boy's father.

He hung his hat on his knee and leaned his head back. He was tired. Weary past bone-weary of all the ugly bitterness. With all his heart he wished for—

He cut off his thoughts with a knife stroke of rigid control. Everything he might wish was an impossibility now. Wishing around the campfire was over. It had gotten a lot of them through some mighty bad times, but it was futile now. Only a fool would torture himself by trying it.

Absently, he touched his shoulder, his knuckles brushing the sour-faced man wedged in beside him. Tossing the dog up to the top of the coach hadn't been smart. His wound was aching like fury. He smiled a crooked smile. He knew he'd do the same thing, again and again, until the big golden dog had safely arrived at journey's end, wound or no wound.

Journey's end. He wasn't much looking forward to his own. A Confederate in the Federal Army was going to have a tough row to hoe. He'd sure as hell keep his mouth closed. Let just one of the soldiers he'd be serving with learn that he'd owned one of the largest plantations in Virginia and worked it with over a hundred people, and the fat would be in the fire. Yes, he'd be sure to keep his mouth shut.

He closed his eyes. Funny thing, that. He called them his people. He knew all of them by name, knew their families, and kept them from being parted—even broke the law and educated them if they wanted.

Just like the white bond servants from England who had indentured themselves in the early days, he had worked them seven years. Then he had freed them if he thought they could make it on their own. Most went to that big colony of freedmen up near Petersburg. Some went north, and some—With a lump in his throat, he remembered those who had refused to go. His body servant, Saul; his butler, Agamemnon, who could easily have worked for wages in the homes of some of Jonathan's Northerner friends, who'd told him so on every visit; even Caesar, whom he had trained as a blacksmith, and who could have made a good living at the trade, had stayed. His people. The men from the North called them slaves.

He steeled himself against the acid that bit into his very soul. Driven to some physical action, he contented himself with massaging his throbbing shoulder. Inside, he twisted and turned, striving to find a position from which his memories couldn't eat him alive.

Catherine watched the man across the coach from behind her dark veil. Though he was far too thin, and the lines of care and bitterness had etched themselves deeply beside his mouth, he was still a very handsome man. His mouth fascinated her. Since he kept such an iron guard over the expressions that would have betrayed his thoughts should he let them reach his eyes, his mouth was his most revealing feature. The lips were finely chiseled, firm, and clean cut. Obviously the man was an aristocrat, she thought with a hint of scorn.

She saw him smile, an odd, self-deprecating smile, and wondered what he was thinking. She saw him touch his shoulder, and suddenly remembered the bloodstained hole a ball had made just there in the shell jacket of the uniform he'd worn when she first met him.

Of course! That wound would still trouble him unless he'd gotten very good medical care for it. If he'd taken the ball just before being captured, however, she knew the chances of that were slight. It was one of the shames she had to share with other right-minded Northerners that Rebel prisoners were not treated well. It was no comfort to her that prisoners of war throughout history had never been treated well.

She shifted her position a bit, uncomfortable with her thoughts. The army said that the Union soldiers in Rebel prisons were on scant rations and went without medicines, and it was true. But it was also true that the people of the South, women, children, and old men—as well as soldiers—were on the verge of starvation because their crops were burned and their land turned into battlefields.

She had heard that Virginia was almost a wasteland, that the armies that moved back and forth across the state had taken most of the trees for forts and campfires and that all the grass had been grazed to nothing by their horses.

When she had read about the trees, she had experienced a tug of regret. She and her beloved Jonathan had honeymooned on his yacht. They had spent the long summer days sailing the Chesapeake Bay and up the James River.

Jonathan had pointed out the huge trees that dotted the sweeping lawns at Harrison's Landing. The Virginians called the huge farm Berkeley Plantation, if she remembered correctly. He'd told her that those very trees had been standing there when the first colonists came to Jamestown.

She remembered the awe she had felt at the sight of the towering giants. Now they were gone. Burned in cook and camp fires when the army had camped there.

To grow food to support that part of the South, only the Shenandoah Valley had remained. Now it, too, was burned over by order of the Union high command.

Her mind turned to the plight of the men who had owned those stately mansions along the James: Westover, Berkeley, Shirley, Brandon, all those huge farms they had sailed past. Were they like this Rebel? Reduced to skin and bones with bitter lines beside their mouths?

Her honest heritage of a puritan conscience attacked her again. Would this one look so worn if he had been given proper food and medicine at Camp Douglas?

Medicines. The South didn't give any to the Union prisoners in the notorious Libby Prison in Richmond, she knew. They might have done so at the beginning, but they certainly didn't anymore. Didn't her own newspapers brag that the Navy's blockade effectively cut off all shipments of medical supplies to the Rebs?

She couldn't, no matter how bitterly she hated those who had taken her husband from her, condone denying Rebel prisoners proper care for such a reason. Not when they were held in the North, where there was still such plenty.

She glanced at her Jonny. She was relieved to see that he looked less uncomfortable now that he'd taken the Rebel's advice and was looking ahead of the horses instead of straight out his window. Tenderness welled up in her. He was so precious to her. Doubly so now that her Jonathan was gone. Fervently she thanked God that she had never had to see him go hungry.

Suddenly she was ill with these thoughts of suffering. Enough. It was all too much for her. There was nothing she could do to change things. In that, she was as helpless as the women of the South.

She squeezed her eyes shut and took a deep breath. Soon it would be over. Her father-in-law said that it was a miracle that the South had held out as long as it had, with no allies and no munition factories to speak of.

Their armies were being decimated and there were no men to replace those who fell in battle. At the same time, the North had a steady flow of immigrants flooding into New York who were aglow with the burning desire to preserve the United States of America at any cost.

The Union army was full of men who might speak little or no English, but they were willing to fight. The South lost irreplaceable thousands of men, yet fought on. There was rarely a battle reported now that the odds were not at least three to one against them. Clayton had told her that with reluctant admiration.

To Clayton Foster the Rebels might be a gallant foe. He might admire their tactics and tenacity, and even so still regard them with bitterness for the son he had lost; but to her they were simply the men who had destroyed her life. They were the men who had killed her husband and taken her son's father from him and in one stroke, irrevocably, horribly, changed her life.

She could feel the tears welling behind her eyes, feel the tightness in her chest that made her want to cry aloud. Teeth clenched, she turned her thoughts resolutely away from the war.

When she had regained control of her emotions, through half-lowered lids, she watched the Rebel. He'd put his hand into his coat. His long fingers barely moved the fabric as he rubbed his shoulder.

She locked her mind against feeling sympathy for him and wondered if she would be able to get the driver or the stage guard to lift Scout down and put him back up on the roof of the coach for the rest of the trip. She was sure the Rebel wouldn't try to do it again. She sighed.

Her father-in-law felt the movement of her shoulders and asked loudly, "Are you all right, Catherine?"

She raised her own voice to be heard over the pounding hooves, the jingle of harness, and the creak of the stage-coach. "Yes, Clayton, thank you. I'm fine."

The Rebel opened his eyes. He listened for a moment to the heavy chuff of the horses' breathing. "We'll be stopping soon, ma'am. It'll give you a chance to stretch your le—ah, limbs."

Catherine could think of nothing to say in response. He looked as if he could do with some stretching himself, cramped as his broad shoulders appeared between the two men on either side of him. She nodded to let him know she had heard, civility demanded that of her, and turned to look out the window.

True to his prediction, the stage slowed a bit and headed downhill into what looked like a village. In minutes, they had stopped and the sweating team was being replaced by a fresh one.

The Rebel eased out of the coach in one lithe movement. "How about a little walk for the lady, driver?" He stood easily balanced on the step.

Above him Scout whined, hung his head over the baggage rail and nuzzled the hand the Rebel had clamped on the edge of the roof.

"It'll have to wait for the next stop. I got a schedule to keep. Rest for the passengers is at the next stop."

Catherine saw his jaw clench. Then she saw him realize argument was futile. It interested her that he was annoyed by his failure to win a respite for them. What had he to do with her—with them? Why did he persist in—was the word "pretending"?—to care for them? They were enemies, after all.

He slid back into his seat, staring down at the sour-faced man who had muttered a curse at having to be cramped again until the man said, "Sorry, lady."

Catherine barely nodded her acceptance of his apology. She resented that it had been procured for her by the Southerner more than she minded the curse that called for it.

She leaned her head back and closed her eyes, vowing she would keep them closed until they reached the next station. Maybe that way she could keep the man across from her from bringing to mind all the thoughts she could do so very much better without.

CHAPTER
Five

THE SECOND STOP WAS A BLESSING WHEN IT CAME. THEY were to eat and have a few minutes to stretch their legs. The community was little more than a wide spot in the road, but it did boast a boardinghouse at which the passengers were to have their noon meal.

The driver and the guard disappeared as soon as they'd disposed of the team, leaving the coach standing in front of the shabby building that housed the next team and the small, dingy room that served as office to the stage company.

Scout barked sharply from his place on the roof. Anxious to get down now that the horses had been unhitched, he circled and barked again.

Jonny went to him immediately, clambering up over the luggage-laden boot like a monkey.

"Jonny! Be careful!" Catherine clapped a hand over her mouth, afraid she would say something more. Clayton and she had often discussed her new tendency to be overly protective of the boy. While they admitted it was only natural, they also recognized it as stifling. They agreed she must fight it, but, oh, how hard it was. He was all she had left of Jonathan.

She was overtired, she told herself as tears threatened again. She'd feel better as soon as she'd eaten.

The tall Southerner walked over to the coach. "Think you can get him to follow you down the way you went up?" he asked Jonny.

The boy flashed him a heated glance. "Scout'll do anything I ask him to!"

The Rebel, hands on his hips and legs spread, cocked his head and waited.

Jonny's face flushed with annoyance. He started down the leather sheet covering the luggage. "Come on, Scout. Here, boy." He slid a little from his position at the top of the leather cover that stretched down at a steep angle from where it was anchored to the coach. "Here, Scout."

The dog looked over the edge at the boy. Then he looked over the side to gauge how far he would have to jump to make it down without following his young master, and whined.

The Rebel moved to just below Jonny's position on the slick boot cover. "Come on, Scout old boy. You can do it."

Scout gave one last bark in appreciation of the man's encouragement and launched himself over the edge of the roof. He hit the leather luggage shield at the point at which his young master clung, and together they made record time of their descent.

Scout landed on the ground at the Rebel's feet and bounded off to see Catherine. Jonny, arriving headfirst a split second later, found his arm grasped in a strong grip that redirected his fall to land him on his feet.

The Rebel waited. He kept his gaze locked pointedly on the boy.

"Thanks," Jonny grumbled at last. It was expected of him, but golly he hated being beholden to this Reb. He'd rather have near broken his neck!

They walked over to the boardinghouse the stage driver had pointed out. The three Fosters clinging together led the way, then the two men passengers that had bracketed Jonathan in the coach.

The drummer, lugging his sample case, and the old rancher were chatting about the changes since the last time they'd been in town. With a quick handshake, they separated to go about their respective tasks, each glad to have reached his destination.

Jonathan lingered behind. His eyes, too long accustomed to reconnoitering not to do so, took in the long, dusty street.

It was stark where the commercial buildings stood in its center, lacking even a hint of a growing thing, but there were trees at both ends. They stood in the yards of the few private residences and offered shade to those passing by.

He took a deep breath and smelled home cooking and flowers and all the things that he hadn't smelled in what seemed a very long time. And there was something else. Something that he hadn't felt for a very long time. There was a feeling of peace.

It pervaded the little town and lay on his weary spirit like balm. He ambled through it like a man reluctant to arrive where he was headed.

He was the last one to seat himself at the long table reserved for the stage passengers in the sunny dining room of the boardinghouse. He kept his face expressionless, oddly moved by the commonplace act of people sitting together at a table with a cloth on it, about to break bread together.

Catherine glanced at the Rebel as he sat. Something had tugged her gaze his way. She noted the quiet, easy grace with which he took his seat.

Jonathan—her Jonathan—had always bounced into his chair as if eager for the companionship he found at their table. Her Jonathan had—Oh, how she hated it that this stranger, this enemy, should bear his name! She loathed the way she had to make some distinction to keep the two so dissimilar men separate! She shook out her napkin with unaccustomed vigor and placed it across her lap.

The Rebel obviously heard the snap of the fabric. He shook out his own napkin gently, a smile playing across his lips.

Catherine felt a flash of anger. Why couldn't he be less perceptive of the people around him? Why couldn't he have been a clod like that terrible sergeant who had been abusing him?

She felt so vulnerable and exposed just now, as if every feeling she experienced could be read on her face by the remotest stranger. Coping with the tragedy in her life was something she would far rather do without an audience composed of one overly understanding enemy.

Angrily she forced herself to acknowledge his helping her son when he fell from the coach. Probably he had kept Jonny from at least spraining a shoulder. Maybe he had prevented the child from breaking his neck.

She owed him her gratitude. Why did it have to be so difficult to say anything nice to this man? She was almost overwhelmed with relief when her father-in-law spoke for her.

Clayton Foster cleared his throat meaningfully and said, "I must thank you for catching the boy when he fell off the boot. You probably saved him an injury."

Jonny glared at the Rebel from his place on the other side of his mother. "I—" he began stormily.

The Southerner interrupted him from his place at the end of the table. "I merely steadied his descent. I'm glad to have been of service." He let his glance slide to the windows that overlooked the back garden of the house, dismissing the subject. Dismissing them all.

Ah'm. He said Ah instead of I. Speech like . . . like what? Catherine wanted to make it a fault, when she knew it was only the slowed speech of men raised in a languid environment.

Oh damn, she thought violently, shocking herself. This infernal war was making her unfair. She'd become prejudiced, and she'd always prided herself on her fair-mindedness. Was that, too, to be a casualty of this conflict of brother against brother? What would be left when this rebellion was over?

Her appetite gone, she stared at the plate of stew that someone had set before her. She watched as the woman serving them paused at the table to ask the Rebel, "Would you be so kind as to ask the blessing, sir?"

Catherine saw his hesitation and wondered about it. Finally she saw him bow his head and heard him say briefly, "Bless this food to our use, and us to thy service, Lord. Amen." He said ah-men. She thought that was Episcopalian; it was at home, where everybody else said a-men, but it could just as well be his drawl.

His face was tight when he looked up again. What had he been thinking? That he had little to be thankful for, this man who must have lost everything? He said "bless," not "thank you." Perhaps he didn't feel he had much to be thankful for.

Unbidden, a little flame flared in her. He was alive! He should be thankful to be alive. Thousands of men would be grateful if they could rise from their graves and be alive again. Back home with their loved ones and—

Oh, God. She resisted the physical impulse to curl up around the anguish that centered in her. *When will the pain stop? When will I begin to be myself again? When will I stop being this vengeful bit of nastiness I seem to have become?*

She forced her hand to bring food to her mouth. Forced herself, as she had so often done in the days after she'd received word of Jonathan's death, to chew and to swallow, making the food go down with a convulsive effort of her throat.

While she attempted to eat the savory stew, she tried not to hate the man at the end of the table. She tried to tell herself it was wrong to hate. She tried to stop.

Until he had come into her life, however, she had made some sort of peace in which she could live—some sort of numbness. He had torn it all away in that awful moment it had taken him to announce his name, and his constant presence was like vinegar poured into a wound. She wondered how she would live through the days ahead.

How would she be able to live through this time when they would be forced to be together? How long would it be before she could put her fragile peace back together again so that she could get on with her life?

In her lap, she felt her fist clench so hard that her nails pierced the sturdy linen of her napkin.

CHAPTER
Six

CATHERINE THRUST HER HAT BACK INTO PLACE FOR THE hundredth time. She had put back her veil hours ago, preferring to risk being improper to sweltering behind it for one more minute.

With an effort, she resisted the impulse to blow at the curls that tumbled into her eyes every time the jolts of the stage shifted her hat and rearranged her hairstyle. She concentrated on trying to avoid staring at the Rebel instead.

It was hard to do, however, when one's knees all but pressed against the knees of the man. Unbidden, an unreasonable irritation grew in her. He sat the bench across from her with the same ease with which he would no doubt sit his horse. His long, lean body seemed merely to absorb the jolts and shocks of the road, while Catherine was sometimes thrown six inches up out of her place.

She couldn't help it; his seeming ease made her even more uncomfortable. She was bruised and tired and cross and dusty and she wanted to blame him for it, fair or not.

The last leg of this first day's trip was almost over. It couldn't come soon enough. Everyone in the coach was heartily sick of being jounced and bounced over roads that grew worse with every passing mile.

Catherine was glad that Jonny had long ago given up staring out the glassless window and sprawled across his grandfather's lap. With the ready adaptability of youth, he was sleeping. The senator held him safely, and had braced his own foot against the seat opposite to ensure their position. How fervently she wished her legs were long enough to do the same, lady or no.

Catherine glanced at her father-in-law and saw that the old gentleman's shoulders slumped with fatigue. It worried her. He was always so full of life, so in control. Everyone had been surprised when he'd retired with the war still on. In the pain and confusion of losing her dear Jonathan, Catherine, usually so independent, found herself leaning on her father-in-law.

It frightened her to see him as exhausted as she was. She watched him with concern. He had his head back and his eyes closed. Was the trip going to be too much for him? Catherine felt guilty, now, at having asked him to see her safely settled at her grandfather's ranch.

In her grief and desolation, she hadn't thought of the cost to him. How could she have let herself collapse to the point that she'd become a burden to Clayton?

Suddenly, the wheels of the coach slammed into something Catherine was sure must be a fallen tree. She flew into the air, and returned to the bench with a punishing thump. Too bad she couldn't brace a foot on the other seat like the senator.

At least the Rebel had left his seat with that one, too. He looked surprised, his winged eyebrows raised over startled eyes.

Catherine's satisfaction at his almost comic expression was short-lived, however, as the coach jerked violently upward again and she found herself in a position more fitting the heroine of one of the new dime novels. As the rear wheels struck and passed over the same sizeable obstacle, she was thrown completely free of her seat.

With a startled cry, she flew through the air and landed in the Southerner's lap. Strong, protecting arms closed around her, holding her safe through four more dreadful bumps. She had quick impressions of a clean masculine scent, a hard-muscled male body, and her own acute embarrassment.

Instantly, she began struggling to free herself from her untenable position. She was hampered by the lurching sway of the vehicle, and her own tangled skirts. She thought she heard—no, she felt, by the rumble in his chest—the man laugh.

Indignantly, she looked him right in the eye. His face was only inches from hers. It was impossible to mistake the glint of amusement in his eyes. Before she could think of something sufficiently scathing to say, he grinned at her and said, "Permit me."

Catherine couldn't hear the softly spoken words over the noise of the coach and horses, but she saw them on his lips and felt them with the hands she was pressing against his chest to keep herself from being thrown closer. She scowled at him and his grin broadened.

Inanely she thought, *How odd, I'd thought him older.* She had put his age at about forty until now, but she could see she had been mistaken. The grin took ten years off him, easily.

Strong hands lifted her gently and put her back where she belonged as easily as if he had been handling a baby. She didn't want to appreciate his assistance; she wanted to rail at him for touching her. She was furious with herself for having fallen, of all places, into the lap of a grinning Confederate.

Striving to remain a lady, she looked at him with as much calm as she could muster. "Thank you," she said demurely, her back teeth clenched.

She watched him struggle to subdue his smile. "My pleasure."

That annoyed her. Didn't anyone south of the Mason-Dixon Line ever say simply, "You're welcome"?

With a regal lift of her chin, she turned her head and looked out the window. The day was fading to rose and golden streaks in the sky beyond. Catherine tried to lose herself in its beauty as she sought to regain her composure.

A few minutes later, with a mighty shout from the guard to alert the hostlers and a jangle of harness as the horses slowed, the stage rumbled into the small town that was its last stop of the day.

The driver kicked the brake on and yelled, "Whoa, there!" The coach, wheels locked, slid to a halt behind plunging horses.

Catherine nearly flew forward out of her seat again, and the Rebel reached out as if he would steady her. She glared.

Three men, half-visible in the cloud of dust made by the coach's arrival, ran out of a livery stable and began unhitching the horses. In minutes they led the tired, lathered team away.

The stage office was little more than the dingy front room of the livery stable, but a neat little man in a well-brushed black suit came out of it and addressed the senator. "I made your reservations as you requested, Senator Foster. They ain't much. The Golden Palace is the hotel, all right. But it's the saloon, too."

His manner was apologetic. "I told 'em to put you in the back. It's a lot quieter." He pointed to the largest building on the short, dusty main street. "Guess you folks'll be wanting to get settled."

He pulled nervously at his string tie. The obvious awe in which he held the senator seemed to all but overwhelm him. "The food's real good there." He twisted his hat in his hands, shifting from foot to foot. "If there's no more I can do to help, I'll just get along home."

"Thank you, sir. Thank you very much." The senator's deep voice lacked its usual vitality, but his sincerity got through.

The little man smiled, and began to back away. At a safe distance, he carefully placed his hat on his head, turned around, and went off to his own place for supper. He'd tell how the great man had thanked him—twice—for the rest of his days.

Up and down the street, lanterns were being lit as twilight settled over the town. The lamplight gave sightless houses eyes to watch the night. A woman walked out onto her porch and called her children. Then her door and other doors clapped closed as people went into their homes for supper.

Their driver ambled over, raising little puffs of dust from the street's surface with every step. He didn't look half as tired as his passengers.

That surprised Catherine. After all, he'd driven all day.

He pulled his hat from his head and addressed the senator. "We'll be locking the stage in the barn, like always. You can just leave your things aboard if ya'd like. They'll be safe."

He looked them over sympathetically. "Get a good night's sleep, folks. Stage leaves at six tomorrow morning. Far as the war goes, we're lucky. The only fightin' is down around Tupelo." He lifted his hat in a parting salute, put it back on his head, then he and the guard meandered off.

The four travelers waited a moment by the stagecoach. The three Massachusetts Fosters stood close together, and the fourth, the man from the South who was no kin, a little apart.

Tired as she was, Catherine noticed the hungry look on the Rebel's face as his blue eyes scanned the street. If she hadn't been so weary, she'd wonder why he looked at towns as if he'd never get his fill. Could it have been that long since he'd seen a peaceful community?

Jonny leaned heavily against his mother's side, more asleep than awake. The senator looked as if he were about to drop, and all of them were covered in dust. Catherine watched him take a deep breath, then he squared his shoulders and moved stiffly toward the spot where the stage people had put their light luggage.

The Rebel, without seeming to hurry, beat him to it, scooping up the boy's and Catherine's bags with his own. Catherine was relieved that he'd not tried to take her father-in-law's. The senator was a proud man.

The Rebel turned back to the coach. Softly, he said, "Come on down, Scout."

Oh, glory! She'd forgotten the dog until this very moment. How could she have forgotten Scout? She must be even more tired than she realized.

With an anxious whine, the big dog slid awkwardly down the black cowhide apron that covered the boot, jumped to the ground, and pressed against Catherine's skirts. He gave one sharp bark when, a minute later, the three men who'd taken care of the team came back for the coach and dragged it toward the yawning cavern that was the center aisle of the livery stable.

The coach's moving off acted like a signal, galvanizing the weary little group to action. They walked diagonally across the wide, badly rutted street toward the Golden Palace.

Loud voices and the sound of a tinny piano spilled out with the lantern light to meet them. Before they reached the wide, covered porch, two men appeared from inside and heaved a third, protesting vigorously, out into the dusty street.

Catherine was too exhausted to react to the incident. None of them could help hearing the raw language being yelled good-humoredly back and forth in the big room.

Catherine threw an apprehensive look over her shoulder to the Rebel, who trailed behind them. Immediately, he answered her unspoken plea and moved ahead. She watched him as he approached the swinging doors, hating the fact that she'd called for him, however silently.

He seemed to change subtly as she watched. Though he didn't really, Catherine felt as if he were going on tiptoe.

Stopping just outside the swinging doors, he looked the place over for a minute. Then he held the door open for her, and said softly, "Over to the right." She obeyed him without question, entering the big, smoke-filled room with him close behind her.

The end of the bar nearest the stairs leading to the second floor had a desk attached to it. Behind the desk were the cubbyholes usually associated with hotel keys and messages and mail waiting to be picked up.

Catherine walked purposefully toward the desk, carefully looking neither to the right nor to the left. It didn't take much imagination to realize the men around her were, for the most part, drunk.

A barman saw them, wiped his hands hastily on a soiled bar towel, and hurried over to them. Showing a missing tooth in his expansive smile he crowed, "You must be that there senator the stage company made reservations for."

The noise level in the room dropped considerably at his remark. "Two rooms on the back. Sign here."

He turned the fly-specked register for the senator to sign. Clayton Foster wrote his name and handed the pen to his son's widow. "Catherine," he invited her to place her name below his own in the ledger.

Catherine signed and passed the pen back to her father-in-law. Just a few minutes more and she could bathe. She was so tired and gritty she could think of nothing but getting to her room and washing off some of the dust she'd been collecting all day.

"We'll need one more room." The Rebel spoke from just behind her. He kept his voice low, picked up the pen from where the senator had placed it on the ledger, and signed J. Foster in a bold hand. He signed by reaching around her, giving the impression that Catherine stood in his embrace.

She felt a stir of self-anger that she hadn't had sense enough to move aside. She decided fatigue had made her stupid. She stood quietly within the circle of his arm, though, not wanting to make a scene to entertain the staring men.

The barman–desk clerk snickered as he reached for another key. "Don't want the boy spoiling any of your fun, huh? I got a single for him."

The room behind them had become quiet; even the tinny piano was silent. Since everybody in town—alerted by the reservations made by the man from the stage company—was curious about a United States senator, the barman's remark was clearly heard.

Catherine's gasp was audible. The senator stepped forward, fire in his eyes.

Jonathan grabbed his arm, stopping him in his tracks. In a steely voice the Rebel stated, "The room is for me. The boy has been ill. My wife wants to ensure his rest."

Each sentence was clipped clean to have a sharp edge on it. His stance was challenging. In an icy voice he added, "Not that it's any of your business, *friend*"—he said the last word with an emphasis that made it a threat—"but I snore."

Catherine was angered that he'd claimed to be her husband. Words rushed to her lips that would brand him a liar.
She was bursting to tell the world that this tall enemy was
not her beloved Jonathan.

Then, amid the anger, she felt something else. From
somewhere, caution rose in her. Somehow, she knew she
was being protected by his outrageous claim.

With one surreptitious glance at the calibre of men to
whom she wished to denounce him, she made her decision.
Wisely, she let matters stand. From beside her, she felt her
father-in-law draw a relieved breath.

The senator freed himself from the Rebel's warning grip,
and shot him an assessing glance. After a long pause, he
decided to go along with him, as well. Fixing the barman
with a glacial glare, he said coldly, "Kindly show us to our
rooms."

The man ducked under an open section of the counter and
started up the steps. Suddenly he noticed Scout, who'd been
hidden by Catherine's skirts. "Wait a minute, now! Where
did that mutt come from?"

The Rebel, with slow deliberation, stepped onto the second step below the man. Still, he leaned down to stare,
narrow-eyed, into the barman's face.

In a voice devoid of expression, he remarked quietly,
"The dog is the boy's. If he needs walking, I'll walk him.
He's a quiet dog, and the boy wants him."

The barman looked up into the tall Southerner's eyes for
a long moment. He understood what he read there, and
instantly, his gaze fell away. "Yeah. Okay." Nervously, he
put distance between himself and this quiet man.

The widening space gave him courage. Hoping to save
face in front of his buddies, he tried to sound belligerent.
"But you pay for any damage."

Nobody bothered to answer him.

An hour later, greatly refreshed by a lengthy sponge bath,
Catherine left her son sleeping, the big golden dog on guard
at the foot of the bed. Poor dear. Jonny was so tired, he'd
slept through her bathing him and hadn't even cared when

she promised to bring him back some supper.

Scout, though, had certainly raised his muzzle from his paws when he'd heard her mention food. She gave him a pat and left the room, locking the door behind her and pushing the key and a fresh handkerchief into the commodious pocket she'd had made in her traveling skirt.

She went next door to her father-in-law's room and knocked lightly. The senator came out looking considerably fresher in a clean shirt. Some of the tired lines had left his face with a good scrubbing, too.

"Ready for something to eat, my dear?" He tucked her hand into the crook of his elbow and smiled down at her.

"Hmmmm." She smiled back and nodded. "I hope the gentleman from the stage office was telling the truth when he said the food was good." Her smile turned naughty and she pressed a hand to her stomach, "I'm hollow."

The senator chuckled in agreement. They turned the corner to the stairway and almost ran into the Rebel. From the glowing look about him, he'd been down the street to the bath house and had enjoyed the unimaginable luxury of a complete, soaking bath.

Catherine couldn't help herself. She stopped abruptly. The senator patted her hand, mistaking her envious resentment for repugnance. His face carefully noncommittal, he stood quietly beside her.

The Rebel, his freshly washed hair still damp, quirked an eyebrow at the senator. "I assume you are going to supper." When neither answered, irritation edged his voice. "I suggest you permit me to accompany you. Some of the crowd down there are a little rough."

Catherine felt Clayton's arm stiffen. Was the Rebel implying she wasn't safe with Clayton for escort? Her dislike of the Confederate rose, prompted by his implied belittlement of her father-in-law.

As if he read her mind, he bowed and said in a tone he would use to instruct a tiresome child, "You're a beautiful woman, ma'am. Some of the men down there are drunk. There'll be less chance of anyone offering you offense if you're in the company of two gentlemen."

Catherine felt the tension drain from her father-in-law's arm. Clayton Foster bowed very slightly to the man he must detest, accepting the man's suggestion as a sound one. He had heard the ribald remarks some of the heavier drinkers had made when Catherine had walked up the stairs, and he was too wise not to agree with the Reb.

Clayton admitted the man's intelligence. Still, he doubly detested the tall Southerner. Never for an instant could he excuse this man for bearing his son's name, nor could he forget that the Reb had worn the uniform of the army that had killed that son. He could not find it in his heart to forgive the man for either offense.

Several men, weaving uncertainly, left the bar when the three Fosters reached the foot of the stairs. Swaying, they approached the base of the stairway, gaping slack-jawed up at the descending trio.

The Rebel nodded and said pleasantly, "Good evening, gentlemen."

His quiet remark halted them in their tracks. Clearly, the last thing leering men expected to be called was gentlemen. They regarded one another owlishly.

In their moment of uncertainty, the tall Southerner whisked Catherine across the broad landing and through the door marked Dining Room in fancy gold letters on one of the panes of glass that flanked it. Too startled to protest the Reb's hand on her waist, she heard the senator echo, "Good evening, gentlemen," and they were safely in the hotel dining room.

A woman who looked as if she could have held her own with the crowd in the barroom led them to a table in front of a window that overlooked the street. The Rebel pulled out a chair for Catherine.

For a moment, rebellion flared in Catherine and she wanted more than anything to sit elsewhere—anywhere but the place he designated—but she refused to make even a small scene. She sat and flashed a look at her father-in-law that told him how little she liked the situation. Clayton's answering glance seemed to tell her to endure.

The Rebel took the chair next to her own.

The dining room hostess told them what was available, and sent a waitress to them. Catherine decided on baked chicken, telling her father-in-law her choice, as was proper.

It was the Southerner, however, not the senator, who conveyed her order to the hostess. Catherine looked at him stormy-eyed. As if he had the right!

The senator gave his own order in the tone of voice Catherine knew he used when he was in a politically touchy situation. She bit back the acid remark she wished she could make to the tall man in the chair beside hers.

Her gaze locked with the senator's. She took a steadying breath. She was rewarded by an approving look from Clayton. He must think the men in the bar were more of a threat than the mere annoyance she found them.

The food was indeed as good as the little man from the stage office had said it would be, and the three of them ate in what onlookers would deem companionable silence. In reality, Catherine wished she could have eaten alone.

She picked at her chicken. The senator ate his trout with the mechanical movements of a weary man, and the Rebel proved to have impeccable table manners.

That annoyed Catherine. After all, hadn't she been told that the Confederate army consisted mainly of nonslaveholding small farmers? Simple men who had nothing to gain from the conflict but their precious State's Rights?

Hadn't she heard that the slave owners were definitely in the minority in their armies? Indeed, in the South. The Rebs themselves called their rebellion a rich man's war but a poor man's fight.

Why, then, did she have to be afflicted with one of the rich ones? She'd much prefer having an honest red-necked foot soldier at the table with her to this handsome man with his elegant table manners and her husband's name.

A simple hillsman would in no way serve as such a constant reminder of her own handsome and well-mannered Jonathan. And her loss.

She could feel tears behind her eyes. She turned her face to the window and pretended to watch the dimly lit street until she regained control. If only she weren't so tired.

Finally, she turned back to find the Rebel watching her quietly. "Would you like me to arrange for something for the boy and the dog?" His soft Southern drawl made his query sound intimate somehow, almost as if they did, indeed, share a close relationship.

Wordlessly Catherine nodded, unable to bring herself to acknowledge his thoughtfulness aloud. When the waitress brought the tray with two napkin-covered plates in response to the Southerner's request, she thanked the woman, averting her eyes from the Rebel's level regard.

Rising hastily, she took the tray from the waitress, assured the senator she could manage, and left the dining room. When she reached the door and passed through it to the spacious landing at the foot of the stairs off which the dining room opened, she became aware of the drunken stares from the bar.

Even as she hesitated, the Rebel grasped her elbow and turned her toward the stairs. He walked up them close behind her, shielding her from the avid gaze of the men.

Catherine could feel the strength and warmth that radiated from the man. She could think of nothing to say. What could she say to a man who continually made himself useful to her and to her family when "thank you" stuck in her throat?

When they got to her room, he took the tray from her hands and waited until she found her key. His blue eyes watched her speculatively as she used it. When the door began to swing inward, he handed the tray back to her and touched his brow in a half-salute.

She heard his deep voice murmur, "Good night, ma'am. Sleep well," as she shut the door in his face.

Leaning back against the closed door, she wondered how men could fight day-long battles. The conflict she felt as her hatred of this tall Southerner surrendered to reluctant attraction had drained her of energy. She wished she could stop it, if for no other reason than to conserve her strength, but she couldn't seem to control her reaction to him. Merely hearing his Southern speech made anger flare in her. Having him wish her well fanned it to flames, but under it all, the woman in her was beginning to respond to him. Had she been on a battlefield, she would never have found the strength to fight.

With a heavy sigh, she began the business of feeding her two charges. Scout, at least, seemed highly appreciative.

CHAPTER

Seven

IN THE COACH THE NEXT MORNING, CATHERINE SMILED wanly at her father-in-law. "Please tell me again why I didn't want to take a ship to Galveston?"

Senator Foster braced his foot against the opposite seat and smiled back. "Because you didn't want to risk running afoul of the Confederate States Navy."

"I'm so glad you're here to remind me." She leaned her head back a moment, heedlessly crushing the fine black straw of her bonnet. Her chest rose and fell with a deep sigh.

Across the coach, Jonathan regarded her from under half-lowered lids. It disturbed him to see that tiny lines of fatigue marked her lovely face.

Even as he watched, she twisted her head fretfully. It didn't take a genius to see that the woman was pushing herself too hard. It was as if she had to reach her destination before she could begin life anew and was driven by some harrying force to do so as quickly as possible.

It didn't take a genius, either, to see that she was utterly exhausted. Stage travel was proving tiring for him, and he was used to long hours in a hard saddle, where constant danger conspired with an empty stomach to keep rest at bay.

He had watched her at their two stops today, and he had seen that she only pecked at her food. Unless he missed his guess, the pretty little Yankee was about done in.

His worried gaze shifted to the senator and the boy. The old man seemed to be holding his own. His bearing spoke of past military duty, so perhaps he was, like Jonathan, no stranger to hardship.

The boy, with the typical resilience of youth, spent much of the time sprawled limply across his grandfather's lap, napping, and the rest of the time staring out the window at the changing scenery. Nothing to concern him there.

The woman was another matter. Her strength was clearly not up to the task of holding herself comfortably in place on the rocking stagecoach. The only time she seemed able to relax was when they slowed to ascend the hills, as they were doing now. The rest of the time she clutched the windowsill for dear life, and was battered about by the conveyance itself. Even the great golden dog riding on the roof seemed to fare better than she.

He frowned. Though he felt concern for her, this was a woman who couldn't even thank him for seeing to food for her boy and her dog the night before. He couldn't seem to overcome the bitterness she engendered in him by being alive, healthy, and well-dressed. Resentment rose in him just seeing the quality of this woman's clothing after watching the women in his own life turn their dresses again and again in a gallant attempt to hide the fact that their clothing became more and more faded as they slowly wore them to rags. He couldn't help feeling it when he saw that northern women had had to make no such sacrifices to field the army that had invaded his beloved South.

When he had been dragged in fetters like a common felon through their land, he had been unable to avoid comparing the Northern women to his own. Well-fed and dressed in fine, sensible clothing that showed no signs of wear, they had gone about their errands shod in proper shoes, not make-do footgear contrived from pieces of cut-up carpet.

His heart twisted in his chest to think of his dead wife and his sisters, so used to the finest of Paris fashions, bravely making do. With an effort, he tore his thoughts away from them, unashamed of the tears that threatened to form behind his eyes. They wouldn't be the first tears he'd wept for his own, and no doubt, they wouldn't be the last before this business was over, this war between the states.

Ports were blockaded so that no medicines or arms reached the South; the army dwindled with no hope of replacements; and the entire Southland starved as Sherman and Sheridan burned their respective paths through it. It was easy to see that his homeland was doomed, and with it went every hope he had of regaining his own status in life.

His sisters would be left to his greatly diminished care, for Diana's fiancé had perished, and Susan, just ten last month, had no one but him to support her, either. It was his cross to bear that he would never again be able to keep them in the manner to which they had, all their lives, been accustomed.

It had been all he could do to spirit them away to his cousins to keep them safe from the lecherous designs of the man he'd come to think of simply as the sergeant. He still flinched when he thought of the near thing that had been.

Again he found he couldn't handle the path his thoughts had taken. Suddenly he needed to get outside and find a physical release for his beleaguered mind. He ripped open the door and swung himself out and up to the roof. Ignoring the startled exclamation of the Northern woman, he let the door swing shut and latch behind him.

Settling on the roof with the dog, he leaned an elbow on a tarpaulin-covered roll of something soft. His easy smile answered the startled but welcoming grins of the driver and guard.

"Didn't think you was the kind to spend your whole life indoors with the ladies." The guard spit a stream of tobacco juice downwind.

"Guess not," Jonathan drawled, ramming his hat further down on his head to keep it safe. The coach reached the top of the hill and began a speedy descent that would have sent his headgear flying.

"Cavenaugh's the name," the driver threw over his shoulder. "This here's Holcomb." He jerked his chin at the guard.

"Foster. Pleased to meet you both."

Neither the driver nor the guard took their eyes off the road and the terrain that bordered it, but the guard nodded his head in acknowledgment of the introductions.

Jonathan smiled to himself, putting them both down as good men. "Do you mind if I ask a question?"

"Nope."

"How is it we stop for the night and haven't had other passengers since those first two?"

Cavenaugh threw him a quick, wry glance. "That's an easy one. After the other two passengers got off, the senator bought up every seat all the way to his destination. You paid all the way to Texas, so he had to do without yours."

"Yeah," Holcomb chimed in, "then he paid what ya call a bonus for making stops at night so the lady and the boy can rest. Cost him a pretty penny, I can tell ya."

Jonathan shook his head in admiration of such extravagance by the senator to try to assure the comfort of his loved ones. He smiled to realize it was exactly the sort of thing he would once have done himself if he would have had to take a stagecoach.

He wouldn't have, of course. He would have made up a small caravan of his own servants, armed it well, and gone at his own pace, just as he did when he took his family to Hot Springs to escape the hottest summer months when disease swept the Tidewater. His smile faded. No more.

Shaking the melancholy that threatened him, he glanced at Scout, and the big dog whimpered a greeting, licked Jonathan's chin, and settled his head across the man's thigh.

The Rebel dropped a hand to the thick fur of the dog's neck and kneaded the animal's tense muscles. Scout gave him such a look of utter devotion that Jonathan was forced to laugh. It felt good. He hadn't had a lot to laugh about for a very long time.

Before long, the sun and breezes had worked their magic, and he was sane again.

By the time they stopped for the night, Catherine was so tired she went to bed without even looking at the appetizing supper the wife of the station keeper had prepared for them. She could barely perform her little nightly rituals, and fell asleep with her hairbrush in her hand before she had even begun her hundred strokes.

The next morning, when a staccato knock sounded on her door, she would have sworn her head had just touched the pillow. Awakened to aching muscles and a lingering fatigue, Catherine dressed as quickly as she was able.

Staring at the tired face in the mirror, she scolded, "You certainly know how to make a fuss about a few sore spots and a tiny headache, Catherine Foster." She twisted her long, dark hair into a coil and wound it into a chignon on the back of her neck.

Healthy all her life, and usually bursting with energy for any task she set herself, she was disgusted to find that a few days on a stagecoach could reduce her to a grumbling, foot-dragging hag. "Pull yourself together, Catherine." She gave herself one last wry look in the small mirror over the washstand, packed her things into the carpetbag that yawned on the bed, and hurried out of the room.

The others were waiting over breakfast at the long table in the sunny kitchen that served as dining room for stage passengers. She was glad to see that they all looked refreshed and ready to go. She stifled a sigh of envy, brushed a kiss on her son's forehead, and murmured, "Good morning."

Her voice sounded as if it hadn't been used in a week. The Rebel shot her a penetrating look, and she stared frostily back at him. She'd be a lot more comfortable on this trip if the Southerner would concern himself less with her and her family.

"The eggs are delicious, Catherine. You must ask how they are done." The senator was smiling at her, willing her to compliment the station keeper's wife.

Even that small effort seemed beyond her just now. She looked at the plate the woman placed in front of her with disinterest. She wasn't the least bit hungry.

There was no way she was going to hurt the woman's feelings, however. Smiling up at her, surprised at the effort it cost her, she said, "They smell delicious indeed. How—?" She needn't have worried that she had to think of a way to ask about egg preparation, as the woman was already talking.

"Why, bless your soul, I'd be glad to tell ya. But you must promise not to be put off by my methods."

"No, of course not," Catherine murmured.

"Well, the trick is to keep the skillet that you do eggs in for other things like onions and peppers and good beef or chicken. Never fish, mind you.

"Always scrape and wipe it out good, but let the flavors of them good vittles stay in the iron of the skillet. Keep it where no bugs or varmits can ever get at it, but never wash it. Well maybe oncet in a while, but not regular." She leaned toward Catherine confidentially, "I figure the heat of the cooking keeps everything safe for people to eat, don't you reckon? Anyhow, I ain't never made anybody sick and I been cooking this way for nigh on to twenty years."

She smiled at the whole table and bustled back to her cooking, proud to have been able to share her secret for such flavorful eggs.

The senator took a rather doubtful look at the eggs he'd just been extolling the virtues of, caught the derisive look on the face of the Rebel across from him, and manfully took another forkful. Finding them as good as before, he frowned to keep from smiling at the Southerner and continued his breakfast with gusto.

Catherine found the eggs good. She had to taste them to avoid offending the cook, regardless of how she felt about the way they had been achieved, but once she had, she managed to eat a creditable breakfast.

The feeling of not quite being there passed away as soon as she had food in her stomach. She was no longer headachy, either. Tonight, she vowed, she would force herself to eat some supper if she fell asleep in her plate doing so. She couldn't risk letting herself become ill. They still had many miles to go.

The driver rose from his place at the far end of the long table. "Time to hitch 'em up, Tolley."

"Sure thing." The station keeper and his tall, lanky son hurried out, letting the heavy door slam behind them.

The guard grabbed one last gulp of coffee, "Darn good coffee, Miz Tolley," and followed them. Mrs. Tolley waved a large spoon in his direction to acknowledge her due.

Jonny scampered to Catherine's side. "Mama, may I go play fetch with Scout? Just for a minute? He has to stay so still on the roof all day." Jonny's face was excited. He'd adjusted to stage travel and looked forward to the new sights each day brought.

Catherine experienced a sudden fear. "Stay near the station, dear. Where the men can see you." The words were no sooner out of her mouth than she wished she'd just told him to have fun.

She constantly forced herself to try to treat him normally, no matter what it cost her—as now, when she wished she could leave the table and go watch over him.

As if he could see what was in her mind, the Rebel rose with the unhurried grace that was one of the things that so irritated her about him, and told her, "I'll keep an eye on the boy, ma'am."

Her "Thank you," nearly stuck in her throat. Then he was gone, his long-fingered hand settling the broad-brimmed hat that too much reminded her of the one her own Jonathan had worn—and of those worn by the men who had killed him.

CHAPTER

Eight

THE REBEL WATCHED AS THE BOY PLAYED FETCH WITH THE big dog. Again and again the short, thick stick flew and was returned by the grinning animal. The boy had a good arm. The last time the Rebel had been north, he had seen a game that Abner somebody had thought up where a man batted at a ball pitched to him. Baseball, it was called.

He wondered if the boy knew about it, and maybe aspired to pitch. From what he'd seen, the players were held in some esteem by most of the youths watching it.

In the next town they reached, he would see if he could find a ball. Then their stops might be less tedious for the child. The boy behaved very well, but the hours spent inside the coach had to be galling, Jonathan knew.

Suddenly, he had an idea. He walked to where the driver stood watching the final preparations. When the man looked at him inquiringly, he asked, "I wonder if it would be possible to let the boy sit up with you part of the next run?"

"Don't see why not. He's a nice little young'un. Long as his ma don't mind." Jonathan touched the brim of his hat and walked back toward the way station.

Before he reached the door, the senator came out and courteously held it open for his daughter-in-law. The woman's lips pursed when it became evident he wanted to speak with her.

Ignoring the irritation he felt at her hostility, he removed his hat and said, "Ma'am, I've spoken to the driver and he says it's all right with him if the boy would like to ride on the box for a while. I'd look after him, but I need your

50

permission before I tell him he might."

Catherine's mind flooded with visions: of Jonny tumbling down the seven feet to the ground, of the wheels of the coach passing over him, of tree branches that swept him from the high perch, of Indian arrows that flew from ambush. "Why must you constantly interfere with our lives!" she burst out.

She hadn't been able to keep back the words, however unfair they might be. Fueled with fear for the only thing she had left of her marriage, they erupted without her volition.

"Catherine!" The senator was clearly shocked by her ungracious behavior.

Catherine passed a hand across her forehead and forced herself to do the right thing. "I'm sorry," she almost snapped. "I know you want to help make the trip better for him, it is just that I'm . . ." She'd literally die before she told this intruder from the enemy camp that she was afraid.

He saved her the trouble. "I understand, ma'am. My wife was the same way about our son. It's hard sometimes for a woman to let them do the things that have a little risk attached." He saluted her with his hat in the act of replacing it on his head and turned away.

Catherine wished for an instant that she could ask him about his son. Then she turned to look at her father-in-law. "Why are you looking at me like that, Clayton?"

The tall, silver-haired man regarded her a moment before answering. "It's so unlike you to be ungracious, Catherine. I wondered if you weren't feeling well."

"I suppose that's your tactful way of telling me I behaved badly." She sighed. "I do, don't I? I can't seem to help it. Every time I look at him, I remember that it was men like him who killed Jonathan."

It was the senator's turn to sigh. "Yes, my dear, I find I have the same problem. But I think he's trying to be kind to Jonny. And, I have to remember that if it weren't for his intervention, we might have had to leave Scout behind in Saint Louis."

"Oh, dear Clayton. How fine and fair-minded you are." Catherine was ashamed.

The senator touched her arm to guide her to the waiting coach. "No, my dear," he said sadly, "I am only trying very hard to be."

Catherine shot him a quick, concerned glance. Why couldn't she be as charitable to the Southerner as her father-in-law seemed able to be? At least then she would cause the senator less distress.

Determined to make amends, she approached the Rebel where he stood beside the stagecoach. After all, hadn't he spoken of a wife and son? They were somewhere far from him. Surely he must miss them dreadfully. "Captain," she couldn't bring herself to address him as Captain Foster, couldn't give him her husband's name. It was all she could do to give this enemy her beloved Jonathan's rank.

The tall Rebel turned to face her, his expression guarded. Had she hurt him? The thought disturbed her strangely. No. Surely not. She had just failed to approve his plan for her son. Well, he'd no doubt feel better in a minute. "Captain, I've had second thoughts about your suggestion that Jonny ride on the box. I'm sure he would enjoy the experience immensely. Thank you for thinking of it."

Duty done, she started to turn away from him, then turned back in a whirl of skirts. She forced herself to say, "Thank you for watching over him up there."

In spite of the tumult she felt about it, she knew that with the Rebel on watch, Jonny would be perfectly safe.

Jonny sat beside the driver, with the guard hard against him on his left side. The Southerner and Scout sprawled in what passed for comfort on the roof of the stage. Jonathan thought it a testimony to the eggshell-like strength Concord built into the stretched canvas roof of its stagecoaches that both he and the large dog with its muzzle on his hip could occupy the roof.

Interested himself, he watched as the boy drank in every word the driver uttered. Jonathan was enjoying learning as much as the lad seemed to be. This stretch of the road was fairly smooth, and he could listen to their conversation easily.

"Which reins go where? How do the horses know which ones you mean?" Jonny looked hard at the fistful of leather ribbons the driver held.

Cavenaugh laughed. "Well, boy, it's simple really, oncet you get used to it." He made subtle play with his fingers to maneuver the team around a large rock intruding on the edge of the road. The team responded perfectly and he threw a triumphant look at the boy. "Just takes a lot o' years to learn to stay off the horses' mouths so you don't make 'em hard. A cold-mouthed horse bores on the bit. Wears a driver out if it don't pull him plumb off the box, and wastes most of the horse's own energy, too. You want to keep 'em soft in the mouth."

"Tell me how! Please tell me how you do that." Jonny was so excited he bounced on the seat once.

"Easy, Button." The Rebel put a calming hand on the boy's shoulder.

Jonny shrugged it off. "Don't," he said in a tight little voice.

The man withdrew his steadying hand and dropped it on the dog's head instead. Scout groaned with pleasure.

Jonathan's face, closed an instant before, softened. With a sigh, he scratched behind the dog's ears. Too low to be heard, he murmured, "Nice to have one friend."

Scout thumped the roof with his tail, his eyes adoring. The Rebel smiled.

The boy asked Cavenaugh again wistfully, "Couldn't you just tell me how you do it?"

"Sure you can handle knowing? Me, I learned from Crandall, the finest driver in the West. Took me seven years of almost constant practice with a reining rig he set up for me. Oncet I knowed, I just had to drive."

Jonny looked at him earnestly. "Well," he said consideringly, "I'm only a boy, you see. It'll be a long time before anybody'll let me drive. So I guess you can show me all right."

Both the guard and the driver laughed. The guard reached around the boy to slap his partner's shoulder. "Gotcha there, hasn't he."

"Yep. Guess I'll have to tell him how it's done." He turned to the boy, easing the horses to a walk for a breather. "You see the teams?"

At the boy's quick nod he went on. "First span are the leaders. The reins for them I hold between my pointin' fingers and my middle fingers. Off side horses—that's your right hand—in my right hand; near side in my left.

"The reins for the swing team go between the middle finger and my fourth finger—the one that folks wear their weddin' rings on. Next," he held his hands so the boy could see, "the reins for the wheelers go between my little finger and the ring one. See?

"To use 'em, I crawl my fingers up the reins," he moved his fingers, inching up the narrow lengths of supple leather. Then, "Or I let 'em slip out a bit."

When he demonstrated this, one of the swing team horses shook its head. Cavenaugh laughed. "They don't much like their mouths played with."

"Then how do you stop them?"

"Why, you've seen me do that a few times already, boy. I just yell 'whoa' to the horses and put my foot on this here brake." He touched the long wooden lever that rose beside him on his right. "No sense in sawing the horses' heads off. Not if you know how to drive."

At that moment, he applied the brake once to slow the descent of the coach as they topped a rise and started down the steep other side at a good clip. His hands never moved from where he rested them near his knees. The brake dragged at the rear wheels, keeping the vehicle from overrunning the wheelers.

On the flat again, the horses moved easily along, tugs and reins loose on this good stretch of road. The single-trees to which their traces were attached swung with their movement.

"How do you do turns with so many horses?" The boy's face shone with eager curiosity. "Left turns look 'specially hard to me."

"That's a good question, young'un. You just have to remember to let your leaders almost pass the place you want to turn in to. Past the center of the space, leastwise. Then you turn your leaders while you hold your swing horses to the right till they get to the same spot. Then turn them while you rein your wheelers right, and when you let them wheelers turn, why, you're done with your turn."

He looked hard at the boy. "You get all that? If you do it right, you're fine. Do it any other way, and your rig will take out the leaders of anybody coming out of the street you're turning in to."

"I'll remember." Jonny's face was serious, a frown of intense concentration marred his forehead as he solemnly promised.

The driver said quietly, "You do that, son."

Without moving his hand to take up or release an inch of rein, Cavenaugh cracked his whip next to the ear of his off leader. "Get your mind back on your work, you lazy slug!"

The big bay scooted back up into his collar, taking his fair share of the load again. Cavenaugh yelled, "Good boy!" and smiled down at the boy at his side.

"Golly. You didn't even twitch the reins when you did that." Awe filled his face.

"Well, son, I guess ya' gotta learn that, too."

Jonny sighed at the enormity of the task.

Suddenly, behind them, the Rebel tensed. Steadying himself on the driver's shoulder, he rose to his knees, peering intently ahead.

"Whadaya see?" Cavenaugh was quick to sense the watchfulness of the man behind him.

"Dust. Up there behind that bunch of rocks."

"Better get the boy inside."

"Right."

"But I don' wanna get back inside. I wanna see what's up there."

The Rebel reached over and grasped the boy firmly. Without comment, he swung him easily up from his place beside Cavenaugh and whirled him, wide-eyed but silent, in a long arc that ended with the boy's feet and legs entering the window on the door of the coach.

"What the devil!" The senator's startled exclamation could clearly be heard by the men outside the vehicle.

The Rebel spoke softly, only the pitch of his voice enabling the senator to hear his words over the rumble of the wheels. "Trouble up here, Senator. Better take the boy in with you."

"I have him."

The Southerner let go when he felt the tug of the senator's grip, and the boy was safely inside. He gave the senator a mental mark of approval. The man caught on fast and acted faster. A good man to have with you in a bad situation.

All Jonathan's attention was focused on the ridge up ahead where he'd seen the momentary swirl of dust behind the rock that jutted so close to the road.

"Got a gun, Reb?" Cavenaugh's voice was like iron. He was peering at the rock, and he wasn't happy with what he didn't see.

"No."

"Here. You can keep it. I won it off a man in Kansas City in a poker game last year. Never had no use for it." He nudged a box from behind his feet over toward the guard.

The guard reached down, flipped the lid of the box back, and fumbled in it without taking his eyes off the ridge. Reaching up and back, he handed Jonathan a handsome forty-four in an expensive tooled-leather holster.

Jonathan expressed his appreciation of the generous gift with a low whistle.

Cavenaugh chuckled, but the sound was grim. "Help us out of this, and you'll have earned that, Reb."

"Let's hope I won't have to use it."

The sound that Cavenaugh made indicated that he didn't think it likely Jonathan would get his wish.

The lead team was even with the rock formation and moving fast when the attack came. Six Indians screamed their war cries as they dashed out onto the road. Sturdy Indian ponies hurled themselves forward. They charged at the team pulling the stagecoach, shoulders ramming the lead horses.

A challenging neigh rang out and one of the swing team reached forward with big, yellow teeth and tore a piece of hide from the rump of one of the Indian ponies. Dust billowed and swirled as the riders of the two ponies fighting to stop the lead horses reached for each of the team's bridles to drag them to a halt.

Jonathan heard a piercing cry from the woman in the coach beneath him as he took steady aim at the Indian dragging at the off leader. Squeezing off his first shot, he looked down and saw a rider grasping the windowsill nearest Catherine Foster. Reversing the gun in his hand he brought the butt down on the man's head with all the force he could muster. The Indian pitched from the back of his pony, his body falling rapidly behind as the terrified horses pulling the coach plunged recklessly down the road.

Holcomb gave a yell that drowned out those of the Indians and felled the other Indian that was dragging at the near side leader. The horse savagely shook his head, whinnied his joy at being freed of the weight that had torn at his mouth, and stretched out flat in a dead run with his companions.

Staying atop the swaying, jouncing vehicle had become Jonathan's major problem. Dropping flat, he spread his long legs wide and braced his feet in opposite corners of the baggage rail around the roof.

If strength of purpose could have achieved it, his elbows would have dug holes in the roof of the speeding coach. Flinging an arm around the yipping dog to stop him from jumping off the roof in his excitement, he fought to bring his gun to bear on another attacker, clenching his teeth against the impatience that welled up in him. He'd learned in the hard school of battle to count and hoard his ammunition, and he knew he only had five shots left.

A third rider fell, and Holcomb gave a wordless shout of satisfaction. He had missed twice, thanks to the wild unsteadiness of the coach, and it didn't set well with him.

The remaining members of the small war party fell back to the safety offered by the roiling cloud of dust left in the wake of the careening stagecoach.

Cavenaugh fought to bring his bolting team under control without appreciatively slowing them. "Easy there, steady there."

His deceptively calm voice slowly penetrated the fear of the horses, and they steadied and began to gallop as a team again. Though their pace didn't slacken, the strident disharmony of their passage smoothed, but the team still took them at a perilous pace along the winding, deeply rutted road.

Cavenaugh filled the air with a litany of curses and prayers and fought to guide them safely around a cliff-bordered curve. Jonathan fought the urge to squeeze his eyes shut as the coach slewed around it, narrowly missing hurtling into the chasm below. "Thanks be to God," the driver shouted as they made it safely. Jonathan fervently echoed his sentiments in silence.

Thunk! Jonathan looked with astonishment at the arrow sunk in the bag next to his shoulder. Thwap! A second arrow hit the box on his other side. He whirled to face the peril hidden by the cloud of their own dust. *They'll get it right in a second*, he thought, and he had a distinct aversion to becoming a pin cushion.

He rammed his back against Cavenaugh's to steady himself and loosed a shot into the dust cloud. How the blazes did they see to let fly their arrows when he couldn't make them out for the dust screen following the Concord?

"Make yourself at home," Cavenaugh growled, bracing him.

"Thanks, I will." Jonathan took aim at a form he thought he could see. "Steady," he rasped. Cavenaugh's back became a rigid support as he fired. There was a sharp cry from behind, and the sound of unshod hooves seemed to drop away.

A final arrow leapt toward him from the dust cloud, and ricocheted off the leather apron covering the boot. Scout yipped, then whined from where he lay pressed against Jonathan's side. The Rebel looked over his shoulder and saw that the arrow had struck the big golden dog. Blood from the wound began pooling on the roof where they lay.

Cursing futilely, Jonathan spun around. The dog looked at him imploringly, his beseeching eyes bright with pain. Jonathan yelled, "Slow down!"

"Are you crazy?" Cavenaugh's voice shot up an octave and he took his eyes off the road for a split second to see what had caused the tall blond man to lose his mind. Seeing the blood and the arrow protruding from the dog's shoulder, he cursed in his turn. "Damn you, Reb. It's only a dog, for God's sake." Nevertheless, he pulled the team down to a more sedate pace that enabled the Confederate to tend the animal.

Working quickly, Jonathan removed the arrow and stuffed his handkerchief into the wound to stop the bleeding. Scout's head lolled lifelessly over Jonathan's lap.

In the coach, Jonny had heard the dog's yelp. "What's the matter with Scout?" he cried. Scrambling free of his grandfather's grasp, he leaned far out the window. "What have you done to my dog, you dirty Reb?" he screeched.

They heard the Rebel say, "It's all right, Button. He got nicked, but it's not too bad."

In no way reassured, Jonny tried to climb out the window to see for himself.

His grandfather snatched him ruthlessly back into the speeding vehicle and slammed him firmly down on the seat between Catherine and himself.

His mother seized his arm as if her very life depended on keeping him at her side.

"Mama," the boy squirmed against her grip, "you're hurting me."

"Better that I should hurt your arm than that some red Indian should put an arrow through you, young man!" She snapped and glared at him as if only his recklessness were at issue. No matter that her heart had all but stopped with fear that the attacking Indians might harm him. Jonny must never know that he had become her reason for this journey. Some things were too heavy for children to bear.

After a moment, Jonny offered by way of making peace, "Will I like it at Three Rivers, mama?" His concern for Scout had now become anxiety for their whole journey.

Catherine smiled, and a twinkle appeared in her eye. "I think so. You were content enough there when we took you to see your great-grandfather when you were an infant."

"Mama! I was a baby then. I don't even remember."

"Well, I think this time you will enjoy the ranch." Her voice softened, and her eyes grew soft with memory. "I always did. I loved riding all over it and watching the ranch hands take care of the herds." She took her son's hand. "I loved just being out there under the big open sky. It felt . . . like I was closer to God than in the bustle of the East. Closer to everything that matters." She looked a little embarrassed, shrugged, and said in a lighter tone, "I love it. I hope you will, too."

Jonny was quiet for a little while, keeping his hold on her hand. Then he squirmed around in his seat so that he was looking up into his mother's face. "What was Great-grandfather like?"

Catherine hesitated only an instant. "He was . . . very tall. A big man. With a shock of silver-white hair . . . and eyes like an eagle." Her voice was husky. "When he spoke, men listened" —she smoothed his hair back from his forehead— "and he held my whole world together for me."

Jonny was silent, awed to see the tears in his mother's eyes. Finally, he said wistfully, "I wish I could have known him."

Catherine clasped him tightly to her. "I wish you could have, too, dearest." She sat holding him and stroking his hair absently.

She was going to build Three Rivers back up to where it had been in her grandfather's day. She had to, for she wanted it for her son so desperately. It wouldn't be easy, she knew, for Texas was a Confederate state, and she was the widow of a Union officer.

Without her son to plan for, she would have stayed in Massachusetts, and dwindled away under her father-in-law's roof. She'd have become "the pretty little widow Foster," with no other purpose in life than trying to comfort the old gentleman for the loss of his son.

Sighing under the weight of her thoughts, she settled back and wondered what it had been like on the roof of the coach. Exposed to arrows from the attackers, thrown about like rag dolls, with no walls to keep them from falling off or being shot, the men had driven off the Indians.

In her mind, she pictured them. Cavenaugh would have had his hands full trying to regain control of the frantic team. Holcomb would be shooting, of course, he was the guard, and that was his job. She'd heard his rifle crack at least four times. How many times had he hit his target? The jolting would have made it difficult to aim.

Reluctantly, her mind returned to the terror she'd felt when that Indian had ridden up to leer at her through the window, hanging tight to the sill. It had been the Rebel who'd smashed him away.

Her heart still thundered at the remembrance of the painted face and the strong, red-bronze arm that drew back for the hatchet stroke with which he would have dispatched her. She owed her life to the tall Confederate with the pewter-blond hair. The obligation to him that his rescue forced on her made her distinctly uncomfortable. Owing him her life—She couldn't even finish the thought.

They pulled into the way station half an hour later. "Whoa, whoa there," Cavenaugh called out of habit. The horses needed no encouragement, they were stumbling in their traces, utterly and completely spent by their efforts, eager to obey the driver's voiced signal and that of the applied brake.

"What the hell ya' done to this team, Cavenaugh?" A wiry little man ran out of a low log building to tend the stricken horses. Two larger men followed. "Walk 'em for a while and be sure they're certain cool before you feed 'em," the wiry man ordered.

The two hostlers began the task of unharnessing the weary, sweat-covered team, darting stern looks at Cavenaugh. It was clear they heartily disapproved of his treatment of the panting horses.

Cavenaugh told the man in charge, "Ran into Indians a ways back, Grisham. Couldn't do no better by the team and still get here with my passengers safe. They're lucky they ain't stuck full of arrows. Just don't water them more than a few swallows till you cool 'em good."

"Don't you go telling me and my boys how to do our job!" Grisham said as a matter of course, his mind on Cavenaugh's news. "What kind of Indians?"

"One is about like another to me. Ask Holcomb." He turned to open the coach and help his passengers descend.

The wiry man moved to where Holcomb was helping a tall man with blond hair lift a large dog down from the roof of the stage. "What happened to the dog?"

The tall man glanced at him briefly. "Arrow."

"Is he hurt bad?"

As Holcomb lowered the dog to the tall passenger's waiting arms, he asked his old friend, "D'you ever hear of being hurt good, Grisham?"

The door to the coach slammed back out of Cavenaugh's hand as the boy rushed to his dog. "Scout! Scout, are you all right?" His eyes were brimming over with tears. He dashed them away with the sleeve of his jacket so he could see for himself how his dog was.

Scout heard him, and raised his head from the Rebel officer's arm. He regarded his young master an instant, then his head dropped back.

"He's dying! Scout's dying." The boy was frantic.

"Easy, Button," Jonathan soothed. "He's gonna be fine. Don't scare him to death with your caterwauling."

"What do you know? What do you know about my dog?" Jonny grabbed the arm the Confederate had under Scout. "Put him down! Put him down so I can see."

Without replying to the near hysterical boy, the Rebel turned and carried the dog toward the log building. "I need some clean cloths and some boiled water," he told the station keeper. "Whiskey, too, if you have it." He called after the wiry man as he scuttled ahead to open the door. "And a razor to shave the fur back out of the way."

Grisham looked at the purposeful way the man walked toward the way station. "My wife will fuss to have a dog brought in," he said aloud. Then he continued in a loud whisper, "But she's soft about animals. You can talk her around easy enough."

Jonathan flashed him a grin. Jonny followed close on their heels, gulping back his tears.

Grisham opened the door, stopped to wipe his feet carefully on the primitive reed doormat, then stepped aside for the burdened man to pass through. "Guess you best put him out of the way in the corner, mister." He moved quickly to show the way across the large common room. "I'll fetch somethin' for you to lay him on."

Jonathan noted that the corner was as far as they could get from the big black iron stove where a short, round woman with a cheery face was inspecting the contents of a steaming pot. The corner looked cozy enough, clean-swept and with no windows near it to cause a draft.

He held Scout while the station keeper brought an ancient quilt for the dog to lie on. Jonathan's glance checked the tattered quilt. Like everything else he saw in the station, it was clean. When Grisham flapped it out, it smelled of fresh air and sunshine. It was quickly folded into a pallet of a size to fit the dog.

"Is he gonna be all right?" The boy's soft voice quavered. His hatred of his Rebel foe was lost in his concern for his canine friend. Kneeling beside Jonathan, he reached out a hand to his dog.

Scout lifted his muzzle just enough to touch his nose to the boy's hand. One thump of the blond-feathered tail, and the dog lay still and closed his eyes.

Jonny jumped to his feet. Seizing the Rebel's shoulder, he shook it hard. "He's gonna be okay, isn't he? He's got to be all right! Scout's got to be all right."

The big dog shuddered and whimpered once. Jonathan rose from his kneeling position and grasped the boy by the shoulders in his turn. "Yes, he'll be all right. But I'm going to have to sew up that tear the arrow made, and I'm going to have to have you help me. Can you do it?"

For a moment the boy looked frightened, and Jonathan knew he'd asked a lot of the child. Then the boy straightened, swallowed hard, and said resolutely, "Scout's my dog." His gaze, full of determination, met Jonathan's. "I reckon I can do what I gotta do to help him."

"Good boy!"

Jonathan heard the soft rustle of skirts and the light scent Catherine wore filled his senses. Turning to meet her as she approached the corner, he saw she had a bowl of water and a small supply of clean rags.

Her eyes met his as directly as the boy's had. In them he saw only concern for her son's pet. All the animosity he was used to seeing was gone.

Dare he hope that her aversion to him had gone for good? The strength with which he wished that were so startled him. He was shaken by the desire to be free of this woman's hate. God knew he had experienced more than his fill of hatred, both that he had felt and that he had received from others. He was weary of hatred. He wanted to be finished with it. Without realizing it, he sighed a great sigh.

Catherine leaned toward him pleadingly. "Scout is going to be all right isn't he?" Anxiety darkened the brown of her eyes until he could hardly discern her pupils. Her lips, usually held in such a stern line whenever he was looking her way, softened and trembled. "Please," she breathed so softly he could barely hear.

For just a beat of time, her face was all that existed for him. He watched, fascinated as tears formed and trembled on her lashes. He felt as if a bolt of lightning had hit him.

She was so beautiful, so brave, this woman who had championed him against the abusive sergeant on the railroad platform in Saint Louis, yet despised him ever since. She was so gallant that he had not seen her shed a single tear for her personal tragedy, but here she stood ready to weep for her son's dog.

The knowledge tore something loose in his chest and melted the core of anger he'd harbored for the last few years. Her tears, even though they were not shed for him, were like a balm to his wounded spirit. It was as if the little Yankee widow had somehow given him permission to live again.

"Scout will be fine." Gently, he took the bowl and the rags from her, striving not to break the spell that held him.

"Do you need anything else? The station keeper's wife told me to ask you, and to tell you she'll come and help as soon as she can."

Her voice was soft, the sharp edge he was used to hearing gone from it. He enjoyed the music of it, lilting clear in spite of her strange accent. "A needle and thread, please," his words were breathless, his sharpened awareness of her had hit him like a blow to the stomach. It was as if he asked her for so much more than items to sew up a gash. His gaze locked with hers as he spoke and his words seemed to hold her in place.

Her lips parted, as if she, too, suddenly needed more breath. A like awareness flickered in her eyes.

The station keeper hurried up, a bottle clutched in his hand. "Here's the whisky you wanted. And the razor." He whipped a lethal looking blade out of a back pocket and slapped it into Jonathan's hand.

The light in the back of Catherine's eyes fled. Its flight shattered the magic.

The boy cried out angrily, "You're not gonna drink before you work on my Scout." He shoved himself between the man and the dog.

The tall Confederate seemed to come out of a daze. "What?"

"If you haven't the guts to sew on him sober, you leave my Scout alone!"

Catherine, fighting her own feeling of unreality, rushed into the unpleasant situation. "Jonny! Be quiet, dear. I'm certain Captain Foster has no intention of drinking anything before he helps Scout." She looked to the Rebel to explain to her son. "I'm afraid I don't know just what the whiskey is for, myself, Captain Foster."

He was clear-headed again. And finally she had called him by his name. He'd thought he was going to have to wait forever to hear her use it. Even though he understood that it must be difficult to call him by the name and rank that had been her husband's, still her refusal to do so had rankled.

Captain Jonathan Foster was his name, too, and he had every right to it. The strange twist of fate that had thrown them together—he and the widow of a man who'd borne his identical rank and first and last names—notwithstanding, he had hated being, as he had been the last few days, denied his own name.

"The whiskey will cut the risk of an inflammation developing in the wound," he explained, weary of the boy's mistrust.

"I'll get the needle and thread." She moved gracefully away, his thoughtful gaze following her.

The boy tugged at his sleeve. "Please, what are you going to do?"

Jonathan yielded to the anxiety in the young voice. "What I've done for more wounds than I can remember, Button. I'll clean the wound, then I'll have to have you hold Scout while I sew him up. Can you do it?"

"Will it hurt him?"

Jonathan didn't answer.

"Yeah. I guess it will." Jonny knelt and stroked the dog's head. "But I can do it," he answered the man. "I can do it because I gotta, Scout." He was speaking earnestly to his friend now. "You have to be brave, Scout." His voice got tight. "And forgive me and him if it hurts."

Jonathan patted the boy's back, then left him to comfort his dog and went to meet Catherine as she crossed the large room bearing the needle and thread.

CHAPTER
Nine

SCOUT WAS ASLEEP, EXHAUSTED FROM THE ORDEAL OF having the wound in his shoulder sewn up in careful stitches by the Rebel. Catherine and her father-in-law sat quietly together at the big table in the center of the room and drank the coffee that Mrs. Grisham had made fresh in anticipation of the stage's arrival for lunch.

"You're pale, my dear."

"I'm fine, really. It was just that it was Scout—and so bloody." She smiled at him reassuringly over the rim of her cup.

"The boy seems to be having a delayed reaction to the operation." Senator Foster gestured with his head toward the door.

Catherine rose hastily when she heard her son gag.

"No, Catherine." The senator placed a detaining hand on her arm and she hesitated. "Let him be. He's in good hands."

Outside, Catherine could see the shadows of her son and the Rebel. The Confederate tenderly held her retching son as the child brought up his breakfast. She started forward.

"Catherine. Let be." Her father-in-law's voice was soft but firm.

As she stood, indecisive, she heard the pounding of hooves faintly in the distance. Before she could reach the open door, two horses came thundering into the yard of the way station.

Frozen statue-still by her recognition of the burly rider on the first horse, Catherine stood back in the deep shadow just beyond the spill of sunlight across the floor. The sergeant! It was the brutal sergeant from the railroad station in Saint Louis. What must she do?

She needn't have worried. Mistreating the Rebel was the farthest thing from the stocky man's mind at the moment. Swinging from his saddle, he reached up to yank his companion, a young corporal with blood streaming down his face, from his horse.

Jonny straightened, his discomfort forgotten. "What happened?" he quavered.

"Injuns," the sergeant shouted to Grisham, not even seeing the boy. "There's a packa redskins three miles west of here." He dragged the fainting corporal toward the door.

Jonathan met him and slung the wounded man's arm over his shoulder to help the sergeant lift him over the threshold into the safety of the station. Catherine held the door wide for the three men to edge through.

Grisham bustled in behind them. He took one look at the arrow protruding from the back of the corporal's shoulder. "Lordamighty!" He hurried out to tend to the soldiers' horses, thankful he didn't have to deal with it.

"Get him over to the table." The Rebel officer took charge without thinking.

Mrs. Grisham, eyes wide in her pale, round face, swept the checkered cloth from the table, and the two men placed the now unconscious corporal facedown on it.

Inspecting the slow-welling hole at the base of the shaft sticking out of the man's back, Jonathan mused, "That arrow will have to come out." He regarded the sergeant levelly across the body on the table. When the man made no comment, he prompted, "What are you going to do?"

"Me?" The sergeant leaped back from the table. "Faith an' bejasus! You don't think I'm gonna mess with that arrow!"

Jonathan muttered a disgusted curse and whirled from the table. His glance met Catherine's. Her face was pale and determined. "Clean cloths and the whiskey again, please."

Mrs. Grisham, in the rolling gait that was as near as she could come to a run, rushed to find the things he needed. "Lordamercy," she wailed as she lumbered away, "Indians!"

Her husband thrust his face into the sergeant's. "Yep, Indians. And I bet you led 'em straight to us, din't ya?" His mustache quivered with outrage.

"What the hell did ya expect me to do? This is the only place within miles," the accused man spat back.

"Calm down," the Rebel ordered quietly. "If they're a war party, chances arc they'd know about the station already."

"Yeah." The sergeant snatched at the reprieve, then plunged into anger. "And who the hell do you think you are, telling me what's what! You're nothing but a damn—"

"Sergeant," the senator bellowed. "The ladies, if you please."

The heavy, florid face turned truculent, but he was quiet. Menace and resentment showed in every line of his bulky body.

Jonathan's voice was like a whiplash, brooking no refusal. "Get outside and stay on the lookout."

The man hesitated only a moment; then, with a snarl and a look that promised retaliation, he obeyed.

Jonathan accepted one of the rags Catherine had brought from Mrs. Grisham. The station keeper's wife hastened off to find the needle and thread again, thinking he would need it because of the stitching he'd done on the dog.

Catherine stood beside him, trying to help him as he cut away the prostrate soldier's jacket. Jonathan shot her a glance, saw she was pale, and asked, "Are you all right?"

"I'll be fine," she assured him, adding inanely, "I helped with Scout, didn't I?"

Jonathan caught the blush that suffused her face. He smiled at her wryly, his voice warm as he said, "You did a good job, too."

The station keeper brought a lantern to supplement the light of the oil lamp hanging over the table. "Looks like that's gonna be a bear to get out."

"Hmmm. We'll have to cut it out, I think."

"Yep. Sure as hell can't push it through to the other side." He remembered Catherine and muttered, "Beg pardon, ma'am."

Catherine was too aghast at the idea of deepening the wound to notice either his profanity or his apology. "What do you mean, push it through?" she gasped.

"Ta git the point. Those heathens put a big barb on their arrows when they—" the wiry man stopped talking when he noticed the hand Catherine clapped to her queasy stomach. "Sorry." He let his breath out in a wheezing gust. "Seems like I got me a new talent fer saying jist the wrong thing," he muttered.

"Yes, well, then why don't you just hush up, husband." His wife was back with two of her sharpest knives. She held one out to Jonathan. "This one's probably gonna be best for that."

"Hold him down," Jonathan ordered the senator as he took the small, slender knife from Mrs. Grisham. Both she and the senator took firm grips on the unconscious man. "You better go see to getting the horses in, Mr. Grisham."

"Already got the boys doing it." He moved to relieve his wife from her position at the head of the table.

Catherine held the rest of the cloths, ready to proffer them as they were needed, and watched the Rebel grip the knife firmly in a rock-steady hand. Wiping away the welling blood with a rag in his left hand, he tossed the saturated cloth to the floor and spread his long fingers against the man's back to steady the flesh around the arrow's shaft.

Catherine felt the blood leave her head as he cut into the taut skin. Her vision blurred and the room started to spin. She jerked her eyes up from the spurting wound and concentrated instead on the Rebel's gleaming hair and strong features. Diverting her thoughts with determination, she tried to put a name to the strange color of his hair. Not blond like that of people from the Scandinavian countries. No, not silver blond. Nor was it golden blond. She knew people who had hair the color of wheat, but that wasn't it, either.

The man on the table bucked and screamed. She jumped and shuddered, her nails digging into her palms, the pile of rags shaking in her hands.

The Rebel had had his hair cut in Saint Louis. She was glad he'd had it cut. She could see the strong column of his neck now that his hair was trimmed to collar length. She locked her gaze on that now, obstinately, as she fought to ignore the sounds made by the writhing man on the table.

The Rebel had a film of perspiration on his forehead. His usually smooth brow was furrowed now in concentration, but she could visualize it clear and wide. After all, she'd been sitting across from him for days now. The man on the table yelled a string of curses, and Mrs. Grisham plunked her considerable weight down on his legs to keep him from kicking the Rebel.

"Steady. Almost done." Jonathan soothed the man much as he would a fractious horse.

Catherine smelled the metallic tang of fresh blood and frantically studied the mouth that had just spoken, pressing her hand harder into her treacherous stomach. He had, she admitted reluctantly, an attractive mouth. It was cleanly chiseled like those found on some marble statues. Fine, but sensuous. For just an instant, her tumultuous thoughts touched on how they'd feel against her own.

With a gasp, she yanked her traitorous imagination back into line. Her chest heaved with the effort to catch her breath, she'd so shocked herself.

The Rebel threw her a concerned glance. "Are you all right?"

The involuntary deep breath had steadied her, and she blushed furiously, angry that her foolishness had betrayed her to his notice. She was in control of herself again. "Must you always ask if I am all right?" she said waspishly.

She saw that his eyes were darker than usual, the blue almost like that of a sapphire. Was it a trick of the light? Or of his own fierce concentration? She refused to believe it was because of concern over her.

Just then the man on the table jerked once as the Rebel yanked the arrow free, then he stopped struggling. He had fainted.

"Here's the needle and thread, sir." Mrs. Grisham reached them toward him as she slithered from where she'd been sitting on the unconscious man's legs to stand on the floor again.

"Thank you, Mrs. Grisham, but I think this is a small enough wound to let be." He smiled at her and the woman basked in his smile a moment before returning it.

Catherine basked in it, too, while she breathed deeply to get her head to stop spinning and her stomach to settle back down. What even white teeth he had. Even her Jonathan's hadn't been as—

The reminder of her late husband brought her to herself with a solid thump. What could she have been thinking of to so admire this enemy of her country? Sternly she reprimanded herself, and when the man turned from ministering to the wounded corporal, she was able to ask, "Why did you not sew his wound as you did Scout's?" She was pleased to hear that her voice was cool and impersonal.

"A deep wound needs the chance to drain. It needs to heal from the bottom up, or it might become putrid. The dog's long gash needed to be held together so it wouldn't pull wider and make everything worse."

"I see." That sounded lame even to her, but the exchange enabled her to return to a comfortable footing with the Rebel. He looked puzzled, but then, he hadn't endured, as she had, her mind's outrageous speculation. Catherine nodded serenely, said, "Thank you," and moved away to help Mrs. Grisham prepare a bed for the injured man.

Mr. Grisham yelled for his hostlers. The wounded man seen to, it was time to think of the Indians. Leading the small group of defenders to a cabinet, he opened it and began to pull out rifles and ammunition. Jonathan noted the number of guns with satisfaction. "Good," he said to the station keeper, "the women can reload the empty guns while you discharge the others. You've enough to keep up a steady fire."

Grisham looked less tense now that Jonathan had taken an interest in his preparations. "I put by plenty of ammunition and plenty of guns, but I sure would like it a sight better if you'd tell us how best to use 'em. I ain't never spent no time in the army."

For a second Jonathan's eyes went still. Then he said softly, "You have the sergeant just outside."

"Yeah, and iffen I had my way, that's where he'd stay. You saw how he ran off and left his man." The wiry little man's eyes narrowed to slits. "He warn't leading yon poor boy's horse in here. The horse was just following along after his. If we hadn't been awatching, he'da let the corporal fall on the ground. That man don't care for nobody but hisself." His stern gaze challenged Jonathan. "You take charge. It's my station, and I want you to do your derndest to keep it safe." He thrust his jaw forward. "Will ya?"

Jonathan regarded him solemnly. When he spoke, his voice was rock steady. "I shall do my best, Mr. Grisham."

"Thankee." Grisham swept his hand around to indicate his wife and the two hostlers. "We all thank you."

"Show me the place."

"Yes, sir!"

Catherine watched the Rebel walk around the large room, test the shutters that Mrs. Grisham was pulling in and fastening, and ask questions about the roof and the big lean-to storeroom behind the building. When the station keeper's wife had bolted the last shutter in place, he stopped to speak to her.

Catherine saw her bob her head in eager cooperation, gesturing to the pump that stood at one end of her kitchen. When Jonathan saw there was an unlimited supply of water in the building, his smile lighted the room. Then he returned to his minute inspection of their shelter.

No sooner had he finished his slow circuit of the place than there was a frantic scrabble at the front door, and the sergeant plunged into the room, yelling, "They're coming! The Injuns are coming!"

Jonathan walked to the door in a leisurely fashion and stood there looking out, studying the lay of the land. The ground immediately surrounding the station was bare. Too many stages and horses and busy feet had scuffed away the grass and growth for there to be any cover for the Indians to sneak up through. There was heavy brush, however, from the edge of the clearing to the edge of the river a quarter of a mile away.

Catherine wanted to scream by the time he turned away from the door and closed it firmly behind him. He'd no sooner dropped the bar into place to secure it than the first arrow plunked into it. Catherine heard her own startled gasp before she thought to put her hand to her mouth to stop it. Without thought, she reached out and drew Jonny close to her.

Clayton Foster gave her shoulders a reassuring squeeze, then straightened his own and walked over to the Rebel. "If you will be so good, tell me where I can be of the most use."

"I'd appreciate it if you'd take a position at that right front window, sir."

The senator nodded, took a rifle, and went to the window indicated.

Jonathan turned to the first hostler. "Get a rifle and take the window at the rear. There's a good chance they'll figure that if they can get into the storeroom, they can use it for cover until they can break through."

Pointing, he sent the second horse handler to his post. "Sergeant, take the window to the left of the door."

"I ain't taking no orders from a filthy Reb!"

"Sergeant!" The senator's voice was like a whip and filled with contempt.

The sergeant walked toward the window, trailing his carbine along behind him, its butt bumping along the floor. The look he threw at the Rebel boded no good.

Jonathan took up a position at the door, lifting the bar and easing it open the little he needed to observe any activity outside. It was eerily quiet. Even the birds had ceased to sing. His whisper carried easily to everyone in the room. "Ladies, I wonder if you would be so kind as to reload for us when the occasion demands?"

Catherine knew that someday she was going to scratch his eyes from his head! Here they all were in mortal peril, and he was still using the stilted, overly polite phrases for which his culture was justly—and in her present opinion, obnoxiously—famous. With great difficulty, she controlled a strong desire to rant at him and moved to where the extra guns and spare ammunition lay.

As she watched, he slid his revolver out of its holster where he had thrust it and forgotten it after they'd reached the station. She was puzzled to see him slip three bullets out of their chambers and carefully place them in the watch pocket of his vest. She thought it a very odd thing to do, but she realized this was not the time to attempt to satisfy her curiosity.

Mrs. Grisham had watched him, too, and Catherine saw her give a grim nod of approval. Evidently the station keeper's wife knew something of which Catherine was unaware. Perhaps there would be time to ask her later. Catherine devoutly hoped there would be a later.

Feeling that she had to have something to do, she went to the rough pallet where the wounded corporal lay. Placing a hand on his forehead, she was glad to find it cooler than when he'd been dragged over the threshold. She hoped it would continue so and that he wouldn't develop a fever.

Suddenly, her thoughts were sent spinning by a series of savage war cries and the sound of galloping hooves. Her gaze flew to where the Rebel stood coolly, half behind the door, his gun pointed unwaveringly at the approaching attackers. "I'll take the center man, the two of you each take the one on your side," he ordered.

Disregarding the arrows that rained against the door, he fired. There was a shriek from the yard and a dull thud as his target hit the hard-packed earth in front of the building. The man to that one's immediate left fell as the senator shot. The sergeant missed, and the Rebel took his man with a second shot.

As the war party circled the sturdy log station, guns spoke from the other windows. The Indians, their enthusiasm dampened by such well-ordered resistance, withdrew.

They came again moments later, the crack of stolen army carbines added to the noise of their attack. The men at the windows fired steadily, and four more Indians dropped to the hard-packed earth in front of the way station.

After that, the Indians' tactics changed. They retreated behind the heavy brush and shot from its protection. The carefully aimed bow shots often entered the narrow apertures through which the stations's defenders shot back. The Indians moved so quietly through the bushes that they didn't even rattle the dry leaves to give the whites a hint of their positions. And their aim got better. The danger to those in the way station had increased tenfold.

"They'll be able to hang out there for the rest of the year if they want to, damn 'em!" The sergeant ducked back as an arrow whistled past his face.

Jonathan closed the door and dropped the big bar back into place as he left his post. He crossed to the corner, and shoved Mrs. Grisham's big food safe out to stand at a right angle to the wall. Next he dragged the big table over to make another right angle both to the food safe and to the other corner wall, leaving only a narrow space for entry. Sending the heavy table crashing to its side, he built a box to protect the women and the boy.

"Jonny, drag Scout's blanket over if you can. Mrs. Foster, you and Mrs. Grisham stay in this area. More arrows will find their way inside now that the archers have a steady aim. You'll be safer here."

Catherine ran to help her son drag Scout to the safety of the nook the Rebel had made for them. As she dragged the blanket holding the big dog back to its safety, she marveled at the calm of the Southerner's voice. If she were to have to speak now, she was sure her voice would quaver. Even Clayton's had an edge of excitement to it as he called out, "Here, let me help you with him!" and hastened to help the Rebel carry the corporal to the safer area.

Two more arrows sped into and across the room to embed themselves in the logs of the back wall with solid thunks.

Their leader asked, "Have you water buckets ready, Mrs. Grisham?" He sounded like a man asking if there were butter for his bread. Catherine found herself calmed by his matter-of-fact tone.

"Just as you asked, Captain." The heavy woman matter-of-factly plunked two buckets heavy with water down just outside the shelter. Then she bent to offer the corporal a drink of water.

"Thank you, ma'am." The wounded man closed his eyes a moment, then said, "I think I can help load if somebody could bring me the guns."

Mrs. Grisham patted his shoulder. "You just talk to the boy, corporal. Keep him from dashing out there where the arrows are flying, and we'll all be grateful."

The man's pale, youthful face lit for a moment. He nodded and again closed his eyes.

Mrs. Grisham whispered to Jonny, "Here, Jonny. Keep him from thinking of his pain if he should want to talk." She gave the boy a little shove toward the man's pallet, and he went to the corporal's side and settled himself in the narrow space between the soldier and Scout with his back against the wall.

Catherine marveled at the simple woman's diplomacy. And at her calm. She herself worked hard to keep her hands from trembling and letting them all know how afraid she was. She was in agony of fear for her son's safety.

Outside it was quiet. Jonathan eased the door open a crack to get a better idea of what the Indians were up to. With a searing whoosh, a flaming arrow embedded itself in the doorjamb inches from his head. He tore it loose before it could ignite the wooden frame and flung it into the yard.

"Be ready with your buckets, Mrs. Grisham!"

"I'm ready, Captain!" The grim determination in her voice transformed the overweight, nondescript woman into a warrior before Catherine's eyes. She hoped she would respond as nobly if the Captain called her to some duty.

Two more fire arrows plunked into the logs that formed the front wall of the building. The tall Southerner grabbed a bucket from Mrs. Grisham, leapt through the door, and doused one and then the other flaming missile. As a surprised roar burst from the throats of the war party, he threw himself back into the station, his long, lithe body literally flying from the porch to the safety of the inside floor. A hail of arrows followed him at shoulder height, passing well over the man, who lay belly down on the rough plank floor of the station. As he hit the floor, he rolled aside and kicked out to slam the door shut behind him.

He was on his feet in a flash, dropping the bar back across the stout door. He picked up the empty bucket and returned it to his hostess with a smile.

Mrs. Grisham glared at him. "I surely do hope you ain't planning on doing that agin. You're enough to give a body a heart attack." She snatched the bucket from his extended hand and started back to the pump to refill it, shaking her head all the way.

Catherine couldn't have agreed more with the woman's sentiments. When she had seen him dash out through the door, she had been sure the Rebel was rushing to meet his certain death. Her relief at his safe return left her dizzy.

"Don't do that again, please." She stood watching him intently.

"No." He spoke softly, looking hard at her. "They'll be waiting for me the next time."

Catherine shuddered and wrapped her arms around herself. She hadn't the courage to ask him if that meant that he planned to dash out again, anyway, if the need should arise. When she continued to stand silent, he said, "Excuse me, ma'am." He touched the air where the brim of his hat would have been, and moved off to confer with the station keeper.

After a moment, Mr. Grisham shouted, "Do *what?*" He stepped back from the Southerner as if he feared the man had lost his mind.

"If I don't," the Rebel argued reasonably, "they can just sit out there and snipe us off or keep shooting fire arrows into the building until they start some part of it ablaze." He lowered his voice even more and asked softly, "Then where will the women be?"

"Tarnation, lad. There'll be a stage in here late this evening. That'll give us a distraction and reinforcements as well."

The Confederate's mouth became grim. "So much more reason for us to get rid of the Indians. What chance will the people aboard that stage have, coming in here sure that everything's as it should be? You can bet the Indians will hear them from way off, even if they aren't keeping a lookout, which isn't likely, you'll agree. They'll be ready for the stage when it gets here. The poor bastards won't have a chance."

Grisham's thin shoulders dropped; he ran a weary hand through his mop of hair. "You're right." He shook his head. "But I don't see how you're gonna do it. They can sit out there and just wait us out."

"Maybe. But not if I can help it."

CHAPTER

Ten

CATHERINE FELT AS IF HER HEART HAD LITERALLY JUMPED up into her throat. Her chest pained her, and she finally realized she needed to breathe. Unconsciously, she had been holding her breath while she watched the Rebel give his quiet orders to the senator and Mr. Grisham.

He had removed the sergeant from his post at the front window to the left of the door and replaced him with the older hostler. He assigned his own post at the door to Grisham. Catherine wondered what the Rebel was planning to do.

As she watched, the younger hostler came in from the storeroom and dumped an armload of things on a small table near the corner Scout had occupied. Her father-in-law and the Rebel immediately went to inspect the pile. Catherine moved closer, deliberately eavesdropping.

" . . . keep everybody firing to get their heads down and keep them that way while I get near the brush," the Rebel was instructing.

With dawning horror, she heard the senator laugh without mirth. "I can see why you replaced the sergeant."

"Yes. I figure I'll stand a lot better chance of getting back in here without a bullet in my back."

The senator threw an assessing glance at the man they discussed. "If I were you, I'd watch my back even after I got back in here safely."

The Rebel nodded solemnly. "Thanks." He grinned a crooked grin. "I'll take your very good advice." Returning his full attention to the items on the table, he quickly assembled them into a bundle.

Catherine saw among the items a feather duster, of all things. Scraps of dirty rags, even strips of an old blanket and a short length of light chain cluttered the table's surface. What on earth could he be doing?

With an economy of motion, the Southerner wrapped the whole jumble into an open-ended roll made from a square of tough, new canvas and secured it with the chain tight around its middle. Catherine watched as he took the odd bundle to the door.

There, Mr. Grisham held an oil lamp, which struck her as quite strange, for there were hours of daylight left. When the old gentleman cracked the door and peered out, then signaled to the Southerner, Catherine surged forward. "Surely you're not going outside!"

The Rebel looked up from his preparations, surprised at her outburst. Smiling without warmth, he said, "Only me, Miz Foster."

"How can you say that as if it weren't important that you were putting yourself at risk?" She could feel the horror welling up in her—the horror that had assailed her since the first maimed men and shipments of pine coffins had arrived in her hometown at the beginning of the war.

Her father-in-law broke in, gently reprimanding her. "This is man's work, Catherine."

She bit her lips to keep her hot protest from rushing out of them. Man's work. How often had she heard that phrase? And she liked it no better each time she heard it.

Man's business. Man's work. Then they went away on long trips or off to war to die and left women behind who were totally ignorant about how to go on. She found their whole attitude beyond bearing. Stubbornly she refused to move away from the men again.

Her father-in-law frowned. The Rebel smiled faintly. The frown left her unmoved, the smile filled her with curiosity. When this was over, she intended to demand of the golden man the reason for his smile. And, if he came up with any kind of a satisfactory answer, she might then ask him why it was "man's work" always to die.

Her mind jolted: if he came back.

She took a firmer grasp on her rioting emotions. She could feel the hysteria that had threatened her ever since word of her husband's death had come to her. She'd fought it often, conquering it by sheer strength of will.

So far, she had won, but this time it was harder.

This time it was insidious. This time it had nothing to do with her own life. This crushing fear was for a man who was not even a friend nor even a simple stranger, yet she was dizzy with the force of the feeling of alarm that beset her.

Confusion washed over her then, and she bowed her head and whirled away from the men, running back to her little safe spot. Running away from her own confused senses, feeling like a coward.

At the door, Grisham unscrewed the brass top of the oil lamp. Jonathan held out the bundle of inflammables he'd assembled, and the station keeper emptied the oil from the lamp onto it. The senator took a lucifer out of a small silver box, struck it, and held it at the ready.

Suddenly Catherine understood what the Rebel intended. She slapped a hand hard across her mouth to keep back the shouted protest that rose in her. He was going to set fire to something outside!

How could he hope to survive the cloud of arrows that would fly at him the moment he passed through the door? She wanted to turn away. She didn't want to see this. She couldn't bear to watch, but she was powerless even to close her eyes.

At the windows, the two hostlers took firmer grips on their rifles and stared intently out at the bushes that hid the Indians.

The sergeant glanced away from the back window he had been set to guard just long enough to flash a look of pure venom at the Rebel. Catherine knew he'd rather see the Southerner dead than have him succeed in whatever the men had planned. A shiver of apprehension passed over her.

Jonny saw her rub her arms. He recognized the gesture.

It was one she made when she was deeply distressed. Throwing his arms around her, he sought to comfort her. "It'll be all right, Mama. You'll see."

Her every nerve screaming, Catherine stood where she could see what was going to happen. She was faint with apprehension and grateful to have her son's arms around her.

The Rebel whipped the door open, said, "Now," in a voice of iron, and stepped through the aperture even as the bundle he dangled from its chain flashed into flame from the senator's match.

As if those flames had alerted the fiends of hell, startled screeches mingled with fresh war cries.

The Indians saw the crazy white man charging down on their position and were stunned to inaction by his daring. However, their amazement was of brief duration. Arrows flew, but their target leapt to one side and came on.

The men in the way station opened up a murderous fire, hoping to keep the Indians from shooting at the Southerner. They were hoping, too, that one of them didn't wing him by mistake. Then he was there, at the edge of the bushes in which the horde of savages lay hidden.

If they seized their chance, the Indians could reach out and overpower the lone runner, but none did, and then it was too late. The dry brush burst into flame as the Rebel swung his blazing burden along its edge.

He ran the whole width of the stand of bushes, slammed to a stop, then doubled back toward the station, zigzagging as he ran. Halfway to safety, he paused, and like a discus thrower, he hurled the flaming bundle back into the center of the brush. It flew high in a wide arc, spewing the burning debris of which it was composed down along the path of its trajectory.

There was a high-pitched cry as the missile plummeted out of sight into the depth of the bushes. As he ran for his life, Jonathan fervently hoped it had proved an especially unpleasant experience for at least one of the attackers.

He flung himself through the doorway that Grisham opened wide for him and stood with a hand pressed to his side, laboring to regain his breath. Grisham said, "Lordamighty, Captain, I ain't never seen nobody run like that before."

Jonathan grinned at him and gasped, "Incentive."

"Whatever you say. But you flat flew."

The men at the windows slacked off firing, straining to see the results of the Rebel's handiwork. Every one of them could hear the hungry crackle as the flames ate up the dry brush.

Crashing into and jostling each other, the Indians fled their quickly burning cover. Through the writhing plumes of smoke that undulated skyward, the defenders of the way station could see them fling themselves on their ponies and dash away.

A single warrior, his face marred by a hideous scar, turned and let fly a last arrow. He shook his fist in their direction, yelling words none of them could understand, then kicked his pony into a dead run to catch his companions. The dust billowed behind them and they were gone.

"Yippee!" Grisham crowed his delight. "Run, you murdering sons of—!" He broke off as he remembered the presence of the women.

"Lordamercy!" Mrs. Grisham patted Jonathan's arm. "You did it, Captain. You got them pesky Injuns on the run. God bless you." Going up on tiptoe, she placed a hearty smack of a kiss on his cheek. Then she went to where her husband stood looking out the door and wailed, "Oh, Jake, I was so afraid the Captain was gonna hafta use those bullets on the boy, Miz Foster, and me!" Then she lay her head on his shoulder and burst into tears. Grisham clumsily put his arms around her and patted her broad back, kissing her on the top of her head.

The senator offered the Rebel his hand. "Thank you, sir." He cleared his throat, feeling his way. "If you felt any obligation for the small service I did you in Saint Louis, please consider the debt more than amply repaid."

Jonathan shook hands with the older man, measuring the truth of his words in his eyes. The color of his own eyes deepened. With a half bow, he wordlessly thanked the Yankee.

Catherine felt compelled to thank him as well, but she sent her son forward to do so, instead. She wanted to teach him to do what should be done, even if the effort to thank him herself was beyond her.

Jonny walked as if he were wading through deep sand, his feet reluctant to deliver him to a task he found distasteful. Arriving at his destination after what seemed long minutes, he looked up at the tall Rebel. "Thank you," he managed, his voice tight with the effort to admit himself beholden to a Rebel. When he saw the amusement in the man's eyes, he turned his back on him.

Nursing his resentment, and careful to keep his back rigid to express his disapproval, he marched back to his mother. He put his arms around her waist and pressed his face against her side, his onerous duty done.

Catherine looked down at her son. She wanted to weep to see him carry such a burden of hatred. Did it have to be this way? Did even the children have to bear the awful burden of the angry emotions engendered by war?

Anguish flooded her. This wasn't what she wanted for her son. Not for Jonny. She couldn't bear to have him tormented so, to have his childhood stolen in this way. He hadn't grown up in an area where he'd been a victim of the awful horrors of the conflict. Never had he had to go without food or a safe, warm shelter, clothes, or shoes. Nothing had touched him personally but the loss of his father. All the rest, the hatred and the bitterness, those tearing, destructive emotions, he'd learned from others. And God help her, she was one of those others.

She looked down at him, smoothing back his hair and looking long at his earnest face. Wasn't that bitterness around his mouth? God forbid that she should further foster such emotion in a child. Especially her own son, the only living reminder of her husband.

The spontaneous celebration of their narrow escape from death at the hands of the Indians swirled around her, but she didn't hear it. Her mind was full of self-recrimination.

Questions that were suddenly of great importance to her filled her mind.

How did adults create bitterness in a child? Surely by example, for bitterness was a sentiment that had been alien to her own young life. If Jonny was beset by it, then certainly it came from her. Her very soul quailed at the thought.

Standing there in the huge, log-walled room with the scent of burning brush in her nostrils, Catherine took a good look inside herself for the first time since her husband had been killed. She wasn't pleased by what she saw.

Quietly, like a lamp wick gently being turned higher, the realization of what she must do came to her. Though she had to force herself to do it, she moved calmly to the little group around the Rebel captain.

With careful dignity, Catherine lifted her slender hand toward him. "Thank you, Captain . . ." Her hesitation went unnoticed by all but the Confederate and herself. " . . . Foster." Her voice was low and steady, and her eyes met his resolutely. "I'm certain that your brave action has saved all our lives today." Smiling with genuine sweetness, she finished, "I am truly grateful."

An astonished Jonathan took her proffered hand and held it too long, his defenses shattered by that smile. For once she had rendered him speechless.

Perversely, she found it a very pleasant experience. She smiled again, savoring his nonplussed expression, and gently withdrew her hand.

CHAPTER
Eleven

SCOUT RODE INSIDE THE STAGECOACH THE NEXT DAY. He sprawled along the bench beside the Southerner, his head across the man's thigh. The man held Scout lightly but securely so that the dog wouldn't tear open the long, carefully stitched gash in his shoulder.

Catherine watched the way the man cradled the great golden dog against the jolts of the road and wondered at the feelings that the sight stirred in her.

Suddenly, she realized that she was calling him "the man" in her mind, now, instead of the Rebel, realized that she'd had to make an effort to even think of him as "the Rebel" since he'd saved them all during the Indian attack. Somehow he'd become Captain Jonathan Foster to her—in spite of her own Jonathan—a man worthy of his own name, no matter what discomfort thinking of him so might bring to her personally.

She watched his long-fingered hand as it stroked the miserable dog. She saw the way Scout shoved his muzzle into the man's—into Captain Foster's—free hand, and wondered why she had been so stubborn. She had always said that anyone upon whom the big dog put his seal of approval was a fine person, worthy of her regard, but she had willfully ignored her own wisdom when it came to this man.

Jonathan looked up and saw her watching him. "He'll be fine," he reassured her. "Just uncomfortable until we get to the end of our trip."

The senator looked from one of the speakers to the other. He noted the dark circles under his daughter-in-law's eyes.

His gaze turned to his grandson, close against his side in the cramped space between, then he looked across at Jonathan. "I think we'll all feel better when we reach the end of this journey."

Jonathan kept silent. He had very little hope that he'd feel better at the end of his trip. In fact, wondering what Sergeant Keefer was planning had him more than uncomfortable, now.

Why the blazes hadn't the sergeant arrested him? He knew that beefy insult to a uniform would love to treat him as a fugitive and continue to escort him—no doubt in chains, again—to Fort Hardy. Surely nothing would give him more pleasure.

Had the senator spoken to the man? Had he offered to guarantee Captain Foster's arrival at the fort? Jonathan's mind chased the subject around and around, searching for an explanation.

He was damned sure that it hadn't been concern for his wounded corporal that made Keefer overlook Jonathan's departure with the other passengers on the stage.

His gaze rested on the tired face of the senator. God, he wished he knew if it was something the senator had done.

He wished he could swallow his pride sufficiently to ask the man. He knew he wouldn't.

There was no sense in worrying about it. He would be at the fort in a few days, and no doubt he would be in uniform by the time Keefer wandered in with his wounded man.

Wearing the Yankee blue was going to be one of the hardest things Jonathan had ever done in his life.

Two weary days later they forded the Red River. The stagecoach and its team of six horses passed easily across its firm bed. The muddy red water, the color of old brick, came no higher than the hubs of the coach wheels at any point in their passage.

Catherine heaved an audible sigh. The Red River had always marked the point that, for her, meant she was truly

on her way home. Home to the grandfather that had raised
her from the time her parents had died in an Indian attack.
Home from the long winters spent in the East in a school
for affluent young ladies, free for a whole summer to be
herself and roam. It amazed her that she'd all but forgotten
the lift that crossing this wide river had always given her
spirits. Somewhere deep inside she felt a sense of release.
She was home.

All these latter years she'd spent in Jonathan's home,
following the dictates of her Eastern training, being the
perfect wife, mother, and daughter-in-law to the staid New
England family into which she had married. She had all
but forgotten the wonderful freedom she had known here
in Texas. Quick tears welled in her eyes to think of those
halcyon days and the big, bluff man had who had made
them possible. She would never see her grandfather again
in this life, but nothing could take away the wonderful
memories that would sustain her.

Jonathan saw a single glittering tear trembling on her
lashes and the softening of her lips. Something twisted in
his chest. Unconsciously, his hand tightened in the dog's
fur, and Scout whined a low protest.

He called himself to order. Surely she had cause to
grieve. She'd lost her husband, after all.

It was none of his business, however. He couldn't concern himself with her, as much as he longed to. His business
was to strive to pull out of the ashes of his own life a life
for his sisters. He had no time to assuage the grief of the
widow of an enemy. Such a gesture would come under the
heading of a life of his own, and that was a luxury he no
longer possessed.

A muscle in his jaw jumped as he strove to convince
himself of this. It was foreign to his nature to see someone
suffer and fail to attempt to alleviate that suffering.

No longer, however, was he the master of a gracious
plantation. This war had changed all that. No longer could
he command vast resources to set things right for others.
All of that was gone, trampled into the morass of the huge
battlefield that had been his native Virginia. He couldn't

even make things right for himself.

His hands were full. There was no more he could do.
Now he was bound to serve in an army that he'd left
because of his principles, siding with his native Virginia
in the matter of her rights. He knew that now the men
he would serve with in that army would demand he pay
for his choice with some form of retribution. He would
have his hands full coping with his own problems. How
could anything that he might offer serve the lovely woman
opposite him?

Repressing a deep sigh, he turned his head and stared out
the window. At least he could spare her the embarrassment
of his regard.

Catherine saw the man across from her tighten his jaw
and turn to look out the window. Surreptitiously, she wiped
away a tear that threatened to fall. No doubt he was comparing her to the women in his life, and her weakness had
disgusted him.

She was sorry, because she had come to a reluctant
admiration of the man. But his attitude angered her, too.
It was true that she had not suffered as had the women of
the South, but her grief was just as real an anguish to her
as any they had felt, and she resented being weighed and
found wanting in Captain Foster's eyes.

Resolutely, she gave one hearty sniff. Then, in her turn,
she looked out into the distance.

At last, when the sun was low in the sky, they were
on her ranch. Three Rivers. Home. They turned into the
meandering, mile-long drive. Back at the last stop, the
senator had offered to pay the driver extra to take them up
to the house.

Cavenaugh had laughed at him. "Holy Saints, Senator.
You already paid for every seat in the coach for every
day of this trip but the first. And for stopping every night.
You got a problem with money burning a hole in your
pocket?"

Cavenaugh had stayed on as their driver. It suited his own
purpose. He had a married niece down on the Rio Grande

that his wife wanted him to check on since the girl hadn't written in a while.

The senator's insistence that they stop every night and keep the same coach—to avoid having to take their chances on regaining a place on the regularly scheduled stages—made the journey for this particular coach a soft one as far as Cavenaugh was concerned.

As long as the senator was a big enough man to pull it off, Cavenaugh guessed he would be safe staying on as driver. It certainly made his own plans easier. His wife Mary's mind would be relieved that much sooner about their niece if he went and saw for himself, and that, in turn, would make his own homelife a darn sight smoother.

Holcomb, as phlegmatic as ever, had said merely, "I'll just come along for the ride." Cavenaugh was even happier to have his old friend riding shotgun.

Neither'd had any objection to delivering the senator's party to their house, as they had dropped off the last mail pouch some time back, and weren't in as big a hurry to get to Fort Hardy as they were curious about the big Three Rivers Ranch house they'd heard so much about.

In the stagecoach, Catherine gripped the dust-coated windowsill and leaned forward to look for the great old house she'd grown up in. She was straining to see it long before they topped the last rise that hid it from view. She was so eager to see the house that she didn't even notice that her son was hanging half out the other window, an indulgent senator keeping a firm grip on the seat of the eager boy's pants.

They topped the last rise, and Cavenaugh slowed the horses. The house was standing, majestic on its hill, but one long wing of the gracious building was charred, the roof timbers collapsed into it.

Catherine gave one sharp cry as if she had received an actual physical wound, and wrenched the door open to leap out.

Jonathan slipped Scout to the floor, grabbed her before she could jump from the still-moving coach, and held her safe.

"Let me go!" Her frantic voice was husky with tears. She fought him to be free, but still he held her effortlessly. He could feel her pain, and it brought back to him the night his own home had been put to the torch.

He held her as he had held Scout, to keep her safe from injury. There was much more in his embrace, though, as he silently willed her the peace and acceptance that had never been granted him.

She struggled against him, striving to pry his hands from her waist. Still he held her. He released her only when the horses came to a stop, steadying her with a firm hand until she was on the ground and walking away like some participant in a nightmare, toward the place that had so long been her home.

Jonathan left her to her grief. Privacy was the only solace he could offer her. He stepped down and turned instead to look beyond the house at the ranch's outbuildings.

The barn was mostly still there. What he suspected had been the bunkhouse was missing its roof and looked to be beyond saving. The smithy was a heap of burned timbers collapsed around the chimney of the forge, and there were a few other buildings so destroyed that he couldn't guess their former uses. The great house blocked his view of the fourth side of the square the buildings formed.

It was going to take a lot of hard work to restore the house to its former grandeur and the ranch to its accustomed level of efficiency. But, he reminded himself firmly, it was none of his business. It couldn't be.

He waited quietly by the coach and watched as Catherine moved like someone in a trance toward the house. "Boy," he growled, and Scout answered him with a short yip from the floor of the coach where he had been hastily dumped when Jonathan had grabbed Catherine. The big dog was willing but unable to get down and come to his new friend because of the stiffness of his wound.

"No, Scout, not you." A faint smile softened his grim features. "You, Jonny." The boy came to the window immediately. "Your mother needs you."

"Grandfather said to wait."

"Your mother needs you."

The boy jumped from the coach and ran to her without further urging.

The senator got down carefully, stiff and weary after so many hours in the stagecoach. "You're right, of course." He rubbed the small of his back and stretched. "I should have seen that myself."

"We're all tired."

"Yes." The senator bit back the observance that the Confederate hadn't missed his daughter-in-law's need, weary or not. He kept his voice neutral as he asked, "You'll be going on to Fort Hardy."

"Yes." Jonathan's voice rumbled on the single word. He regretted thus revealing the depth of feeling that shook him. He fervently wished he had an alternative, but he had given his word to a caring friend, and short of death, he'd keep it.

"We could use you here, you know." The senator watched him carefully.

He let his gaze travel the extensive ruins. God knew he'd rather stay here where he could help rebuild something than to go and endure the life he knew awaited him at the fort— a solitary Southerner among men who hated him.

He was too disciplined to release the sigh that rose in him. Turning without another word, he went back to the coach and helped the whining dog to the ground.

"Sorry." He truly was, more sorry than the Yankee senator could imagine, but he'd promised his old friend from the Point that he'd faithfully serve in the Western army if granted his freedom, and so he must.

He saw Catherine snatch up her skirts and run toward the house. A round woman that put him in mind of Mrs. Grisham, the station keeper's wife, flung open the front door and rushed across the veranda to meet the graceful figure in black. Smiling, he saw the slender woman enveloped in the comfortable embrace of the heavy one.

An instant later, he saw two riders charge into the side yard and dismount, shouting greetings to the widow. The sight of them did a lot to relieve his mind. She did have men around the place. Until that moment, he hadn't realized how responsible he felt for this Mrs. Foster, late of Massachusetts.

Smiling a twisted smile, he went and sat back where he could not be seen in the shadows of the coach. There he listened to the good-byes Cavenaugh and Holcomb shouted as the coach pulled away, and never saw Catherine Foster start toward it, her momentarily unguarded expression one of acute loss.

Cavenaugh drove into Fort Hardy with a flourish. As the dust swirled around the well-traveled vehicle, Jonathan slipped out of the door on the side away from the crowd that had gathered around the stagecoach, eager for news of the war in the East.

The thick dust finally settled, but by that time, Jonathan was a good distance from the coach and headed for the long, low adobe building that had a Union flag flying bravely above a wheel-mounted canon in front. Ambling over to join himself to a group of men heading for the door, he entered the headquarters building with them.

Just inside, there was a bulletin board with a clutter of papers speared through and attached to it by whatever came to hand. He glanced at it in passing. One of the papers affixed to the crude board was a flyer that pulled him up short. "Wanted for Desertion, Jonathan Foster." Incredulous, he read the notice of his own desertion from the Federal army. He stared at it, his mind refusing to take it in. He hadn't even reported for duty in the blasted Federal army yet.

Shocked, he read and reread the text. The picture—he fervently thanked God—was an unrecognizable drawing of a scowling brute of a man purported to be him. The gist of the notice was that he, a dangerous rogue Confederate, had broken his parole and nearly killed the sergeant escorting him in a blatant attempt to rejoin his Virginia cavalry unit.

He read that he was armed and considered dangerous. The paper urged that if it were not feasible to bring him in to the fort to be hanged for desertion, he was to be shot on sight.

For a moment, his blood ran cold. Then it was heated to the boiling point by his anger. How dare that swine Keefer claim he had broken his word?

Through all the abuse and the beatings, he had stayed at the sergeant's side, determined to keep his word no matter how cruelly the man sought to force him to break it. Now that overstuffed bastard was trying to make the army believe—he corrected himself with bitterness—*had* made the army believe that he, Jonathan Parke Foster, was a deserter.

Suddenly he began mentally berating himself for being slow. Of course! This was the reason Keefer had not taken him back in tow. To do so would have given the lie to this piece of chicanery. The bastard!

Anger blazed high in him and his fists clenched and unclenched at his sides. A man near him looked at him askance to hear Jonathan's teeth grate with the force with which he clenched his jaw.

Alerted to the peril of his situation by the man's stare, Jonathan looked quickly around the room. No face was familiar. Best of all, the face of that lying skunk Keefer wasn't there, either.

It struck him that it might be a very good idea to make his escape. Obviously, if he stayed here, he'd be gallows bait before long. Civilians with military bearing had a tendency to stand out in an outpost fort.

Pulling the brim of his hat low over his eyes, he moved nonchalantly toward the doorway he'd just entered, slumping a bit as he went. When a small group of soldiers led by a burly sergeant approached from outside, Jonathan's heart skipped a beat, but it wasn't the man he was coming to think of as his archenemy. Then they were past, and his way was clear.

Forcing himself to walk slowly and to move with an easy slouch, he stepped off the wooden porch into the dust of the square. Diagonally across from post headquarters, he saw the livery stable and headed that way.

Pulling out his handkerchief, he clapped it over his nose and mouth as if to keep himself from breathing the dust kicked up by a troop of horse soldiers returning from patrol. He felt as if time crept as he crossed the open space. Gaining the doorway of the livery stable, he kept the handkerchief close to his face and pretended to sneeze now and again.

A man loomed at him from the dim interior of the livery stable. "Kin I hep ya?"

Jonathan wheezed to disguise his voice. "I need a horse." He followed the statement with a couple of convincing coughs and paid the man the full price he asked for the first horse he brought out and showed him. Thank God that Tom Dunston's parents back in Saint Louis had forced him to accept the loan of more money than just what he had needed for his stagecoach ticket.

"Yer lucky I'm honest, mister,'cause ya'd sure be an easy hombre to cheat." He shook his head sadly over his customer's lack of bargaining skills. "Sure be easy. Almost wish I hadn't showed you the best horse first."

Jonathan wondered if the man lamented the ease of the sale. For his part, he was glad he had gotten the big bay gelding at something near a fair price. Horses were in great demand right now, had been since the war in the East had been killing them off by the thousands.

Mounted and on his way out of the fort, Jonathan put away the handkerchief he'd hidden behind and turned the head of his mount in the opposite direction from the ranch called Three Rivers. If the man at the livery stable should be asked about any stranger, he wanted the man to remember the false direction he seemed to take.

Jonathan could navigate well enough by the night sky, so he wasn't worried about his ability to double back to the ranch later on. The only problem he could foresee was one that troubled him considerably. How was he going to explain his presence at the ranch once he'd arrived there?

CHAPTER

Twelve

IT WAS DARK AS PITCH AS HE APPROACHED THE BARN. "Dammed lucky if I don't get my fool head blown off," he whispered to his newly acquired horse.

The horse smelled hay and pressed toward the dark structure. "Okay, boy. I get your point. I'm pretty hungry myself."

But hunger lost the battle to weariness, and after he'd seen to his new mount, he sought out a hidden spot in the hayloft. He was asleep before he'd decided whether or not he was comfortable in the deep hay.

Catherine woke with the dawn. Stretching lazily, she smiled. She had rested well in her old familiar bed. She'd been able to push all her worries aside in her joy at being back on the ranch. Now they returned with a rush, and she felt the weight of them settle on her spirit.

She washed her face in the water that had grown cool overnight in the pitcher on the washstand. Its temperature both refreshed her and chased away the last vestiges of sleep.

Moving quietly so that she wouldn't wake the others sleeping away their travel weariness in adjacent rooms, she found one of her old split skirts and a shirt and slipped into them quickly. Looking into the large mirror her grandfather had gotten her for her sixteenth birthday, she drew her hair back away from her face and secured it with a ribbon from the copious supply that still rested, a tangle of colors, in a box in the top drawer of her dressing table.

She looked so young. Without her hair in the bun she usually wore, and free of her somber widow's weeds, she looked like a girl again. She smiled at her reflection, pleased.

Quietly she made her bed, something her grandfather had always insisted on in spite of his numerous servants, and crept down the wide staircase and out the front door. A ride was just what she needed to get the kinks out of her from the long days in the stagecoach.

How did passengers who traveled in the usual way bear it? she wondered. Without the senator's largesse—and influence—she would have had to stay in her seat night and day except for the brief rest stops. Consulting her various aches and twinges, she wasn't certain she would have survived the trip if she had been forced to travel that way.

She was well aware, though, that passengers who gave up their seats to snatch a night's rest sometimes had to wait days to find another place on a passing stage. She must make sure to let the senator know how much his thoughtfulness meant to her.

She hesitated on the edge of the veranda, waiting for Scout to catch up with her. "Hello, boy. Feeling better?" She scratched him under his chin and smiled to see the plume of his tail in easy motion.

Then her attention was all for the ranch. Now that she was back on the land that had nurtured her, she was suddenly alert and thinking again. The dark cloud of grief that had so oppressed her since word of her husband's death had begun to lift.

She looked around and saw not only the destruction that had upset her so last evening, but also all that remained standing. The barn and the house were the most important things on the ranch, and they were still here.

The house had sustained damage, and that had all but undone her yesterday. She had sorely needed the comfort of Ellen's welcoming embrace then, but today she was rested and more herself than she had been in a long time. This was such a huge house that they could easily manage without the burned-out wing. It had been made up only of bedrooms they had used for guests, after all.

The bunkhouse would certainly pose a problem if there were any hands to sleep in it, but the two vaqueros who had whooped into the yard to greet her when she arrived were all that were left of the men who had worked the ranch, and they lived in their own place, the house that she would always think of as Maria's house.

Ellen had told her how Maria's husband, Carlos, and their son Juan had driven off the raiders that had tried to burn the ranch buildings. They had fired from the protection of the thick walls of their low adobe house.

Catherine said a quick prayer of thanksgiving. She would have been devastated if anything had happened to Maria. She had known Maria, who was four years older, all her life. They were playmates, and when Maria's parents had retired from Catherine's grandfather's service and gone back to Mexico, she had wept for days. For a while after they'd gone, Catherine had even been horrid to the new housekeeper-cook, her now very dear Ellen.

Then, Maria had married at fifteen, and she'd brought her husband Carlos back to the ranch, stubbornly insisting that she had always lived on Three Rivers and that the patron would be glad to take him on as a ranch hand.

Catherine's grandfather had taken one look at the worried face of the young Mexican and had hired him on the spot. He had figured if the lad wanted the job as badly as he seemed to, he would make a good hand. Carlos hadn't disappointed him. Now he and his son, who had been born nine months after his parents had come to the ranch, had saved Three Rivers from being burned to the ground.

How grateful she was to the two of them, and how worried she was that they were working harder than anyone should. They would try not to neglect the work on the herd, she knew, and there was more to be done with the cattle than it was possible for two men to do.

All the other hands had either gone off to fight the war or—she remembered Ellen's news with a grim face—been chased away by her Confederate neighbors. It was all more than she was ready to face just now.

Her ride. She refocused her thoughts on her determination to ride. All the other things would have to be dealt with, but not just now. Not on her first day home.

She stopped in the shade of a tree to say, "Stay Scout," and the dog dropped to lie there out of the sun. Catherine walked on.

The barn door was far enough ajar so that she didn't have to fight its massive weight to gain entry. Once inside, she stood smiling as she watched the dust motes float lazily through the shafts of sunshine that penetrated the cracks between the vertical boards of the barn walls.

Throwing back her head, she inhaled the dry, sweet scent of hay and the warm, earthy smells of the barn. A horse hung its head over the half-door of a stall, and she went forward to see if it was one she knew.

No, she didn't recognize the big bay, but that wasn't odd, considering how long she'd been away. Neither her husband nor the senator would hear of her traveling during the war, and her grandfather had echoed their sentiments.

But she was here now and—Suddenly she tensed, her eyes opening wide in shock. She had heard something! There was somebody in the hayloft! The noise that had startled her was too heavy a sound to be just one of the barn cats.

Oh, why hadn't she brought the little gun her grandfather had insisted she wear when she rode about the ranch?

"For varmints," he'd said when he'd given it to her. And then he'd carefully explained that there were more varmints than just rattlesnakes before he'd buckled the scaled-down holster and belt around her slender waist.

Now that she had a need for it, she'd forgotten and left it in a drawer in her room.

She was halfway up the steep stairs to the loft before she thought that it might have been a good idea at least to let Ellen know what was going on. She hesitated for only a moment at the thought.

No, she'd see for herself. It was her barn and her responsibility. She could always screech like a banshee if the need arose. All the windows were open up at the house. They'd hear her and run to her rescue.

Stealthily she continued her climb. She heard a low moan from whomever slept in her hay, then a restless sound as if the person were on the verge of awakening. Taking up a pitchfork that stood jammed into the hay—just in case— she rounded the stack of bales from behind which the moan had come.

There was a blur of movement, and before she could even register its source, the pitchfork had gone flying and she was flat on her back in the hay, a lean hard body pinning her down.

She looked up at the man she had called the Rebel for so long. His handsome face was flushed with sleep, his sensuous mouth still soft with it. His eyes, though, were very much awake. Alert and ready for battle, they blazed down at her, threat in their blue depths.

"Oh," she breathed softly into a moment that had become suspended in time. She heard the quick intake of his breath as he recognized her. She felt the movement in his body, pressed tight against her own, as he inhaled. Sudden warmth suffused her face as she realized the intimacy of his position atop her, one of his long legs between her own.

She should push against him, encourage him to move off her body. But she seemed paralyzed by a strange languor. It was almost as if she drew comfort from the weight of his body pressing her down into the hay.

Embarrassment flooded her at the thought. Anger at her acceptance of their position filled her mind. Twisting beneath him, she bared her teeth at the man whose face, eyes changing subtly to something she feared more than she feared the threat of attack, was mere inches above her own. "Let me up!"

Jonathan fought the army of sensations that had swarmed through him in the last few moments. Aroused from the deep sleep of exhaustion to full battle alert, then all in one instant aroused in quite another way by the soft body he'd thrown beneath his own, he found himself reeling with reaction.

God, it had been so long since he'd known a woman. His senses swam with desire, his body shouted his need.

Remorselessly he crushed his reaction to the girl that twisted beneath him. *Keep still!* his mind shouted. What the blazes was she trying to do to him?

He altered his gasp to a laugh as she said again, "Let me go." Even as he rolled off her, he noted that her voice had a breathless quality that didn't seem far from that of his own. It gave him great satisfaction.

"Sorry." He took a deep breath to counteract the breathlessness of that single word. His voice normal again, he continued, "Never startle a sleeping soldier, ma'am." Sitting in the hay, he leaned on one arm behind him, drew up a knee and rested the other arm across it.

Catherine said crossly, "I didn't expect to find a sleeping soldier in my barn." She made the words a challenge.

"Yes, well, I do have to apologize for that, don't I?" He watched her pull hay from her hair and brush at it on her shoulders. She stood and slapped at the back of her divided riding skirt, trying to be rid of more, staring at him.

"What are you doing here? I thought you'd gone to the fort." She twisted to see if the back of her skirt was free of hay.

He watched her and told his body to be still as she unconsciously displayed herself to him. She had changed. It was as if, in discarding her mourning clothes, she had discarded several years, and was again the girl she must have been when she had lived here. He wondered how the two sides of her would work out living together in a single body.

Rising, he pulled from her hair a stem of hay she had missed. She pushed his hand away irritably, and her pique amused him. He laughed and suggested with a wave of his hand that she precede him, and together, single file, they descended from the loft.

Skilled as he was in the ways of women, he recognized and enjoyed her reaction to him. Watching the slender woman move across the loft, his gaze fastened on her slightly swaying hips, he took pleasure in knowing that for just an instant, she'd responded to him as a man.

Cold reality hit him as she started down the steps. He muttered a mild curse softly under his breath.

For a moment he had forgotten who he was. Who he had become, rather. No longer was he the desirable owner of vast acres, wealthy scion of one of Virginia's oldest and most illustrious families, he informed himself nastily. Now he was just a penniless nobody. He had nothing to offer this woman nor any other. He clenched his jaw and followed her, all feeling consigned to the realm of yesteryear.

"Did you say something?" Catherine half-turned back to him as she asked. She was shocked by the coldness of his face.

His answer was like a fall of ice. "No."

With an effort she tore her regard from his closed visage. The word "oh" came inanely to her lips, but she lacked the breath to say it. Thanking the good Lord for small blessings, she turned and tried not to stumble as she led the way down the rest of the loft stairs and out of the barn.

The senator was awake, and had just checked on Jonny when Catherine and the Rebel came in from the barn. With the practiced ease of a statesman, he kept from showing his surprise at seeing the Rebel and walked down the stairs from the open upper hallway to meet them.

His eyebrows rose slightly to see the bits of hay both of them wore, but knowing his daughter-in-law as he did, he was able to wait patiently for an explanation.

Catherine said with little grace, "We have a guest for breakfast, Clayton. I found him sleeping in the barn."

The senator said dryly, "I see."

Catherine blushed and pulled another piece of hay from her hair. "When I found him, he was asleep and I startled him."

"Never startle a sleeping soldier, Catherine." Her father-in-law offered his advice in a neutral voice.

Relieved that he wasn't going to probe into what had happened in the loft, she said, "So he told me," and went to tell Ellen they had company.

"Last night you went to the fort." The senator gave the Rebel a starting point in the explanation he obviously expected.

Jonathan's every sense alerted. Weighing each word carefully, detesting the lie he was constructing out of half-told truths, Jonathan answered him. "They don't want me in uniform at the fort." That was true. They wanted him in a long pine box and six feet underground. "The war will soon be over." That truth nearly tore him apart. The next one came only a little easier. "Soldiers will soon be flooding back to the West. More than they will have need of."

That was the best he could do. He could hardly say that he was a wanted—no, a condemned—man. That Keefer had lied and made him a fugitive would be of no matter to a Yankee senator. The man would probably see it as his duty to return him to the fort for swift justice.

No, he admitted. That was not so. That was a lie born of bitterness. The senator would probably try to straighten things out for him.

But Jonathan had learned a lot about justice for Southerners at Northerners' hands in the last few months, and he was unwilling to experience any more, thank you. No matter how well-meaning the senator might be, there were other Yankees involved. A lot could happen to a man while he cooled his heels in a cell. Jonathan could already attest to that.

Catherine came back into the room. "Ellen says she's got breakfast ready." She regarded the Reb—Captain Foster— with cool curiosity. She was completely recovered from whatever had overcome her in the barn.

It must have been some product of the exhaustion induced in her by her long trip. At least that was the way she intended to think of it.

The men followed her into the dining room. Catherine took her place at the head of the table, gesturing Jonathan into the place at her right. The senator took the chair opposite him.

Catherine watched the two men with interest. Captain Foster wore a wary expression, as if he waited for some attack.

The senator regarded him with a thoughtful expression, but when he spoke, it was to Catherine. He seemed to weigh his words carefully. "The Captain has been refused at the fort. It seems that they anticipate a flood of replacements from the war in the East shortly and have no need of him."

Jonathan quietly let out a long breath, hiding it by looking down as he placed his napkin in his lap.

Catherine looked from one to the other, feeling almost as if she were watching a duel.

She saw some of the strain leave the Rebel's face. A part of her mind wondered at the significance of that, but another distracted her by addressing the fact that he was "the Rebel" once more.

She was displeased to notice herself thinking of him as "the Rebel" again. Was it, she asked herself, because she wished to reestablish the distance that had existed between them? Had the scene in the barn thrown her that far out of kilter?

Her son spared her the necessity of answering her own unwanted questions. With the crash of a door upstairs and a rush of footsteps down the stairs, he hurtled into the dining room. "Am I late?" he asked anxiously. "I thought I smelled bacon." His glance touched the Southerner. "Oh." His expression became guarded. "What are you doing here?"

"Having breakfast with your mother and grandfather." Jonathan's cool, firm tone showed his displeasure at the boy's attitude. In the South, all adults took the responsibility for properly rearing the young.

"Sit down, dear." Catherine indicated a chair. "And please watch your manners. We have never been ungracious to guests at this table."

The boy had the good grace to blush. "Yes'm," he mumbled to the plate in front of him.

The senator regarded the man across the table for a long minute, then asked, "If you are free from your obligation at the fort, what are your plans?"

Jonathan looked at the older man levelly. "I guess at this point, I don't have any." Color began to rise in his face.

Senator Foster shoved his scrambled eggs around his plate, appearing to consider his next remark. After a sip of coffee, he spoke. "You'll remember that just before you left last evening, I told you I'd like you to work for us." He raised an eyebrow inquisitively.

"Yes, sir." Jonathan kept his face impassive, but his stomach knotted with apprehension. With fall coming, he had to get his sisters out of the South. When the gardens stopped producing, there wasn't going to be enough food for them to share at the cousin's with whom he'd left them. He needed a job in a hurry. Holding his breath, he prayed he was being offered one.

The senator saw the tension in the Rebel and thought perhaps he understood. The man's financial resources must be pretty well drained by now. Three Rivers Ranch wasn't his, however. He turned to his daughter-in-law. "Catherine?"

Catherine was having difficulty sorting out her feelings. Would she want to have with her constantly a man who'd aroused such feelings in her as this one had done in the hayloft? She thought not.

At the same time, help was nonexistent, and she knew she couldn't run the ranch with just Carlos and Juan. In her mind she argued. He was a Rebel, an enemy. But then, so were most of her neighbors. Perhaps that would make him an asset.

She passed her hand over her eyes. Why did she have to make this decision before she'd gotten settled in? Why was Clayton forcing it on her?

Clayton Foster saw her gesture but was determined to have his answer. Good hands were hard to come by—any hand was hard to come by—and this man had more than proved his mettle at the way station. He wondered what ailed the girl. "Catherine?"

"Yes?" She made her voice vague, stalling for time.

"Have you a job for Captain Foster?" Out of the corner of his eye, he saw the Confederate officer's color deepen further. Obviously being hired was a new and decidedly uncomfortable experience for him.

"Can you work cattle, Captain?" Her voice bordered on scornful.

Putting his pride in his pocket and hating her for forcing him to, Jonathan answered her through clenched teeth. "I can learn." His eyes bored into hers, unyielding.

Clayton interrupted the tension between them. "Catherine, we need men to work this place. I'm sure the Captain will do a creditable job at whatever he turns his hand to."

The senator was as surprised as his daughter-in-law to hear himself champion the Rebel. What the devil had gotten into him? Must be he wanted to discharge the obligation he had felt to the man since the episode at the way station. Damned if he'd admit he was affected by the man's plight.

"Very well." Catherine sounded confident now that her mind had, she thought ruefully, been made up for her. "Fifty dollars a month and found." Seeing him bewildered, she said, "Found means room and board, Captain. Is that agreeable?"

The pay was better than twice what he had gotten in the cavalry. He hesitated only an instant before answering, "Quite."

Catherine looked at him in mild astonishment. In all her days at the ranch, she didn't think she'd ever heard a hand sign on using the word "quite."

CHAPTER
Thirteen

THE NEXT FEW WEEKS SPED BY WITH CATHERINE WATCHing the Rebel's progress carefully. Carlos and Juan had had no objection to teaching him. In fact, they were overjoyed to have another hand to help them. They were not very happy, however that Catherine had rehired her old foreman, Kirby Morris. She hoped they would come to understand the man was sorely needed.

Though Captain Foster might not know anything about cattle, he rode like he was part of his horse, worked like a demon, and wasn't afraid of anything. Carlos and Juan gave her glowing reports of him, so she was in complete charity with her father-in-law again.

"Good morning, Catherine." Clayton smiled at her over his coffee. He waited until Ellen had put Catherine's breakfast in front of her to say tentatively, "The Rebel seems to have fallen into the routine of the ranch pretty well."

Catherine's smile disappeared. "Yes, he seems the kind of man used to making himself at home in whatever situation he may find himself."

Clayton was amused. "And that offends you?"

She shrugged. "It smacks of opportunism." She buried her nose in her coffee cup and refused to meet his eyes.

Clayton was surprised at her attitude. "Great Scot, Catherine. The man has lost everything. His holdings were in Virginia, after all, and most of that state is little more than a trampled battleground at this point."

He struggled with exasperation, shocked to find himself

forced into the position of defending one of the enemy. "He's spent the last three years in situations that nothing in his upbringing could have prepared him for, and you find it strange that he's adaptable?" His face was a study in disbelief.

Catherine was astonished.

Clayton laughed shortly. "Forgive me, my dear. I can't imagine what came over me. Startled, I guess." He returned his attention to his breakfast, wondering why he had jumped to the Rebel's defense.

Catherine smiled at him. Her voice held a grudging note. "Yes," she said like a little girl carefully righting a wrong, "he is fitting in quite well."

She reached for his cup and poured him more coffee. "Morris says he learns fast. Grudgingly of course. Morris, I mean, not the Captain."

"You're glad to have Morris back, aren't you?" He thought he'd detected a note of hesitation in her voice.

"Yes, he's a good foreman. He knows cattle." Her troubled gaze met the assessing one of her father-in-law. Catherine looked at him a long minute. "I just wish he'd stayed on here after Grandfather died."

There was a long pause before the senator spoke. "Kellerman offered him the same salary, and it didn't come with the difficulties that he'd have had to face here." He put a hand on hers. "Things got pretty uncomfortable when the neighbors learned your grandfather had left the ranch to a Yankee widow."

"Those neighbors have known me all my life."

"Feeling runs high in wartime, my dear."

"Carlos and Juan stayed."

"Yes, but Carlos is married to Maria, and Juan was born here. And they nearly had the place burned down around their ears."

Catherine stared out the window. Her sigh could have been heard in the next room.

Jonathan peeled off his rawhide work gloves and thrust them into a hip pocket. He looked down at the palms of his hands with a rueful half-smile. He had thought riding with the cavalry in all kinds of weather had toughened them, but the new blisters he was forming disabused him of that notion in a hurry.

His rueful smile became a grin. He wondered what his body servant, Saul, would think. Massa was learning what it meant to put in a day's work with his very own hands. His grin widened. It was a pretty good feeling, he was surprised to find.

"Hey, Gringo! You ready to eat or not?" Juan's face appeared around the side of the barn.

Jonathan grinned again at the cut. It had started when his ignorance about roping and branding had forced the exasperated little Mexican to shout to his father, "What good is this stupid gringo, anyway?"

Jonathan had learned fast, however. Finally, he'd won Juan's grudging approval. Carlos's had followed less reluctantly. Much to Carlos's displeasure, his son had persisted in insulting his new friend, and Gringo had become the Southerner's name, as far as Juan was concerned.

Jonathan picked up the reins of the big bay he'd bought. "Come on, boy." He led the big horse to the trough in the center of the square formed by the ranch buildings. While he washed off under the pump, the horse drank from the trough it fed, watching him with great, soft eyes.

The horse had won both Jonathan's admiration and gratitude. The animal was undoubtedly familiar with ranch work and had taught his new rider much of what he'd learned about handling cattle.

Jonathan had named him Creole after the horse Robert E. Lee had ridden in the War with Mexico. He could think of no greater compliment to bestow on the animal—nor any more subtle way to cut back at Juan for calling him Gringo.

He tossed his water-darkened hair back. "Let's go, Creole. I've been angling for a long time for some of Maria's cooking."

Leading his horse, he walked diagonally across the square

yard, eyeing the ranch buildings the raiders had destroyed. He had hoped he was finished with destruction, but now he had found it even here.

He looped the big gelding's reins around the hitching rail in front of the low adobe house that Maria Rodriguez ruled with an iron hand. Later he'd ride him to make his customary patrol of the range immediately surrounding the ranch house before retiring for the night. Night patrol had become a habit that cleared his mind and settled his spirit for sleep.

Removing his hat, he approached the door and stomped his boots free of dust. Maria's daughter, Consuelo, came to invite him in shyly, her eyes modestly downcast.

Jonathan murmured, *"Gracias,"* and waited just inside the door.

A cheery feminine voice called, "Come in, come in. Do not wait to be led by the hand, Señor Jonathan. I have all I can do to cook enough to keep you men from grumbling." Maria waved a long-handled spoon at him, then used it to point to a place at the table. "Sit, sit. I am Maria. *Bienvenido a mi casa."*

"Thank you, señora." He smiled at her, as he took the place opposite Juan. "It was *con mucho gusto* that I received your invitation."

Carlos and Juan grinned at each other and said teasingly, "Ahhhhh!" Juan waggled his eyebrows.

Maria whirled away from her cooking, eyes wide. "Ahhhh." And hers was sincere. "The señor is most kind." She looked him over with bright interest, this gringo her men admired.

As the men exchanged small talk, Maria and Consuelo put the food on the table, then took their places. "Carlos," Maria commanded, and in melodic Spanish her husband asked a blessing.

The food was as good as any Jonathan had eaten, and he told Maria so. "Gracias, señor." She shot an arch look at her husband. "It is so nice to have one's work complimented."

Carlos had the grace to blush before growling, "Do not be foolish, woman."

Jonathan asked quickly, "Were you here when the raiders came, señora?"

"Call me Maria. You are helping my Catherine. And at the way station, you have saved her life, I think."

Jonathan registered that comment with surprise. How could Maria have known about his actions at the way station? He'd be interested to know if Cathy Foster had told her.

Maria went on, eyes glittering with malice, "Yes, I was here when the filthy cowards came to burn Three Rivers, *el diablo* take them. It was our good fortune that we were all here in the house. Juanito had barely come in from his chores in the barn, but he was here, *gracias a Dios.*" She began passing the huge platter of chicken and rice, thrusting it forward like a weapon.

"Could you tell who they were?"

"They wore bandannas over the lower parts of their faces, but I think it was that man Kellerman and his crew." Her voice showed her disgust with the raiders' stupidity. "The horses, they did not wear bandannas. Juan recognized them."

Jonathan frowned. "But I was given to understand that this was the work of Confederate neighbors. I hadn't heard Kellerman was a Confederate."

"No more is he. He has been careful to take no side in this war, that one. Now that it is obvious who will win—" She drew in a quick breath to see the look of pain that crossed her guest's face at her careless comment, and was grateful for the way he ducked his head to spare her feelings. She went on more softly, "—Mr. Kellerman is beginning to make himself sound as if he supported the North.

"Not too loudly, of course. Not yet. But you can believe that is the only reason he has let Mr. Morris come back to Three Rivers. If things had turned out differently, you may be sure that Señor Morris would still be at the Lazy K."

Carlos grunted agreement from the head of the table.

"Are you saying that Morris is Kellerman's man, Maria?"

"*Sí.*"

"What do you think he's doing here, then?"

Maria saw the blue of his eyes deepen as he watched her. She said, "Three Rivers and the Lazy K have always been rivals. That is all I can tell you. That and that I distrust Señor Morris. It is all I know."

Jonathan sat scowling. Finally he asked, "Is Kellerman after the herd? Or the ranch? Or both?"

Maria and Carlos exchanged glances. Even as close as Maria had been to Catherine in her youth, it was not the way of her people to speak of the business of the patrons. Not to a *norteamericano*, at any rate.

Jonathan held his tongue and waited. White flecks appeared in the deep blue of his eyes. His patience broke the reticence in Maria. The ice in his eyes goaded her. "We," she burst out, "fear that Kellerman has greedy eyes on the ranch, *sí*. We hope he does not look at Señora Catherine," she took a long, shaky breath and grimaced. "But he has long been a widower."

Jonathan's face went still.

Maria saw the subtle change in him and stopped worrying so about her Catherine. "We do not know what having Señor Morris back at Three Rivers means, but we are troubled. He was not one to care for the ranch nor for Catherine's welfare once the patron died. We are all *muy* suspicious of his new helpfulness."

Jonathan looked at her steadily. "But you haven't told them up at the house."

"No." Maria shifted uncomfortably. "There is enough to bear at the house just now."

"Thank you, señora. Now that I know these things, I'll be watchful."

Maria laughed, attempting to lighten the atmosphere in the room, "You almost speak as if you were one of us!"

Juan grinned, aware of his mother's purpose. "After all this *arroz con pollo, madre*, perhaps he thinks he has become one of us. ¿*No es verdad, Gringo*?"

Jonathan grinned back at him *"Es verdad, muchachito."* And it was true. Somehow he felt bonded to these people who looked after Cathy Foster's welfare. He wondered how it had happened. He wondered, too, when he had begun thinking of her as Cathy.

CHAPTER

Fourteen

MARIA HAD GIVEN HIM A LOT TO THINK ABOUT AT DINNER the previous night. He was still trying to figure out what, if anything, Morris was up to as he rode to join Carlos and Juan on another section of the huge ranch.

He spotted the old hacienda that had been the beginning of Three Rivers Ranch—only it had been Tres Rios then—and swung right along a barely defined path, just as Morris had instructed. Ten minutes more should bring him to the place Carlos and Juan were working, over on the edge of the ranch.

Taking a shortcut through a draw, he told his big gelding, "Steady, Creole," as he trotted into the depression. He spoke more to hear a human voice than of any necessity. The horse had more savvy about this terrain than he did.

"Captain Foster!"

Startled, he halted his horse and looked in the direction from which he'd heard the call. There, not fifty feet up the draw, he saw Cathy crouched over the still form of a cow.

Hurrying to her, he saw in a glance that the cow had died giving birth to a calf, and that Cathy was trying to pick the weak little thing up.

"Hold on, Cathy. You'll hurt yourself!"

Startled at his calling her Cathy, she watched the lean Southerner's graceful dismount. His skin was deeply bronzed by the sun now and his strange pewter-blond hair was bleached to a lighter shade—or had his prison pallor just made it seem the color of gold-shot ashes?

He was devastatingly handsome, whatever the cause, especially now, with his eyes bright with interest and his lips soft with concern.

He was beside her in an instant, kneeling to look the calf over. He glanced at the dead cow. "Young heifer. Just couldn't make it to the end of her time." He turned his full attention to the calf. Somehow it was free of the sac it was born in. That was why it was still alive.

When he looked back up at Cathy, his eyes were grave. "This one hasn't much of a chance, Mrs. Foster."

She returned his regard silently. He'd said "Cathy" before, when he hadn't given it any thought. No one had ever called her Cathy except her grandfather. Hearing her name thus shortened again filled her with warm memories.

She let that knowledge slide through her, wondering if she minded this man calling her that. It had been a slip, of course, but did she mind, or did she like it?

When he had spoken again, he had called her Mrs. Foster, not even Miss Catherine, as the rest of the ranch did. She wondered if he felt Miss Catherine was too familiar, or, and she felt it more likely, too subservient. At least he had stopped displaying that wry smile every time he spoke to her. She wondered about that, too.

She turned her thoughts back to the calf, getting up gracefully from where she knelt. "Let's take it to the barn. Maybe Jonny and I can raise it. It might be good for him to have something to do."

He looked into her eyes. "And if the calf doesn't make it?"

Catherine hadn't thought beyond getting the poor little thing back to the ranch. She felt as if her arms were half out of their sockets from her futile attempts to lift the limp calf.

She'd been so relieved to see him ride into the draw. Now all she wanted him to do was to take it to the barn for her. She didn't want him to remind her that her son might have a hard time if it died. She didn't want to be torn two ways.

She looked down at the still-damp calf panting in the dust at her feet. She knew there was no way she could abandon this frail creature. A life was a precious thing, and you fought to hold on to it.

Catherine had grown up here on Three Rivers, and this wouldn't be the first time she had worked to preserve the spark of life in some creature too weak to fight for itself. It was a part of her own life to do so, a vital part.

To her grandfather, all life had been sacred, and he'd passed that belief on to her. Evidently it was now time for her to be sure her son understood it, and the calf would help her.

She turned abruptly. The hem of her riding skirt touched his arm as it swung. Glaring down at the kneeling man who seemed always to upset her, she ordered. "Take it to the barn. We'll put it in the empty stall next to Rosie."

His eyes narrowed at her tone. "Yes, ma'am." He gave the words an icy edge. He'd never once heard her leave off the word "please" when she gave Carlos or Juan an order. The omission rankled.

Catherine fought down an exasperated sigh. She had made her words an order deliberately. Now why, in Heaven's name, should she be distressed that he'd taken them just as she had intended him to?

She was upset, and it was all the fault of the tall man rising effortlessly from the ground with the calf gently cradled in his arms.

She watched as he approached his horse and murmured, "Steady, Creole." The horse became immobile. There was no more than the flick of an ear, the flare of a nostril, as the Southerner thrust his booted foot into the stirrup and swung up into the saddle. He made it one fluid motion, even with the calf in his arms. He made it look easy.

Catherine knew better. She found herself watching the play of muscles in his back. Under the blue fabric of his work shirt, glued as it was to his back with the warmth of the day, she could see them clearly. Though he had gained some weight and was no longer the pitifully thin man he had been, he still lacked flesh enough to hide the definition of his muscles.

His work denims, new just a few weeks ago, were getting

worn, and in becoming so, they molded themselves closely to his long legs. Under their fabric Catherine watched the lean muscle in his thigh bunch in the powerful motion that lifted the newborn calf so easily onto the horse's back with him.

He might be too slim still, but he seemed to have regained his full strength. She was glad for that, for she still remembered the effort it had been for him to lift Scout onto the roof of the stagecoach.

She remembered, too, the pain it had caused him, and the stained, torn shoulder of his tattered Confederate uniform that had told her he had been wounded there. She recalled the time in the coach when he rubbed his shoulder as if it pained him, and the scrupulous care he took never to do it again when he caught her watching him.

At the remembrance, suddenly somewhere inside, she felt strange, as if she were melting, painfully melting, to think of the cost to him of his valiant efforts on her family's behalf. The strength of her reaction to her thoughts confused her.

Refusing to give them her attention a moment longer, she mounted quickly and rode her mare out of the draw ahead of him.

When she had mastered her emotions, she slowed her horse until he caught up and was riding beside her. Just because she was troubled by the feelings he engendered in her was no reason to be rude to the man. Those feelings were, after all, hardly his fault.

As the silence drew out between them, she found she had to make some effort at conversation. They were still miles from the barn. "Your horse has an unusual name."

He smiled at her, his eyes twinkling. "He's named after the horse General Lee rode in the War with Mexico."

"I see." She did, too. All Southerners, and a great many Northerners, as well, revered Robert E. Lee. Lincoln had been about to ask him to command an army when Lee resigned his Federal commission on the grounds that he could not lead men to invade Virginia's sister states. Catherine didn't want to think about the war and changed the subject quickly. "Have you ever worked with an orphan calf?"

"No. Never."

She looked at the easy way he held the animal and smiled. "You do very well for someone with no experience."

"I like animals." Then he laughed shortly, deciding to help her with the effort she was making to pass the time and added pleasantly, "Though I'm beginning to think maybe cows are one of the least likeable."

Catherine smiled without looking over at him. "They can certainly be cantankerous." Her face became serious, and she glanced his way. "And if they take fright and stampede, they can be dangerous."

Suddenly she remembered that he wasn't really a cattleman, and her concern for his safety was overwhelming. She realized she must warn him, and she turned full face to him now, her eyes wide. "Carlos and Juan have told you that you must get your horse and yourself out of the way if a herd stampedes, haven't they?"

She shuddered, and Jonathan saw the shadow in her eyes, and the play of emotion over her expressive face. "Our old foreman, Charley Watts, was killed that way." Her face saddened. "He had been with us all my life."

Jonathan saw the tears gather and sought to distract her. "If was around cows that long . . ." He let his voice trail away.

She dashed her sleeve across her eyes. "We don't know what happened. He was out by himself when . . . when it happened."

"I'm sorry. It must have been a sad time for all of you."

She nodded, and they rode a little way without speaking, the only sound the horses and the creak of leather. Now, though, their silence was companionable. Jonathan let it touch him for a long minute, breathing deeply the scent of the dry mesquite around them, savoring the moment. But there was something he wanted to know, and he said, "And then your granddaddy hired Morris."

"Yes." The word was almost curt. Her eyes, large and dark, were a little startled at his remark, curious. It seemed to come from nowhere, and hang between them, out of place. She found she didn't want to pursue whatever bent his thoughts were taking, and pushed her curiosity away.

Jonathan made a mental note of the shortness of her answer. There was no praise for the man, no relief at having him back. Maybe Maria didn't have as much to worry about as she thought she did. It seemed to him that there was not a lot of liking for Morris in Cathy Foster's single word.

She didn't speak again and long before they reached the barn, his idle mind had begun suggesting puzzles. The most interesting one of them was that there just might be a connection between Charley Watts's death and the hiring of Kirby Morris.

One part of his mind thundered, *Preposterous!* But another filed the ugly thought back away in that part of his brain that had brought it up, the part that had kept him alive in many a tight situation.

At the barn, he shook off his thoughts to follow his employer's instructions about the calf. She dismounted and walked toward him where he still sat his horse. "Hand me the calf." She held out her arms.

He looked at her as if she had lost her mind and swung his leg over the saddle horn to drop lightly to the ground with the bawling calf in his arms. "I can manage."

She almost wanted to slap the amused look off his face. He made her feel like a ninny standing there with her arms outstretched while he slid to the ground. Even so, she wondered at the strength of the resentment he caused in her. She found him a very annoying man.

Turning, she moved into the cool interior of the barn. She walked to the stall beside the milk cow's and looked inside. "It's clean."

She stepped aside for him to enter the stall with the calf. Holding the door open put her in close proximity to him as he passed. She found his light scent pleasant, and it tingled her senses.

Clenching her teeth with self-aggravation, she let the door close behind her. As he stood waiting to lay the calf down, she bent down and fluffed the bright, shiny straw in the center of the stall. "There, that should do."

"Very nicely," he said, his gaze locked on her slender figure. His voice was a mellow rumble that caused the tiny calf in his arms to bawl.

There was an answering sound from the stall next door, and the calf turned a searching face in that direction. Catherine gave an inarticulate sound of sympathy. "Milk. Would you please get some milk from Rosie?"

Cathy remembered the "please" this time, he noted. No, he corrected himself, she had forgotten to omit it for his benefit. He sat back on his heels and regarded her for a moment.

She was a strange little thing, this beautiful Yankee widow, not at all like the women he was used to, the women of his world, who ruled the lives of the people around them with a combination of charm and a steel will covered in honey and velvet. Briefly, he wondered what his sisters would make of her. He rose easily.

"Milk." She put a lot of impatience into that one word. She watched in amazement as he turned as red as a beet.

"I'm sorry, Mrs. Foster." He sounded embarrassed. He was embarrassed to be caught daydreaming over her and because of the confession he must make. Taking a deep breath, he got at it. "I understand that the calf needs milk and that you'd like me to get it. I know there's probably plenty and to spare next door in that cow you call Rosie." He nodded at the stall beside the one in which they stood, and the color in his face, which had almost receded to a normal level, rose again. "But," he said apologetically, "I have not the faintest notion how to get the milk out of the one and into the other."

If he had been anyone else, Catherine would have laughed aloud at his charming diffidence. Instead she said sharply, "You can't milk a cow." She didn't make it a question, she made it an accusation.

He raised an eyebrow and made it look like a reprimand. Carefully he bit out, "I never needed to know how to milk a cow."

She heard each word separately as it fell into the tense atmosphere between them. "No!" she flashed at him. "You had black slaves to do that."

His voice cut her off like a whiplash. "Servants. Servants in my house and in my barns and in my dairy. Hands in my fields. Just like you have hands on your ranch, Mrs. Foster!"

"No! Not like I have hands, Captain Foster! My hands can leave if they want to."

White-faced with anger, he stared at her. "What do you know about it?" His eyes blazed at her, and she saw he relished the way she took an involuntary step backward. "It was your Northern ships that stole the poor wretches away from their homes. Then you found you couldn't keep them healthy in your cold climate." He whirled away from her and grabbed the top of the stall door, clenching his hands so hard on it she feared he'd break the wood. "But you didn't care that they weren't much use in factories, you had your own white wage slaves to do that work. People you could just throw away when you saw they were sick, or too old.

"So you sold us the blacks so you could keep your molasses and rum trade going. You never worried about their welfare then."

He wrenched open the low stall door and stormed out. Turning, he glared at her over it, taking hold of it again as if to steady himself against the anger that shook him. "Have you ever nursed them through influenza? Smallpox? Have you ever visited the old retainers in the cabins you retired them to, to see that they had all that they needed? That they didn't feel useless or forgotten? Have you ever even talked to a real honest-to-God Southern slave, Mrs. Foster?"

Shocked into silence, she could only stare at him.

"No. You haven't. You probably never even talked to a Southerner until you had to talk to me."

She made a feeble gesture. She had talked to Southerners on her wedding trip, and had found them charming and hospitable. She had seen that their slaves seemed healthy and well-clad, too, but she knew instinctively that she had better not say anything to interrupt his white-hot outpouring.

He went on without pause, leaving her no time to answer. "No, Mrs. Yankee Foster. You don't have the vaguest notion about the South and its peculiar institution.

"You probably don't even know that Virginia had been working for years on a way to free the slaves." His voice filled with heavy scorn. "Oh, no, not because we were so noble of spirit, my dear." He made it sound as if she were anything but his dear. "No, madam. It was because they had become a financial drain that far surpassed their worth.

"When England solved her problem in a way that worked, we took hope. Their government paid two hundred million dollars to British slave owners to guarantee the release of their slaves. But did your wonderful Yankee statesmen want to consider that option? No, the few stupid bastards who cared at all about the subject wanted us to just set them free.

"A good field hand represents an investment of two thou sand dollars, Mrs. Foster. Would you like to give away that much of your family's fortune, multiplied many times over? Would you like to give away your children's security? No! I thought not.

"And how about them? Those men and women who have no means of livelihood?"

His voice was scathing. "But slaves weren't the issue. We both know that. Tariffs that forced us to buy shoddy Northern goods instead of the good English products we'd always bought, tariffs that in turn forced us to sell to the North for lower prices than we got in England, were at the heart of it, Mrs. Foster. So we exercised our right—our *right*!—to secede." Catherine heard his teeth grate together as he fought to stem the flow of words that seemed to erupt like a volcano's fierce release of intolerable pressures from his lips.

He bogged his head down between his shoulders, leaning forward, his nails sinking into the whitewashed wood he gripped. He struggled to speak more reasonably, but the frustration of years shoved him on.

He sounded a little calmer, though, maybe even a little

weary, as he said, "And if you cared so much for my people, madam, why didn't you and your kind set up an almighty howl when you read Mr. Lincoln's Emancipation Proclamation? Why didn't all you pious Yankees make him free all the slaves with his presumptuous proclamation? How in Heaven's name did you countenance it when he freed only the slaves in the rebellious states? Tell me that, Catherine Self-righteous Foster. Is it more acceptable to live as a slave as long as one does it in the North, madam?

"Tell me," he lifted his anguished face to her. "A Yankee colonel took some of my people from my home. Will they live free or will they be his slaves?"

Catherine sensed the agony behind his question and it surprised her. She had no answer for him, and she would have been afraid to voice it if she had one.

She looked at him more closely. He had certainly had her full attention before, but she had watched him in the slightly unfocused way that its prey watches a snake. Now she saw he was worn out with the fury that had fueled his outburst.

He pinned her with his blazing blue eyes. His voice was soft now, exhausted. "Would it interest you to know that two of my field hands who had been enticed to try your famous Underground Railroad asked me to send for them? The blessed Abolitionists had gotten them away to the North, pronounced them free, and left them to starve in the streets. And I'm not there to take care of them now. I can't help them anymore."

He lifted a finger at her, and though there was half a stall between them, Catherine felt that he thrust it into her face. She saw strength flow back into him. "So don't you ever, ever presume to talk to me about my past again." He snatched the door of the stall open with his newfound strength, and for one wild split second, Catherine feared he was going to come for her, but he'd opened it only so he could slam it. Then he was gone.

Catherine's knees gave way and her legs crumpled beneath her. She plopped down in the sweet-smelling straw beside the calf. It lifted its head weakly and dropped it into her lap.

For a minute, she could only stare at it. Then she shook her head to clear away her daze and murmured distractedly, "I must get you some milk."

CHAPTER

Fifteen

THAT NIGHT AT DINNER, CATHERINE WAS UNUSUALLY QUIet. Lost in thought, she mechanically served the family from the steaming dishes Ellen placed before her.

Clayton looked over at her with concern. "Is something the matter, Catherine?"

She glanced up, distracted. "Did you say something?"

Jonny stifled a giggle with his hand, looking from his mother to his grandfather. At a stern look from Catherine, he sat up straighter and put a serious expression on his face. Clearly his mother had something on her mind, and he knew better than to giggle again.

"Is it true that the British government designated money to buy their slaves from their British owners?" she asked his grandfather.

"Yes, my dear. Somewhere around two hundred million in our currency, if I remember rightly."

"Why didn't we do the same?" She looked at him steadily. She was astonished to see him shift uncomfortably and look away.

"Things weren't that simple, Catherine. The abolitionists were kicking up a dust. They didn't want the South to be recompensed for the loss of their slaves." He turned his gaze back to her face, feeling he was on safer ground. "They hold that slavery is wrong and that people shouldn't be property."

Catherine interrupted him. "Nobody should be owned by anyone, that goes without saying. I think most of us feel that way, but the Constitution still holds that slaves are property." She looked troubled, "Wrong as that is, doesn't that make the Abolitionist Party's attitude illegal?" A frown of concentration furrowed her brow. "At least until they might amend the Constitution?"

The senator heaved a sigh. "Things are never that black and white in politics, Catherine. You have to understand."

Catherine lifted an eyebrow, and he held up a hand, stilling her objection to his use of the trite phrase. "Men were running for election. The Abolitionist Party was strongly supporting Lincoln.

"Politics!" Catherine had lost any illusions she ever had about statesmen. Her voice was scornful.

The senator plowed on. "Lincoln's a good man, but when he got elected, the South thought he would bow to the party that put him in power and free the slaves without remuneration."

He smiled at her as if he were apologizing for the weakness of men. "You can't expect men to stand still and have their fortunes stripped from them. Much of the wealth in the South was in its slaves." His voice firmed. "Besides, they are ardent States' Rightists. They hold that it's none of our blessed business to tell them what to do in their own states." Clayton gave up trying to eat his dinner, put his knife and fork across his plate, and sat back. Under his breath, he murmured, "And I doubt we'd like their interference in our lives any better if the shoe were on the other foot." He expelled a long breath.

Catherine charged into the gap. "Would Lincoln have done that?" She went on without giving him a chance to answer. "No. He wouldn't have. Lincoln's a Unionist, not an Abolitionist. If he'd cared all that much about the slaves being free, he'd have declared them all free in his Emancipation Proclamation, wouldn't he have?"

"Catherine," Clayton weighed his words, "President Lincoln would have done, indeed, would do, anything to preserve the Union. So would Jefferson Davis have, and Lee, and any number of good men on either side."

Jonny cried out, "Jefferson Davis! But he's the Reb President."

Catherine turned his way to glare him out of the conversation, but his grandfather looked across the table and told him quietly, "Jeff Davis made one of the most moving and convincing pleas for the preservation of the Union that I've ever heard, Jonny."

"When?" his grandson challenged, the word scornful, but his eyes alight with interest.

"When Mississippi seceded, son. Davis stayed in the Senate as long as he could, fighting for a way to reconcile the differences between North and South."

His grandfather let the boy's mild insolence go uncorrected in the interest of helping him understand history in the making, so Catherine followed suit.

"Really?" Jonny watched his grandfather nod gravely and finally said, "Oh." Digesting this, he asked, "Then why didn't the Union stay together?" He was frankly bewildered.

Catherine would love to have an answer to that, too. She leaned forward, her dinner forgotten, and asked, "What did send the South down such a disastrous path?"

"The argument was States' Rights. Cooler heads were trying to work things out. Lincoln sent forces to Fort Sumter in violation of the truce—"

"What truce?" Catherine had heard nothing of a truce.

"There was a truce at Fort Pickens, the other Federally held fort in Southern territory." He waved the fact aside to continue to make his point. "Lincoln only intended to show national authority by sending troops to Sumter. I know personally, for a fact, he never intended to go to war."

"Then what happened, Grandfather?"

"Hotheads happened, Jonny." The senator sat back wearily. "Then the die was cast."

"What's a die?"

"One of a pair of dice." His voice held a note of irritation for an instant, then he accepted his responsibility for instructing his grandson. His words rushed through his explanation. "Caesar said, 'The die is cast,' meaning it was too late to turn back, when he crossed the Rubicon to fight Pompey."

"Where is the Rubicon? It's a river, isn't it?"

His grandfather, tired of the conversation that had brought back to him the agonies of mind that he and many other right-minded men had long suffered, suddenly decided he was glad of this digression. He answered shortly, "You'll learn all about it in your studies of Latin."

He placed his crushed napkin beside his plate and rose. "Now, if you'll excuse me, I'll go out and smoke my cigar."

Catherine watched him go, then excused her fidgeting son absently. She pushed away her own gold-rimmed plate. Elbows on the table, she folded her hands and dropped her chin on them.

So. Much of what Jonathan Foster had said in the barn was true, then. Why didn't she want it to be?

Obviously, you wanted the side you were on—in anything—to be totally right, but her attitude went beyond that. She wanted him to be wrong, not just his cause, she realized with a start. She wanted him to be someone she could dismiss from her mind without a second thought, for dismissing the tall Southerner from her mind had become something that was increasingly difficult for her lately.

The image of his tortured posture came to her mind. She could clearly see him gripping the stall door as he bent over it. There had been real pain in his voice when he spoke of his responsibility to his people. That's what he had called them, as if they were family. How could that be, when she had read . . . But then, there were things that she hadn't read. Things that she had just confirmed with her father-in-law that had never seen the light of day in the newspapers she had read.

How was one to make fair judgments when the very news one studied to do so lied? By commission or omission, as the Book of Common Prayer said every Sunday. That made the news she read propaganda, not facts. The very thought shocked her to the core.

With an exclamation of aggravation, she threw her balled-up napkin down next to her plate. There were still two questions she wanted answered.

Striding across the large parlor, she let herself out onto the porch. "Clayton," she asked without preamble, "what provision did the Abolitionists make for all the slaves they brought up the Underground Railroad?"

The senator sighed. He knew better than to tell her not to trouble her pretty little head about it, but God, how he wanted to. "None, Catherine, which is but one of many problems we face. People in the North consider them competition for their jobs. That was what gave rise to the riots in New York when the Emancipation Proclamation came out.

"Many have starved and many others have formed gangs that rob in order to put food in their mouths. It's a deplorable situation, one none of us is proud of."

She didn't ask him her second question. She didn't want Jonathan Foster's opinions and feelings to color her own.

It was ever so much simpler just to read the newspapers and believe the Rebels were monsters of iniquity.

In the corner of the barn loft that Jonathan had turned into his home, he stood scowling at the clean shirt that lay on the bunk he had built against the wall. He would have to apologize, of course. His behavior had been inexcusable. He had even used foul language.

Try as he might, he could not remember ever having spoken to a woman as he had spoken to Catherine Foster. A sense of deep shame filled him. An accusing glance into the broken mirror he had brought from the burned-out bunkhouse showed his color high with it.

What the devil had come over him? It was as if she were some sort of catalyst that turned his cool reserve to molten anger. He had only to be in her presence to begin to burn. She had but to appear, and he was longing to . . . to what? He glared at his reflection, and watched it scowl back.

This strange lack of understanding his own feelings that assailed him was no excuse. Whatever was happening to him, he owed Cathy Foster an apology.

Juan came leaping up the steep stairs to the hayloft with a big smile on his face. "Hey, *Gringo*. You want to go into town? See if we can scare up a little excitement among the ladies? They're real lonesome now the army can't come to town."

Jonathan grinned and let out a long breath, suddenly relaxed. Of course, that was at least half his problem.

Glory! How long had it been since he had been intimate with a member of the fair sex? Juan's suggestion might be the very solution that had eluded him. "You bet, Juanito. I'll ride into town with you and keep you out of trouble."

He dove into his clean shirt. Cathy Foster would just have to wait for her apology.

They raced the first half of the trip to town. His big bay and Juan's flashy palomino took turns holding the lead for the first half of the way, and they spent the last half of it walking the horses to cool them out.

"Ayiee, Chihuahua, amigo, wait until you see the girls at the Longhorn." Juan touched the tips of his fingers to his lips and threw the kiss in the direction of the little town.

Jonathan smiled at his friend's extravagant gesture and felt a tightening in his body. He hoped the girls were all Juan claimed. A night with one of them might be just the thing to take the edge off him where his employer was concerned.

"You may choose any one but Rosarita," Juan instructed. "She belongs to me"—he grinned at his friend with a merry shrug—"and to several dozen other men as well, but tonight we do not consider that."

Jonathan grinned back. After two years as a widower faithful to the memory of a wife who had been little more than a girl, an encounter with a woman wise in the ways of pleasing a man sounded like a fine idea.

They saw the little town as they crested the next hill. With a wide, dusty street running straight between two rows of buildings, it sprawled away from them to end in a group of frame houses. These were gently lit with the glow of oil lamps, and they clustered around the single spire of a church.

They were the homes of the town's citizens, the people who owned or worked in the bank, the mercantile, the unpretentious restaurant-hotel, and the Longhorn. There were small trees in that end of town, as if its occupants were beginning to make their homes permanent.

The saloon was brightly lit, the light spilling out through two huge windows that flanked the double swinging doors and through the doors themselves. From the babble of sound that met them as they rode in, the Longhorn was as busy as most saloons on a Saturday night, in spite of, according to Juan, the army's being temporarily forbidden its precincts for busting it up the week before.

Jonathan and Juan dropped their reins over the crowded hitching post and loosened their cinches for the comfort of their horses.

They paused just inside the swinging doors: Juan with the caution that all smart Mexicans used when they entered public places in Texas, Jonathan with his usual habit of reconnoitering.

Instantly Jonathan's eye was drawn to a table in one corner where the foreman of Three Rivers sat with his late boss, Kellerman. The whiskey in the bottle the men were sharing was half gone, Jonathan noted with interest. Obviously they'd been talking for a while. The thought disquieted Jonathan. Why, though, did he object to the two men maintaining a friendship? What was it about Kirby Morris that made him distrust the foreman?

Suddenly, his thoughts scattered as with a glad cry, a tiny brunette detached herself from the arm of a big drover and flung herself at Juan. "*Querido mío*! Where have you been? I have missed you so."

Juan grinned down at her and all but preened himself. He turned her toward Jonathan, showing her off, his grin turning cocky. "Rosarita, this is my friend, Jon. Who have you to . . ." He shrugged, smiling, and wiggled his eyebrows suggestively.

Rosarita laughed at Juan's delicacy. With a quick look over her shoulder, she lifted a hand and a tall blonde moved purposefully toward them.

Jonathan waited for his expected response to the girl. She was tall and slender with breasts that would have done credit to a much larger woman. A man would have to be a cigar store Indian not to respond to the warm, knowing look she was giving him. He felt the hair on the back of his neck rise with his own appreciative animal response to her.

She slipped an arm through his and gave him a smoldering glance from beneath artificially darkened lashes. "Buy me a drink?"

Her perfume enveloped him and his breath shortened as he smiled down at her. The round firmness of her breasts lit a fire in him as he answered, "My pleasure . . ."

Without warning, the words conjured up a face framed in the black of a widow's veil. Cathy's face, fussing at him for using those very words, and he knew with a chill of disappointment that a drink was all that he'd buy for or from this woman who clung tightly to his arm, pressing her full breast against it.

He cursed himself. Cathy Foster! Of all the inappropriate women he could be smitten with, she had to be the one to castrate him as far as the willing blonde was concerned. He must be out of his mind.

No, it was simply that he had been too long in camps full of men. Then prison, again full of lice-infested men, and then the first woman he had been thrown together with for any length of time had been Cathy Foster.

He fought to keep his attention on the blonde. No, he told himself desperately. There was no way the thought of Madam Foster was going to keep him from sating his long denied masculine needs with this luscious blonde tonight.

Deliberately he looked down the front of her dress as the girl purposefully leaned into him. He could see all the way down to the rosettes on the toes of her shoes. With a quick intake of breath, he registered the fact that she was naked under her dress. That ought to do it. He let his breath go in a whisper of appreciation.

He waited for the expected response in himself. He waited in vain. Dear God, he must have lost more than his mind! He didn't want this delectable morsel. The hunger that was tearing him to pieces was for another woman altogether.

He looked around the big room, gulping air to fill his starving lungs, and realized he'd been holding his breath. Sorrowfully, he disengaged the startled blonde.

He looked for a possible threat to his friend. There didn't seem to be anyone looking at Juan with a jaundiced eye, so he could get the hell out of here before he embarrassed both himself and his young friend without worrying that Juan might need him later.

He slipped a gold piece into the girl's hand, kissed her quickly but thoroughly on her painted lips, and said, "Some other time." With purposeful strides he headed toward the swinging doors.

By the time Juan caught up with him, he'd mounted and turned Creole's head toward home. "Hey, Gringo! *¿Que pasa?* What is the matter with you? Where you going?"

"Back to the ranch, amigo. And don't call me Gringo. Call me Sitting Bull."

"What?" Juan and Rosarita cried in unison, but Jonathan had kicked the big bay into an indignant gallop. He needed to find someplace to go for a swim, preferably someplace with cold water.

CHAPTER

Sixteen

CATHERINE STRETCHED OUT HER ARMS FOR THE CALF, AND suddenly, meltingly, it disappeared. Instead the Rebel Captain Foster, in full, crisp Confederate regalia stepped down from his horse in his habitual single fluid movement and stood, his body inches from her own.

She looked up into his face and saw the burning hunger in his eyes. Desire, stronger than any she had ever known, exploded in her, tearing away every vestige of restraint. She flung herself against him, her arms clasping him about the neck, insistently forcing his head down toward her own.

Hungrily, his lips fastened on her mouth. The kiss was searing. His hands moved from her waist up her sides until they rested high on her rib cage, his thumbs just under her breasts.

She quivered with the strength of her yearning to be one with him. Digging the tips of her suddenly bare toes into the ground, she pressed herself closer against him.

He swept her unclad body into his arms without breaking their kiss, and carried her effortlessly into the cool, dark barn and up the stairs to the hayloft.

Falling on her, he pressed her deep into the fragrant hay, ravishing her body with kisses, setting her tingling flesh a-quiver. Then he rose to his knees and began to remove his yellow sash, his shell jacket, then his shirt, and she saw the smooth perfection of his chest and shoulders. A moment later, he was completely nude and over her and she was—

With a strangled gasp, Catherine Foster, respectable widow and devoted mother, catapulted from her dream, bolt upright. "Oh!" she gasped. "Oh dear."

One hand at her throat, her eyes still unfocused in remembered passion, she leapt up to stand on the bare floor, hoping that leaving the warmth of her bed would cool her heated blood. She pressed her other hand to her chest to still the racing of her heart and heard a voice she scarcely recognized as her own say, "This will never do!"

She was breathing as if she had just run a race, and she adamantly refused to acknowledge the tenderness and electric awareness of her body. Never had she had such a dream. Never had she even known there were such dreams.

This dream had certainly been a far cry from any she had ever had before. Until now, she had experienced only the chaste, maidenly dreams she and her friends at school had shared with one another. Those had been sweet, innocent dreams about happening to meet one of their beaus on a deserted path somewhere and exchanging one sweet, forbidden kiss.

Why, this dream had gone beyond her most intimate experience of marriage! She was shocked.

She wondered if she were suddenly losing control of her emotions. That thought certainly didn't appeal to her, however, and she threw it off.

Obviously, she told herself reasonably, she just felt a mild attraction for this other Jonathan Foster. After all, the voice in her mind explained, he'd done some things she thought rather heroic, and naturally she admired that in him. As for the rest of it—her mental voice became stiffly virtuous—she had just brought her wifely knowledge of the ways of a man with a maid into her dream, and—

"And what, Catherine Foster? And what?" she demanded of herself fiercely.

And you just had an attack of carnal desire for the man, didn't you? She would never speak those words aloud. She went on scolding herself in her thoughts, her mental voice implacable, now: *Be honest with yourself. You never used to be such a liar. You had a dream, and in it you fantasied about . . .*

But right there her mind balked. She had to force herself to go on. *Go on, Catherine*, her mental voice snarled. *About what? About dreaming of lying with a man in the heat of a passion you never felt for your husband?*

"No!" She spoke sharply aloud again. There was no way she was to allow this shocking sort of thing to occupy her thoughts a minute longer.

There was no way she was ever even going to think about this dream again. She was going down to the river, and she was going to stand in the coolest eddy she could find until her temperature was back to normal and she had her mind back, for she had absolutely no doubt that she had temporarily lost it.

Halfway back to the ranch, Jonathan finally slowed his horse before he ran it into the ground. A heavy rack of clouds passed overhead and obscured the moon, and Creole began picking his way carefully. His ears were steadily pricked forward now. They had been flicking nervously back and forth as his rider had tried to voice every curse he'd ever heard in three years with the Confederate cavalry. But Jonathan was calmer now, and Creole was beginning to relax.

"Hope you want a bath, boy, 'cause you're gonna get one." Jonathan headed his mount for the bluff over the deepest part of the river. He figured there was a good chance that was where the water would be coldest.

Catherine arrived at the river's edge, slipped out of her dainty Moroccan leather slippers, and dipped a toe into the water. It was hardly cold, but she felt that its contrast to the unaccustomed warmth of her body would be sufficient to restore her equilibrium.

She tossed her cotton robe over the branch of a tree. It was the same old tree that she'd used to hang her clothes on since she was seven years old. She slipped, unencumbered, into the water.

Looking for the cool eddy she had promised herself, she swam smoothly away from the bank. The water felt delightful as it flowed around her, almost like a caress.

She knew the river was deepest under the low bluff on the far side. That was probably where it would be coolest. While her need for a lower temperature had lessened, she still found it an appealing thought.

With sure strokes, she swam to the foot of the bluff. Treading water, she ascertained that it was indeed cooler here, but the current was stronger, too, and it was only by swimming that she could stay in place.

After a few minutes of lazy paddling, she decided to swim in closer under the bluff and hold herself in place by grasping one of the low-hanging branches of the trees that grew from its foot. *There*, she thought as she held a sturdy branch, *that makes things simpler*.

Reaching wide, she grasped another branch and balanced herself between the two, her arms straight out and back from her shoulders. Lying here on the surface of the cool water, her wet body gleaming pale in the shadows as it floated out from the tree branches she held, she could relax and be comfortable—and comforted.

Jonathan arrived at the edge of the bluff, hesitated a fraction of a second to discard his hat and gun belt, then urged Creole to leap out, away from the edge. They plummeted the twelve feet into the river, the water closing over them as their combined weight drove them deep.

Under the bluff, Catherine cried out in shock at their sudden appearance and the dark bulk of them flying over her to the surface of the river. Their splash left her sputtering and clinging tighter to one of her branches. With quick modesty, she turned her back to the intruders. Anxiously she waited for them to reappear. They must not see her, whoever they were. She watched for them over her shoulder. She was well aware that the man might prove a far greater threat than just to her modesty.

As they popped back to the surface, she was forced to make a lightning decision. She could hardly admit her presence, unclad as she was. And there was no way she could swim to her clothes, nor, in fact, gain the far bank where they were without being seen by the man who had just jumped his horse over her into the river.

As the man still sitting the swimming horse tossed his wet hair back out of his eyes, the clouds that had obscured the moon's bright silver light passed, and she saw with relief that the intruder was the man of her dreams.

Her mental voice instantly began scolding her again. Man of her dreams, indeed! While it was literally the truth, that was the only way it was true, and she certainly wasn't going to have that particular phrase associated with this man who consistently made her existence one upset after another.

Man in her dreams wasn't much better. Intruder, was more like it. Intruder in her life, intruder in her dream, now even intruder in the place in the river she had always considered her own private retreat. Like a ninny, she felt tears threaten. What was the matter with her? Why was she so out of kilter where this man was concerned?

Catherine saw Jonathan dive off his horse into the water. The horse swam to the bank, shook mightily like some gigantic dog, and was soon grazing through the brush. Thankful that the animal hadn't gone up the gentle slope of the bank where her clothes were, Catherine treaded water while she smoothed her long hair back off her face. She looked back to see what Rebel was doing.

She watched as he swam briskly, seeming to work at tiring himself out. As he settled to a pattern, she let go of her branches and began cautiously working her way toward the bend of the river, timing her movements to his. If she could get around the bend, she could cross to the side where her robe hung. It would only take her a second to put it on, grab her slippers, and perhaps get away from the river without him being any wiser.

She swam slowly, resisting the urge to stroke out strongly and accomplish her aim more quickly. She knew that if she set up any splashing, he'd detect her presence. She was determined to avoid that. The last thing on earth she wanted was to be caught in the river in the altogether by that man. She would rather face another Indian attack. Two!

She got out of sight around the bend, crossed to the opposite bank, and was swimming stealthily, dark head barely above the water, to the tree where her robe hung, when there was a strong surge in the water beside her.

She heard a surprised, "Cathy! What the blazes are you doing here?"

Slamming his feet to the bottom of the river, he stood. Catherine watched in helpless fascination as his shoulders, then his chest emerged from the water. She saw the way the river water clung like crystal beads in the moonlight to the crisp hair that marked his chest and disappeared downward.

Unable to look away, she saw the water recede from his slim waist. Oh, dear, suppose like her, he was not dressed? Her mental voice was frantic this time.

She almost panicked as the water parted over the tops of his naked hips. Then, like a benevolent last-minute reprieve, she saw the dark fabric of his denims riding low on them. *Oh, thank Heaven,* her mental voice chirped and died away.

He hitched his pants up an inch and extended his hand to her. "You shouldn't be out here alone like this, Miz Foster." He frowned when she shied away from him, heading back toward deeper water.

"Like what?" Catherine heard herself demand truculently. Dearest Lord, could he know she was naked? She fervently prayed he wouldn't find out. She pulled her hair forward over her breasts.

"Alone in the middle of the night. What else? These are times of some unrest, madam." His tone was censorious. "There are marauders and Indians, and . . ."

At that moment, the night breeze picked up, and the skirt of Catherine's light cotton robe fluttered for an instant, pale in the moonlight. His horse gave a startled whinny, then moved out of sight.

The man spun toward the movement in a flash, every sense alert for danger. Catherine watched his muscles tense and ripple under the skin of his back. Then—horror of horrors—she saw him relax completely and turn toward her, grinning. With a quick intake of her breath, she saw not the smooth perfect chest of her dream, but the ragged scar on his left shoulder. She heard him finish his comment in a much changed tone, and became breathless for another reason altogether. " . . . and stray cowboys who just might find the idea of their boss lady skinny-dipping a pretty exciting prospect."

Catherine sank lower in the water, letting it lap her lips. At the same time she moved backward, away from him. Never for one instant did she take her eyes off him.

When he bent and laid his arm along the surface of the water, she thought fleetingly of turning and swimming with all haste to the deep shadows under the trees at the base of the bluff. She found, however, that she lacked the courage to take her eyes off him.

Even as she watched, the upper part of his body followed his arm out toward her and he seemed to blend with and become part of the water as he cut through it in her direction without a sound.

With a little yelp, Catherine spun around and started swimming with all her might toward the shadows. She wasn't going to let him get close enough to see that she was indeed skinny-dipping, not if she drowned herself getting away from him.

She was a good swimmer, and she had a twelve foot or more head start. She was driven, too, by frantic need, and she reached the shadows under the bluff ahead of him.

Suddenly he overtook her. Whatever she had expected, it wasn't to be caught up in a viselike embrace and to be crushed hard against his lean body. As her mind screamed a bewildered protest, his hand clamped across her mouth, and he dragged her deeper into the shadows at the foot of the bluff.

Dear God, what did this attack mean? What did he intend to do? From his grip on her, she had no doubt that he was well aware that she was nude. His arm encircled her body just under her bare breasts. Did he think she had tried deliberately to entice him? Could he feel justified in this attack? Was he intending to . . .

She felt his breath hot against her cheek, and was dizzied by his nearness. It was a moment before her clamoring senses stopped sending out alarms, and she heard what he was trying to tell her.

"Look. Indians. Be still and hope to God they don't see us."

Her body froze. She even stilled her breath. His grip slackened as he realized she'd seen and understood.

In the clear moonlight on the opposite bank sat the scar-faced Indian that had led the attack on the way station. As he let his horse drink its fill, his eyes searched the top of the bluff under which they hid. He held an army rifle easily in his right hand. His companion merely watched his own horse drink, but he, too, held a rifle.

The horse raised its head and looked away toward the spot at which Catherine had last seen Jonathan's bay. *Dearest Lord,* she whispered in her mind, *don't let him whinny. Please God, just don't let him whinny.*

The horse flared his nostrils, inhaling deeply to call to the horse he suspected was nearby, but his rider, probably eager to escape detection so near the ranch house, stopped him with an urgent hand. Then, turning, the two disappeared.

Jonathan held her close another moment. He told himself it was to be sure she was safe, sure she would keep quiet. But in truth, the delight of feeling her soft, naked body down his own lean length was more that he could force himself to forgo.

Any earlier doubts he may have had about his masculinity fled. He sighed a ragged sigh of relief.

His body's eager enthusiasm at Cathy's naked nearness quickly disabused him of the fleeting notion that he'd become a useless old man during the war. He bit back the moan that rose in his throat at the strength of his reaction to her. Reluctantly, he ordered himself to let her go.

Catherine was so frightened to see the Indians on the bank that she had forgotten the impropriety of her situation. When the captain tried to let her go, she was anything but helpful.

The last thing she wanted was to relinquish her hold on his neck. She was almost desperate to prolong the wonderful feeling of safety his nearness engendered in her.

Finally, unable to withhold it, Jonathan moaned low in his throat, his senses reeling. "Cathy." He was proud to hear he didn't gasp. "Let me go. I have to go see where they went." That sounded like a good excuse to him.

Fear for the safety of those at the house made her let go. Relief combined with regret in him as she complied. "Don't move until I call for you."

With a smooth surface dive away from her, he disappeared underwater without a sound. Urgently Catherine watched for him, but he didn't break the surface again until he was well under the far bank, hidden from anyone who was not standing on the very edge.

The thought that Jonathan might meet the Indian as he came out of the water struck terror through her. Her unblinking eyes stung as she anxiously scanned the area. Fortunately, there was no one on the river's edge. She began to breathe again.

He disappeared in the direction the Indians had taken, keeping low and running from one place of concealment to another for as long as she could see him. It seemed that a decade—a century—passed before Catherine saw him return. Somewhere he'd retrieved his hat and gun.

He signaled her to swim to him. She struck out immediately. She was painfully aware that she still had nothing on, but her family was asleep and defenseless. Having a man see her in the nude for the brief moment it would take her to reach her robe became insignificant against the necessity of warning them.

When she could touch the bottom, she stood and waded out of the water. The man on the bank held her robe out to her. He held it in such a fashion that the garment shielded her from his eyes. She slipped into it quickly, grateful for his gallantry. "Thank you."

From the huskiness in her voice, he knew that she was thanking him for preserving her modesty as well as assisting her into her robe. He wondered if she would have been so quick to ascribe noble intentions to his gentlemanly gesture if she could have known what he was thinking.

With his eyes averted so she couldn't read his thoughts in them, he lifted her to his saddle, mounted behind her, and headed Creole back to the ranch house. "Don't fret, Cathy. The Indians cut wide of the house. Your family's safe."

Catherine felt the rumble of his deep voice under her cheek, in his chest. She was worn out with the emotions the night had sent tearing through her. She leaned against him, grateful for his support.

Jonathan held her in his arms and fought down the fierce desire to turn her face up to his and kiss her until she wanted him as much as he burned for her. He had learned one useful thing in that Yankee prison camp. He had learned patience.

CHAPTER

Seventeen

THE HOUSE WAS QUIET, JUST AS JONATHAN HAD PROMISED, and a deep feeling of relief shook her. His arms tightened around her and she thought he feared she would fall. She turned to smile up at him. "Thank you. Thank you for . . ." She hesitated as the magnitude of all she owed this man hit her.

She had so much to thank him for. First, for being sure that the Indians had posed no threat to her family, for she had noticed that when he returned for her, he had his gun on.

And, of course, he had saved her life again. Or perhaps he had saved her from worse. She certainly hadn't known the Indians were there on the bank of the river. Only his quick action had kept her from speaking and giving them both away.

She owed him her thanks, too, for his tactfully preserving her modesty when she came up out of the river. She finished her sentence lamely. " . . . for everything." She knew it was woefully inadequate, but she had no idea what more she could say.

Anxious to check on her sleeping son, she slipped out of his arms and down from the horse before he could assist her. She lingered for only a moment, her hand on his knee, and said softly, "Good night, Captain Foster. Thank you from the bottom of my heart."

She couldn't read his expression in the shadow the brim of his hat cast across his strong features, but she wondered why he didn't speak. When he finally nodded, she gave

145

a little shrug, turned, and crossed the veranda into the house.

Just inside, she felt strangely drawn to look back at him one more time. He was like some bronze equestrian statue in the pale light of the moon. She waved and softly closed the door.

Jonathan sat as if he were indeed poured in bronze. Shocks ran up and down his nerves, and the place where her hand had rested upon his knee felt as if he had been branded.

Smiling without mirth, he acknowledged that she had no idea what her nearness had done to him—no idea at all, or she would never have risked touching him.

As it was, Catherine Foster had narrowly escaped being swept up again into his arms and charged off with. The worn-out little-girl simplicity with which she'd thanked him had been all that had stopped him from at least kissing her silly. Her trusting, unconscious touching of his knee had nearly overthrown even that restraint.

The little Yankee widow was playing the very devil with his senses. He said a quick, ironic prayer that the good Lord grant that either he could manage to avoid her until he'd cooled down a bit, or, that if they did meet, she would have the good sense to keep her hands off him. He certainly lost any good sense he might have at her slightest touch.

He gave a short laugh of self-derision, then spoke aloud to his horse. "I hope you're ready to take me back to the river, boy. I think I could use another swim."

In the week that followed, Jonathan used the long days of hard work to wear himself out and subdue his body's insistence. He made it a point to avoid Cathy, and he rarely saw her, though he heard her come to the barn to feed the calf late every night.

If he could just make it through the next few weeks, the calf would be old enough not to need that late feeding, and he would be able to sleep without being made to toss and turn with thoughts of Cathy Foster. Carlos and Juan would just have to put up with his foul temper until then.

Even in the dust and heat, while he was out branding cattle, he thought of her. There seemed to be no way he could drive the woman from his mind.

"Hey, Gringo! You gonna take a strain on that lariat or no?"

Jonathan stopped interfering with his mount and backed Creole away from the bawling steer, cursing softly. His mind clearly wasn't on his work.

Carlos glared at him as he applied the Three Rivers brand to the steer's hip. The animal bawled, and the smell of burning hair and hide rose into the hot, dry air. "We got a lot of work to catch up on, Jonathan. What's your trouble?"

Jonathan shrugged. He was well aware that the ranch work had been neglected for the duration of the war, and there were hundreds of steers that had never been branded. He looked out at the herd they had gathered from all over Three Rivers's range. Maybe thousands.

Carlos and Juan had had their hands full just keeping up with the castrations. They needed his assistance, and he needed to keep his mind on giving it to them.

"Ha! The gringo has skirt problems, *padrecito*."

"*Dios,* Juan," Carlos put the branding iron he'd just used back in the fire with the others and watched the two men flip their ropes free of the rising steer. "Take him into town and have Rosarita find him a friend." Carlos looked from one to the other impatiently, waiting for another steer.

"I'll go." Jonathan moved off to cut out and rope the next candidate for branding so he could drag it to Carlos.

"He didn't like Rosarita's friend." Juan looked hard at his father.

Carlos stared back at him, weighing the possibilities. Pushing his sombrero back, he scratched his head thoughtfully. "He must come again to dinner. Maybe your *madre* will know what ails the man." Carlos had seen Rosarita's blonde friend. That remembrance made him worried about Jonathan.

By early afternoon, the situation was deteriorating badly. Carlos was fuming. He ordered Juan to take his place at the branding fire and climbed up on Juan's stocky roping horse, hoping to steady his new friend.

It didn't work. Going to fetch the next steer, Jonathan got a bad rope burn when, his thoughts on Cathy, he dallied late and caught his hand in his own loop.

"You are lucky you still have all your fingers, *mi amigo*," Juan taunted his cursing friend. Then, laughing at Jonathan's discomfort, he reached carelessly for his next branding iron. "*Dios mio!*" he yelled, looking down at the smoldering palm of his glove.

Jonathan stopped muttering curses over the raw, red streak on the top of his hand and threw back his head, taking his turn laughing.

"*Basta!*" Carlos shouted at the two of them. "Enough! We are through for this day." He shook a fist in their direction. "*Estúpidos!* How will I get the work done if you two vie with each other to see who is most clumsy? Tell me that!"

Jonathan and Juan looked at Carlos's red face, then at one another. Both knew the time for laughter had passed.

"Home! Go home!" Carlos shouted at them, glowering, his voice like thunder. "And don't neither one of you be late for dinner!" He shook his fist at them, then shooed them away like chickens. Muttering darkly, he began kicking sand on the branding fire. For such a small man, Jonathan noticed, he could kick a lot of sand.

Jonathan decided to stable his horse and look for something to put on his rope burn before he washed up and changed his shirt to go to dinner at Maria's. The damn thing burned worse than he'd expected. He squeezed his wrist with his good hand to take away some of the pain. Doing so distracted him just enough so he didn't realize Cathy was coming out of he barn as he went charging in.

The resultant crash would have sent her flying if he hadn't grabbed her. "Sorry," he barked, holding her shoulders fast in a hard grip.

"Oh, I do beg your pardon. I should have watched where I was going." Inadvertently, she touched his hand.

He winced when her fingers hit the rope burn. Then he said gruffly, his breath gone from the touch of her hand. "So should I."

She noticed him flinch. "Have you hurt your hand?" She reached for it, and short of being rude, he saw no way to avoid her taking it.

She looked at the oozing red streak across the back of his hand and winced. "These rope burns hurt something awful. Come up to the house and let me put some salve on it. They don't hurt as badly if you keep the air from them."

"It's fine." The last thing he wanted was to have Cathy Foster fussing over him so close he could smell the scent of her hair and see how smooth the skin on her cheeks was. He was hurting enough without adding the particular discomfort that her nearness caused him.

He pulled his hand out of hers. "I have to clean up."

She was surprised by his brusque attitude. She knew there was no way that air hitting his raw rope burn could be anything but painful. She knew, too, that the chance of a cowhand having any sort of healing salve among his things was just about nil. Why was he refusing to let her dress his rope burn?

"Of course," she said stiffly, releasing his hand. Her eyes met his, challenging him, demanding an explanation.

"I've been invited to Maria's for dinner." He stood staring down at her lips. How tantalizing they were. Even though her voice had become brusque, her lips were still soft, inviting. Irresistible.

There in the cool shadows of the barn, Catherine suddenly felt as if she knew how a rabbit must feel when facing a snake. Except that a snake was the last thing she meant. It wasn't that kind of danger she sensed, she thought inanely, her knees weakening.

Without volition, she swayed toward Jonathan, her own eyes fastened on the sensuous curve of his underlip. She saw his eyes change, cloud with his intent, and half close. He began to lower his head toward her. As naturally as

a sunflower following the sun, she lifted her mouth to
him.

"Mama," Jonny's voice broke the spell like a dash of cold
water. Her face flaming, Catherine jumped back a step and
turned toward him as he entered the barn. "I've brought the
bottle," he went on, unaware of the tension that crackled in
the air. "Can we feed the calf now?"

"Uh, yes, dear," she heard herself answer automatically
from miles away, her hands flying to her hair as if she
thought she might find it disheveled from the force of the
emotions that ran through her.

Jonathan laughed a low, quick chuckle. She thought he
sounded as breathless as she felt. Like someone waking
from a trance, she watched his rapid retreat up the loft
stairway.

Uncomfortable with her thoughts, she put them from her
and tried to tell herself she was grateful that her son had
provided her with the distraction she was busy convincing
herself she needed. Refusing to consider whether or not she
was truly glad of his interruption, she threw an arm around
the boy.

She took the calf's milk bottle from him and they went
together into Rosie's stall to fill it. Greedy little snuffling
noises from the calf in the next stall caused them to grin
at each other as Catherine milked.

Filling the bottle took only a minute; then she and Jonny
moved to the calf's stall. There the tiny heifer's moist little
nose had appeared, just barely, over the top of the door as
she thrust it up in greeting.

Jonny beamed his delight at his mama as she opened
the door just enough for him to slip through and push the
eager calf back so that she could enter. The warm glow
of happiness she felt to see her son so content and happy
filled her to overflowing.

How glad she was to be back on Three Rivers. In spite
of the difficulties she was striving to deal with, she was
certain now she had made the right decision to come. If
only her grandfather could still have been here to see this
with her, her happiness would have been complete.

They had only had the heifer a week, and some of that time it had been touch and go with the little runt, but they had pulled her through. With a combination of lots of loving attention from Jonny and lots of milk from Rosie in the stall next door, they'd brought her along to the point that she had decided to stay with them, after all.

Jonny was absurdly attached to the calf. Scout was even a little jealous.

Catherine took a deep breath and savored the smells of warm animals and fresh hay. Content, she settled herself in the clean straw next to the stall wall, and leaned back against it.

Watching her son play gently with the wobbly calf, Catherine resolutely set aside the memory of her encounter with Rebel Captain Jonathan Foster and smiled over the tiny calf's head at her son. Again she thought how glad she was that she had decided to come home. Here he was recovering from the terrible shock of his father's death much more quickly than he could have done at the senator's. There, they would have been constantly reminded of the war and their loss.

The calf showed them that her manners hadn't improved one bit since her midday bottle. She left off playing with the boy and began butting first one and then the other of them, demanding more milk.

Catherine asked with a laugh, "Are you sure this isn't a piglet, Jonny?" She pushed the calf away and struggled against it to regain her feet.

The boy laughed happily back at her. "I don't know, Mama. I'm just a city boy, you know."

Catherine took the bottle and left him to go to Rosie's stall. "Just a little more, please, Rosie. Be a good girl."

Rosie turned huge, liquid brown eyes full of patience to watch Catherine squirt half a bottle full of milk. Totally unconcerned, the cow pulled another bit of hay from her rack and chewed on it thoughtfully.

Catherine slipped back into the orphan's stall and was instantly charged by the calf. Jonny held valiantly around her neck, striving to impede her determined progress toward her second course.

"Here. Quick!" She thrust the milk at her son, letting him think his actions were saving her real distress. She smiled at the way he expanded his chest and stood tall, thinking he'd saved his mother from being trampled at least.

When they had finished feeding the orphan, Catherine smoothed Jonny's hair back from his forehead and, ignoring his grimace, kissed him there. "Don't stay down here until you're late for dinner. We don't want to make Ellen cross."

Earnestly he looked up at her. "Especially before dessert." Jonny thought Ellen made the best desserts in the world.

Catherine laughed and left the barn, heading for the house in strides longer than any she'd ever used back East. Of course, she had greater freedom of movement in her split skirt. It wasn't just the split skirt, however. It was being home. Under the wide skies of Texas her spirits seemed to soar. Somehow, she felt free.

Jonathan, in the loft above, exhaled a long breath. Maybe now that he wasn't straining to hear and savor every word, every movement the two below had made, he could go down to the pump and begin getting ready for another of Maria's fine dinners.

As good as the food was that Ellen put on the tray that she left on the bench at the back door for him every evening, there was still something better about eating even a simple meal with friends. It was something that couldn't be surpassed even by food prepared by the best chefs in Europe.

As he pumped water to wash, he wondered why the Yankee widow made him so blasted awkward about washing up when she was within watching distance. He had never been shy. . . .

It came to him as he put his head under the strong stream he coaxed from the pump that it wasn't shyness he was suffering; far from it. It was pride. A man used to every luxury, he simply didn't want the woman to see him washing at a horse trough.

He had had everything. Every luxury that life provided had been his to enjoy—and to offer a woman. Now he had nothing.

He slammed the pump handle down to the fullest extent of its stroke and stalked back to his new home. There it loomed before him in all its grandeur. A barn.

He lived in a barn, like an animal. He could hear the boy playing happily with one of his housemates.

He owned one horse—he who had owned hundreds of the finest thoroughbreds in Virginia—his saddle, and the clothes on his back. Nothing else. All the rest was gone. Was it any wonder he couldn't bear the thought of the beautiful widow seeing him bathe at her horse trough? He thought not.

He heard the boy leave the barn as he dressed. Good. He wasn't feeling much like talking to the child just now.

The discomfort he was feeling as he arrived at Maria's went far beyond that engendered by the raw rope burn on the back of his hand. All his problems seemed to rise up and converge and seek to overwhelm him. That was what came of dwelling on the negative thoughts he had had at the horse trough.

When he got to her door, Maria met him, obviously aware that he had hurt himself. He was led in and clucked over by his hostess as if he had sustained a major injury.

It was with deepest gratitude that he submitted to her motherly ministrations. The stinging wound on the back of his hand was one thing that could be made to feel better, at any rate.

Maria told Consuelo to tend to the cooking and led Jonathan to the pair of cowhide chairs that Carlos had made for her when she was a bride. There they sat knee to knee while she worked on his hand.

When she had finished bandaging it, she sat back and looked at him. "And so, my friend, what else can Maria help you with?"

Jonathan smiled a crooked smile. "Thank you for fixing my hand, Maria. It feels much better."

"And the rest. What is it that so troubles you?"

He looked at her levelly for a moment, considering the problem that he must come to grips with soon.

"Come, Jonathan," she chided him. "Two heads are always better than one."

"Yes, I suppose you're right." He smiled at her for her kindness. "It's my sisters. I must get them out of where they are, and I have no idea where to settle them." He frowned. "I want to get them out of the South, entirely." Bitterness crept into his voice. "Invaders are filling the South." He gave her a rueful smile. "And I can't go back for them, to help them."

"*¿Por qué no?* Why not?"

"I gave my word that I wouldn't go East again while there was fighting there."

He looked so grim that Maria's heart went out to him. "And your sisters cannot remain where they are until the fighting is finished?"

He laughed shortly. The sound was without amusement. "No. My last letters in prison were from my sister, Diana, and the cousin with whom I left them. It seems she is having the same difficulties from which I rescued her before. Only this time she is not the target for a lecherous enemy, but for the moonstruck son of the house."

He said in the disgusted tone he'd have used to say that his sister had terrible manners, "Diana is extremely beautiful." He frowned. "My cousin says she cannot keep the girls. She refuses to have her peace disrupted any more than the present difficulty with the North is destroying it." He quirked an eyebrow at his friend. "She insists that Diana and Susan must be gone before winter comes. She can't abide the idea of being caged up in the house with the situation."

He said honestly to Maria. "I wondered how they would feed the girls, once winter came. I hoped that sending them my pay would help them all."

"That is very generous."

"No," he raised his eyes to her, "they're family."

"Now, however, you must find a place for the sisters, *sí?*"

"Yes."

"In town there is a boardinghouse."

"Maria, the Yankee sergeant that I rescued my sisters from in the first place is stationed somewhere near here. I can't risk them bumping into that swine. Not when I am powerless against him."

Maria decided that there must be some things about being a Confederate where the Union was in power that were much like being a Mexican in Texas. She thought hard. "What about the senator? If you brought them here, he could keep them safe, and you could have them near you."

One look at Jonathan's face told her how well he would like another man taking over his responsibilities. "Besides," he said as he saw she understood, "how long could they impose on Cathy's hospitality?" He shook his head. The answer was no.

Finally Maria said, "You need a place of your own."

"Yes," he admitted heavily. "I do. And we both know my chances of getting it."

He rose and reached out a hand to her. "Come, your family's looking at us like ravening wolves. You must feed them."

She permitted him to pull her up as she permitted him to change the subject. Looking at his gallant smile, she felt her heart take up a burden for him. She would put this man in her most serious prayers.

CHAPTER

Eighteen

CATHERINE WALKED SLOWLY OUT TO THE BARN TO FEED the orphan. She saw Jonathan ride out on his nightly check of the range. She found that his patrol, as she thought of his nightly excursion, gave her a sense of security that was comforting. It was nice that something the disturbing man did gave her a sense of comfort, she mused.

The little heifer was asleep when she got to her stall. Catherine smiled as she stood and watched her sleep, sprawled out flat as she'd never have done out on the range. Soon, she would give up this feeding, and Catherine could go back to getting a full night's sleep.

She was debating whether or not to wake the calf when it sensed her presence and raised its head to look at her. Getting up hind quarters first, the calf came over to the door and regarded her solemnly.

"Hello, sleepyhead. Shall I get you your milk?"

The calf bawled, and Rosie answered from the next stall. Catherine decided it would be best to get the milk, even if the heifer didn't seem interested at the moment.

It only took her a minute to procure the bottleful from a cooperative Rosie. Then she was back, and the calf did, indeed, manage to dredge up some interest in the proceedings. "It won't be long before you'll be sleeping through the night," she told the calf as she held the bottle.

Scratching the heifer between its wide-set eyes, she said, "Good girl. Tomorrow night I'll be even quieter when I come, and we'll see if you can sleep through until morning."

The heifer looked as if she were ready to lie down again, so Catherine gave her one final, very gentle pat and quietly left the stall. Turning down the wick until her lantern was almost out, she lifted it off the hook, blew down the chimney to extinguish it, and carried it back to the house.

From the back porch, she took one final look around the square, filled with contentment. "Yes, I'll have to rebuild a bit," she whispered to herself, "but it's still Three Rivers, and it's still home."

She smiled at the barn where Rosie and the heifer were, and thought with a warm feeling of the man that would soon be sleeping there, too. Life was going to be worth living again; she knew it.

She was still smiling when sleep came to her in her grandfather's huge four-poster bed.

Twenty minutes later, the barn burst into flames.

Jonathan was taking longer than he usually took to make his circuit of the ranch. Something just didn't feel right. Too many times in the past he'd had this same feeling, and every time, only great caution had saved him from disaster.

Eyes narrowed, every nerve on the stretch, he rode toward the wooded depression beside the rocks that marked the place he usually turned back to the barn. Out of the corner of an eye, he caught a slight movement.

Dismounting, he ground-tied Creole and hoped the big horse wouldn't nicker when he left him. Slowly, placing each foot with infinite care, he approached the spot where he'd seen the brush move counter to the wind.

An Indian lay on his belly, watching the ranch complex. His rifle lay at his side. Approaching him from behind, Jonathan couldn't see the man's face, but his gut feeling was that he was looking at the Indian with the scarred face.

Turning carefully, willing silence, Jonathan scanned the surrounding area. Where was the other Indian? The one that had been with Scarface on the riverbank?

Suddenly, while Jonathan was turned away, Scarface exploded into action. He lunged up off the rock on which he'd lain, and hurtled down the hill toward his pony.

Jonathan let go a curse and started after him. Instantly he realized he would never catch the Indian on foot. A piercing whistle brought Creole to him. Flinging himself into the saddle, he raced in pursuit of the Indian.

Scarface cut parallel to the river. His pony, surefooted in the light of the moon, flew over the flatter terrain nearer the ranch house. Creole, not to be outdone, stretched out and snatched great lengths of ground with every stride.

The Indian's pony was fast, but the big bay gelding was taller by several hands and his longer stride began to make the difference. Down past the place in the river where Catherine and Jonathan had swum the night before, on past the bluff from which he had jumped Creole, and on out to the open range they raced.

The only sounds were the pounding hooves of their mounts and the heavy breath each took as his leading hoof struck the ground. Slowly, inexorably, the larger horse gained on the Indian pony. Soon they were almost even, and when they were, Jonathan launched himself into the air toward Scarface to bring him down.

The Indian tried to turn his horse away swiftly enough to leave his attacker clutching thin air, but the path wasn't wide enough for the maneuver, and Jonathan tore him from his horse's back.

The horses ran on, dust billowing from their passage, but the men hit the ground with a terrible force that sent them rolling over the edge of the path and down the rocky hill beside it.

First one and then the other slammed into the dry, hard, rock-strewn earth as they grappled with one another, each seeking the advantage. Over and over they turned until a boulder as big as a house brought them up short and they both lay dazed for a moment by their rough descent of the hill.

Jonathan blinked away stars with a shake of his head, and reached for his gun, but Scarface was up and over him, his knife drawn. Before Jonathan was half up, the Indian slammed down astraddle him, his knife at Jonathan's throat.

Jonathan grabbed the wrist of the Indian's knife hand, forcing it up and away, striving to turn it upon his attacker. Suddenly, to Jonathan's utter bewilderment, the Indian used the strength of Jonathan's push to rise and stand towering above the fallen white man.

Slowly, making a great show of the action, Scarface sheathed his knife. Jonathan's hand, his gun half drawn, stopped its movement. For a long minute the two men stared at one another, then the Indian folded his arms across his chest.

Jonathan figured out that the Indian was waiting for something, but he was damned if he knew for what. Slowly he shoved his forty-four back into its holster and removed his hand from his gun butt. With equal deliberation, he rose from the ground and stood easily facing the Indian. He waited for the Indian to make the next move.

Scarface leveled a hand at him. "Brave Warrior. Burn bushes. Brave."

Jonathan waited for more. It came. "Brave Warrior and Red Hawk have enemy. Enemy kill Red Hawk's squaw and Red Hawk's son. Give Red Hawk this." He touched the hideous scar that disfigured what was still a noble face. "Red Hawk kill someday."

"Keefer." It was all Jonathan could think to say.

"Tonight, Sneaking Coyote, as we call Keefer, will try to kill Brave Warrior."

Jonathan listened for an instant to the bruises clamoring for his attention and thought it more likely that Red Hawk had tried to finish him off, but he kept his mouth shut. How the devil did the Indian figure Keefer intended to harm him?

As if he had read his mind, the Indian lifted a hand again and pointed to a spot just over Jonathan's shoulder. "See."

Jonathan whirled around to face the danger, and forgot the Indian's existence. Almost a mile away, he could see the barn that was his home, burning brightly.

Catherine stirred uneasily in her sleep. She was dreaming that she heard the lowing of cows. She frowned, then sat bolt upright as she heard a horse scream. As her eyes opened, she could see the red light of a fire dancing on her walls.

"Jonny! Clayton! Ellen! Fire! Fire!" She was rushing from the room, stumbling into her boots, even as she shouted. She became aware, as sleep retreated, that it was the barn that burned, not the house,

Then panic hit her. Jonathan! Jonathan slept in the barn.

She shoved her feet into her boots, grabbed her robe, and ran out of the house and across the square and into the burning barn.

Frantically she searched for Creole. Relief rushed through her as she saw his vacant stall. Even so, she checked to see that he wasn't lying down. "Thank you, dear God!" she breathed. Jonathan hadn't gotten back yet.

She used her robe to wrap around her own terrified horse's head. It was the only way she could lead her out of the fire.

The panicked horse threw her this way and that, tossing her head to free it of the blindfold Catherine had made of her robe, but she hung on grimly until she had latched the mare safely into the corral, knowing that horses run back to their familiar stalls when they are mindless with fear. Then she stripped the robe from the horse and ran back to get Rosie.

The milk cow was bawling, her eyes rolling in her head, but true to her training, she followed where she was led, and stood quietly when Catherine tied her to the tree by the smithy. Catherine blessed her sincerely, and ran back to the barn.

Thank God there was only the little orphan heifer left. The calf! Would she have the time to rescue the little heifer? She knew she would never be able to lift it, and it had never been taught to lead. Bless God, there hadn't been time to teach her anything, she was so young. Would she follow Catherine? With the same determination with which she had brought the calf home and fought for her, she was going to fight for her now. She plunged her singed rag of a robe into the horse trough, then wrapped its sodden length around her head and shoulders and dashed back into the barn.

"Mama!" Jonny's agonized cry rang out in the night, but Catherine didn't hear it over the crackle of the flames. She was too busy dodging balls of flaming hay as they exploded down from the hayloft.

The calf! She could hear its frantic cry, see it outlined against the light of the straw that had caught and now flamed on the far side of the stall.

Good! With fire behind her, perhaps Catherine could persuade her to come away from the place she'd been taught she was safe and out into the safety of what was to the orphan, the unknown dark.

Catherine wrenched the door to the stall open and reached toward the terrified calf.

Outside, Jonny, with a wail that tore at his grandfather's heart, raced into the burning barn after his mother. He knew which way she would go. He knew she'd try to save his calf, and he headed in that direction.

Through the heavy smoke he could barely make her out, but she was there, coaxing the calf to follow her. Jonny started to run to help her.

At that instant, the hayloft collapsed and hid his mother and the calf from him in a blazing wall of flame.

Jonathan had never ridden as he now rode to reach the burning barn. Miracle after miracle occurred to keep his horse from falling as he galloped over the rough, unpredictable, and unseen terrain between him and the burning barn.

Slamming to a halt in the square, his duty done, the great horse screamed his terror of the fire. His cry was echoed by the human shrieks made by Maria and her daughter as they ran, looking like specters in their long white nightgowns, toward the barn.

Several yards ahead of them, the senator rushed toward the inferno. Jonathan stopped him and spun him around roughly. "Cathy and the boy. Where are they?"

"Let me go, damn you! They're in there!"

Jonathan ordered, "Hold him!" Ellen, Maria, and Consuelo grabbed and held the senator.

Jonathan took a running, bone-jarring leap into the horse trough, rolled once to get as wet as he could, then was up and running for the barn in a flash.

Ten feet inside the door he was as dry as if he'd never heard of water, but he was inside, past the worst of it, and headed for the place he was sure Cathy would have gone. Leaping through a wall of fire, praying he would make it through, he erupted on the other side within feet of the orphaned calf's stall.

From the light of the brightly burning straw that had been the bed of the calf, he could make out three huddled forms. Cathy, the boy, and the calf pressed against the wall as far from the flames as they could get, coughing and staring bright death in the face.

"Come on!" He grabbed the two up roughly and shoved them toward the back of the barn with one hand; with the other arm, he scooped up the bawling, kicking calf and herded the woman and the child before him to a section of the barn not yet part of the general conflagration.

Putting the calf down and yelling, "Hold her," more to give them something to keep their minds off their terrible danger than because he hoped they'd be able to hold the terror-stricken calf, he looked around for something to break through the back wall.

Picking up a heavy keg of nails, he began to batter the wall. The long boards of the wall splintered, then cracked away in large enough sections so that they could push the boy and the calf through.

Cathy squirmed through next, then their rescuer shoved out, gasping for air for his smoke-filled lungs. With inhuman strength, coughing and retching from inhaled smoke, he dragged them mercilessly around to the front of the barn.

Someone yelled, "There! They're safe!"

"Thank God!" The senator stopped struggling with Carlos and sat weakly on the ground.

Catherine realized with sudden clarity that it was only their timely appearance that had stopped her father-in-law from rushing into the collapsing barn in search of his grand-son. She owed the Rebel Captain even more.

"Gracias a Dios," Maria cried and fell into a fit of weep-ing. Consuelo, pale-faced and shaking, stood and patted her shoulder awkwardly, trying to comfort her, while Carlos and Juan ran to help the stricken trio to a safer distance from the tottering structure that the flaming barn had become.

An instant later, with a sound that was almost a human groan, the huge barn twisted and fell into itself, sending sparks flying a hundred feet into the night sky.

CHAPTER

Nineteen

DAWN HAD BROKEN BEFORE THEY WERE ALL TREATED FOR their burns and scrapes. Jonny was the first in line for salve and bandages, then was immediately sent to bed. They could hear him complaining through the giant yawns that overcame him all the way up the stairs to his room.

When the boy was cared for, Catherine insisted that Jonathan remove his charred remnant of a shirt. He merely looked at her.

"Come," she told him firmly. "This is foolish. You obviously must have salve put on your injuries, or you will be of no use to anybody when your burns become infected." Putting it that way protected her against the emotions that were tearing at her behind her cool façade. Could she touch him without her hands shaking? Could she feel his hard flesh under her fingertips without trembling?

Finally he relented, and she watched him, trying not to be caught staring. The muscles in his chest and back worked and glided like silk under his skin as he removed and folded his shirt.

She wondered briefly at the scrapes and bruises on his back. Forcing a laugh, she used it to hide the way her lips had parted involuntarily when he'd finished removing his shirt. "Why do you take such care? It's only a rag in its present state."

He turned and smiled tightly back at her. "Rag to you. My only shirt to me. My other went up with the barn, remember?"

His mind was no more on the words they exchanged than

hers was. He was so glad that he'd been in time to save this glorious woman who had risked her precious life to save an orphan calf, that the familiar bitterness that leapt up to remind him he had once owned many dozens of the finest shirts was easy to ignore.

"But . . ." She looked troubled. "Surely I pay you enough to buy shirts. Why had you only two?" She blushed as soon as the words were out of her mouth. It was none of her business how he spent his money. She hoped madly that he was still paying for his horse, and not spending his money on whiskey and women.

Disarmed by her blush, Jonathan answered before his pride had time to remember that his problems were none of her affair. "I must see that my sisters are resettled comfortably. I save every penny I can for that." Then it was his turn to color, as he realized he had revealed more than he wished these Yankees to know.

"How many sisters do you have?" she asked in breathless fascination. "Why don't you settle them with your wife and son?" She was so intent on learning all she could about him while he was willing to talk that good manners followed caution, flying to the winds.

His expression changed. It flickered briefly through terrible pain before it settled into suppressed anger. "I hardly think my *two* sisters," he answered her prying question with ironic good manners and a mocking bow, then went on coldly, "would be comfortable in the cemetery, Mrs. Foster." His voice was arctic and he turned from her before he even finished his sentence.

Catherine was left to sort out feelings that ranged from mortification at her gauche behavior, through relief about his married state, to tearing pity at having caused him such pain.

There was nothing she could say. No apology she could offer for what she'd done. No comfort he would accept. All she could do was stand there in abject shame as he walked away from her.

A soft voice spoke at her shoulder, "Señora Catherine." Maria put a gentle hand over hers and enfolded it comfortingly. "He will get over it. It is the fact that he cannot be with his family to protect them that rides him like a devil."

"Thank you, Maria." She took Maria's offered hand in both her own. "It's just that . . ."

"I know, Catherine," Maria said in a whisper. "I know." She wasn't simply offering comfort, she was telling her friend that she had guessed how she felt about the tall Southerner.

Catherine turned to stare at her childhood playmate and saw that she did, indeed, know. In Maria's eyes, Catherine faced, for the first time, the truth of her feelings, and a tremulous warmth blossomed through her and pushed away her fears.

Maria knew that she loved the Rebel. Until this moment, Catherine hadn't truly known, herself. Until now, she had called the attraction she felt for the quiet man anything from annoyance to—since her disturbing dream—need.

Now she would have to come to grips with the fact that it was something infinitely more. And she wasn't the least bit sure that she was ready to do so.

At breakfast later in the morning, Catherine and the senator put together a long list of lumber, nails, and tools needed to rebuild. They had no idea where they would get the men. Now that the barn was gone, however, it was impossible to wait any longer to rebuild the destroyed buildings that had made up the square behind the house.

"I think that's got it. And I think that maybe our own Rebel may be able to talk some of the Confederates around here into coming and building—if we promise to stay out of sight," he finished wryly.

Catherine grimaced, then nodded, picking up her coffee cup. *Our own Rebel.* She wasn't going to think about that remark. Neither the warm feeling it gave her, nor the enraged one she was sure the Southerner would feel if he'd heard Clayton.

She breathed in the warm aroma of Ellen's fresh-brewed coffee with a half-smile of appreciation. After a sleepless night, it would help her get started.

The senator sat back in his chair and looked at her levelly. He brushed aside her assent to his plans for building, taking it for granted, and got to his next point. "Catherine, I've been thinking."

She smiled indulgently at him. It would be a rare moment when he was not thinking, but she didn't say so. "Yes?"

"About the Rebel's sisters," he began, and suddenly Catherine was all attention, the drowsiness that had assailed her a moment ago forgotten. "We owe the man more than we can ever repay."

His daughter-in-law nodded agreement, hastily swallowing the last of her coffee and clinking the empty cup into its saucer with no trace of her usual grace nor any regard for the antique Minton china.

"We could make it so that he could have his sisters here with him, and thus repay him in a small way."

Catherine scowled thoughtfully. "He'd never let us invite them, Clayton. He's far too proud to permit his sisters to be the objects of anyone's charity, much less ours," she finished with a hint of bitterness. "And I couldn't bear the thought of taking in boarders, even to assuage his prideful feelings."

Clayton burst out laughing. "I wasn't suggesting you set up as a landlady, my dear. What I'm suggesting is much more in line with the man's continuing and, if I may be permitted to say so, heroic service to this family."

"What you say is certainly true, sir. What is your point?"

The senator was accustomed to the way his son's widow met him man-to-man in serious discussions. Her forthrightness was her principal legacy from her grandfather. He didn't even blink anymore.

"What I am suggesting, Catherine, is that you deed the old hacienda and a few hundred acres to the man as a reward for saving your life." He paused to let that sink in, then he nodded. "Yes, and my life and Jonny's and all the rest of us at the way station, as well." He rushed through the list impatiently and got back to the point before Catherine could prompt him to. "Then he would be able to have his family, what's left of it" —he ignored her flinch— "with him and still be here where he can not only earn the money to keep them, but still be of service to you.".

He regarded her, bright-eyed, ready to gauge her response. "For my part, I shall send for his sisters. I remember their address, as I have sent several letters for him since we've been here."

Catherine sat back in her chair, still stunned by his proposal. Part with a piece of Three Rivers? Her grandfather would spin himself to a splinter! And of course she'd have to make it clear that if he left, the property would revert to the ranch from which it came.

She smiled wryly. Obviously she had made her decision. That was simple to see from the road her present thoughts traveled.

But how did she really feel about always having him nearby? She gently probed her emotions. She had to fight the sudden elation that threatened to sweep her away on one hand and the fear that rose, unbidden, on the other.

Hitherto, she'd always known that someday he would move on. This decision would change that. Now how would she console herself when thoughts of him overwhelmed her? She felt almost as if she were about to begin gambling with her own sanity.

She frowned. Maria's single look had shatteringly pointed out to her that she was hopelessly . . . She refused to say the words, she was still fighting against admitting the truth of them. Quickly, she substituted *attracted to* the tall Southerner.

She could certainly excuse herself for her flash of elation in light of that, but she didn't know how she was going to cope with having him near for the rest of their lives when the barrier of their differences made things so hopeless between them.

None of that was under discussion, however, and she made her decision without considering her feelings, past, present, or future. Rebel Captain Foster more than deserved this gesture of appreciation. She said calmly, "Yes. It's fair and it's more in proportion to what he has done for us than anything I can think of. Thank you, Clayton."

She put her napkin on the table and started to rise. She was amazed at how good she felt, considering she was parting with a piece of her heritage. She supposed that it was because now she could stop feeling so beholden to Jonathan. Her grandfather would approve of that, at least. For whatever reason, her spirit felt lighter, and she was grateful to Clayton for making it so.

The smile she sent him was almost impish. "I leave it to you to find a way to get the stiff-necked Rebel to accept. I'll go draw up the deed." She shoved her vacated chair back under the table. "I think five hundred acres is all our miserable hides are worth, don't you?"

He smiled back. "Most generous, my dear."

"Thank you. Now you have to do the hard part."

He looked up at her with a puzzled frown.

Her smile became absolutely devilish. "Now you have to make him take it."

The senator made his preparations, then went in search of the Rebel. He found his quarry down by the river. Evidently, he'd just washed the soot from the rag that was all that was left of his shirt, for he was holding it up, dripping, while he looked at it critically.

"Captain." The senator spoke loudly enough to be heard over the sluggish movement of the water. He watched as the Rebel leapt to his feet and turned. He was alert, but not threatened. It was a good fighting man who could instantly judge what came up behind him.

Jonathan stood easily, hipshot, and hooked a thumb in his belt while the other hand dangled what had been his shirt. His eyes were curious. "Good morning, Senator."

"Yes, it is a good morning, since we are all alive, thanks to you." He held out a bundle. "I brought you a couple of shirts." When Jonathan took the shirts from him, he walked over to a rock near the standing man and sat on its edge. "I wonder if we could talk?"

Jonathan bent down and looked into the shadow under

the edge of the senator's rock. Straightening, he tossed the remains of his shirt onto a bush to dry, put the package down, and folded his arms across his bare chest. Gravely, he nodded.

With his own expression as serious, Senator Foster broached the subject he'd come to discuss. "Catherine and I would like to find a way to say thank you for what you did last night." He saw the man tense. Obviously he was braced to refuse any gesture of gratitude from them.

Very well. The senator hadn't spent years as a politician without becoming pretty adroit at talking people around to his way of thinking. He felt sure that it would be a chilly day in the nether regions when he couldn't. "You know, we sure are getting to be mighty beholden to you, Captain." He smiled to take any sting out of the words and said, "Not a very comfortable feeling, that. Catherine and I want to find a way to even the score."

"That's not necessary."

"Are you trying to tell me you don't chafe when you owe somebody something? Or that you can turn your back on a debt?"

Jonathan said, "No. I guess I'd feel it as galling as you seem to." His tone was guarded.

"The burden of a gratitude one can't repay can be an onerous one, can't it? Gets oppressive after a while, don't you agree?"

"Yes." Jonathan's expression was wary. It wasn't hard to guess the senator was up to something.

"Yes, indeed." The senator rose from the rock. "Well, thank you for understanding how we feel. Both Catherine and I appreciate it." He brushed at the seat of his pants casually. "By the way, why did you look under this rock?" Before Jonathan could answer, he added, "Oh, when Catherine figures out some way to even the score a bit, you won't make it difficult for her, will you?"

"Rattlesnake," Jonathan said evenly, his eyes glittering.

For a second the senator thought the Rebel had caught him at his game and was calling him a snake. Then he realized that he had just been told that in his citified ignorance he might have sat down on a poisonous reptile.

Neither idea appealed to him much.

Catherine was waiting for her father-in-law when he returned to the house. She was standing in the cool interior, looking fresh and pretty in a white muslin dress, and she was very impatient. She had a heavy sheet of paper in her hand. "Did you get him to accept?"

The senator hung his hat on the rack by the door and stood smiling at her. "I began. He's not an easy man, you know."

Catherine made an impatient noise.

"At least I got him to agree that being obligated to someone isn't comfortable. The next move is yours." He went on without a pause. "What's for lunch? And by the way. Where is the Captain going to live until the new barn is finished?"

A thoughtful expression appeared on Catherine's face. She tapped her lips with the edge of the heavy paper that was the key to the Rebel's future. "You'll have to ask Ellen what she's serving for lunch," she murmured absently.

Her mind wasn't on food. Clayton had just given her an idea of what she might do to get Jonathan to accept the deed she'd drawn up giving him *Tres Rios* hacienda.

She whirled, and in a flurry of soft white skirts, passed Clayton and called out, "Ellen! When Captain Foster comes for his lunch, tell him I want him to ride out with me."

She spun back, almost bumping into her startled father-in-law. "Sorry!" Then she called back over her shoulder, "Tell me when he's finished his lunch, please."

"Yes," Clayton said plaintively, "And please tell me what's to eat."

Ten minutes later, she was back downstairs, ready to ride, looking very workmanlike in her leather split riding skirt and man-tailored shirt. The only trace left of the elegant woman who'd met the senator when he'd come in was the soft style in which she wore her abundant dark hair piled on top of her head.

Clayton smiled at her from his chair at the table. "No man in his right senses could refuse you anything, Catherine."

"Let's hope Captain Foster is not quite in his right mind, then." She pulled on her riding gloves.

"I didn't say *mind,* daughter."

Very slowly, Catherine raised her regard from her gloves and turned it on her father-in-law. Never before had he called her "daughter." Always it was "Catherine," or, when he introduced her, "daughter-in-law."

She didn't trust herself to say a word. She hadn't any words to say. All she had was the wonderful feeling that she and Clayton had become real family at last. She felt the joy of that knowledge flood her heart.

After a long moment, she tore her gaze from his smiling eyes, and fearing she might burst into tears, turned and all but ran for Ellen.

Ellen looked up from the piecrust she was rolling out on the big table in the center of the kitchen. "He hasn't finished eating his lunch, Miss Catherine."

"Oh. That isn't why I've come." Catherine was flustered. "I knew you'd call me."

Ellen really looked at her then. She set aside her rolling pin, draped a damp linen tea towel over her dough, and wiped the flour from her hands with a dry one.

That finished, she held out her arms to Catherine. "Here, dear." Then she patted Catherine's back as the younger woman clung to her. "You've had an awful shock, dear. That's all this is." Ellen hugged her employer fiercely, as she had been doing since Catherine was eight years old.

Catherine took hold of her suggestion avidly. "Yes," she said, wiping at her eyes, "I'm sure you're right. That is exactly what it is." She smiled at Ellen, "Thank you."

Ellen patted her arm. "You'll be fine presently. You'll see." She looked beyond Catherine through the screen door onto the porch. "Looks like he's finished his lunch."

Catherine started. How did Ellen know it was the Rebel who caused her distress?

Ellen peered at Catherine sharply. "You asked me to tell you when the Captain had finished his lunch, Miss

Catherine." And suddenly she wasn't at all sure that her Catherine's problem was the shock of losing her barn. Not sure at all.

She watched pensively as the slender woman quickly left the house.

Catherine watched him closely as he looked around the patio of the hacienda. "Do you think you could fix up enough space to live here comfortably until we get the bunkhouse rebuilt?"

The smile he turned her way made her heart speed up. This was the first time she had seen a smile of delight on his face. It made him, instantly, ten years younger.

Had it been so long, then, since anything had pleased him that the simple suggestion that he sleep in a decaying adobe ruin could bring that smile to his face? As she watched the eagerness with which he strode across the broad expanse of square, red tiles that were all but covered with years of dust blown in through the tall iron gates, she nursed the warm feeling that came with knowing that, someday soon, the hacienda would be his.

It had stood empty since her grandfather had decided to build closer to town, and it had fallen into disrepair, but on seeing it up close, she realized that time had not ravished the adobe building as it would have a wooden structure.

Her grandfather had always forbidden her to come near it when she was a child, then she had been too busy, and finally she had gone away as a young woman. Now she felt the enchantment of exploring the sprawling old edifice as keenly as her companion did.

"Why? Why would anyone just leave this place?" He gazed around in wonder.

"My grandfather wanted to be nearer the town."

"He left this to be only half an hour closer?" By his almost scornful expression, Catherine could tell this man would not have relocated if he'd been the owner of the graceful, sprawling building.

Pushing aside her reaction to his implied criticism of her beloved grandfather, Catherine smiled, wondering how he would react when he found he was the new owner. Thunder and lighting, she had no doubt.

It occurred to her that it might be wiser to wait and enlist the aid of his sisters when they arrived. She still had vivid memories of the furious tirade he had unleashed on her in the barn the day they rescued the calf. Perhaps she would do well to enlist his sisters' protection, as well. She would probably need protection from the fit she felt certain his overweening pride would throw.

Pride of her own, and a curious, exultant merriment bubbled up in her as she watched him. What a many-faceted man he was. Only he could have caused her to so quickly tuck away her husband in that region of her heart that sheltered and cherished memories. The force of this man's personality would allow for nothing else.

"Look!" He easily lifted a heavy, wrought iron candle stand as tall as he from where it lay on its side in the dust. Carefully he kicked aside a pile of dry cottonwood leaves and set the stand on its feet. He regarded her expectantly, his usual reticence cast aside.

Her heart swelled. She pressed her hand to the front of her shirt to keep it from bounding free and ending up literally in his keeping. "Yes, it's lovely. I'm sure it was left because it wouldn't fit in with the things grandfather ordered for the new house."

She smiled as she joined him in his enthusiasm for discovering any other abandoned treasures. "Let's see what else is here that you can use to make a home for yourself."

She saw him hesitate when he heard her say "home." And with a sinking heart, she saw some of the shine leave his face as the memories flooded in. Then, thankfully, she saw him give himself a mental shake and decide to enjoy the moment.

He held out an imperious hand, and she slipped hers into it wonderingly. It was like a gift, this unconscious sharing he offered. Even through their riding gloves, she felt such a shock of electricity at his touch that she cried, "Oh!" and forgot what to do with her feet.

He turned and caught her as she stumbled. "Are you okay?" He laughed down into her eyes, and she found she was having difficulty with her breathing, too.

Somewhere she found enough breath to say, "I'm fine," and to laugh back up at him, "just clumsy."

His grip on her hand tightened and he drew her closer to him, causing their arms to contact firmly for the whole length of her own, as if he intended to guard against having her stumble again. Leading her, all but pressed against his side, across the huge main room, he passed the yawning cavern of the fireplace and bent to retrieve the twin of the candle stand he'd stood on the other side. "Would you look? They're both still here."

Catherine felt sadness try to touch her: Obviously things were not often "still here" in the war-torn South, or his voice wouldn't be so full of amazement that no one had violated her property. The armor of her joy at being here with him turned the sadness away. Even as she refused to let the feeling ruin this time for them, she marveled that it was she and not the man at her side who had felt it.

"What a beautifully proportioned room." His eyes traveled it. "Who built this?"

"A man called De Vargas. When his family all died of smallpox, he sold to my great-grandfather and went back to Spain."

He tugged at her hand, one eager child leading another. To the left of the fireplace there was a huge time-blackened door. He ran his fingers over the pattern of heavy, square-headed nails with which it was ornamented, tactilely enjoying the craftsmanship.

Drawing her close against him, he positioned her so that she would see what lay beyond the door at the same moment he saw it himself. She watched the muscles in his arm tighten and bulge with the effort it took to open the door. It took a great deal of strength, but his hand forced down the lever that released, with a screech of neglected metal, the heavy wrought iron latch. Then he pushed at the door.

It refused to budge, and Catherine waited, willing him not to relinquish her hand so that he could manage it. She felt a sharp pang of regret as she waited for him to.

Instead, Jonathan put his shoulder against the door. He had no intention of loosing Cathy's hand and breaking for them both the magic of sharing. He was filled with it. Floating on it. And he knew unerringly that she felt it, too. If he had to, he would kick the door down.

One mighty shove did it. The door creaked slowly open. They were staring into an immense room filled with shelves. Bookshelves. And like a miracle, the books were still there. Jonathan was drawn like metal to a magnet by the books on those shelves: hundreds of them covered with dust, festooned with cobwebs, their bindings beginning to crack, but still there.

Dragging her along, he strode across to the nearest. Reverently removing a single volume from the shelf, he lifted their joined hands to support its spine as he carefully opened it.

"Shakespeare! *The Sonnets.*"

Catherine heard the reverence in his voice. She watched his face as his eyes devoured the page. New knowledge about this man filled her mind. He read. And he obviously had not had anything to read for a long time if she could judge by the avidity with which, finally breaking himself away from the one in their hands, he stared at the books around them.

"Why are they here?" He demanded, frowning at her as if their presence, so far away from the hub of the ranch, were a crime.

"I don't know." She felt she had to distance herself in his mind from the responsibility for this neglect of the wonderful library. "I was never allowed to come here. I suppose grandfather didn't read a lot. There were only a few bookcases in the big house." With her free hand, she pulled cobwebs away from the shelf.

"You should move them to the house. This room has stayed surprisingly tight." He looked to the snugly closed casement windows along the end wall, and back at the door that was so well fitted in its jamb that he'd had to fight it open. "That's the only reason that the field mice haven't ruined them." His eyes went back to feast on the books.

Catherine watched him. The same feelings flooded her that filled her when her son looked into the window of the big toy store in Boston.

These books were Jonathan's. He had found them and fallen in love with them, and she was going to see that they became his. She was elated that it was in her power to see to it that he had this, at least, from his past—his love of reading and the ability to sate the appetite he clearly had for it.

"Books," he was saying reverently. "All the knowledge, all the thought, all . . ." he broke off, looking a little embarrassed. His voice became brusque. "You'll want to get them to the house as soon as you can have shelves built."

She wondered for a moment if she should let him think that she would take the books to the house. It would certainly add to the effort he would put into convincing men to come to build if he thought he was getting them to build bookcases, it seemed. But it wouldn't be fair.

She took a careful breath and said as nonchalantly as she could, "No, I'm sure they'll be safe with you living here." She tried to ignore the way her heart behaved to see the pleasure her words brought him. Even so, she could feel the rosiness that it caused to flood her cheeks.

Catherine stood quietly, waiting for him to direct their next move. She was unwilling to break the spell they were caught in by even the slightest suggestion.

He smiled down at her and led her out again into the main room. He looked up at the balcony, then passed under it and into a wide hall from which the steps to it rose. They could see a huge dining room beyond.

Keeping her away from the wrought iron hand rail as if he feared it might no longer be sound, he pulled her up the tile-faced adobe steps behind him. Still he held her hand. She hoped he would never let go.

At the top of the steps, he turned and took her to another strong oak door, this one carved with figures. She hadn't time to identify the figures before Jonathan pushed the door open and they saw the large, light-filled room behind

it. Almost every wall was filled with windows. Even the
fireplace was set in a wall full of windows. Only the wall
against which the oversized bed stood was limited to a
mere four.

The bed stood on a dais. It had no footboard, but the
headboard, heavily carved with sweetly smiling cupids,
almost reached the high ceiling.

Catherine heard Jonathan murmur under his breath, "God.
What a place to—"

He caught himself, and she saw him flush slightly. Pretending she hadn't heard, she delighted in his unspoken
thought, for indeed, this would be a most wondrous place
to make love. She blushed at her own thoughts.

She looked from his face to the bed and felt herself
deluged with a powerful tide of longing. What would she
do if by some wonderful chance he . . . She grew dizzy at
the very thought.

"Cathy." Her name was only a breath, but suddenly she
couldn't find her own. She watched him lower his eyes to
her breasts as she fought to breathe again.

He understood, of course, and his gaze flashed to her
face. She knew desire had to be plain to see there. The
magic of the hacienda had combined with the depth of her
feelings for him to overwhelm her ability to hide her love
from him.

His free hand came up to cup her face. Slowly he turned
until his whole body was close to her own, and flame ran
along her veins. She turned her face to the roughness of his
rawhide work glove, and brushed a kiss into the palm.

Slowly he moved his fingertips to his mouth and she
watched his strong, white teeth seize on the fingertips of
his glove. Then the glove dropped away and staring straight
into her eyes, unblinking, he recupped her face and waited.

Her eyes locked with his, she slowly turned her face and
kissed the bare palm of his hand.

He exploded like lightning. Instantly she was swept hard
against him, her ribs almost cracking with the hungry
strength of his embrace.

He pushed her back against the wall next to the door

and held her there, pinning her with the lean length of his hard, muscled body. His hand free—for the other had never relinquished her own—he plundered her body.

The contrast to the silkiness of her skin as his work-callused hand plunged into the front of her shirt and cupped her breast, drove her to gasp, "Jonathan." He groaned aloud, and caught the moan with which she echoed his passion in his open mouth.

Finally, he let go of the hand he had held so long, but before she could register the sense of loss, he had lifted her effortlessly against his chest. With determined strides, he approached the huge bed.

Letting her slide tantalizingly down the length of his body, he held her firmly in the circle of his arm. He never took his eyes from her own. Reaching out for the dust-laden bedcover, he swirled it to the floor in one fluid, powerful movement.

Catherine saw the dust fly into the shafts of sunlight from the windows and the myriad motes were as stars to her, brightening this moment. She heard him laugh low in his throat at her maidenly gasp, as, pressed against him by the desperate force with which he held her, she felt the strength of his need for her.

She entwined her arms about his neck, wanting him more than she had ever wanted anything in her life. More even than life.

He lifted her high again, cherishing her against his chest, looking into her eyes with a fierce possessiveness. With one, speaking look, her eyes answered him. She told him all he waited to know as, without hesitation, Catherine gave him the gift of herself.

In movements that seemed to take forever, his eyes claiming her own, he lowered his head to her. Her fingers tightened in his hair, and she pressed her aching breasts against the hard wall of his chest. She saw his mouth open, saw the tip of his tongue between his even white teeth, and opened her own lips in breathless anticipation.

As he kissed her with a kiss that she was sure was stealing all that she was from her, he lifted a knee to the bed and turned to fling her on it to bury her beneath his urgent body.

And when he did, with a crack of time-dried wood, the huge bed collapsed. The headboard, with all its smiling cupids, came smashing pitilessly down upon them.

CHAPTER

Twenty

CATHERINE NEVER KNEW HOW THEY GOT TO THEIR HORSES. The bed falling had been like having the Almighty dump a bucket of cold water on their passion.

Jonathan, dazed by the crash of the heavy headboard, had hauled her from the wreckage of the big bed and out onto the balcony over the main room before he'd spoken.

"Oh, God! Cathy, are you all right?" His voice had been shaking with concern. Though he knew he had shielded her with his body from the brunt of the falling headboard, he had to hear her say she was all right.

She had merely nodded her head to answer him, too embarrassed to speak. In the aftermath of the bed's collapse, she was completely roused from the wonder of his touch, and she was mortified to have been so wholly, wantonly committed to the experience they'd been about to share.

It was gone now—all the wonder, all the magic of the day—and the two of them sat their horses and tried to look anywhere but at each other. When they had ridden a mile or so back toward the main house, Jonathan cleared his throat and said, "Catherine, I feel I should apologize for my behavior. I . . ."

She stopped listening immediately, as, wooden-faced, he plowed on. Silently she raged at him. How dare he apologize? She flashed him one angry glance and refused to respond to a word he said.

Her horse carried her on. The sun began to slip toward the horizon. The evening might be cooling, but Catherine's anger was not.

Jonathan was quiet now, still as death on his tall horse.

Suddenly she could bear it no longer. She dug her boot heels savagely into her mare and galloped off, leaving an angry Jonathan fighting his startled horse in the cloud of her dust.

Cursing fluently, he sent Creole after her. He was careful to stay far enough behind her not to further incur her wrath.

When he'd seen her safely back to the ranch, he planned to take another long swim.

The next morning and for long days after, Catherine avoided Jonathan. She managed not even to see him for the better part of a week.

He was busy all day somewhere out on the range, and at night he must have been at the hacienda, because Ellen told her he picked up his breakfast when he came in to get his orders for the day from Morris.

"When he comes in for his breakfast, he's been saying that he won't be back till the next morning," Ellen told her. "I stick something on his tray that he can take with him to eat later, though. Wouldn't want a considerate gentleman like him to go hungry."

Catherine was annoyed. "He's a cowhand, Ellen." It wasn't true; she just wanted to snap at somebody. She'd been feeling absolutely waspish lately.

"That man's a gentleman, no matter what he does to keep body and soul together, Miss Catherine, and well you know it." Ellen gave the biscuits she was rolling out a thump with her rolling pin.

Ellen's remark did nothing to improve her employer's temper, but Catherine lingered, waiting for a glimpse of Jonathan as he came for his breakfast.

When he did, Ellen gave her a knowing glance and paid her back for her smallness. "Captain," she called as she crossed the big kitchen to the door, "you're mighty welcome to come in here and eat at my table anytime you've a mind to." She threw an arch look at Catherine as she listened to his melodious voice thank her prettily.

Ellen hissed, "Gentleman," then nodded her head with satisfaction at the sight of Catherine's retreat. She went back to fixing more biscuits for the family and that Morris who lived in the abode house opposite Maria's. Every night he ate the food Ellen took there at a proper table. She grumbled aloud, "While a gentleman eats on the back porch." Ellen gave a disapproving sniff.

A moment later, she took two more biscuits out to the Captain. Steaming hot, dripping butter, and with her best preserves on them.

Jonathan finished the breakfast Ellen gave him and smiled at her as he returned the dishes. "Those were the best strawberry preserves I've had since I was a boy, Ellen, and I surely do thank you."

He left Ellen smiling fondly and had just gathered up Creole's reins when the ranch foreman came out from his own breakfast.

"Hey, Foster!"

Jonathan looked toward him without expression. Morris took a perverse pleasure in calling him by his last name. It hadn't taken Jonathan long to figure out that he liked to pretend he was bossing the owner, since the name was the same.

"Today you work with the men building the bunkhouse." He jammed his fists onto his beefy hips and eyed the quiet Southerner. "I don't cotton to the idea of you camping out at the old hacienda. Seems to me you might get used to living better'n a hired hand ought to." He watched Jonathan through slitted eyes, his look measuring.

Jonathan regarded him without expression. He'd seen Morris's sort too many times to rise to his bait. If Morris was curious about how he was accustomed to living, let him ask. He wouldn't get an answer. "Whatever you say, Morris." He deliberately omitted the "Mister" that everybody else used. He led Creole back to the rough lean-to he had thrown up to shelter him since the barn had burned and began to unsaddle the big gelding.

"No need to do that. I can use him as a spare today." Morris stomped after them.

Jonathan kept unsaddling. "Creole's mine."

"All the horses on the ranch belong to any hand on the ranch, Foster." The foreman glared hard at him.

Jonathan sighed. He wondered what it was about him that made the beefy men of the world think they could walk over him. He finished taking the tack off Creole and said patiently, "I didn't mean I chose this horse. I meant I bought him. He's mine. I own him."

"But you don't lend him." Morris's voice was flat.

"That's right, I don't." Jonathan's was flatter.

Morris scowled, "You go work with the carpenters today," he said again. "Get that bunkhouse up. I don't like my hands living all over the place." He gave Jonathan a meaningful look. "I want you out of the hacienda."

Jonathan replied in a voice full of bored insolence calculated to drive the heavy man wild, "Anything you say." He moseyed with provoking slowness over to the bunkhouse.

Catherine had heard the exchange from one of the dining room windows. Angry as she was—reasonably or not—at Jonathan, she still enjoyed Morris's discomfort. She knew the man was something of a bully, and it pleased her to see him meet with opposition.

In the days that followed, Catherine realized she shouldn't have been so pleased. What she wasn't so pleased about was that now, every time she looked out a window anywhere on the back of the house, Catherine saw the Rebel.

His bronzed skin sleek with sweat, the muscles working under it easily, he toiled beside the men he'd gotten to come and build. Worse yet, sometimes they sang—usually when Morris, whose Union sympathies strengthened with every victory the Federal army won against the depleted, starving armies of the South—was around to be offended by it.

The songs they sang as they worked were always "Bonnie Blue Flag," "Dixie," or, if they really set out to get the foreman's goat, that States' Rights song, "Battle Cry of

Freedom." Sometimes, as night approached and they were packing up their tools to leave the ranch for the day, they sang "Lorena."

That was how Catherine learned that Jonathan had a very fine baritone. True and clear, it carried on the evening stillness above that of the other men when they sang the plaintive campfire song.

Their singing disturbed her as much as it did Morris, maybe more, for it called up for her all the horrors of war and reminded her too sharply of the man for whom she feared she no longer grieved sufficiently.

One song in particular sent her scurrying for her bed to press her pillow over her ears. That was the awful parody someone had made of "Listen to the Mockingbird." The men sang of listening to the parrot shells in the first verse, and of listening to the whizzing of the minie balls, those deadly French bullets, in a second, and to her, even more horrific verse.

That one they sang with such gusto and mighty hammering, that she couldn't hear Jonathan, if he happened to be present, at all, anymore. But Rebel songs got the buildings up, and neither she nor the senator heeded the foreman's requests that she forbid them to sing.

"Damn fool, that man," the senator said to her. "Does he think they'd stop singing because a Yankee told 'em to? Or that they'd do a lick of work if they did?" He shook his head.

Standing there beside Catherine at the window, he mused, "You know, I wonder why Morris is so all-fired eager to get the Captain out of the hacienda and back to the bunkhouse."

Catherine looked at him, startled, then turned back to watch the men working. "They'll be finished soon, so it won't matter about the singing or Morris's wanting Jonathan out of the hacienda."

"You thinking of ordering him back to live in the bunkhouse?"

"I think I'll leave that up to him. After all, he owns the hacienda now."

The senator snorted. "He doesn't know that."

"He will when his sisters get here."

"Yes, well. About that, Catherine."

She turned away from the window to smile at him, "What about that?"

"There you go again. It isn't ladylike to be as direct as a man, my dear." He held up a hand to forestall her comment. "About that, is that I've had a wire from one of the telegraph operators along the way, and those girls are less than two days off."

Catherine brightened. "Wonderful. I'll ask Ellen to bake several cakes so they'll have a choice of desserts their first night here. Cakes will keep that long and be the better for it."

"Wait just a minute. Have you told their brother, is more to the point than Ellen and desserts, Catherine."

She sighed. The senator waited expectantly. Finally, she surrendered. "No. I've racked my brains, and I simply can't think of a single excuse for interfering in his life as we have."

The senator exploded. "Now you think of that! For God's sake, Catherine . . ." He sputtered to a stop. The ends of his mustache quivered.

She put a hand on his arm. "No, dear, for the Captain's sake. For the sake of the man who saved all our lives— twice. Mine and Jonny's three times. It's all for his sake."

Her expression changed fleetingly. "Besides, all I did was deed him a place. You're the one who decided to send for his sisters."

The senator stood there with his mouth opening and closing, but no words came. Catherine took her opportunity. "Will you excuse me, Clayton? I think I hear Jonny calling me."

Clayton looked out to where Jonny and the Captain were trying to get Rosie to let the calf nurse. Jonny hadn't the faintest intention of calling his mother and getting told to get out of Rosie's makeshift corral before he got hurt, but the senator hadn't spent years honing his diplomacy for nothing. "Certainly, my dear."

*   *   *

"She won't let her!" Jonny shoved his hair back off his forehead and glared at Rosie. "Why won't the dumb old cow let Daisy get her own milk? She lets us get it for her."

Daisy, as the boy had named the orphan heifer, butted the cow's udder again. Rosie eyed her with distaste and raised her hind foot threateningly.

"Don't let her hurt Daisy!" Jonny looked beseechingly at Jonathan.

"Easy, Button." He smiled down at the boy, secure in the knowledge that he had picked up from working with the cattle. "They're just working things out."

"Rosie's gonna kick her. I know she is."

"Rosie's a good sort. She won't kick her very hard."

"I don't want her to kick her at all!" He started forward, but the Southerner pulled him back, grabbed him under the arms and swung him up to sit on the top rail against which the man lounged.

"Stay put and watch, Jonny."

"But what if Daisy gets kicked?" The boy's plaintive wail was loud enough to be heard all over the square. Neither of them saw Catherine come out of the house in response.

"Sometimes we get kicked when we're learning, son. Sometimes that's the only way some of us do learn." He ignored Jonny's murmured, "I'm not your son," accepting it as the boy's automatic tribute to his dead father, and continued, "It won't help anything for you to get in the way and get hurt. This is Daisy's problem."

Ruffling the boy's hair he told him, "Cows have to work things out just like we do, Button."

Catherine's voice cut in on them, "Captain Foster. Why are you encouraging my son to take such chances? He might be hurt in there."

Jonathan looked up at her. He let her see that he understood that her attitude came from the anger she felt for the man, and not the concern she felt for the boy. His Cathy knew very well that neither Daisy nor Rosie would ever do anything that could hurt her son, and she knew even better that he'd never let anything hurt the boy.

He didn't bother to answer her. He knew as sure as sunrise that no matter what he said it would only upset her.

Not saying anything turned out to be an even sorrier choice, he figured, when he saw the storm brewing in her eyes. With frank appreciation, he watched the movement of her breasts as she took in sufficient air to lay him out.

He was so busy being fascinated to see Catherine's lips part to deliver her tirade, that she was the first to hear the coach.

With the thunder of hooves and the rattle of harness, a stagecoach appeared over the last hill in the road into the ranch. Scout raced to greet it, barking furiously, his tail wagging a mile a minute.

Jonny popped down from the fence, Jonathan pushed away from where he lounged against it, and Clayton came out of the house, a decided look of nervous apprehension on his face.

Clayton hurried to the Southerner's side. "There's something that I've been meaning to tell you, Captain," he said urgently.

Catherine interrupted him, "Can't you see it's far too late?" She went, with long strides, to meet the coach.

The senator said helplessly. "Don't know what's gotten into that girl. She's so out of sorts lately."

Jonathan looked at him, well aware that he would never know what had happened to make his daughter-in-law behave as she was. He had certainly shared her experience, intimately, and wasn't feeling too even-tempered, himself.

The senator cleared his throat. "Jonathan, there's something I think you should know."

Jonathan looked at him in surprise. The senator had never called him by his given name. He could tell, even now, that it cost the older man to call him by his dead son's name.

The senator must be under considerable stress. Jonathan wondered what could have put him in such a state.

Then, all their attention went to the man flourishing his whip on the box of the stage. Cavenaugh! Jonathan grinned to see him again. While everybody else seemed suddenly to have grown roots, Jonathan strode forward to greet the doughty old driver. "Cavenaugh! By all that's holy, what brings you back here?"

Some of the shine left Cavenaugh's wide face. He darted a look beyond Jonathan. "You mean you don't know? Nobody told you?" He seemed caught between consternation and amusement. "Well, if that don't beat the Dutch."

Jonathan stopped and stared at the man, puzzled. Before he could make another move, something barreled out of the coach in a welter of skirts and flung itself against him. Strong, wiry arms squeezed his middle, hard. Incredulous, he stared down at hair the exact color of his own.

When he had enough breath back to speak, he asked tentatively, as if there was not the slightest chance of an affirmative answer, "Susan?"

The head buried in his stomach rubbed a violent affirmation against it. He clutched his little sister even closer, his emotions threatening to unman him.

Just then the door of the stagecoach opened a second time, and a radiant goddess stepped out of it.

"Diana!" He gasped. He was stunned. What were his sisters doing here? How did they get to Texas? His mind seemed to have lost its ability to function, and he simply stared as the lovely vision walked over and kissed him gently on the cheek.

The senator rushed up, struggling not to yield to the urge to actually push them into the house so that he could explain to Jonathan. "So glad you ladies made it safely. That's my daughter, Catherine. She'll take you to freshen up."

The older girl looked at the stunned expression on her brother's face and the pleading one on that of the silver-maned man beside him. Understanding instantly that there was something that needed only the gentlemen present, she pried her younger sister off her brother and glided over to the attractive brunette, a gracious smile on her perfect lips and Susan firmly in tow.

Catherine all but gaped at her. Jonathan had said she was extremely beautiful and Catherine had supposed the superlative had been an exaggeration. Instead she was finding it a gross understatement. The girl was a vision of loveliness.

Catherine smiled and invited them in with as gracious a gesture as she could manage. Suddenly she felt as if her face needed washing, her hair needed combing, and her dress, compared with the almost threadbare one the goddess invested with such beauty, needed to be put in the rag bag.

She cast a nervous smile at the serene girl, seeing her glide along as if she never touched the slightly uneven turf under her feet. How in Heaven's name did this lovely girl exist in the everyday world?

Suddenly she was filled with relief at having given the hacienda to Jonathan. Gratitude be damned. She might have deeded it to him for saving her life, but she was even more glad now that she had done so. At least it meant that she wouldn't have this vision underfoot all the time making her feel like a hag.

CHAPTER
Twenty-one

THE NIGHT WAS COOL AND DARK, THE SKIES SAPPHIRE velvet set with jewels. Catherine and the Rebel, however, were impervious to the beauty of the setting. Toe to toe they stood glaring at one another on the bank of the river.

They had held their respective tongues until they had marched as far as the river out of respect for their loved ones. They were quietly preparing for sleep after a lovely dinner from Ellen, which they had enjoyed, unaware of the awesome force of the storm brewing.

Now it was about to break.

Jonathan began in a voice of deadly gentility. "It was rather interesting to see my sisters here in Texas, Miz Foster."

She matched his tone. "It was . . ." she began, then swallowed her next words. She decided not to tell him bringing his sisters here was all Clayton's idea, even though it was. Not while she knew that, in spite of the deceptive calm of his present attitude, the storm was coming. " . . . my pleasure," she finished sardonically, using the phrase she hated to hear from him.

She'd give her father-in-law's generosity full credit when this argument was over. Sooner or later, Jonathan had to come to understand that his sisters belonged where he was.

She began again. "We thought it would be a nice surprise," she said, neatly shouldering half the responsibility. "That you'd all be happier together." She added defensively, "And it's clear your sisters are."

191

When he didn't speak, she added, almost apologetically, "We meant to tell you about it, but Cavenaugh got them here two days before we expected them."

His rigid control broke then. "But you expected them. You knew they were coming while I rode around chasing cows completely unaware of that fact." He took a deep breath to steady his temper. It didn't work.

He only succeeded in adding to his agitation by filling his nostrils with the sweet, heady scent of her. His need of her flashed through him, knotting his hands into fists and goading him to rant at her. "What makes you think, Catherine Foster, that you have the right to move my family around without my permission? Without my knowledge?"

He whirled away from her, then whipped back around to tower over her again. "Blast it, Cathy. You can't mean to have them here as boarders, certainly. And you sure as hell don't think I'd let them stay as long-time guests!" She saw the white sparks in his eyes. He went on, his voice rising. "Surely you don't think I want to put them in town at Mrs. Bender's boardinghouse where every bluebelly in the area can harass Diana, do you?"

He thrust his fingers through his hair. "Just what in blazes did you intend me to do with them? At least at home they were among friends who would keep an eye on them if anything happened to me." Remembrance of the flyer—"dead or alive"—rose in his mind, driving him to the edge of desperation.

He prayed Cathy would never learn of that lying, shaming piece of paper. He had no intention of telling her about it. Not ever.

He tried instead to make her see that he had few options when it came to the care of his sisters. "It wasn't much, Cathy, but putting them near friends was the best I could do." He watched her intently, and she saw that frustration was tearing at him.

What did he mean, though, if something happened to him? Surely he was in no danger now that he wasn't fighting in the war and the army didn't want him for fighting Indians. She felt her stomach twist, and knew she couldn't bear even the thought of anything happening to him.

Surely, too, he knew that she and the senator would befriend his sisters. And the neighbors hereabout were all Confederate sympathizers. The two girls would have lots more friends than she had been able to make, and she had been born and raised here.

Perhaps if he knew he had a place of his own in which to keep them, his mind would be eased about having them here. She knew the time had come to tell him about the deed to the hacienda, but this wasn't the way she wanted to go about it.

She sighed deeply, recognizing the hopelessness of her position. She had to tell him, of course—and blast it—she had to tell him now.

She took a deep breath. "Jonathan."

He frowned. She had his full attention already. Why was she asking for it?

"How are you doing at the hacienda?"

"Fine." He looked puzzled. Why the devil was she changing the subject? Avoiding things wasn't like Cathy. "It just needed cleaning up. There's hardly any damage. My pleasure."

He saw her little grimace at the phrase she so resented, the phrase she'd used to him so mockingly earlier. He also saw she was hanging on his every word.

Her interest made him continue. "I work on the place every night. When I'm tired, I read."

He looked into her eyes and saw the softening and the gladness there and relented a little. His voice lost its hard edge. "It's . . ." he searched for a word that would adequately express his feelings, and finally said merely, " . . . pleasant to have books to read again."

He grinned faintly, boyishly, as if he were confessing a weakness. "I sit up all hours reading."

Catherine thought her knees were going to melt at the crooked little grin. Why did this man have such power to affect her? She'd never had such trouble with her anatomy before. Never.

She remembered, then, the faint smudges she'd seen under his eyes when she fussed at him about Jonny and the cows that afternoon. She understood them now that she realized he was giving up his sleep to read. That touched her deeply. She counted reading, after her family, her own greatest pleasure. They shared another bond. Her smile became soft.

He looked hungrily at her lips and remembered the big bed at the hacienda. Suddenly he wanted more than anything to tell her that he had fixed it and slept in it every night, haunted by the memory of her. But he knew of no way he could.

"You like the hacienda, then?" She made a little face as if she thought she had said the wrong thing.

"Of course." He frowned at her, puzzled again. "Cathy, what is it?"

"It's the hacienda." She turned her back to him. "Look, I'm not very good at this, and I'd bet my last dollar you're not going to be very good about it, either." She shrugged off the hand he placed on her shoulder, as if his imminent anger could be conducted through it like electricity to strike her down. "No, let me finish, because your stupid pride is going to make you mad, and I'd just as soon get it over with."

"Cathy," his voice was like warm honey sliding down her nerves. "You know there's nothing you can say that will make me angry with you."

"Good." She turned to face him, amazed that he could say that in the face of all the minor explosions that had taken place between them. "Then I'll just tell you right out . . ." her eyes searched his face, her own defiant " . . . that I've deeded the hacienda and five hundred acres around it to you." When he didn't speak, she said the rest of it in a rush. "In appreciation of your services to my family." She heard him take a deep breath, and she babbled, "As a thank-you for saving our lives."

She watched as his expression changed from stunned to wrathful. In a movement so fast it was a blur, he grabbed her shoulders. Some part of her mind registered that he was a very beautiful man. It wasn't the part that had to face his anger, however.

"You what!" He shook her until her hair fell free and tumbled down her back. "What do you mean you deeded me part of your ranch?" His face looked like that of an avenging angel. "Do you think I want to be beholden to you for the rest of my life?" He shook her again and then pushed her from him. She stumbled back, caught her balance, and stood resolutely braced against the storm of his temper. Her own flared as it caught fire from the unreasonableness of the man.

"Oh," she snarled at him. "So it's all right for us to be obligated to you for all eternity, but not for you to accept a gesture of appreciation from those whose lives you saved. What's the matter, Captain? Was it too easy to save us? All three times that you saved my son and me? That last time, wasn't the fire hot enough?"

She advanced on him, driving him back a step now. "Or is it just that we aren't worth a few hundred acres and an old abandoned dwelling?

"What about the others? The Grishams and Cavenaugh and the others. What about all those lives? Aren't they worth a little land to you? Does it make it better if I throw them in, too?"

His face was as hard as iron. "That's not the point. You're twisting things."

"No. You're the thing that's twisted. All you can see is the house and the land, and the fear that there might be strings attached to what is merely a simple gesture of gratitude. A way to even the intolerable burden of being so damned grateful to you!"

"Is that the problem, Catherine?" She saw he wasn't angry now. He spoke as if she'd hurt him. "Can't you stand to accept from me what I am still able to give: my strength and my courage?" The expression on his face almost killed her. "I haven't anything else to offer."

Her knees dissolved again and tears formed behind her eyes. She dug her nails into her palms and forced herself to answer in the way she knew she must. Her stomach hurt with the effort it cost her not to fling her arms around him and beg his forgiveness for anything she might have done to bring that vulnerable, hurting expression to his dear face.

But Catherine knew what she had to do, and she did it with all the strength her yearning body had. "Oooh. That was clever, Captain Foster!" She watched his face close against her again, and knew she had accomplished what she must, even if it half-killed her to do it. She went courageously on with the job. "You are so stubborn. It is precisely because we did accept those things from you, yes, and more—your caring and your assistance in the little ways, too—like throwing Scout up on the roof when your shoulder pained you to do it. Like getting Jonny up on the box. Like bashing that Indian's head in."

She passed a shaking hand over her eyes and faltered. Dear Lord, how she wanted him to take her in his arms and comfort her. She choked back those tears, too. "Though I don't suppose that was really a little thing."

He growled, wanting to shock her, "Men kill. It's a little thing."

"You don't mean that. You don't. And it certainly wasn't a little thing to the Indian." She reached for his hand, but he snatched it away in a childish gesture. "Oh, blast you, Jonathan. It's a gift. Take it. It's yours. Make a future with it."

He was still as a stone.

She tried another tack. "I took you there the other day hoping you'd like it. To persuade you to like it."

His eyes blazed at that. "So that was what your grand seduction scene was all about. You hoped to persuade me to forget my pride. To maneuver me into accepting your bounty." His face became hard and his lip curled. "Or was it your intention to make me accept the hacienda as payment for services almost rendered—until the bed collapsed?"

She swung her hand with all her might and slapped the sneer from his face. She was so angry that she was gasping for breath. Her seduction scene, indeed! As if he'd been . . .

"How dare you!" she screeched at him, hurt to the point of dying. Furious to the point of doing murder.

The force of her blow had cut his lip and she was savagely glad to see the tiny drop of blood. Then he touched the tip of his tongue to it and desire raced through her and almost undid her.

She was beside herself with anger and took refuge in it. "You swine! How dare you imply such a thing?"

Inside she wept as something so beautiful was ripped from the special place she'd held it enshrined in her heart and thrown into the dust at their feet.

Tears began to course down her cheeks. From the burning center of the hurt he'd done her, she raged at him.

She had no regard for his masculine pride now. If she trampled it—yes, and him with it—flat into the dirt under her boots, it would be a fate far too good for him.

Cold anger flooded through her and brought her to her senses. She marveled that she could speak and make sense again.

So she would speak and make sense and use words like daggers against the man in front of her, to cut the very heart from his body, to cut away at his pride until she could make him accept her gift and his only hope for a future. And so she did, with acid dripping from every word.

"My very foolish, selfish Captain Foster," she blazed at him breathlessly. "If you had a single coherent thought in your head, and the slightest care for the future of your sisters, ya would take my gift and thank God you had it.

"But no, you can only think of your false and foolish pride, and how it feels to accept something of any value from a mere woman.

"Well, permit me to enlighten you, Jonathan Foster. What I have given you is as nothing compared to the gift of friendship"—she was glad she didn't choke on the so very inadequate word for what she felt for him—"that you have just sullied. It's as nothing at all compared to the comfort of the two lovely girls you profess to love but refuse to think of.

"You, Captain, are a fool. You've gone through three years of a war without learning that it isn't things that are important. It's people who are important, Captain. People.

"Things can be replaced, but the people we are fortunate to have to love and to have love us in return are the true treasures in life. Without them, all the land and possessions in the world have absolutely no meaning."

Tears were streaming down her face, but when he reached for her she slapped his hands away. "No! Don't touch me! You are sick and twisted, and you care for no one. Not even yourself. Only for your pride. Your stupid, stubborn pride.

"Well, keep your pride Mr. Rebel Captain Foster. But you take it as far from me and my son as you can get it. Go take it to your hacienda, and you keep it there. I hate you! And I never want to see you again!"

Jonathan stood there by the river long after Catherine Foster had stormed away, long after the moon had gone down and the stars had begun to fade. Then, wearily, he walked back to the main house to get his horse.

CHAPTER
Twenty-two

"OH, JONATHAN, IT'S BEAUTIFUL. SIMPLY BEAUTIFUL." Diana's soft voice held such delight and awe that he put aside his anger at the untenable position Catherine had contrived to place him in by giving him the hacienda and sending for his sisters.

Diana turned a radiant face toward him. "Jon, it's wonderful." Tears filled her luminous blue eyes. "I never thought we'd have a home so lovely ever again."

Jonathan held her while she wept softly against the front of his shirt. Dear Diana, so like his lost Melinda, so soft, so quiet.

Against his will, he found himself thinking of Cathy, involuntarily comparing the fire and fury of her when they stood on the riverbank the night before to the clinging girl in his arms.

Suddenly he found himself grinning. God, that little Yankee of his was something.

And she *was* his.

Life was such, however, that he would never do anything more than admit to himself his love for her. The passion that had swept him away that day in the light-filled bedroom upstairs was something he would guard against carefully from now on.

Never again would he allow to occur an interlude such as the one that had enchanted them with the magic of that never-to-be-forgotten golden afternoon. Knowing that she was his, and his for the taking, still didn't change the fact that he had nothing to offer Catherine Foster, and more importantly, that he was a wanted man.

She was right. The things that she had thrown at him in her anger last night were true. He was prideful. That pride had been all that had sustained him through the loss of most of what he held dear and the terrible months he had spent in the brutal care of one Sergeant Keefer. Like a knight who valued the armor that preserved his life, so he cherished his pride.

"Susan!" Diana shoved herself away from her brother and cried in horror, "Come down from there this instant!"

His reverie shattered, he whirled to see his younger sister standing on the outside of the wrought iron balustrade of the balcony.

"Hey, Jonathan! Gosh! This is a wonderful house. Have you counted all the bedrooms down the other end of this balcony?"

"Susan," he spoke quietly as he moved to stand just under the child, "please climb back over where you belong. We don't know that the railing is safe." He was careful to keep his voice reasonable. He didn't want to frighten her.

"Oh," Susan called gaily down to him, "it's safe. Watch." She hooked the heels of her shoes on the narrow ledge on which she stood, flung herself forward the length of her arms, and holding tight to the railing, shook her body vigorously. "See?"

The iron of the rail sang, Diana gasped faintly, "Susan!" and swayed dizzily, and Jonathan found himself bellowing, "For God's sake stop that and get yourself back on the proper side of that railing before you fall!"

He ran for the stairs that would take him to her. He caught a glimpse of Diana's set white face as he rushed away from her and under the balcony to the hall and its flight of steps upward.

Taking them four at a time, he arrived at the spot where his little sister had hung so perilously over him a minute ago and found it empty.

His heart plummeting, he looked over the rail to find only Diana, pointing off to his left, her other hand over her

mouth as if she were sick from the shock that Susan had
given them both. He ran down the length of the balcony,
glancing into each room until he found her.

His fingers twitching with the desire to do something,
anything, to make this moment sufficiently memorable for
the girl that she would never frighten them so again, he
stood glaring.

Susan turned to face him, smiling and holding out something to him. She said in a soft little voice, "Look, Jonathan.
I have found a doll. Do you think I might have it? All of
mine are gone, you know."

And in that moment he understood what Catherine had
tried to tell him. It was people who counted. Not just
counted, but who were all that mattered.

He let out the breath he had been holding and opened his
arms to her. She moved trustingly into them, and lay her
head against him.

Fiercely hugging her, he said, "Yes, honey. I'm sure it'll
be fine for you to keep the doll."

Standing there, holding Susan in his arms, and gazing
at Diana, where she stood breathless in the doorway, he
knew that he would have to apologize to Catherine Foster
yet again.

Catherine continued to fume every time she saw the
Rebel come in with the other men for orders. There were
four more hands now, thanks to his persuading several of
the local Confederates to ride for her to earn money to
pay their taxes. Even in the larger group, though, try as
she might, she couldn't ignore him.

It was even harder for her at lunchtime when he rode
up to the bunkhouse to chat a few minutes with the men
working there.

Sometimes he came to return Creole to his lean-to to
rest while he rode a fresh horse to finish whatever task he
was doing out on the range that had worn them both out.
Then he'd rest a few minutes, leaning against some part of
whichever building the men were working on.

Today there had been laughter before he had left the

group, and she found herself resenting the fact that he could laugh when she was so thoroughly miserable. She spoke sharply to herself: "Obviously, Catherine, you need to find something to keep you busy. We can't have you turning into such a nasty person. How could you resent the fact that someone's happy? Especially," she said before she thought, "someone you . . ." She wouldn't finish her sentence.

She went in search of her son. She'd take him on a picnic. It was a couple of hours before lunchtime, and they could really explore for a picnic site.

She hadn't made an adventure for him for some time. They had been so exhausted when they first arrived, and seemed to be too busy, or too much in crisis, for her to have thought to do so since.

Walking quickly into the kitchen, she put her plan into action. Her cook was busy preparing one of those desserts her Jonny thought so much of.

"Ellen, I wonder if you would mind packing a picnic for Jonny and me? I think this is a lovely day for one, don't you?"

"What a nice idea, Miss Catherine. I bet he'll love it." Ellen beamed at her over the piecrust she was rolling out on a flour-covered spot on the big table. "Say. Why don't I pack a lot of food, and you could have your picnic with those nice girls out at the old place." She stopped and waved the rolling pin at Catherine. "I bet they haven't had time to stock up. I bet it would come in mighty welcome to see you arrive with a basket full of good food."

She made a disgusted face to Catherine, and fanned at the fine cloud of flour that her wave of the rolling pin had dispersed into the air between them. "You know darn well they don't have any good vittles. Men, even gentlemen like Captain Foster, don't have sense enough to think of those things."

She put her hands on her hips, marking her dark dress behind her apron with flour, the forgotten rolling pin in one hand. "In fact, I guess I'd say men like him would be the worst at thinking of such things, him not ever having to have thought about it." She scowled, "And not having his mind on his belly all the time, like some I could name," she finished darkly.

Catherine smiled to herself. She had no doubt that the cook was talking about the ranch foreman. Ellen had taken an instant disliking to the man years ago and hadn't seen a reason to change her mind since.

"All right, Ellen. You get the basket ready, and I'll go see if I can locate a pack mule big enough to carry it."

"Oh, go on now, Miss Catherine. I don't intend to give 'em every bite of food in the house." She cocked her head, thinking. "But maybe I'd better send a mite. I don't know how them girls are going to go shopping when they haven't even horses to ride, much less a buckboard." The look she gave Catherine was full of meaning.

"All right," Catherine chuckled at her old friend. "I get the hint. I'll offer them the use of the buckboard when I take them their lunch." She gave Ellen a quick hug and turned to go. "Better get busy. With a pack mule, it'll take me the better part of an hour to get there."

"Aw, Miss Catherine. You can be the worst tease." Ellen shook her head and went back to rolling her piecrust thin, planning the picnic lunch she'd pack.

Catherine left the big, sunny kitchen smiling. She felt a lot better. Ellen had given her something worthwhile to do, and just like working to keep away the dismals, it had lifted her spirits.

Now all she had to do was to find Jonny and choose two horses they could ride who would tolerate the huge baskets she was sure they would both be carrying.

Half an hour later, Catherine had saddled both her horse and Jonny's and they rode together to the back door of the big house to pick up the picnic. True to Catherine's guess, they each had two baskets to manage. Those Ellen gave Jonny to hang from his saddle horn were only a little smaller than those she tied together and slung across Catherine's saddle.

The horses looked at their burdens with some interest, but Catherine had chosen them well, and they stood quietly.

Catherine thanked Ellen, and Jonny and she left the yard at a walk, giving their mounts time to get used to the huge, scratchy lumps that bumped on their shoulders.

"Golly, this is going to be fun, Mama. I like Susan. She's not at all bad, for a girl."

Catherine was surprised into a wide grin. Not bad for a girl, indeed! Susan had looked like quite a lively handful to her.

No doubt it would be good for Jonny to have a playmate. When the clouds of her most recent quarrel with the Southerner cleared, perhaps the two children could see each other regularly.

Jonathan spotted them while they were still a good ways off. "Diana! You have guests."

Diana came running to his side at the gate of the spacious patio. Her lightly shod feet merely whispered over the tiles. Susan, hair flying behind her, came dashing after her.

"Who is it?" They spoke in unison, but were too interested in who was coming to realize it.

"Looks like Miz Foster."

Diana glanced up at him, "Oh." Her face was full of distress. "That must be very hard for you to say, dear." She laid a sympathetic hand on his arm.

"Sometimes," he answered laconically.

They watched Catherine and Jonny slow their horses to a walk to avoid bringing a dust cloud with them, then their company arrived at the gate in the tall adobe wall.

Jonathan was busy holding baskets while they dismounted, and looking thunderously at Catherine for this latest evidence of her penchant for playing lady bountiful.

Catherine gave him a withering glance, turned pointedly away from him, and said to the elder of his sisters, "My cook thought that a bachelor's home might not be very well supplied. She was worried about you having something more than canned beans to eat."

Diana smiled graciously at Catherine, thanking her sweetly for her thoughtfulness and asking her to be sure to convey her thanks to the cook as well. Susan capering around them, Diana led Catherine and Jonny into the hacienda.

Jonathan scowled after them as he saw to the horses. His eyes lingered possessively on Catherine. When they were out of sight, he led the horses toward the low adobe stable in back of the hacienda. Might as well make the horses comfortable. It looked as if she had come to stay a while. Besides, stabling them would also make it tough for Catherine to rage away from him again.

"Can I help?" Jonny skidded to a stop beside Jonathan. He had run to catch up after he said his obligatory hellos to Diana and Susan.

"Sure."

"I've never been here before. It's neat." He looked around the adobe buildings. "It's in a square like our place."

"Yes."

"I guess that's because my great-grandfather grew up here. I guess he just copied the square over to the new place. Do you think maybe it works best, or something?"

"Your great-granddaddy must have thought so."

"Then I guess it does, huh?"

"I guess it does." He affirmed his comment with a nod, handed the boy the horses' bridles, and pointed to the hooks to hang them on.

Jonny went to his task eagerly. "Gosh, look at how fancy these are. Golly." He hung the bridles from their crown pieces and looped up the reins.

Jonathan gave the little iron horse heads a glance as he heaved the saddles onto racks and spread their blankets to dry. "They are interesting, Button. Thanks for showing me."

"You mean you never seen 'em before?" He looked at Jonathan suspiciously.

Jonathan stopped and returned his look. "Sometimes grown-ups just get so busy flying around trying to get it all done that they don't take time really to look at things. Like I said, thanks for showing me." He smiled down at the handsome little boy.

An awful sensation of loss assailed him as he remembered his own son. Trip would have been this age.

He fought down the emptiness and smiled at the lad, "Shall we go up to the house, Button?"

"Aw, do we have to?"

Jonathan just laughed and steered him in the right direction.

When they got to the house, it was clear they hadn't been missed and that Catherine had been busy. Jonathan fought to keep his face from betraying his annoyance when his sisters regaled him with Catherine's string of thoughtful offers.

"Catherine has invited us to use her buckboard to go into town tomorrow for supplies, Jonathan. Isn't that thoughtful?"

"Very." His eyes threatened to burn a hole in Catherine, but she refused to meet them.

"She's gonna give us horses to ride, too! Isn't that wonderful?" Susan jumped up off the window ledge on which she sat and ran over to him. "Do you think I can learn to ride western style?"

"I shouldn't wonder." Nobody but Catherine noticed his lack of enthusiasm. He saw by the straight line her lovely back made against the light from the window behind her that she was aware of his disapproval of her plans for his family.

They all settled carefully on the tile floor for their picnic. Ellen had outdone herself; there was enough food for an army.

Studiously, Catherine avoided looking at Jonathan. "You know, Diana, I think a lot of the furniture for this house is stored in the attics at the new house. Why don't you come and take what you want? No one will ever use it unless you do. It's all furniture that was made for the hacienda. It didn't look right once it was in the new house—just as grandmother had known it wouldn't't." She fluttered a quick glance in Jonathan's direction. "So grandfather sent East for what's in the house now, and put the hacienda furniture in storage."

Diana's pride warred with the long months she'd done without, thanks to the war back home. Furniture for the hacienda would mean she could serve her new friend lunch on a table the next time she came, instead of on a blanket on the hard tile floor, picnic or not.

More furniture would mean, too, that her beloved brother wouldn't have to sleep on the floor so that she and Susan could have his big, cupid-decorated bed. It took only an instant for her woman's practicality to win over her family pride.

With a wide smile she accepted Catherine's offer. "You are most gracious. And of course I hope you will help me to choose and to place things." Her smile became diffident. "Spanish haciendas are a little out of my experience."

Catherine hesitated only a moment. To acquiesce meant that she might run into Jonathan more than she was ready to, but she had prayed for something to do to keep her busy, and this would be fun. "I'd love to."

Jonathan left them as soon as he could wolf down enough lunch to pass for having eaten and went back to his current task of putting the hacienda stables to rights. Jonny and Susan tagged along, having eaten as quickly as he in their eagerness to play.

They bickered for the better part of an hour about what a boy could do that a girl could not. After listening to them all that time, Jonathan was considerably relieved when Catherine, accompanied by a smiling Diana, finally came to collect Jonny for their return home. Seeing the women approach, he said, "Better get the bridles, Button."

Jonny raced for them while Jonathan lifted the saddles off the racks and started for the stalls that held the horses. Jonathan halted in mid-stride when he heard Diana call, "Wait. Please wait to tack them up. I must see how it's done! Catherine is lending me a horse to ride."

Jonathan bit down a caustic remark about charity from strangers. How could he ruin his sister's pleasure in her newfound friend? Instead he said ungraciously, "Then you'd better learn to ride bareback."

Catherine spoke without thinking, "But I'll lend you the tack, too," and wished she'd bitten her tongue. She saw Jonathan's face flush and knew that he'd taken her offer as another proof of what he could no longer do for his family.

She wanted to sigh aloud. Her heart actually ached: she could feel it. Would things never come right between them?

"You'd better learn to ride bareback because you'll never lift one of these as high as a horse's back." He hefted Catherine's saddle with one hand, lifting it up for Diana to really see. "And we haven't servants to do it for you."

Diana's eyes flew wide at the cold acid in his voice. Then she looked from him to Catherine and back again. Wisely she didn't say a word.

Catherine jumped into the breech with her teeth clenched and her eyes narrowed. "Never mind, Diana. I'll teach you. After all"—she shot a venomous glance at Jonathan— "though your brother may not realize it, I'm a woman, too."

Jonathan whirled to look at her. "Now, what the devil is that supposed to mean?" She knew damned well he was aware—painfully aware—that she was a woman, and there was not a chance in hell he'd ever lose sight of the fact, either. What the blazes was she nattering about?

Diana's voice brought him back to himself, "Jonathan," she said sharply. "You cannot speak to a lady like that."

He saw that his sister, still trailing the soft trappings of Southern womanhood about her like invisible veils, had no idea how he could speak so to this woman whose mere presence was torment to him. This woman was a steel-spring combination of Yankee directness and Western freedom. Diana hadn't been here long enough to realize the difference. Hell. Diana might never understand the difference!

He muttered an abrupt, unrepentant apology and turned back to his task of readying the horses, then gathered their reins and led them out into the stable yard without a backward glance.

Let his sister lecture him about his manners until nightfall. Just now he was going to concentrate on getting the thorn in his side up on her horse and out of here.

CHAPTER
Twenty-three

CATHERINE THANKED THE NEW COWHAND THAT HAD hitched up the buckboard and tacked up the two horses she had chosen for the Foster girls. She was sorry she didn't know his name yet, but he was so stiff with her she was afraid to ask. His sympathies were Confederate, of course. He wouldn't be working for them at all, nor would all the others, if it hadn't been for Jonathan.

The young man secured the reins of the two horses to the back of the buckboard. He stayed back there and watched her get herself ably up on the seat with an expression of relief.

Catherine thought sourly, *There's one more Rebel that doesn't want to touch me. There's getting to be quite a crowd.*

She picked up the driving reins from where they were twisted around the handle of the brake, lifted them to signal to the team to start, and bowled out of the yard and off toward the hacienda at a pace that rattled the buckboard.

Half an hour later, she was waving hello to an excited Susan, who'd seen her coming and was running as fast as she could down the road to meet her. "Hey, where's your boy?" Grinning widely, she trotted along beside the buckboard.

Catherine pulled in the team. "Come on up, you'll wear yourself out."

Susan scrambled up. "Diana would have said I'd get all dirty. Where's Jonny?"

"Home. He knows we'll go back by there on the way to town. I'm sure he'll join us then."

Suddenly her spirits sank. That was true. She would have to drive back past the house to get to town. That meant that every time Jonathan had to go to town, he'd pass her house. That might not be too comfortable if things didn't improve between them.

Very well, she'd just have to try to see to it that things did improve between them.

"Are those the horses you're lending us?" Susan asked very shyly, almost as if she were afraid she were being rude.

"Yes. I chose them for you myself. The skewbald is pretty well matched to Jonny's pony." She smiled impishly, and turned to look straight at Susan. "Maybe just a little faster."

Susan's eyes lit up with that piece of information, but she only said, "Skewbald." The child considered it, then giggled. "What a funny word."

Catherine's smile widened, remembering when she'd first heard the word. "Isn't it? Means brown and white. Piebald's black and white. Jonny's pony's a piebald."

Susan absorbed that without a comment, then asked, "What's the other horse like?"

"Ah. The sorrel's a bit of a handful," she looked to where the mare switched her tail in irritation at being tied behind the buckboard, "but your brother said Diana is a good rider, so I chose Firefly for her. She's a feisty little mare, but she hasn't anything sneaky about her."

"She's very pretty," Susan told her.

"Yes, she is. Besides, with that mane, she just had to be Diana's, didn't she?"

Susan giggled, "Yes. Firefly's as blond as we are. She'll fit right in."

Catherine realized that she liked this child very much, and was glad. She had never given a great deal of latitude to people merely because they were shorter than she. She demanded the same courtesy from children as from adults.

She eased the brake on and called, "Whoa!" They had arrived.

Diana was waiting at the gate. Her excitement at the prospect of going into town glowed in her eyes.

Behind her, Jonathan stood quietly. Catherine caught his eye and saw that he was still annoyed by her telling him to escort them into town today. She had deliberately waited until she was mounted and riding off to give him the order.

She wondered if she had thought he would have refused if she had asked him to drive them. Or had she, deep in her heart of hearts, feared he would refuse to go even in response to a direct order from his employer if she hadn't ridden off without giving him the chance?

She hadn't risked it. Was that because she feared she might not have these few hours with him? She clenched her teeth. Loving this man was so much more tumultuous than loving her husband had been.

Looking him straight in the eye, she said coolly, "I brought your sisters' horses so they'd have them to ride first thing tomorrow." When he didn't say anything, she added, "I can drive the buckboard, if you'd rather ride." She turned to look at Diana. "I hope you'll ride with me so we can get to know one another better." But her attention was still on Jonathan, and her skin tingled under his gaze.

"I'd love to." Diana came to the side of the buckboard and looked helplessly at her brother. He stepped forward immediately and swung her up beside Catherine. "Thank you, dear."

Jonathan nodded and said, "I'm sure Miz Foster could have just pulled you up, but I'm glad to have been of service."

Silent laughter exploded through Catherine. He was annoyed that she had driven herself and brought two horses without masculine aid. Well, at least his annoyance was better than his cold indifference.

She was glad that she had gotten his goat. What was it her grandfather had always said? If someone gets your goat, it shows you that you have a goat.

She smiled almost fondly at Jonathan. She saw from the look that he sent back at her that she certainly had gotten his goat.

He popped a squealing Susan effortlessly over the side of the buckboard and onto the the blanket-covered bale of hay that Catherine had put in the back to give the children a place to sit. Susan bounced about getting settled, and the sweet smell of hay wafted over them.

Moving to the back of the vehicle, Jonathan untied the horses and led them away to the stable. Catherine and Diana were chatting amiably by the time he had settled the horses and returned.

As his long strides ate up the distance between the corner of the house and the buckboard, he kept his eyes locked on Catherine Foster. His Cathy was earnestly trying to draw Diana out, trying to make her feel welcome.

He decided he would drive them, after all. He put a boot on the hub of the wheel next to the brake. "Slide over, Miz Foster."

Catherine started. She'd been so interested in what his soft-voiced sister was telling her that she hadn't heard him approach. Reluctantly she made room for him, wondering why she was hesitant about it.

Perhaps she didn't like the idea of riding all the way to town in such proximity to him. Obviously, she thought, registering the way her breath had shortened when his arm brushed and remained against hers, she was too affected by his touch. She promised herself that she would see to it that Diana sat in the middle coming back.

The town was as dusty as the ranch, but there was enough of a bustle to make Diana look around with a great deal of interest.

"Let's go to Marston's first," Cathy suggested.

Jonathan chose to interpret this as an order and guided the team in the direction of the general store with a curt, "Yes, ma'am."

Catherine didn't find his attitude amusing anymore, but his attempt to sound short with his soft manner of speech made the corners of her mouth turn up slightly.

She ignored him—or pretended to—and said to Diana, "I thought you'd like to shop while you're fresh. We can pick up the grain later." She noticed that Jonathan was pulling his hat lower, and followed his gaze to a pair of soldiers from the fort that were just mounting up and riding out. She was puzzled.

Just then, Jonny shot up off the bale of hay and vaulted over the side of the buckboard into the street. She opened her mouth to reprimand him, but Jonathan spoke first. "Button! Don't ever do that again."

The boy began to turn red and Jonathan went on. "Think of the example you set for Susan. While you'd be careful to see there was no danger, she might not."

He ignored his sister's outraged protest. He wanted to preserve Jonny's fragile pride. He wasn't the least bit worried about Susan's.

Jumping lightly down, he walked to the head of the team and tethered the near horse to the hitching rail. Smoothing a hand down its sleek hide, he walked to the wheel and stood waiting for Diana to get her skirts in order. She reached for his shoulders and he lifted her down.

Catherine used the time to decide whether she'd follow Jonny's example and get down on the street side, thus avoiding contact with Jonathan, or whether she'd let him lift her down, just to see his discomfort at having to do so.

Today was a day for imps with Catherine. Careful to keep her expression demure, she moved to the end of the box and reached her hands out to Jonathan.

His eyes were shooting sparks. She wondered if he could read her mind. An instant later, she wasn't wondering anything. Her thoughts all went flying as Jonathan reached up and seized her in his arms. Swinging her free from the buckboard, he held her like a child in his embrace, hard against his chest.

The look he gave her sizzled. She could feel the pounding of his heart against the arm trapped between their bodies, and when he let her legs down and slid her tantalizingly down his lean length, she thought she'd swoon.

As from a distance, she heard him ask in a casual voice, "How's that, Miz Foster?" and she was glad that only she could detect the mockery in his tone.

With a superhuman effort, she kept herself from smoothing her hair and skirts. She knew she only felt disheveled by the strength of feeling his action had engendered in her, and refused to react, at least so he could see.

The mockery in his blue eyes took on a hint of admiration.

Catherine fumed, but her voice was completely cool and impersonal as she murmured, "Thank you, Captain," as if he didn't matter any more to her than some faithful servant.

She moved forward and tucked her arm through Diana's. Together they went into the store, the children impatiently following at their heels.

Glancing back over her shoulder, she saw with satisfaction that Jonathan looked absolutely sullen—and smoldering. Her heart fluttered.

She was torn: One part of her yearned longingly to take him in her arms and comfort him, and the other part wanted to gloat. She remembered how distant he'd been since the night they had quarreled—since that magical day that they had shared exploring the hacienda, in fact—and she decided to leave him uncomforted for a while longer.

Then the thought came that perhaps he would refuse any offer she might make to close the chasm between them. The spring went out of her step.

Diana felt her lag and stopped. "What did you find?"

"Oh! Uh," Catherine focused quickly on the table they were passing. "Sunbonnets. Here they are, and you and Susan should probably have them because our sun is much stronger than the sun back East."

"What a good idea. At least for Susan." She gave Catherine a mischievous smile. "I prefer hats. The sillier the better."

Catherine smiled back. "I like these." She reached a hand behind her and touched her wide-brimmed man's hat where it hung from its *barbaguejo*.

Diana looked thoughtfully at Catherine's hat, pulled it back up to the position in which Catherine wore it, and her gaze became speculative. "Hmmmm, yes. The contrast definitely does something."

Catherine laughed, "Yes, it keeps more sun out of my eyes than a lady's hat would. Come on, you have to shop." She brushed her hat back off her head.

She moved to the counter. "Mr. Marston, please put this lady's purchases on the Three Rivers account."

"That won't be necessary." Jonathan's hard voice was immediately behind her.

She had offended him again. It made her angry that it was so easily done, and she whipped around to face him. "It's just a convenience for Diana. We can settle later."

She could hear his teeth grate. "I'll take care of my own debts, thank you, Mrs. Foster."

He must really be angry to manage not to say Miz, her mind registered. She wanted to sting him. "I can always take it out of your wages," she said carefully, her stomach in a knot.

He whirled away from her and the high heels of his western boots slammed the floor with each step that took him to the door. "I'm going to get a haircut. I'll be back for you."

The door closed behind him firmly, and Catherine was left feeling bereft. Why had she done that? What made her want to claw at him all the time now? She had certainly never had such feelings ever before.

Diana held something up for her to give an opinion on, and she turned her attention, as well as she could, back to her new friend.

Jonathan returned, his hair neatly trimmed to just touch his collar, before they had finished the last of Diana's list. They rushed through to the end of it. "Linens, next," Diana's soft voice read.

"No," Catherine's voice was firm. "There are too many at Three Rivers. Ellen told me just the other day that she and Consuelo found it hard to keep most of them from yellowing with disuse. We have linens."

Diana nodded, as if Catherine were family and she could casually accept the use of her household goods. Jonathan felt his jaws lock.

"I'll wait for you outside," he ground out and left them again.

The two women hurried to find and check off the last item. They thanked the owner of the store and left him staring after Diana as if he'd never been dazzled before.

Outside, Jonathan helped them both up into the buckboard. Catherine first, *as if he were doing age before beauty,* she snapped to herself.

He looked at neither, unsure with which one of them he was most upset.

Untethering the team, he climbed easily up to the buckboard's seat, took up the reins, and waited for the children to jump themselves up onto the tailgate. Without comment, he drove around the corner to the feed store.

"I'll be right out." It irked him that the women were so deeply interested in their shopping that they hardly noticed he was gone. It salved his raw feelings a little when both children decided to follow him.

Left in peace, Catherine told Diana. "Ellen's soap is much nicer. You'll be pleased that you didn't buy that." She chuckled. "And we're still working on her supply from two years ago, so you needn't worry about disfurnishing us. When Ellen makes soap, Ellen makes soap!"

Their merry laughter caused three men on the corner to look their way.

"There's plenty of French soap for your and Susan's face, as well. Though I honestly think Ellen's attempt to duplicate it worked pretty well, and I'll give you some of that, too. I'd like your opinion."

A rough voice interrupted. "Well, now, what are two pretty ladies like you doing out here alone on the street?"

Catherine stiffened and kept her eyes carefully on Diana's. Thankfully, the girl didn't shift her gaze, either. True to her upbringing, she ignored the men who stood just beside the buckboard.

"Wha'sa matter, girlies? Think you're too good to talk to us?" The second voice was no better than the first.

Still, Catherine kept her back turned toward them. Diana's lips parted, but she kept her gaze riveted to her friend's. Catherine saw fright in Diana's eyes and looked beyond her into the gloom of the cavernous feed store. There was no one in sight, not even the children.

A hand appeared at the corner of her field of vision, and she was snatched roughly around to face the three men. "Hey, girly. We're talking to you." The man stood on the hub of the wheel and leaned toward them.

Diana's voice rose sharp and clear. There was no trace of its habitual softness. "But you shouldn't be, you know. We have never been introduced, and it is exceedingly improper of you to attempt to engage us in conversation."

Diana hardly knew what she was saying. She was only sure she had to try something to get the man's filthy paw off Catherine's arm.

Her gaze went frantically to the street from which they'd come. A lone rider on a too-thin horse glanced their way.

"Well, now. Ain't she the one." The men laughed coarsely. The other two pressed nearer the man who clutched at Catherine.

Fear for her friend stirred in Diana. "My brother will be back at any moment. Please let her go."

Catherine tried not to glare at the men. They were not the sort of men one provoked. She said calmly, "We don't want any trouble."

The man kept his grip.

"Let go, please." Catherine's voice was quiet but firm.

The man looked at her curiously. "You ain't skeered."

A new voice spoke. "Was that your intention? To frighten ladies?"

The scorn in the man's tone was like a whiplash to the bully holding onto Catherine. With a growl, he released her and spun around to face the lone man on the skinny horse.

The man leaned an arm on the high pommel of his McClelland saddle and looked mildly down on them. "I think it would be nice if you left the ladies alone."

The three hoodlums erupted into profanity and started for him.

Diana grabbed Catherine in a desperate embrace and started screaming for her brother at the top of her lungs. "Jonathan! Jonathan! Help!"

The thugs pulled their rescuer from his horse and started swinging at him. The sound of fists hitting solid flesh sickened Catherine, and she cringed against Diana.

The thin man was no match for them, but he fought them bravely and with skill. The three attackers kept getting in each other's way as they jostled one another for a chance to hit the stranger. As a result, he was inflicting almost as much damage as he was taking.

It was clear to the two women watching that the stranger wasn't fit, and his strength was beginning to fail when Jonathan hurtled out of the feed barn and threw himself into the fray.

The biggest two turned on him. A blood-curdling screech that sounded like it came from the bowels of the earth rent the air. It bounced off the walls of nearby buildings and curdled Catherine's blood.

Instantly, it was echoed by the man who'd come to their aid. The addition of a second voice made it sound as if they were surrounded by the fiends of hell.

Catherine clutched at Diana, and was amazed to see calm exultation on her face. Her attention left the fight momentarily as she gasped, "What was that!"

"Catherine, honey, that was a Rebel yell!" Diana informed her, cheeks flushed and eyes flashing with the light of battle. "Get him, Jonathan!" she yelled into the melee.

Catherine blinked and turned back to the fight in a daze. She sought and found Jonathan, and was shocked again, this time by the expression on his face.

Teeth drawn back in a smiling snarl and narrowed eyes alight, he was obviously enjoying alternately pounding the two men in front of him. One fell quickly after a shattering blow to the jaw, and he made short work of the other.

Immediately, he turned to help the stranger, whose meager strength had failed. Ripping his assailant back off him, he sent the man to the ground with a single well-aimed blow.

The stranger grinned at him and wiped the back of his hand across his bloody mouth. "Thanks." He sagged back against his scarecrow of a horse. Humor lit his eyes, "I guess I'm not as tough as I used to be."

Diana, not in the least in need of any assistance when the men were busy elsewhere, jumped lightly down from the buckboard and flew to the man's side. "It is we who should thank you for your timely intervention. Catherine and I were frightened to death! And there was no one to rescue us, for my brother was far out of earshot." She kept her eyes modestly downcast, her voice sweet and breathless. "Now you just let me take care of your wounds." She brushed his hand aside and dabbed at his split lip with her pristine little handkerchief. "I'm Miss Diana Foster." Her huge blue eyes flashed to his face, and then were demurely veiled by long golden lashes as she waited in breathless anticipation to hear his name.

From her place on the seat of the buckboard, Catherine watched, fascinated. She'd heard of Southern belles and their wiles, but never before had she seen a champion in action. She was more than a little impressed.

The man took her tiny hand in his and said, "Now don't you go soiling your dainty little hand with my unworthy blood, Miss Diana."

Dear heart! Catherine found she was in the presence of two champions, for there was no missing the man's soft Southern drawl, nor the light in his eyes as he skillfully joined in the game. She could feel her eyebrows rising of their own accord.

Jonathan, however, was used to scenes like the one before him. He stuck out a hand and offered, "Jonathan Foster."

The man straightened with an effort, "Taylor Ashworth, sir."

Jonathan frowned. "Any kin to Stuart Ashworth?"

"My cousin on my daddy's side."

"And a good friend of mine at the Point."

Catherine sat through the glad recognition and the exchange of news. She watched Diana totally captivate the man without another word, and wished the seats of the buckboard were padded.

In the end, Taylor Ashworth was forced to accept the Fosters' hospitality. Jonathan tied Taylor's exhausted horse to the back of the buckboard and asked the children to shift their seats to the bags of feed that Jonathan finally got loaded.

That left the blanketed bale of hay for Diana to invite the stranger to join her on. She did so with the grace of a queen offering to share her throne.

Jonathan took the reins back from Catherine with an easy smile. She was dumbfounded. Was a good fistfight all it took to restore a man to a reasonable mood?

Heaven knew she would never really understand him, but she found that she was grateful, nonetheless, to find herself back on amiable terms with Jonathan once more.

CHAPTER

Twenty-four

CATHERINE COULDN'T GET JONATHAN FOSTER AND HIS mercurial moods out of her mind. All morning she had been thinking of him, trying to figure him out.

Finally, the senator had managed to drive him from her mind. He told her that the foreman had issued him an invitation, and she was strangely disquieted about the senator riding out with Kirby Morris to look over the herd. It was silly, she knew, but she couldn't shake her uneasy feeling.

"Clayton, why in the world do you want to ride out there in all that dust and grit to look at a bunch of cows? You hardly know which end the hay goes in." She could hear the edge on her own voice.

"Now, little lady," Morris broke in, "I'm sure the senator knows a great many things that could benefit our operation." He turned his ingratiating smile on the senator. "Any help would be appreciated, sir."

Catherine fought a tide of annoyance. After all, the senator knew next to nothing about cattle, and Kirby Morris's attempts to defer to him might do no more than bring a twinkle to her father-in-law's eye, but it made her suspect that the man had an ulterior motive.

"I really wish you wouldn't waste your time, Clayton. You know you don't ride much now. You'll just be uncomfortable later."

Her father-in-law grinned at her. He was well aware that he didn't have a thing to contribute to Morris's knowledge of cattle ranching, but he was curious to discover why the man was going to such lengths to flatter him, and he was determined to go.

Catherine saw his determination and gave up.

She walked out to the horses with them. "Be careful, Clayton."

Jonny came running up to wave good-bye as the two men mounted. "See you at dinner!"

Catherine ruffled his hair. "You always have your mind on food these days, don't you?"

He smiled up at her. "Chasing around with Susan is hungry work, Mama."

With their arms around each other, they went back into the house. There was a fond smile on Catherine's face, but in her heart, there was a sense of foreboding.

Jonathan let Creole have his head, and after two days of rest while Jonathan settled his sisters, the big gelding ate up the miles from the hacienda to the part of the ranch where the herd had been gathered for tallying. They crested a hill, and there it was spread out before him: a great, moving mass of brown hides and white faces filling the range almost as far as the hills a mile away.

"Whoa, boy." They stopped and just watched. Jonathan whistled. "You don't see a sight like that very often, Creole. Pretty impressive, isn't it?" The horse flicked an attentive ear back at him.

As he watched, two men rode into his line of vision. One was the heavyset foreman he disliked, but who was the slender man with him?

"That's the senator!" Surprised, he spoke aloud. "I didn't even know the old boy rode anymore, Creole."

He looked around for Carlos or Juan, or any of the men he'd hired for the Fosters, but they weren't in sight. As he scanned, however, a movement in a draw to the east of him caught his attention. Narrowing his eyes against the sunlight, he peered closer.

There were three men there, bandannas over the lower part of their faces as if to protect them from breathing dust. But Jonathan saw they weren't working cattle and there wasn't any dust where they were.

He threw a glance at the spot where he had seen the senator and found him crossing the herd with Morris. Seeing the man there made him uneasy. In the time he had been on the ranch, he had learned better than to cut across a herd that way, even if it took a while to ride around it.

Looking back at the men in the draw, he saw them moving forward and spreading out on his right. Before he could guess what they were up to, they had drawn their guns and, whooping and firing into the air, had begun spooking the cattle toward where Morris and the senator were riding.

Vividly, Catherine's terror of stampede rushed into his mind. Then his mind filled with his own terror, as he saw Morris push the senator from his horse and wheel away leading it, leaving Clayton afoot in front of a herd on the verge of stampede.

Spurring Creole, Jonathan aimed the big horse at the spot where the senator had gone down. Morris hadn't seen him and was heading his way almost nonchalantly with both horses.

Snarling with rage, Jonathan charged down on him. Expertly, he rode Creole into the horse Morris was riding.

With grim satisfaction, he swung his arm down as if he had his cavalry saber again, and he knocked the beefy man from his saddle an instant before the startled foreman completed the act of bringing his gun to bear on Jonathan's chest. Morris's horse squealed and went bucking away.

Jonathan caught up the senator's mount and tore off in Clayton's direction. He could just make him out through the dust made by the milling cattle. Any minute now they'd break and stampede. Those where Morris was down were already circling around on the edge of panic.

He stood in his stirrups and looked back to where he'd seen the men who had tried to start the stampede. They had turned tail and were running off in a tight pack. Kellerman's crew, he'd bet.

He slid the horses to a stop beside Clayton. "Hurry! Mount up!" He held the dancing horses in an iron grip while they jittered and plunged, watching with rolling eyes the points of the horns tossing so near them.

Clayton yelled at him over the bawling of the steers, "You don't have to invite me twice, son." He scrambled aboard his horse with no regard for form or dignity, and they were off, the horses running flat out for safer ground.

There was a cry over to the left of them as they rushed to safety, but Jonathan let Morris take the chance he'd given the senator. If the man made it safely out of the herd, he would be in trouble for attempted murder, anyway. Maybe he would even hang for the murder of Catherine's grandfather's foreman, Charley Watts.

They pulled up on the hill where Jonathan had paused just minutes before. He looked at the white-faced senator. Clayton pressed a hand to his chest. Then Jonathan saw him extract a small paper envelope from the watch pocket of his vest, take a pinch of powder from it, and wash it down with water from his canteen.

Presently the gray left his face and his color returned. Jonathan didn't have to be told the senator had a heart problem. He looked off into the hills to give the old gentleman time to compose himself, and his own heart sank. Unwelcome, the thought came: Without the senator, Cathy would be all alone.

Finally, he asked, "What was that all about?"

"Damn it, boy. Give a man time to express his gratitude before you start bullying him for explanations." The senator scowled at his rescuer, said, "Thanks," and told him, "That lousy skunk said, 'Maybe Kellerman can get that bitch off this spread without you around,' and then he sent me flying."

"I guess that makes it clear enough." Jonathan's face was grim as he looked in the direction of the Kellerman ranch.

"We can't prove a thing unless we have Morris and he talks," the senator said mildly. He sat looking blandly at his companion.

Jonathan looked back at him levelly. Then he cursed and turned his horse back toward the herd. It had settled down a lot since Kellerman's men had stopped harassing it, but the steers around the spot where Morris had fallen were still dangerously restless.

With a disgusted sigh, Jonathan headed Creole down the hill to that spot.

Her continued uneasiness forced Catherine out on the porch just before lunch. She found herself staring off in the direction of the huge dust cloud that hung low in the sky and marked the location of her herd.

Jonny came out on the porch. "You looking for Grandpa?"

"Yes, dear, I suppose I am."

"Me, too. I wish he hadn't gone off with that Morris. I don't trust him."

Catherine couldn't think what she should say to her son, so she didn't say anything. She just stood there, taking comfort from his presence.

When Jonathan and Clayton came over the hill, Jonny let out a whooped, "Grandpa!" and ran to meet them. Morris was being led behind them on his horse. He looked a bit the worse for wear.

Catherine had all she could do to keep from running to meet them, herself. When they got near enough, she could see that Morris was quite battered, and she could hear the steady stream of curses he was muttering.

"Shut up, Morris. Don't make me sorry I went back for you," Jonathan snarled.

Morris stopped cursing, but Catherine hardly noticed. She had eyes only for the long gash in Jonathan's forearm. "You're hurt!" There was blood all over his left forearm and hand, and down the side of his horse. For an instant, she wondered if she'd faint.

Jonathan didn't issue any denial, and she hurried to his side to inspect the wound more closely. "A horn did this, didn't it?"

He nodded, the grimness leaving his face as he looked down at her.

"Come into the house and let me clean that good and get a bandage on it." She tugged at his knee, urging him to dismount. She had to wait as he drew his revolver out of its holster and tossed it to the senator. "I'd feel better if you had my gun to take care of that snake if you need to."

"Thanks." Clayton caught the gun deftly and gestured for Morris to get down.

Catherine got insistent. "Please, Jonathan, come now. Terrible things can happen from wounds made by cows."

Jonathan went with her into the house, catching the drip of his blood in his good hand to save her carpets. They headed for the kitchen. Catherine hurried him along. "I want to pump water over that for a few minutes. We must be absolutely sure the dirt's all out."

She took him to Ellen's well-scrubbed sink, turned back his ripped sleeve, and pushed his arm under the steady stream of water she was pumping. Jonathan stood quietly, inhaling the scent of her and watching how the light from the window broke colors free in the shine of her dark hair.

When she was satisfied that she had all the dirt out of the wound, she asked Ellen, who was watching the proceedings with very wise eyes, to bring her the whisky.

Ellen bustled off to do so, and Jonathan laughed down at Catherine. "Not planning to sew me up, are you?" Catherine's cheeks paled and he was sorry he'd said anything.

"Yes," she said, her lips tight.

Jonathan was doubly sorry he'd brought the subject up.

Ellen arrived with the whiskey, and Catherine sent her for needle and thread. Once Ellen was out of earshot, she poured the whiskey into the long gouge on Jonathan's arm. Her stomach tightened at the grunt of pain she elicited.

When Ellen returned with the needle and a spool of white thread, she dropped both into a pot of water Ellen had boiling on the big black iron stove.

"Miss Catherine, that's the water for tonight's mashed potatoes!"

"I have to be sure there's no dust on them." Washing her hands thoroughly with Ellen's good soap, Catherine fished the needle and the spool of thread out with a spoon. She laid them on a snowy linen dish towel.

Along the table's edge, she put down another, and ordered Jonathan to lay his arm on it. She felt her lips go bloodless as he calmly sat down on a kitchen stool and placed his arm for her to sew up.

Could she do this? She'd been so sure she could. "Maybe we should send for the doctor." Her voice sounded wispy.

Jonathan smiled at her. "You can do it," he said softly.

Tears filled her eyes, and she looked down suddenly at the wound to hide them from him. The gash was long but clean, the muscle exposed but not torn. He had so little flesh, still, that there was little more to it than to pull the skin together and sew it.

She set about the task as gently as she could.

Jonathan simply sat and watched her. With her full attention on her task, she could hardly look up at his face, so he let himself love her with his eyes.

He studied the way her hairline grew, and the blue and deep red and black of the hairs that were scattered through the thick dark brown of the heavy mass she'd drawn back from her face with a ribbon that matched the soft blue of her shirt.

He let his gaze go where his lips longed to, along the line of her jaw, over the softness of her lips, down the lovely column of her throat. . . . He yanked his eyes up and drew a deep breath.

Catherine looked up at him anxiously. "Did I hurt you?"

He saw the drying tears on her lashes, and the compassion in her beautiful brown eyes, and if Ellen hadn't seen the look on his face and said, "Oh, dear," he'd have kissed her.

Instead, his glance flew to Ellen's rapt face, and he grinned at her, admitting to all she'd seen, and shook his head, pledging her to silence. Then he schooled his face and turned his attention back to Catherine.

"Almost finished," she murmured. "Almost done, now." She soothed him as if he were a child. He was amused, he who had deep saber slashes sewn up by men who could have cared less if they hurt him, so long as they could get

to the next wounded man quickly. And he was touched. He
loved her so, his Cathy.

From the doorway, the senator cleared his throat.
Jonathan's gaze shot to him. The senator stared at
him evenly for a long moment. There was no doubt in
Jonathan's mind that the man, too, had read his feelings
from his face.

The senator saw the depth of love the Rebel felt for his
dead son's wife. He wondered for a long, painful space of
time how he would handle this. Then he cleared his throat
a second time and said into the fragile silence, "I'm sending
Bob, here, for the sheriff." He indicated the new ranch hand
waiting for orders. "Do we need the doctor to check on your
needlework as well?"

Catherine's head came up, and she looked, puzzled, from
Jonathan to her father-in-law to Jonathan again. What had
she missed as she worked so hard to secure the end of her
thread so carefully?

Jonathan and Clayton were looking at her so seriously.
She could almost feel the air between them crackle.

While she wondered what had occurred as she bent over
Jonathan's arm, Jonathan told Clayton, "Just ask Bob to get
some powder to stave off infection." He looked at Cathy,
"Cathy's done as good a job as Doc Farmer could have
done."

The extent of the pleasure she took in such a quiet statement surprised Catherine. She was smiling as she took the
two linen cloths she had used back to Ellen.

CHAPTER
Twenty-five

"YOU'RE SURE HELL ON MY SHIRTS, SON," CLAYTON TOLD Jonathan as he helped him ease the arm Catherine had bandaged into the left sleeve of yet another of his shirts.

Jonathan grinned at him. "Sorry, sir."

Jonny watched the two men with interest. He thought he detected a subtle change in his grandfather's attitude toward the Rebel.

It seemed his grandpa had accepted the man, somehow. He thought about that for a minute, probing around in his own mind to see how he felt about it. After a bit, he decided that he felt pretty good about it, because of Daisy and Susan and all. But it took some getting used to.

He offered his own observation, "If you ask me, he's just hard on shirts, anyhow. Remember he burned up one of his own."

His grandpa looked at him, and one corner of his mouth quirked up in a smile. But it was his eyes that sent Jonny scurrying off to pester Ellen for a treat. His grandpa's eyes looked like he was proud of his grandson for something. That was the kind of thing that could make a body squirm.

Ellen came blustering into the parlor before Jonny got all the way out of the big room. "I've fixed a snack for everybody." She shot a glance around the room to be sure her thoughtfulness didn't include Morris.

Clayton interpreted her look with a wry smile. "I'm afraid that you'll have to take a tray to the foreman, Ellen." He watched her grow with the size of the outraged breath she

229

was taking. "Oh, and spoon feed him, too, as he's tied to a chair in the office."

"On the coldest day that ever happens you-know-where!" Ellen flashed at him.

The senator permitted himself the luxury of a laugh. Catherine joined in, having overheard Ellen's mutinous comment, as she came into the room in a fresh blouse, and Jonathan's chuckle died in his throat at the sight of her.

Her hair was done up on top of her head again, in that loose, seemingly careless way that intrigued him, and her face was aglow, all traces of the tears she had cried as she stitched his arm washed away.

Her glance caught his, and for a breathless moment, they stared at one another, their feelings naked for all to see.

Ellen said, "Oh, dear," as if she had intruded on something very private, and Catherine's lashes dropped to cover the warm expression in her eyes.

All of a sudden, the Rebel found his entire attention was needed to try to button the cuff of his right sleeve. He was slow and clumsy with his injured arm.

Catherine watched him as if she could hardly bear to let him do anything without her, much less try so hard to do something she knew must pain him. As her hand reached out to him and she started to go to his side, the senator cleared his throat and stepped over to perform the simple service.

Clayton saw that the Southerner's gaze had been drawn from his task to his daughter-in-law's face. Clayton felt something twist in his chest. Something he felt certain he didn't need the little envelope of white powder in his vest pocket for.

"Come on, Captain. Food will do us all good, and if I know Ellen, you won't need a lick of help cutting anything up." He looked the Rebel straight in the eye. "But I guess if you do, you can count on me to help you do it." That was as close to a declaration of friendship that the senator had ever come.

Jonathan followed the family into the dining room enveloped in a warmth that he hadn't felt for some time. Until now, except for the time he spent working with the men rebuilding the square, he'd sorely missed the feeling that he was among friends.

The senator was right. Ellen served them soup and sandwiches and big glasses of milk, as if they were children who needed it to grow. Jonathan flashed her a warm smile of appreciation for her thoughtfulness. There was nothing he would have a problem with, stiff arm or no.

Ellen went back into the kitchen flapping her apron to cool her suddenly hot face. If anybody was to ask her, Miss Catherine's goose was well and truly cooked. There wasn't a woman in the whole state of Texas who could resist a man with a smile like that!

Bob got back with the sheriff just as they were rising from the table. Catherine sent Jonny to ride over and play with Susan to get him out of the way.

"Don't tell them about my arm, Button. You'd just upset Diana."

Jonny assured him that he wouldn't, but he let it be known by the way he slumped and dragged his feet that he really, really wanted to stay and watch the sheriff in action even more than he wanted to go play with his new friend.

A severe glance from his mother sent him on his way. Then, and only then, was Morris untied and brought out of the small room off the foyer that served as the ranch office.

After the introductions had been performed, Clayton stared hard at the law officer and told the short, square Texan matter-of-factly, "Sheriff Tate, this man tried to murder me." Succinctly, he related the events that led up to his sending for the law.

The sheriff looked hard at the senator. "You seen to have something more on your mind, Senator Foster."

Clayton weighed the man carefully, liked the bluff openness he saw, and decided to bring him into his plans. "Sheriff, do you know much about Kellerman?"

The senator liked the faint look of distaste that crossed the sheriff's face before he schooled it to neutrality.

"Yes, sir. I'm familiar with Mr. Kellerman." His voice was devoid of expression.

The senator found himself liking this stocky Texan. "Jonathan," he nodded to where he stood, "says that the men who tried to start the stampede looked like Kellerman's to him. He told me at lunch that he was keeping an especially sharp eye out because he's brushed up against some of 'em out near his place, and figured they hadn't any business there. He has the old De Vargas hacienda."

The sheriff looked at Morris.

The Rebel caught Morris's eye and touched his bandage, tacitly reminding him he'd swing for that little fiasco if Jonathan didn't like the way he answered the sheriff.

Sheriff Tate asked Morris, "Do you know of any reason Kellerman men would be hanging around the old place?"

Morris began to sweat. "He's . . . borrowing cows from this ranch. A lot of 'em haven't been branded. Not enough cowhands. That's the way he takes them out. Past the old De Vargas place."

"Well, since our new foreman" —Tate ignored Jonathan's surprise when he nodded again in the Southerner's direction— "risked life and limb to go get Mr. Morris out of the incipient stampede Kellerman's men started, I imagine Mr. Morris will be happy to tell Mr. Kellerman that that sort of thing is to cease." His brows snapped down. "Immediately."

He cocked his head. "Maybe some sort of written statement to the effect that Mr. Morris, having worked for Mr. Kellerman, was cognizant of the . . . er, borrowing of cows from our herd. And that he was party to it," the senator raised and admonitory index finger, "as was a group of Mr. Kellerman's men party to the beginnings of a certain stampede.

"That sort of document in my safe, with a copy in the safe at your office, might serve as a handy help for the, shall we say, restoration of friendly relations between Three Rivers and the Lazy K. Don't you think?"

Jonathan stirred restively, like a horse on too tight a rein.

"You had something to add, Captain?" The senator did the asking, but it was obvious Sheriff Tate was curious to know what ate at Jonathan as well.

"No 'restoration of friendly relations' until we get our cattle back." Jonathan's expression brooked no argument.

Catherine looked at him pensively, enjoying the way his jaw jutted forward just a little as he challenged the other two men, reveling in the sheer masculine power of him. He added quietly, upping the challenge, "Not if I'm foreman here."

"Just how do you plan to get the cattle back, Captain?"

"I plan to ride over and look at his herd. Anything with our brand, or that looks like our cow and doesn't have a Lazy K on it comes home with me. Unless he's been branding mighty fast, I should recover some."

"Well, now, Captain," the sheriff looked at him calmly, "seems to me that Kellerman might have some objections to that."

"Sir, I do truly hope so."

"Have you any plans that might make him agreeable to letting you bring home cows from his place?" Tate's face was grimly serious. "Plans that I wouldn't have to interfere with?"

"Well, I figured after you got that statement from Mr. Morris, I just might take along a copy of it." He grinned evilly. "Or Mr. Morris himself."

Kirby Morris looked uncomfortable. The Southerner had never called him mister before. He was sure it boded ill for him that he was doing so now to the sheriff. His eyes darted from one man to the other. Perspiration rolled down his temples.

Catherine said conversationally, "As owner of Three Rivers, I think I should go along. After all, they're my cattle."

Jonathan turned quickly toward her, his face set. "Cathy, there is no way I am going to allow you to come with us." His tone was adamant.

Clayton marveled that his daughter-in-law didn't flare up.

She smiled serenely, "But you say they're my cattle. Surely the owner should be present when his, or her, property is recovered."

Clayton wondered what it was she was up to. This quiet conversation didn't fit his idea of Catherine Foster when she was full of determination to go somewhere. He looked at her searchingly. Her expression was carefully bland.

Jonathan stated, "You're not going, Cathy, and that's that."

The senator waited for the fight. When it didn't come, he shook his head in disbelief. She was up to something. He'd lay odds on it. He knew he'd never find out by asking, however, and got on with his own problems. "Okay, let's get this paper worked out."

When the wording was acceptable to Cathy and the senator, the paper was shoved over to Morris to sign. The senator copied out one more and got it signed as well. He handed it to the sheriff and watched him fold it carefully and put it in the breast pocket of his coat.

"We need one more," Jonathan insisted. "I want one to take with me when I confront Kellerman."

The senator ignored the squirming Morris. "Sound like a good plan to you, Sheriff?"

Sheriff Tate nodded. "Guess I'll ride along, too, to be sure there aren't any misunderstandings about what's going on here." He regarded the tall Southerner levelly. "I wouldn't want there to be any gun play."

"There won't be, Sheriff. That paper's all I'll need." He smiled easily. "Now, if you'll excuse me, I'll go pick my men," Jonathan told him.

He stopped just before he got to the door. Turning, he walked back to the stocky law officer.

He unbuckled his gun belt and handed it to the sheriff. "There," he said, "You hold it, and if there's any shooting and I'm not around to testify, you can hang Kellerman for me."

He heard Catherine's gasp as he sauntered out into the yard.

CHAPTER
Twenty-six

CATHERINE FOLLOWED JONATHAN OUT ONTO THE PORCH. "Captain!" Her voice was husky from a moment ago when he'd alluded so carelessly to the possibility of getting killed.

She was determined, however, to win her point. She had no intention of letting her woman's heart distract her from her intention.

He halted abruptly and turned back to her almost impatiently. "Yes?"

She looked at him intently, her heart in her eyes. Suppose this was the last private moment she would ever share with him? There was no guarantee that Kellerman wouldn't . . . Her mind refused even to form the rest of that thought.

He saw the yearning on her face and took the few long strides that brought him back to her. Against his will, his hand moved up to touch her cheek. "Cathy, what is it?"

She fought a battle not to turn her face and kiss his hand as she had on that day in the hacienda. That day that seemed so long ago. She won her fight, but her lips quivered.

"Cathy, angel, what's the matter?" He bent his head to her, then caught himself and straightened. There was no way he could gently kiss that quiver away. Not in broad open daylight with the sound of voices clearly carrying from the house.

There was no guarantee he could keep the kiss gentle, either, the way his blood was beginning to pound through him at the feel of her silken skin. He had to go before the mere sight of her standing there looking up at him unmanned him.

"I have to go, Cathy." Even to his own ears his voice sounded hoarse with emotion.

"I know," she whispered. "But be careful." Her fingers touched and clung to his own. "Come back to me."

He stared long at her, imprinting her face on his mind, fighting the urge to crush her to him and cover her face with kisses. What if that fool Kellerman or one of his men did get trigger happy? He'd never see her again. Never have another chance to hold her in his arms.

His jaws locked with the effort it cost him not to snatch her to him and bury his face in her hair. He managed to grate out, "I've got to go, Cathy. I have a job to do."

She shook her head hard and moved away from his hand. How typical of the man. He had no idea that the casual reference he had made to Sheriff Tate about his possible death had upset her.

He probably thought it wasn't worth being upset over. No doubt he considered the possibility of anything happening to him remote. But she had already lost one man she loved— one who had been just as sure that nothing could ever happen to him. Men could be so thoughtless. It made her angry.

She looked him straight in the eye, her anger giving her courage. "The sheriff, Clayton, and I are coming." She kept talking over the protest that erupted from him. "We'll watch from the bluff over Kellerman's house."

Jonathan subsided when he realized she would be far from any potential danger. "All right."

He hung there another instant, as if bound to her by invisible cords. His eyes said all his voice refused to express, then he spun on his heel and strode out into the sunlight, calling for his men.

Catherine sat her horse gracefully, back straight but relaxed. She conversed easily with the sheriff and her father-in-law as they waited on the bluff that overlooked Kellerman's big house. Soon they saw Jonathan and the five men that rode with him approaching.

Inside she felt like she was dying.

She saw the man on the porch get out of his chair and meet the riders at the hitching rack. Jonathan made no move to dismount. Instead, the man scurried back into the house, and returned with Kellerman.

Kellerman stomped out to the hitch rail, his choppy strides full of anger. She saw Jonathan speak to him at some length. Kellerman blustered and shook his fist.

Her heart almost stopped when the sheriff drew his forty-four just as Kellerman's man reached for his weapon.

Kellerman turned on the man angrily, and the man put away his gun. She could see when Kellerman turned their way that his face was red.

Her eyes flashed to Jonathan's face, and she was filled with a fierce pride to see his cool confidence. He said something to Kellerman, and drew, very slowly, from inside his shirt, the paper Morris had signed.

Kellerman took it and read it. An instant later it was confetti on the ground. Kellerman turned half away from his tormentor and stomped the pieces into the dust. She saw his lips draw back from his teeth as he snarled something at Jonathan.

Catherine's heart threatened to burst from her chest when Jonathan laughed at the apoplectic man. Then he said something to him with a gesture that indicated that he was through talking and intended to go recover her cattle.

Insolently, he turned his back on Kellerman. Next, he indicated with a hand command strongly reminiscent of the cavalry, the direction of Kellerman's herd.

She watched him as he rode away and knew that if anything happened to him, she would never survive her loss.

Juan was so angry he could hardly remember his English. "*Très* hundred head! They took over three hundred head of cattle from us." He looked at Jonathan as if he wanted him to deny it.

There wasn't any way his friend could. There was no doubt that the herefords on Kellerman's ranch had come from Three Rivers. Kellerman ran a mixed herd, none of them remotely resembling the purebreds Catherine's grand-father had been raising.

Jonathan had ignored the protests of Kellerman's herders. He had cut out every one. Kellerman's men knew who the cows belonged to. There was no resistance beyond the mild protests.

As far as Jonathan was concerned, his mission had been a success. Catherine would have her cows back. He was full of proud satisfaction that he had been able to get them for her.

Then suddenly, galloping around a bend in the road from the man's ranch house, he saw Kellerman. The man rode to within a few feet of him and skidded his horse to a stop.

Kellerman was breathing as if he had just run a mile. His eyes glared at the man who had thwarted him with a mere piece of paper.

Jonathan reined Creole in and waited for him. His narrowed eyes were cold and expressionless.

Lips drawn back in a snarl, Kellerman spat, "You've won today, Foster, but I don't want you to be too happy about it."

He smiled venomously. "Morris and I know of a way to be rid of you, you bastard. And I'm riding over to the fort to look for a certain sergeant I know right now!"

With that he brought his quirt down hard on his sweating horse's rump and galloped away. The dust billowed up in his wake.

Jonathan sat his horse, his face like stone. Kellerman knew. So did Morris. And they both knew Keefer.

He'd been living in a fool's dream of fancied safety while the two of them had just been waiting until a moment of their own choosing to bring him down.

Now that moment had come.

The entire herd had meandered past him by the time he pulled himself back to reality and gave Creole the signal to move.

So it had come. This was to be the end. Kellerman would find Keefer, and Keefer would come for him.

He smiled grimly. He hadn't spent all that time in the sergeant's care not to understand the man. Keefer had the tenacity of a bulldog.

He would come for him. Of that Jonathan had absolutely no doubt. And when he came, he'd haul Captain Jonathan Parke Foster, C.S.A., back to the fort to be hanged.

Catherine rode down from the bluff as fast as it was safe. Then she went flat out across the range to the where Jonathan would reenter Three Rivers.

She corrected herself quickly: Tres Rios. The hacienda belonged to her dear Southerner now and so did the five hundred acres around it.

Her heart was pounding at the thought of the fight she anticipated. The fight she had deliberately set up when she demanded to be present when the cattle were reclaimed.

She hastened to cut off Jonathan's cattle drive as it entered his property. Outwardly she appeared perfectly calm as she waited. A few minutes later, her father-in-law rode up to keep her company.

"Sorry, my dear. I simply do not ride as recklessly as you do."

She caught the implied criticism in his remark, and smiled gently at him. "I'm sorry if I worried you."

"Hmmm, well, yes, you did. Apology accepted." Clayton admired the way she had drawn his fangs.

Next, from the direction of her own ranch, Carlos arrived at a gallop. "I found it at last, Señorita Catherine." He showed her the object, smiling widely. "*Dios*, but there is much in that attic!"

He took up a station on her other side. Catherine smiled at him. "Thank you, Carlos. Do you know what I intend to do?" she asked when it looked as if he would burst.

"*Sí*. I have guessed."

"You don't sound glad about it." That puzzled her. "He's your friend."

"*Sí, muchachita.* But a very proud one. The Captain is . . . how do you say? . . . *muy macho*."

Catherine looked annoyed. She sighed and was about to

give him her opinion of *macho*, when the first of the cows came into view.

She saw Jonathan riding at the front of the drive, tall and straight, and she smiled. Yes, he was proud. Impossibly proud. How was he going to accept her gift of the cattle?

He was probably going to blow up in her face.

Very well. She would just have to survive it. She had survived his temper before.

She remembered the day they found the orphan calf. He had been magnificent.

He had finally gotten over the gift of the hacienda. . . . Well perhaps, not quite . . . but well enough to touch her face this afternoon on the porch. He would come around. She would bring him around.

But now here she was complicating things again and it might take a little longer. She could wait. They had a lifetime.

Perhaps if she could make him see how advantageous for his sisters it would be for Tres Rios to have a herd of its own again, with its own, long-forgotten brand to mark them until Jonathan could design his own.

She turned to look at Carlos. With the long branding iron carried across his thighs, he sat quietly, worriedly, on his horse beside her. Every now and again he glanced down at the iron she had sent him to find before she, Clayton, and the sheriff set out for Kellerman's.

Catherine followed one of his glances. The Hacienda Brand it was called. It was one of the most unusual in the West. She could hardly wait to show it to Jonathan, in spite of the apprehension she felt.

He saw her then, and his horse shot forward. She watched as he came to her, her smile radiant.

He reined in while he was still a world away. At least eight feet. Too large a space to reach across.

"Cathy." He spoke her name as if he had never said it before. As if he never expected to be able to say it again.

Something in his face caused her heart to stop, and without her even willing it, her mare carried her to his side. When she spoke, he could barely hear her.

"Jonathan." There was a world of meaning in the way she said his name. With this utterance she surrendered the last reluctance she had harbored at calling him by it. For the first time it was his name and his name only.

The other men from the ranch rode by and spoke to her respectfully, but she didn't hear them. Diana, Susan, and their single hand, Taylor, rode up, too, drawn by the dust cloud the cattle made in passing. Still, she never took her gaze from Jonathan's intent one.

Unaware of Diana's low laughter in response to Taylor's "I think we're intruding, Miss Diana," Catherine sat wrapped in the magic of Jonathan's regard. She was oblivious to all else.

His eyes told her more than words would ever express. Only when the cattle began to back up and mill around them as the senator and Carlos relayed to the drovers her order to hold them at this spot, did she stir. She was more than reluctant to return to the here and now.

Jonathan gave up his intent study of her face and turned his attention to the milling cattle. He frowned and opened his mouth to give an order.

Before he could speak, Catherine said, "No, Jonathan. This is where the cattle are to bed down. You refused to let me go to retrieve them, so they are yours."

Ignoring the play of emotions that crossed his face, she went on, " 'To the victor go the spoils,' if I'm not mistaken." She lifted her chin and said coolly. "And you refused to even let me be present to share in the winning of a victory. You went, so they're yours." She watched him, braced for his explosion.

But to Jonathan, pride and cattle had come to have no meaning at all. Only Cathy had meaning for him.

The pride would die with him in the next few days, and the cattle were only a nice legacy to help his sisters survive. Thank God for sending his old friend Stuart Ashworth's cousin Taylor to help them. Funny, he thought, how things fall into place.

He looked over the herd. Then he looked over the land and off to the hacienda in the distance, all so newly his that he hadn't really grasped that he owned it yet.

He took a deep, shaky breath and looked to where his sisters sat trying to pretend they hadn't noticed his odd behavior, and finally he looked at Taylor, who already seemed healthier in just the few days that Diana had been looking after him.

It was a good life. And Cathy had made it for them. More precious than rubies, his Cathy.

He felt his masculine pride stir and attempt to catch his attention, to urge him to taint her gift, but he ignored it. Instead, he smiled tenderly at this paragon of all women and said, very softly, very simply, "Thank you."

CHAPTER
Twenty-seven

KELLERMAN RODE HARD, SO BY THE TIME HE REACHED THE fort, his horse was staggering. He didn't find Keefer there, but he did learn something of interest, something that added urgency to his mission.

"What happened to the flyer on that escaped Rebel deserter?" He thumped the bulletin board as he demanded an answer from the sergeant on duty.

The sergeant looked him over with a military man's contempt for untidiness. His answer was all that Kellerman cared about, however. "A Major Williams, whose father-in-law is supposed to be a close friend of President Lincoln's, has made some inquiries into the matter of Captain Jonathan Foster." He considered and deliberately omitted the "sir" that he accorded most civilians out of courtesy. "The major said in his letter to the commandant that he was at West Point with Captain Foster.

"The commander ain't a West Pointer, but he knows how they stick together there, despite this here rebellion." He ran an assessing eye over the pudgy man in the expensive clothes and decided to finish the matter. He didn't try to keep the note of boredom out of his voice. "So the flyer's been taken down, pending investigation into the matter by the major himself. He's due at the fort before the end of the month."

He turned back to the stack of papers on the scarred desk, dismissing Kellerman. There wasn't much to like about the red-faced man.

"One more question. Where will I find Sergeant Keefer?"

The man at the desk's eyes grew still. "What do you want him for?"

"That's none of your business." Kellerman realized his mistake, and tried to recover, "He's a friend of mine."

The man's look told him what he thought of Kellerman's friends. He yanked a finger over his shoulder. "He's gone to pick up a boy that got into trouble from the civilian jail."

Kellerman spun around and left.

"You're welcome," the sergeant said sarcastically to the empty room.

Kellerman was still cursing. The man at the livery stable had been disgusted by the condition of the horse he'd ridden in on and had refused to rent him a horse. The one he traded for Kellerman's was a rough-gaited, ill-tempered beast, but the man had refused him any other. He hadn't ridden far, however, before he saw a group of soldiers in the distance.

"Good thing," he muttered to the ewe-necked horse under him. "I'm about sick of your rotten hide."

Riding hard to meet the soldiers, he saw, with relief, that it was Keefer who led them. He started right in. "If you want that Reb, Keefer, you'd better hop to. Some major with connections has cottoned to what you did to the man. He's on his way from the East to straighten it out." He laughed unpleasantly, enjoying the shock on Keefer's face. "Maybe he's gonna straighten you out, too."

"Shut your face, Kellerman." Keefer gestured the two men with him to take the prisoner, a fresh-faced recruit, and drop back a bit. "What's this all about?" He looked slyly at the man beside him. "It ain't like you to come running to save anybody's plans but your own. What's goin' on?"

"None of your damned business." Kellerman spurred his horse, reining it in cruelly so it jumped but wouldn't move forward against the pain in its mouth. "If you want that damned Rebel, you just better get him hanged quick, is all, or you'll miss your chance." He released his grunting horse and shot away from the detail, leaving the four men in blue looking after him.

To a man, they were full of curiosity about the man's appearance out here in the middle of nowhere. One of them, the fresh-faced recruit who had gotten into trouble for his loudly vocal support of Jeb Stuart against the attack of the barman in the Golden River Saloon, wondered what kind of business Keefer had with anybody he called "the Reb."

Catherine pulled her long tresses forward over her left shoulder and dragged her hairbrush through them. She watched her own eyes in the mirror. "Catherine," she asked herself aloud, "what happened to him? What made him behave so strangely this evening?"

She sighed and the face in the mirror frowned, easily recognizing as a distraction to thinking clearly the warm feelings that flooded her at the very thought of him. "His behavior was so unlike him. Why did he accept the cattle so calmly?" The frown on the face of the girl in the mirror deepened; she made a little move of disgust. "All my clever machinations were unnecessary."

She looked away from her reflection out into the deep, sapphire night. The scent of jasmine wafted in through her window.

She remembered the day her grandfather had brought the vine to her for planting under her bedroom window. A wave of nostalgia touched her, and she willed herself to let her mind float away on it, but it refused and returned to the puzzling problem of Jonathan's unusual behavior.

She gave herself a scowl in the mirror. "Catherine, he'll come to the house tomorrow morning." She ignored the way her pulse quickened.

He would report in, as he called it, first thing in the morning to give them the numbers from the tally, which had gotten finished in spite of all the confusion yesterday, and tell Clayton and her what he planned to do with the day. She told the serious face in the mirror, "You can get a better idea of what's going on then."

Resolutely, she nodded at herself in the mirror, finished making the long braid in which she kept her hair at night, and put herself to bed. She would keep her mind on her prayers and that would put her to sleep in no time.

But she didn't. Thoughts of the Rebel and the long-ings they engendered in her kept her awake far into the night.

Dinner at the hacienda earlier had been a gala affair. Susan, Diana, and Taylor were so elated by Jonathan's acceptance of Catherine's gift of the herd that they didn't even notice his strange mood.

"Why," Diana bubbled, "I'll bet if we had grass like at home, we could have all three hundred of them eating it and never have to buy hay!"

Taylor looked at her with male patience for female lack of knowledge. "We'll never feed three hundred cows on five hundred acres of range. One steer needs almost seven acres to browse."

She looked at him for a long moment, considering how best she could instruct him without trespassing on his mas-culine prerogatives. And, of course, without losing one iota of her own femininity.

While she very much admired Catherine's forthright atti-tude, she firmly recognized it as an attribute that, while it might become the Yankee girl, simply wasn't her own style at all.

She began her patient work. "Well, I know that we can't do it on such dry land, but I'll bet you and Jonathan could think of a way to irrigate the pastures with some of the water from our three rivers." She blushed, a skill she had learned at her mother's knee, and fluttered her lashes at Taylor. "I mean, it wouldn't be polite to divert all the water, but I don't think anybody'd notice if you just took a little stream off each river, do you?" She made her voice anxious, her eyes wide.

Taylor just watched her and waited for her to finish. After all, he had learned a few things at his mother's knee, too, and he knew that the resolution to the problem she was presenting was soon to follow.

"Well, couldn't you just sort of lead some of the water onto the land now and again? I mean, isn't the difference

between here and home that home has so much more rain-
fall? If the river water acted like the rain, wouldn't more
grass grow?" She lowered her eyes and her voice. "I mean,
doesn't it stand to reason?"

Jonathan came out of his trance to watch his sister's
ploy. He had missed that. She had always been a delight
to watch, pretending that any man was smarter than she. It
never lasted after she really got to know him and let him
see her intelligence, but Taylor was not that far along yet.

She turned appealingly to him, "Doesn't it, Jonathan?"

Smiling, he answered, "Yes. Back home we could keep
a cow on half an acre of good grass." He looked at Taylor.
"Diana's idea is sound. I think you ought to give it a
try."

"Me?" Taylor asked, laughing. "Hey, don't you want to
do it yourself?"

Jonathan stood abruptly. "I need to check on Creole and
the rest of the horses." He placed his napkin on the table
beside his half-finished plate. "You and Diana draw up
some plans. I'll look at them later." Smiling faintly, he
turned and left the dining room.

Diana listened to the sound his boots made across the
spacious main room of the hacienda. Her expression was
strained.

"What's the matter, Miss Diana," Taylor teased, "aren't
you going to tell me how to do the job?"

But Diana didn't answer his question. She turned eyes
wide with concern to him and said with a little trace of
fear, "Something's wrong."

Across the table, Susan, eyes glued to where her brother
had just disappeared, burst into tears.

Jonathan stood at the entrance to the hacienda, a shoulder
against the huge post that held one of the massive gates.
From where he stood, the land flowed away in a gentle
sweep down to one of the three rivers that had given Tres
Rios its name.

He would keep the name as a tribute to the bold Spaniard
who had brought his family here, built the hacienda, and

established his vast ranch. It would be a memorial to the man's family.

The place was beginning to come to life again under the determined efforts of his sister. He smiled to think of all Diana's plans, especially the newest one for irrigating pastures. He looked around at the land flat enough for that to be feasible. He hoped she could make it work. He wished he'd be here to see.

Maybe it would work if she put banks up every now and then, to make the gentle hills terraced, like the rice fields at their South Carolina cousin's. He let his mind toy with the problem.

Windmills like those he had seen near Amsterdam might do for the power to lift the water. He would be sure to tell Diana. Her idea just might work. If it did, they could run a thousand-head herd.

He chuckled. Diana might end up being a Texan Jethro Tull. Somehow he didn't think she would like that idea very well.

God, he was grateful to Cathy and Clayton for giving him this opportunity to see his sisters again, to have this little time with them before . . .

Taylor came up behind him. "Is something the matter, Jon?"

Jonathan looked at his friend for a long while before he spoke. "Taylor. That scarecrow horse of yours is beginning to look pretty good."

"Shows you what food can do."

Jonathan nodded and they stood quietly, Taylor knowing there was more coming. "Taylor, I'm counting on you to stick around here and keep a good eye on things if anything should happen to me."

"What the devil could happen to you?"

"I have something to straighten out. If I manage to set the record straight, nothing will. If I don't, I'll need your promise that you'll take care of Diana and Susan."

Taylor stood silent, the question burning in his throat, but he didn't ask it. Jonathan would tell him when—and if—he got ready.

Finally, Taylor said, "I'll stick."

"Thanks."

Taylor sensed that Jonathan wanted to be alone, so he went back to reassure the girls; falsely, he was sure.

Jonathan stood studying the midnight blue of the night sky. The jeweled constellations held a new fascination for him. Their familiar forms were as if he saw them for the first time. He watched until the stars faded at moonrise, then he turned and went inside to sleep.

CHAPTER
Twenty-eight

RED HAWK WAITED IN THE ROCKS LESS THAN A MILE from the fort. It was a place he lingered often, hoping for a glimpse of his enemy. If ever Keefer left the fort alone . . .

Tonight, Red Hawk had sent Running Deer to the fort to listen. Running Deer knew well the tongue of the white man, and had a craftiness that enabled him to transform his lithe, warrior's body into that of a lame and twisted creature.

In the past, Running Deer had learned much. He counted the information he was able to bring his chief ample compensation for the abuse he suffered at the hands of some of the soldiers.

Patient hours later, Red Hawk saw Running Deer leave the stockade on the ancient pony he rode as part of his deception. His heart lifted as he saw Running Deer raise an arm in salute to the sentries as he passed through the lantern-lit gates of the fort. Exultation fired Red Hawk. That gesture meant Running Deer had news!

Red Hawk flung himself on his own pony and set it hurtling to the last bit of cover that would conceal his presence. His friend arrived only minutes later.

"Running Deer has word for Red Hawk?"

Running Deer answered, "Your enemy has asked for men to go with him at first light to bring the white man we call Brave Warrior back to the fort to be hanged."

"Running Deer brings good news. Red Hawk thanks his brother. Many are the places along the trail to Three Rivers to hide. From one of them I will make fly the arrow that will pay the bluecoat sergeant for what was done to Shy Doe and Shining Eagle."

Running Deer nodded slowly. "Running Deer would be with Red Hawk when he avenges his family."

Red Hawk shook his head. "The death of Red Hawk's woman and son will be avenged" —he tasted the new word and liked the feel of it on his tongue— "but it is for Red Hawk. Alone."

"What then can the friend of Red Hawk do to help him?"

"It is not certain the one we call Sneaking Coyote has the men?"

"Not when I left the fort to bring you word. The chief of the soldiers will tell him tonight."

"Return, then. If men are given, Running Deer will camp outside the stockade and let his campfire be bright." He turned and walked into the stand of trees beside which they stood. Hacking at a tangle of dead branches with his tomahawk, he proffered an armload of fuel for Running Deer's campfire.

"If Sneaking Coyote no get men, sleep cold, my friend." He clamped a hand on the younger brave's shoulder.

Running Deer looked at him resolutely. "I will hope to use these, Red Hawk." He took the armload of small branches and turned his pony back toward the fort without another word, and without a single backward glance.

Hours later, Red Hawk saw the light of a campfire blossom just outside the stockade. It burned brightly. Red Hawk grunted his satisfaction and went to make his preparations for the morning. Sergeant Keefer would never return to the fort alive.

Catherine rose early, dressed, and crept downstairs with her boots in her hand. Just because she could no longer sleep was no reason to wake the others.

The sun would be up in a little while. Already the sky was lightening in the east.

In another hour or so, Jonathan would come. She laughed
to feel the eagerness that surged through her.

Closing the back door quietly behind her, she crossed
the porch on tiptoe and walked across the square to the
new barn. Slipping in through the man-sized door beside
the big closed double doors, she inhaled the scent of newly
cut wood and warm animals on clean bedding.

It was wonderful to be here again. She had never let
herself realize how very much she had missed Texas. Now
she just let her joy at being home wash over her.

Immediately, her mind went to Jonathan. How in the
world she would get him to realize that nothing was as
important as their being together, she didn't know, but she
knew she must.

She remembered the first time he touched her, really touched her, and her gaze lifted to the barn loft. She
blushed. Had she known she loved him then?

Standing here in the semidarkness of the barn, she finally admitted that she began to love him when she first
saw him, when he stood in chains with his head unbowed
and refused to tell Clayton that the sergeant had beat-
en him.

She drifted over to Rosie, who got up from where she lay
chewing her cud and came over to have her head scratched.
"Remember the day he said he couldn't milk?"

Rosie closed her eyes and leaned into Catherine's
scratching.

"He was magnificent that day, wasn't he?" She smiled,
thinking of the way she had actually quailed before his
anger. She laughed again, delighted. There hadn't been
many men who could frighten her with no more than words.

She left Rosie, looked in at the sleeping Daisy, and
drifted over to her mare. "Good morning, girl. You're
all bright-eyed this morning." She picked up a brush and
currycomb, went into the stall, and began the grooming the
mare so enjoyed.

She was singing softly as she worked. One part of her listened for the sound of hoofbeats that would herald Jonathan's
arrival.

*   *   *

Hoofbeats thundered as the detail left the fort. The sentries at the gate saluted the shavetail the old man had sent to head up the group of mounted soldiers. Sergeant Keefer rode a little behind and to the left of the new young officer.

After a few minutes, the men began to relax. "Where're we goin', Sarge?" a rawboned private called out over the sound of the horses.

"To hang a Reb."

"A Reb out here? Thought they was all back East."

"Not this one."

"What's he done worth hanging for?"

"We'll be hanging him for desertion." Keefer laughed aloud. "Yesiree, boys. We'll be hanging this Rebel bastard for deserting the Union army." He threw back his head and laughed louder.

The young second lieutenant flushed and said, "That'll be enough, Sergeant," and Keefer sullenly subsided.

Keefer neither noticed nor cared that the six men riding behind him didn't find anything to laugh about in the thought of watching a man kick his life out at the end of a rope.

The sun was just beginning to rise.

Halfway between the fort and the ranch that was Keefer's destination, Red Hawk lay atop a boulder and peered in the direction from which he knew the man who had murdered his wife and child would come.

Before long Keefer and seven other men came over a distant rise. Red Hawk raised his face to the sky to entreat the Great Spirit, then he turned and picked up the powerful bow he had the medicine man bless for this purpose. Nocking the arrow with the point he had dipped into every manner of filth, he sighted down the long, straight shaft to the barrel chest of his enemy.

Patiently he waited until the man had come well within range. The beginnings of a low chant murmured from his lips.

Suddenly, the face of Brave Warrior swam in his vision. Startled, he considered its meaning. Lowering his arrow's tip, he let the tension on the bow ease. What was the Great Spirit saying to Red Hawk?

The soldiers were very close now. He must understand the wishes of the Spirit quickly or miss this chance for revenge.

He had waited so long for this, it was like pain to withhold his arrow. Then, in a flash of understanding, he knew what he must do. He withdrew stealthily into the shadow the trees cast over the rocks.

His thoughts were clear with new purpose. Keefer rode to the ranch to catch the white man the Indians from the way station raid called Brave Warrior.

Brave Warrior was to be brought to the fort to be hanged. Sneaking Coyote would then be victorious over the noble Brave Warrior. That was not something Red Hawk's respect for Brave Warrior would let happen.

Much greater the victory for Red Hawk to both kill his enemy and to make it possible for Brave Warrior to escape. Keefer would die knowing that he had failed to conquer the gallant white man he hated. Red Hawk's revenge would be all the sweeter.

In the deep shadow at the back of the rock, Red Hawk smiled and let his mortal enemy pass by unmolested. Then he rode to gather his braves.

Catherine heard the hoofbeats she had been waiting for since she had come out of the house. She left the barn and ran to stand by the old smithy where she knew he would enter the yard.

All around her the inhabitants of the various buildings slept. The bunkhouse windows were still dark, and Maria's house was without light as well. The little world of the square belonged to her and to her alone.

Catherine smiled and reveled in the fact that Jonathan had come much earlier than ever before. They would share this quiet time before the bustle that began the day. Fancifully, she wondered if her yearning for him had drawn him to her.

Jonathan saw her standing there in the dim light of predawn. His heart thundered a response to her presence.

The strength of his longing for her caused his hand on the reins to tighten. Creole tossed his head in protest.

Neither of them spoke as he closed the distance between them. Catherine smiled, her eyes alight. She felt as if she had prayed some special prayer and it had brought him to her.

Jonathan leaned from his saddle and swept her into his arms without speaking, without taking his eyes from her own.

The kiss was unlike those devouring, joyous ones they had shared in the room with the cupid bed. This kiss searched her very soul for a response she knew would be eternal.

When he raised his head, he stared for a moment into her dazed eyes. "Cathy," he whispered hoarsely. Words burst from him without his volition, shattering the hold he had on his honor. He spoke words he had no right to say to her. "Did ever a man love a woman as I love you?"

The question was a cry from his heart. Her own answered it with a passionate burst that left her clinging to him weakly, wishing the moment would never pass, wishing they could cling together here under the stars forever.

Presently, lights appeared in the bunkhouse. On the calm air of morning, they heard Maria's melodious voice calling Consuelo to help with breakfast.

Up on the slight rise in the big house, the huge hanging lantern over the big worktable in the kitchen flared to life from Ellen's match. They had only minutes now before someone would step out into the square and break the spell they were under.

Slowly, he rode with her up to the porch that wrapped around the big house. There he lifted her down, bending low out of his saddle to place her booted feet carefully on the ground as if she were somehow too precious to jolt in any way.

He let go of her there just in front of the steps, and she felt curiously abandoned as he stepped down from his big bay gelding and moved to drop his reins over the hitching post.

He took her hand. He held it in the same manner in which he had held it the day they had explored the hacienda, with their fingers interlaced, and his arm, strong and warm all along the length of hers. Memories of that day rushed, blazing, through her.

Somehow this was different. This felt . . . desperate.

She shrank away from that word: desperate. A little shiver passed fleetingly over her. Why had that word intruded upon her happiness? What had desperation to do with them? They were safe at Three Rivers and, like two especially blessed people, had found each other in the boundless reaches of time.

He opened the front door for her but never released her hand. Even when Clayton appeared on the stairs and walked down to meet them with a pleasant, "Good morning," he didn't let go.

They all went into the office. There, very reluctantly, Jonathan turned her hand loose, and the business of the day shoved into their lives to prevent any more magic.

Catherine choked back a deep sigh and lifted from its cubbyhole in the rolltop desk the ledger to record the tally.

Jonathan's wonderful voice spilled over her. She wanted to purr like a cat at the caress of it. It was almost as if he touched her. She smiled a small secret smile and gave herself over to the sensations his nearness created in her.

Why did every sense she possessed seem strangely heightened today? She thought she could feel the texture of the very air around her.

She made an effort to pull her foolish thoughts together. This day was no different than any other, she told herself. It was just that she was a woman whose love for her man invested everything with the wonder she was feeling.

Neatly she entered the tally figures Jonathan gave her in the leather-bound ledger. She found herself smiling at him over her work. She saw reflected in his eyes, the glow in her own. As soon as the ink was dry on the page, she closed the ledger and slipped it back into its customary place.

"You will join us for breakfast, won't you?" She couldn't believe her voice sounded so shy.

He accepted with a nod.

The senator said heartily, "Good. Ellen's making hotcakes, unless my nose is lying to me. Do you like hotcakes, Captain?"

"*Pan*cakes have been a favorite breakfast with me since I was a little boy, sir."

Catherine looked at him quickly. His smile was there, and he was teasing Clayton about the difference in regional terminology for the food Ellen was cooking. Why then did his voice sound so sad to her? Surely she was imagining it.

She flashed a glance at Clayton and found him looking a little puzzled even as he chuckled and said, "I hope they are pancakes, then, that Ellen's going to serve, Captain."

During the meal, Jonathan ate little, in spite of saying the pancakes were the best he had eaten in a very long time. Instead of doing them justice, he stared at Catherine as if he could never get his fill.

Uneasiness began to stir in her. When Jonathan put his hand into his shirt, she remembered that she had felt the crinkle of paper there as she rested against him in the rosy light of the early dawn. She had been too enthralled by the magic between them to wonder at it then. Now, at the sight of it, a nibble of fear attacked the back of her mind. "What is that paper, Jonathan?"

He ignored her and looked straight at the senator. "This is my will, sir. I wonder if you would be kind enough to keep it for me."

The senator's face was sober. "Of course, Captain. I will place it in the ranch safe with our other documents of importance. Will that suit?"

"Admirably. Thank you."

Catherine experienced a chill, but she refused to entertain the feeling of dread that followed it. "Ugh," she attempted lightly. "What a terrible subject for breakfast." Her gaze went from one man to the other. She smiled bravely, fighting a terrible foreboding. "Shouldn't men exchange wills over cigars and port after dinner, rather?"

Jonathan gave up all pretense of eating breakfast. "Cathy," his voice was ragged with emotion. Seconds passed before he tore his gaze from her and transferred it to Clayton. "Senator. There is something you both must know."

Catherine looked wide-eyed to her father-in-law. She was shocked to see by his expression that he had expected this.

Jonathan spoke solemnly. "I told you that the army had no place for me. That was not the truth. Sergeant Keefer reported me as a deserter, and I have been sentenced to hang.

"I came to work for you knowing that I was a condemned man." He took a deep breath and looked at each of them in turn. "I suppose I knew it was just a matter of time, but . . ." He broke off and cleared his throat.

After a moment, a moment in which Cathy felt a cold numbness creeping over her, he continued quietly, his expression grim, "Last night Kellerman rode to find Sergeant Keefer."

He saw that the senator understood, and the knowledge was a strength he could draw from. He smiled a twisted smile in acknowledgment and said softly, "The army could be here any minute."

Then his lips tightened and his voice became formal. "I apologize for bringing such unpleasantness to your home."

Catherine sprang out of her chair. "Why didn't you tell us!"

Jonny appeared in the archway from the hall, "Tell us what?"

Nobody answered him.

Jonathan didn't answer Catherine, either, and she railed at him. "Why didn't you tell us? Why didn't you try to clear yourself? The charge is absurd." She turned a white face to Clayton. "Isn't it?"

Clayton's eyes were full of sympathy, but he, too, vouchsafed no answer.

"Jonathan, why?" Her voice was a wail.

In response, Ellen ran in from the kitchen, her eyes round. "Cathy, I am a deserter now," she heard the Captain say.

She muttered, "Oh, mercy," and twisted her apron into a ball.

Nobody noticed her.

Catherine accused Jonathan, "But you weren't when you got here. You went straight to the fort. You even refused to work for us because you had to go report for duty." Her eyes begged him to explain it all away.

Instead, he told her patiently, "And when I got to the fort, the first thing I saw was a flyer offering a reward for me, dead or alive, for desertion."

She remembered how he had pulled the brim of his hat down when they had seen the two soldiers that day in town. He had been hiding. "But you could have told them . . ." The look on his face stopped her. She looked away from the blaze that leapt up in his eyes.

His lips twisted in a scorn not meant for her. "I had ample experience with the treatment the Union army metes out to its foes. It didn't give me any delusions about the outcome of any efforts I might have made to clear myself."

Catherine threw an anguished glance at her father-in-law. What she read in his face collaborated everything Jonathan said. "But," she burst out, "we could have vouched for you."

"Do you think it would have done any good?" The hand that rested next to his plate became a white-knuckled fist. "You didn't know me. I was the enemy and had merely shared a stagecoach ride with you. You knew nothing of me."

"No!" Her voice rose on the word. "I knew that you were good and true and kind." Tears trembled on her lashes, and she said as if it would prove that he was no deserter, "You saved my son having to leave his dog behind."

"That's true, you saved Scout," Jonny thrust in, eager to help the man he had come to think of as his friend.

The big dog thumped his tail at the sound of his name.

Jonathan's face softened at the boy's interruption, "Yes, Button. It was my pleasure. Scout's a fine dog."

"You saved us all at the way station," Catherine threw at him. "And Cavenaugh said that it was you who spotted the Indians before, when they would have stopped the coach and killed us there." She flung out her hands and her eyes begged Clayton to help her.

Jonathan said quietly, "They will just point out that in doing so, I saved my own life as well."

She stomped her booted foot and flung the napkin she still clutched down onto the table.

She turned on her father-in-law. "Clayton, say something."

"There is very little I can say, my dear." His eyes were pitying, and she hated that. "The Captain has said it all. There is very little chance that he would ever be given even a fair trial, with matters as they stand."

Catherine regarded him. Silent. Stricken.

He turned to Jonathan. "Maybe your best chance is to run."

"No, sir." His voice was firm. "I'll stand fast and attempt to clear my name. I've written my friend, Major Garrick Williams of the Union army, and explained how I was prevented from keeping my word to him that I'd be a bluecoat. There's a chance, if my letter reached him, that he's trying to do something to help."

"Will he be able to help?" Catherine broke in, grasping frantically at anything that could keep Jonathan from being taken from her—from them. He was a part of all their lives, now. "Will he help?"

"Of course, he'll help." He hesitated, then said, compelled by honesty, "If he gets my letter."

His smile flashed at Cathy. "Cathy, don't fret. The only thing I feared was that you"—with difficulty, he tore his gaze from her face and looked at the others—"all of you—would despise me when you knew the truth. Now that I can see that you don't—"

Catherine all but screamed at him, "How can you stand there and tell me not to fret? Fret! Damn you! Don't you dare tell me that you don't care whether you hang or not just so long as I think well of you! I don't want you to hang! I've lost one man I loved. That's enough! Enough." Then, she thought of a way to save him. She gestured wildly,

"Run. Please run. Go to Mexico! I'll come later when I have enough money for all of us to have a big ranch down there. Go." She pointed to the back door and stomped her foot. "Go!"

Jonathan's smile could have lighted the yard on the darkest night. With a spitfire like Cathy on his side, there wasn't much a man couldn't get through.

Slowly, laughing a little to see her in such a state in his defense, he pushed back his chair and rose to go to her. Before he got around the table, his head snapped around as he looked toward the front of the house.

"Gringo!" The cry rang through the house. "Señorita Catherine! Soldiers! Soldiers are coming up the road to the house."

Juan's excited face showed at the door an instant. Then, with a look of fierce purpose, he was gone.

CHAPTER

Twenty-nine

EXPRESSIONS ON THE FACES AROUND THE TABLE RAN THE gamut from horror to grim determination. Jonathan rose without a word and walked purposefully toward the front door.

By the time Catherine could make her body obey her, he was standing at the top of the steps, outwardly calm, waiting for the small detachment of Union Cavalry that were coming smartly up the drive at a trot.

The senator put an arm around her, but Catherine, after a quick return of his embrace, broke free and ran out to stand a few paces behind and to one side of the waiting Rebel.

Almost on her heels, she heard Clayton and Jonny come out together, and saw them take places on the other side of Jonathan. It was as if they had arrayed themselves for battle.

The troopers were almost to the house now and Catherine saw a fresh-faced young officer at their head. A sense of relief flooded through her. He looked like a decent man.

Then she saw Keefer, the brute of a sergeant that had mistreated Jonathan, just behind the young officer.

Frightened, terribly frightened for Jonathan, she thought, *Thank God Keefer isn't in charge.* Watching him come, she could see the unconcealed malice he directed toward Jonathan festering in his eyes.

Unconsciously, she lifted her chin.

The officer raised his gauntleted hand and the small detail came to a halt. Catherine looked from one to the other of them. Except for the sergeant, they seemed a usual group of soldiers, just men sent to do a job.

A little prickle of fear ran through her. The job they had been sent to do just might include hanging Jonathan.

The officer spoke to her, touching the brim of his hat. "I'm Second Lieutenant Winthrope, ma'am." His voice tightened, and his concern for her showed in his eyes. "My men and I have come on an unpleasant mission. Perhaps you'd rather go back inside."

Catherine was proud to hear her voice calm and steady as she replied. "Thank you for your consideration of my sensibilities, Lieutenant. It does you credit as a gentleman." She answered his smile with a tight one of her own. "I am, however, the owner of Three Rivers, and as such, I am accustomed to dealing with whatever problems arise on it."

"Ma'am!" The lieutenant paid her the heady compliment of a salute.

Catherine inclined her head graciously. Outwardly she appeared perfectly calm. Under her apparent composure, however, her heart was racing.

She saw the way Sergeant Keefer's gaze never left Jonathan. She saw how he gloated.

She knew they had come for Jonathan. How could she stop them from taking him?

Her woman's heart, even as she felt it breaking, cried out, *Oh, why didn't you run, my love?* With an effort, she stopped herself from turning her head to look at him. She knew he was standing there proud and straight. *What if I should lose you? How would I go on?*

She forced herself to ask, "What may we do for you, Lieutenant?"

"We're looking for a deserter, ma'am." His gaze locked on Jonathan. "His name's Captain Jonathan Foster."

Her voice was so husky she hardly recognized it. "But my husband's name is Jonathan Foster, and I can assure you he is no deserter."

On the other side of Jonathan, Jonny gulped hard. He stared at his mother, then at his grandfather. Why weren't they making this right? Why didn't they send the soldiers away?

He flung himself to Jonathan's side. Slipping his arms around the silent man's waist, he looked up into his stern face and cried, "What is it, Papa? What do these soldiers want?" Boldly he stared at the troopers. "You leave my father alone!"

Jonathan dropped his hand to the boy's head and ruffled his dark hair. His eyes traveled the young face, and a slow smile transformed the sternness of a moment ago.

He didn't speak. He couldn't trust himself to. He was so choked up to hear the boy—this same boy who had worked so hard for so long to hate him—attempt to save him.

He hugged the child to him in a silent expression of appreciation, a silent farewell.

"Lieutenant." Clayton stepped forward to the edge of the steps. "I remember seeing this sergeant in Saint Louis with a ragged Rebel. He held the man prisoner. Even had him in chains. Is that the man you're looking for?"

"Yes, sir." The officer frowned slightly, wondering whom he addressed.

Catherine told him with a ring of pride in her voice. "This is my father-in-law, Senator Clayton Everett Foster, Lieutenant."

"Sir!" The lieutenant snapped Clayton a respectful salute. Relief showed in his youthful face. "I'm honored, Senator. Perhaps you can straighten this out."

Clayton's face flushed, then, as he wrestled with his conscience, blanched. His distress increased as he found himself on the horns of a dilemma. His office demanded that he speak the truth. His humanity demanded that he protect this gallant man who had more than once risked his life to save Clayton's beloved family.

In his mind, with lightning speed, he made his decision. He was framing careful words that would protect the Rebel, when the sergeant piled down from his horse and shoved himself forward.

"You ain't gonna get away with this," he snarled up at the group on porch. "This is that damned Reb that got away from me in Saint Louis, and you can't keep me from making him pay."

"Are you saying, Sergeant, that you want to revenge yourself on this man because you had a prisoner escape in Saint Louis?" Catherine spoke with deliberate light scorn.

Behind her cool façade, Catherine could feel the undermining stir of panic. She fought it as resolutely as she fought this horrible man. "I remember both of you from the train station in Saint Louis. Surely you can see there's only a superficial resemblance between this man and the man you mistreated in Saint Louis?"

Outwardly she remained calm, inwardly she raged at herself. She had carefully said "had escape" instead of "let escape." Why then did she have to let slip the word "mistreated"?

She bit the inside of her cheeks to keep from speaking further words that might enrage the sergeant and make it impossible to save Jonathan. She might have saved herself the effort.

The sergeant was almost out of control. He shouted at her, "I'll hang him, if it's . . ."

The lieutenant's voice cut him off in mid-threat. "Sergeant, that will be enough."

"But, Lieutenant!"

"Sergeant!"

Keefer subsided, muttering protests.

Clayton spoke directly to the lieutenant, his voice reasonable. He carefully ignored the choleric sergeant. "Everyone in this area knew that my daughter-in-law would someday bring her family back here to Three Rivers ranch, Lieutenant. I suggest to you that she has done so."

It was more than the vengeful Keefer could bear. "You think you're pretty damn smart, don't you!" The sergeant dashed forward, his hands like claws stretched out toward Jonathan. "Look! The Reb'll have scars on his wrists from the manacles, I know! I made them myself!"

Jonathan looked over the man's head at the lieutenant. "If he touches me, I'll kill him." His voice was almost conversational.

The sergeant stopped dead in his tracks.

Catherine closed her eyes, and took a grip on one of the turned posts that supported the porch roof.

"Sergeant!"

The burly man turned to look at his officer, his eyes burning with rage. Military discipline held and he ground his teeth and shut up. His eyes were murderous.

Jonathan refused to let it go on. Catherine and the boy shouldn't have to put up with this. "Lieutenant, if you will promise me an opportunity to be heard, I'll accompany you to the fort quietly."

The sergeant's fragile self-restraint snapped. He ranted at Jonathan. "You ain't got no choice, you dirty Reb! No choice 'cept to swing right here!"

Jonathan lifted his gaze from the red-faced shouter. He let it travel the yard casually. He looked first at Juan, who had run to alert the others, and his look conveyed his thanks for the loyalty of a friend.

His gaze passed on to Carlos, and the older man tightened his grip on his carbine. Jonathan let him see what his friendship meant before he glanced away.

He smiled a crooked smile at the men he had hired for Cathy, who held their rifles leveled at the military men. These were the sons of Confederate families, and here lay danger. He felt it a good idea to say, "Steady, boys. Three Rivers doesn't need any trouble with the military."

The lieutenant and the entire detail snapped their heads toward the ring of determined men. They were impressed by the single-mindedness on the faces of the men who surrounded them.

Jonathan looked back at the flabbergasted lieutenant. "At the Point they never told us that things are a little different here in the West, did they, Lieutenant?" He smiled at the officer. "You'll get used to it."

The boy-officer lifted a hand to point behind Jonathan, "Not to that, I won't," he murmured in a nervous voice.

Jonathan turned to see Ellen standing in the front doorway squinting down a rifle pointed straight at the lieutenant. "Ellen," he said in his velvet voice.

In response, Ellen lowered the rifle from her shoulder. The young lieutenant noticed, however, that she still kept the business end pointing his way.

Lieutenant Winthrope sought to defuse the tense situation. "You were at West Point?"

Jonathan nodded. "Class of fifty-four."

The lieutenant glanced around the yard. The situation didn't look any better. None of the armed men had lowered their guns. They didn't look as if they were going to, either.

He looked at the man he had come to arrest. "Could we talk?"

It was Catherine who offered instantly, "Would you like some tea, Lieutenant?" She shooed Ellen and her rifle into the house with a gesture. "There's coffee, too, if you'd prefer."

Ellen went, muttering, to prepare it, her rifle still firmly in her hand.

The lieutenant relaxed visibly. "Why, thank you, Mrs. Foster. I'd love a good cup of coffee. Can't say much for that we get at the fort." He swept his hat from his head, dismounted, and ordered his men to stand easy.

As he walked to the door with Jonathan, he said too low for Catherine to hear, "I don't much fancy getting shot today, Captain." Then he turned and brusquely told the seething sergeant, "Any trouble while I'm inside, and you'll face a court-martial, Sergeant. Stand the men down."

Catherine led the way to a comfortable group of overstuffed chairs arranged around a low table in one area of the spacious parlor. "Please make yourself comfortable, Lieutenant. I'll just go tell Ellen what we'd like." She glided from the room as if she hadn't a care in the world other than that of a hostess.

The dazzled lieutenant was left to decide how to handle the encumbrance of his saber. He heard Jonathan laugh a low, warm sound and turned to look at him inquiringly, even as he marveled at it. "She has the same effect on me."

The lieutenant grinned sheepishly. "She's a mighty beautiful lady." He solved the problem of his saber by taking a chair to the right that faced the one they left for his hostess and sitting in it slightly sideways to accommodate his scabbard.

Jonathan asked him, "While Mrs. Foster's gone, could we discuss the chances of your seeing to it that I get a fair hearing when we get to the fort?"

Lieutenant Winthrope shifted uncomfortably. He shot a troubled glance at the senator. When his gaze returned to Jonathan, his eyes were grave. "Sir, I wouldn't give you a ghost of a chance."

Jonathan absorbed his words like an unavoidable blow. He looked as if he'd expected no better, but the senator paled noticeably.

"I'm sorry." The lieutenant looked miserable. "The colonel lost a nephew in the war, and isn't what I'd call a charitable man. In fact, he recommended . . . uh, that we . . . uh, hang you here rather than bring you all the way back to the fort." His voice got very soft. "He wasn't very happy when I refused."

"Good man, Winthrope," the senator boomed at him. "Who the blazes is your colonel?" He dragged out of his breast pocket the flat little notebook he always carried to keep track of things he felt needed looking into to write it down.

"Barkins, Sir, Colonel Wilfred Barkins."

Catherine came back and they stood until she settled herself, then the men sat, the lieutenant managing his saber as cleverly as she had her skirt.

"Do you take sugar in your coffee, Lieutenant Winthrope?" Catherine inquired as Ellen bustled in with the heavy tea tray and plopped it on the table with a ringing rattle, a gimlet eye fixed on the young officer.

"Yes, ma'am. Thank you."

"Hmmmph," Ellen muttered on her way out of the room, "He comes to hang the finest man he'll ever see, and puts sugar in *my* coffee."

"Black, please," Jonathan responded when Catherine looked his way. He sat back in his chair and smiled at Winthrope. "Even if I didn't like it black, I lack your courage, Lieutenant."

"My ignorance, you mean." Winthrope cast an eye in the direction Ellen had gone.

Catherine offered a plate of delicate sandwiches; then, duty done, turned her eyes to Jonathan. She saw the smile that lingered after his exchange with his intended captor, and something snapped in her.

How could he . . . how could they all . . . how could she act as if everything was all right, as if this were a normal social occasion?

The lieutenant had come here for a single purpose. He had come to arrest the man she loved and take him back to the fort to be hanged. She looked wildly around their little group.

Clayton said, "My dear . . ." as if he were going to ask her if she felt all right, or if she had a headache. She couldn't believe . . . She rose abruptly, one hand at her throat, her breath becoming ragged as emotions exploded in her mind.

Then, suddenly, there was a clatter at the front door. Catherine spun to face it as it slammed back against the wall. The men all rose from their seats.

Sergeant Keefer stood clinging to the doorjamb, panting as if he had run a mile. His burning gaze ferreted out the Rebel, and in a flash he lost the battle he had been waging to control himself. His face contorted with fury.

"What the hell is going on here? Are you having a damn tea party?"

"Sergeant!" both the senator and the lieutenant shouted in outraged unison.

Keefer refused to be corrected. "You bloody little bastard! No wonder they sent you out here to the West instead of where the real fighting was. You haven't got the guts it takes to lead men. You don't even have the guts to hang one stinking Rebel!"

He grabbed the hat rack next to the doorway and viciously sent it crashing to the floor. Jonathan started toward him. Catherine threw herself into his arms, clinging, preventing him from advancing.

"You can't hide behind her, Reb. The colonel and me, we've got the guts to see to it you swing." He spun around and headed back out the door. "To hell with you, Lieutenant. I'm riding back to the fort for a real officer. I'm going for Colonel Barkins!"

Lieutenant Winthrope charged across the parlor, but by the time he reached the door, the sergeant had flung himself on his horse and torn off down the ranch lane in the direction of the road to the fort. Cursing under his breath, Winthrope stormed out to the edge of the porch.

Jonathan joined him there.

Furious, the lieutenant ordered, "Mount up, men!"

Jonathan detained him with a strong hand. "Wait! Look there."

The lieutenant jerked his gaze away from his insubordinate sergeant and looked to where Jonathan pointed. "My God!"

The ridge that separated the ranch from the road was lined with Indians. They had appeared silently, and silently they sat their ponies. To a man, every eye among them was on the sergeant as he rode up a hill into sight again as he galloped down the lane.

The sergeant reached the road and wrenched his horse left toward the fort. He disappeared from view behind the ridge.

Every brave on the ridge drew his bow. A whistling flight of arrows rained down on the road.

The two men on the porch and those in the yard with the horses knew beyond a doubt that the arrows found their target in the vengeful rider. Every one of them stood frozen. No one spoke for a long moment.

No man of them removed his hat. Sergeant Keefer's sudden death drew no mark of respect from the watchers.

Out on the ridge, the tallest Indian raised his feathered lance to Jonathan in a gesture of farewell. Jonathan raised his arm in reply as he took a single stride forward.

As if they had never been, the braves were gone.

Slowly, the soldiers reacted to what they'd seen, murmuring among themselves. The lieutenant turned to look at Jonathan. His voice was hushed. "Who was that Indian?"

"Red Hawk," Jonathan replied, "settling an old score."

"Then you don't expect any trouble here from him?"

"No, I don't, Lieutenant. I doubt that we'll ever see him and his braves again."

The lieutenant opened his mouth to say something, but before he could speak, hooves pounding up the road to the house took their attention. A series of whoops and yells resolved themselves into a cry for Lieutenant Winthrope.

"Lieutenant! Orders from the fort!" The rawboned corporal he had brought with him approached the porch.

Winthrope, honoring the chain of command, demanded, "What is it, soldier?"

"Rider from the fort, sir!"

The solitary horseman spilled off his lathered horse and used his momentum to carry him past the corporal to the young officer, his spurs clinking. Clearly under stress, he blurted, "Colonel says you better not have hanged that damn Reb, Lieutenant, or the whole blasted company will be riding out of Fort Yuma as scouting parties by this time next month!"

Catherine walked over to Jonathan, not daring to hope, her heart in her eyes. She could hardly breathe.

He pulled her into his arms, and she rested her head against his chest. She closed her eyes tight. Breathing in his scent, she drew strength from him.

Putting his own cheek on top of her hair, Jonathan stood quietly and let the tension begin to flow out of their bodies.

The lieutenant told his man, "Watch your language, Parker. There's a lady present."

"Yes, sir. Begging your pardon, ma'am." He bobbed his head at Catherine, but his full attention was on getting an answer from the lieutenant. "Tell me you ain't hanged that Reb, Lieutenant." Anxiety tightened his voice. "Ever since all the soldiers got sent to the war from outta Arizona, them Apaches think they got the territory back. Scouts out there at Fort Yuma don't last more'n about two weeks. And they don't die pretty!"

"Calm down and tell me what's going on, Corporal Parker, or you'll be doing your scouting as a private."

The corporal snapped to attention and gave his report. "Yes, sir! Lieutenant, sir. A Major Williams has arrived at the fort, sir. He claims that we've been misled about the Reb. Brought a paper from President Lincoln, just in case we need convincin' to listen to him, he says. Got a lotta statements from a buncha the guards at Camp Douglas, too. Don't know what's going on," he dropped his stiff brace and told his officer earnestly, "but I know if you've hung that major's friend, we are in one deep pile of—" he stopped short as he remembered Catherine—"trouble, sir."

"Thank you, Corporal. And the word is hanged."

"Lordamighty, Lieutenant!" The corporal was goaded beyond endurance. "Nobody cares what the word is, jest have you done it?"

Lieutenant Winthrope took pity on the man. "No, Corporal, Captain Jonathan Foster is safe."

Safe! Catherine heard the word and felt tears of relief start to her eyes. Blessed word. He was safe, her Jonathan was safe.

Jonathan sighed and touched Catherine's hair.

She looked up at him. "Your letter. It has saved you."

"My friend has saved me." His voice was deep with feeling. His eyes were as brilliant as her own as he looked down into his beloved Catherine's face. Saved. He was to have the chance to make a life with his adored Cathy, after all.

Swallowing hard, he tightened his embrace, hardly daring to believe. His heart filled.

The messenger was not in the least concerned with the miracle the couple were experiencing. "Thank God! All the way here from Fort Hardy, I could see my scalp plain as day flying from an Apache lance!" Removing his kepi, he mopped his forehead with a bandanna. "Finding Sergeant Keefer back there in the road looking like a pin cushion didn't help, either." He mopped his forehead, no more concerned with the sergeant's death than were the soldiers in the detail.

"Begging the lieutenant's permission, I'll take word back to the fort about Captain Foster."

"Exchange horses with Saunders and take it easier going back." The lieutenant turned back to Catherine and Jonathan.

His eyes warmed. Sincerely he told them, "I can't say how glad I am that this has turned out as it has." He extended his hand, "I hope you will forgive me, sir," he said to Jonathan.

Jonathan smiled at the young officer over Catherine's head. Words weren't necessary, the firmness of his grip said it all.

Together Catherine and Jonathan watched the detail ride out of the yard at a leisurely pace. Just before the crest of the first hill, the lieutenant turned and lifted his arm in a farewell salute. Jonathan responded in kind.

Peace returned to the square as the ranch hands, their rifles held loosely now, drifted off to put them away and get back to their jobs.

Catherine and Jonathan stood looking at the end of the lane until they saw the soldiers reach it and turn in the direction of the fort. Then they looked into each other's eyes. All the world faded away, and there was only the other for each of them.

Clayton smiled indulgently, then slung an arm around his grandson and started back into the house.

"Gosh," Jonny said, "This has been really exciting." Unaware, he shattered the spell that bound the lovers. "Mama, can I ride over and tell Susan?"

His only answer was the relieved laughter of the adults.

CHAPTER

Thirty

ALL OF THEM HAD COME. ALL OF THEM. IT WAS THE HAP-
piest day of her life.

Catherine stood beside her brand-new husband and fought
to keep the tears of gratitude that burned behind her eyes
from spilling over. Her heart sang thank-yous for the return
of her friends, and beyond that, soaringly, for the man
beside her.

Pressing her shoulder closer into his arm, she looked
around the cleared Three Rivers parlor. There was Lorelei
Wilcox, with whom she had played as a child. She was
Lorelei Masters, now, and expecting her third baby.

And there was Buck Stolley, who had brought his little
twin sisters over to play at Three Rivers occasionally when
they'd all been children. And Julia Lansome, whose four
brothers and husband had ridden off to fight for the cause
and left her to run the Flying L with just her three children
to help her.

All of them were her neighbors, and they had once been
and were now again her friends. The war had torn them
apart when Catherine had married her northern Jonathan.
Now, in the waning months of the war, her marriage to one
who belonged to the South, as they did, was bringing them
back together.

Jonathan slipped a possessive arm around her. She smiled
up at him.

"Are you all right?" he asked into the lull between people
wishing them well.

"Oh, yes."

"I love you, Cathy."

She threw him a startled glance. There had been a world of new meaning in his words. She looked at him questioningly.

The tenderness in his usually guarded face almost undid her. His voice was full of hard-won understanding. "There are those in this world who might be bitter at having been so long neglected by their friends."

Something flinched inside her, some little part that wanted to resent her long separation from these people. She forced herself to consider the emotion calmly. "Yes," she said after a pause, each word carefully considered as she strove to share with him her innermost feelings. "I could resent their turning from me because of my first marriage, when all the while I knew that I was still the same person inside. But I don't, Jonathan. I understand. I'm just truly glad to see them here once more." She faced him earnestly. "You know, ranch work made the times any of us could be together few, but the isolation and the hardships gave us a sense of belonging to one another that I have sorely missed."

His arm tightened around her. Pride shone from his eyes.

She turned in his embrace, oblivious to the people who filled the large parlor. "I am blessed, dearest. And I owe it all to you."

Startled, Jonathan looked down at her and saw the sincerity in her eyes. "To me?" His voice sounded so incredulous to his own ears that it made him grin.

Catherine reached up and touched his cheek, enchanted. He looked so young when he grinned. So young and dashing and devil-may-care. She felt as if her very heart would burst with joy at being his wife.

Smiling, she turned again without answering so that she was standing beside him instead of in his embrace. As she did, she noticed the indulgent smiles of a great many of their guests. Of course, she and Jon were the subject of everyone's regard this night—their wedding night.

Every person there knew they would soon be leaving for the hacienda. They all offered her their best wishes as she made it her new home.

She blushed, uncomfortable to be the center of attention, and looked to where Susan and Jonny, dressed in their best and trying so hard to be grown up, were entertaining their youthful guests. Just as she looked, Jonny pulled Susan's hair.

Diana, in her newly acquired status of hostess at Three Rivers, and with Taylor Ashworth at her side, started toward the children to see to Jonny's good behavior, and Catherine smiled. She was free to leave this house without regret now that Diana and Susan had decided to move in and coddle Catherine's father-in-law in her absence.

Suddenly, fancifully, she felt like a container for the gladness that filled her. Giddily, she wished she were translucent so that her joy could shine out on all of them. She looked up at Jonathan and laughed.

Just then, Martha Stolley struck up the strains of a waltz on the piano. Old Jed Williams, still spry though he was past seventy, joined in with his fiddle and the assembled company moved back toward the walls to leave the floor clear for the newly wedded couple to dance the first dance.

Jonathan swung Catherine into his arms and it was as if Providence had given her an outlet for the sweeping joy that inundated her.

They danced onto the rectangle of lighter flooring the removal of the huge Oriental rug had left on the parlor floor. Jonathan guided her skillfully. Though it wasn't a ballroom, the generous dimensions of the parlor gave ample room for Jonathan to startle Catherine with his prowess at the waltz.

Held tightly to him, Catherine flew around the room, her ivory satin gown shimmering in the lamplight as they danced, turning and turning. She fixed her gaze on his luminous smile and abandoned herself to the rhythm of the waltz and the masterful ease with which her husband — *her husband*—danced it.

All around them, their neighbors watched and smiled with pleased indulgence.

As the waltz lilted toward its final bars, Jonathan swept her out of the parlor and through the tall foyer. He threw a gallant salute to the assembled company as he opened the door.

With laughter, the applauding guests bid them farewell. As the door closed softly behind them, they heard the senator still the spate of conversation and invite everyone to the huge table of food that Ellen had prepared.

Then all sound faded as they stood outside on the porch, alone at last. Without a word, Jonathan pulled her close and, bowing his golden head, he kissed away the joyful tears that trembled on her lashes.

It was a tribute to the understanding they shared that he didn't speak. He knew.

Catherine reached up and gently drew his face down. Tenderly, she kissed him. It was a silent affirmation of the strength of the bond they had forged between them.

Jonathan's hands moved along her back, molding her to him. He buried his face in her hair, and she felt the depth of the breaths he took as they crushed against her with each expansion of his chest.

"Cathy," she heard him whisper. The whisper had the reverent quality of a prayer. She trembled with the wonder of it. He lifted her then, and carried her out of the shadows of the porch into the yard to his horse.

There in the moonlight, he placed her on Creole's back and stood looking up at her as if he would seal the image of her indelibly in his mind. Then he mounted behind her.

Seemingly of his own volition, Creole started for the hacienda.

Catherine lay back against her husband's chest, turning her face up so she could see his, strong and handsome in the silvered light of the moon.

Jonathan looked down at her. His arms tightened around his treasure.

Catherine felt his heartbeat quicken, and turned so that she could place her cheek against his chest. Listening to the strength with which his heart pounded sped the rhythm of her own.

In silence they rode to the hacienda she had given him

what seemed a lifetime ago, each lost in quiet contemplation of the other.

When finally they arrived, he gathered her in his arms and dismounted. There was magic in the air around them. Even Creole shared their mood. As if sensing the solemnity of the moment, he stood quietly and watched his master walk away with his precious burden.

Jonathan carried her over the threshold and placed her gently on her feet. She was home.

Catherine's blood flamed as he slid her down the length of his hard-muscled body. She met and matched the depth of his soul-claiming kiss.

A breathless instant later, he lifted her again, and moved purposefully across the immense front room of the hacienda to the hallway and the wide, easy steps leading up to their room.

The stairway was dim, and when he shoved the door to the master bedroom open with his booted foot, never releasing her from the gentle cradle of his arms, their eyes were dazzled.

Moonlight flooded the spacious chamber, bringing the smiling cupids carved in the tall headboard of the wide bed into sharp relief. Through every window it seemed to spill and burn in silver trails that all led to the bed.

Catherine was sure she felt the touch of moonglow on her skin. It tingled. She looked up at Jonathan and saw that he felt it, too. They shared the heightened sensations that grew out of the love they had for one another, out of their longing to be one.

Jonathan lowered his head, and his lips claimed hers. She went faint with desire as her body responded to the molding of his lips over her own.

The sweetness of his kiss pledged tenderness and passion, more than just the tantalizing promises of physical love. His touch branded her very soul, claiming it as his forever.

Twining her fingers in the hair at the nape of his neck, she answered him with a passion that sealed their belonging for all time. She moaned with a sense of loss when he took her hand from around his neck and led her toward the bed.

There he turned her gently away from him and began to unfasten the tiny buttons down the back of her dress. On every inch of her silken skin that he uncovered, he placed a kiss, part fire, part benediction, until she was wild to turn and embrace him.

Slowly, gently, he slid the sleeves down her arms. When he had pressed the heavy satin down over her hips, he allowed her to turn. He held her hands to steady her as she stepped out of the shining ivory puddle her gown made on the dark oak floor.

She was grateful for his steadying hold, for her knees threatened to betray her. She swayed when Jonathan reached out and touched the full swell of her breast above the lace of her chemise. But his fingers merely brushed there an instant as he pulled undone the tiny bows that held it together.

She heard his quick intake of breath as an echo of her own, then she almost cried out in protest as he stepped from her. She fought her desire to throw herself into his arms, and stood watching as his beautiful, long fingers moved to his shirt and began with infinite slowness to undo the buttons there.

Catherine could bear it no longer. The need to touch him drove her to brush aside his hands and finish the task they had begun.

He stood motionless as she unfastened the first one, but when she reached the third, and slipped her hand inside to caress his smooth chest, his breath sounded raggedly through the room. When she pushed the fabric of his shirt off his shoulder and pressed her soft lips to the scar, he cried out, "Cathy!" and tried to take her in his arms.

She pushed against his chest, keeping him away, and touched the buckle of his belt. His nostrils flared, and she thought she could hear the thunder of his heart over the quick beating of her own. She smiled to realize she had such power over him.

She placed a hand against the flat, hard muscles of his stomach, commanding him not to move with the gesture, passion lighting in her to feel his racing pulse under her hand.

Then she unbuckled his belt.

With that action, she lost all control of her Jonathan. With a deep-throated growl, he swept her to him and covered her smile with a kiss that demanded absolute surrender.

She felt his hand, shaking with the urgency of his need, tear away the fine silk of her chemise and find her breast. The world spun and the moonlight became a blur as he called from her body a response as passionate as his own.

Weakly she clung to him. All thoughts were gone. She was lost to the heightened feelings his hands aroused in her.

She quivered uncontrollably as he drew off the rest of her clothes. He held her away from him, and she fought down a whimper. She was afraid she would collapse, for her legs were beyond doing her bidding.

Jonathan's touch was gentle as he took her hands to hold her up. He held her arms out away from her sides so that nothing was hidden from his gaze. His eyes feasted on the sight of her glorious body for a breathless instant before he lifted her onto the bed.

As he moved, Catherine's eyes disobeyed her modesty. She saw, for the first time, the beauty of his whole body. His wide shoulders and broad chest with their scars of battle gave her a feeling of helplessness she had never experienced before.

As he stretched out on the bed beside her, Catherine knew a moment of panic. It had been so long. And she had never felt this way before! Never had she been aflame with a fire that licked at her senses until it threatened to overwhelm them.

Then Jonathan turned toward her, and all her reservations were swept away. With his hard body half over hers as he kissed her, and the evidence of his desire pressing against her thigh, the last vestiges of control flew from her.

Catherine moaned into his mouth as his tongue stroked her own, and she knew that whatever he wanted of her, she would give. She knew as his hands caressed her body that she would never be able to resist his every demand.

While his hands drove her to frenzy, his mouth claimed her cries.

As the moonlight silvered his magnificent body, poised above her own now, a greater light seemed to build behind her eyes. And when he joined them, the light swirled and grew until her mind was lost to everything but sensation. She was his, completely his.

She looked up into his face, so close above her own, and saw it taut with need. His eyes were smoky with passion. He was hers, all hers.

They were one.

She arched to meet him as his strong movements lifted her higher and higher. Possessing her very soul, he carried her with him to heights of rapture she had never known.

She could bear no more. Surely her heart must burst with the ecstasy tearing through her!

And then, with a final, shuddering thrust, he sent them soaring together to completion. Her wild, glad cry mingled with his shouted "Cathy!" and he slumped, spent, beside her, pulling her even closer into his arms.

When their racing hearts had returned to their regular beats, he whispered into her hair, "I love you, wife."

She gave a little whimper and buried her face in his neck. "I love you, too. Husband."

They laughed, then, both amused at the simplicity of the words they had just used to express the towering emotions that existed between them. Words that the youngest of children learn at their mothers' knees. Simple words. Words belonging to a child.

When he spoke, all the days that had gone before, all the loss and heartbreak, and all the pain fell into their proper places as he said the words that said it all: "I love you."

Outside their many-windowed bedroom, the moonlight waned, and a million stars shone in the midnight-blue velvet of the Texas sky.

If you enjoyed this book, take advantage of this special offer. Subscribe now and get a

FREE
Historical Romance

No Obligation (a $4.50 value)

Each month the editors of True Value select the four *very best* novels from America's leading publishers of romantic fiction. Preview them in your home *Free* for 10 days. With the first four books you receive, we'll send you a FREE book as our introductory gift. No Obligation!

For if any reason you decide not to keep them, just return them and owe nothing. If you like them as much as we think you will, you'll pay just $4.00 each and save at *least* $.50 each off the cover price. (Your savings are *guaranteed* to be at least $2.00 each month.) There is NO postage and handling – or other hidden charges. There are no minimum number of books to buy and you may cancel at any time.

Send in the Coupon Below

To get your FREE historical romance fill out the coupon below and mail it today. As soon as we receive it we'll send you your FREE Book along with your first month's selections.
